Praise for

The Goddess Rules

Praise for

Dog Handling

By Clare Naylor

Catching Alice

Love: A User's Guide

Dog Handling

The Second Assistant
(co-author Mimi Hare)

The

Goddess Rules

The
Goddess
Rules

A NOVEL

Clare Naylor

Ballantine Books New York

2006 Ballantine Books Trade Paperback Edition

Published in the United States by Ballantine Books, an imprint of The Random House Publishing Group, a division of Random House, Inc., New York.

BALLANTINE and colophon are registered trademarks of Random House, Inc.

Originally published in hardcover in the United States by Ballantine Books, an imprint of The Random House Publishing Group, a division of Random House, Inc., in 2005.

LIBRARY OF CONGRESS CATALOGING-IN-PUBLICATION DATA
Naylor, Clare.
The goddess rules / Clare Naylor.
p.   cm.
ISBN 0-345-46341-2
1. Women painters—Fiction.   2. London (England)—Fiction.
3. Lions as pets—Fiction.   4. Actresses—Fiction.   I. Title.
PS3614.A95G63 2005
813'.54—dc22   2004054531

Printed in the United States of America

www.ballantinebooks.com

2   4   6   8   9   7   5   3

Book design by Laurie Jewell

And above all, watch with glittering eyes

the world around you. Because the greatest secrets

are always hidden in the most unlikely places. Those

who do not believe in magic will never find it.

—Roald Dahl

The
Goddess Rules

Chapter One

Kate Disney was having sex with her ex when the legendary Mirabelle Moncur first came into her life. Actually she came into the
wooden garden shed that Kate called home just as Jake's naked bottom appeared over the top of the sheets in anticipation of his last
few enthusiastic thrusts. It was the moment that Kate had been
waiting for since she and Jake had broken up a month ago. Since
that Sunday night she'd existed in a fathomless abyss of pain, memories of Jake, and tears. Until about an hour ago, when Jake, in
answer to her prayers and a good deal of amateur witchcraft, had
shown up on her doorstep on his way home from a night out.

"Hello, angel, I've missed you." It was three in the afternoon and
he smelled of whiskey and cigarette smoke, his shirt was half unbuttoned, and his jacket was torn.

"Jake." Kate had been cleaning her paintbrushes when she'd
heard the tap on the shed door. She'd wiped her hands down her
old T-shirt and unbolted it. Jake was the first and last person she expected to see standing there.

"It was my birthday yesterday," he told her, and propped himself
up in the door frame. "And the only present I really wanted was
you."

"Jake, you're drunk," Kate said. Though she knew he wasn't.

"You've got paint in your hair." He leaned forward to touch her bangs. Kate shrank back but knew that she'd already lost the battle. She knew that she was going to let Jake in. "You look terrible," she lied.

"Don't I even get a birthday kiss?"

"You're lucky I haven't punched you."

"I love you." Jake looked at Kate and she felt her will dissolve. Maybe he really meant it this time. Because even though she and Jake had been together on and off for almost three years, he had told her that he loved her only once before, the same night that he'd been signed to a small record label. And that night he really had been drunk.

"We're only going to talk," she said, and stood back to let him through the door.

"I know." Jake pretended to believe her.

"I'll make some tea." Kate turned her back on him and with shaking hands filled the kettle in the large butler's sink in the corner. This wasn't how she'd imagined it would happen—Jake coming back to her. And she *had* imagined it—night and day, waking and sleeping. She'd hoped that it would be a bigger moment—that it would involve a declaration and a diamond rather than a cup of tea at the end of a long night out. But then after three years with Jake, Kate was accustomed to being underwhelmed. Thankfully the sex wasn't underwhelming. It was fabulous. It was even more fabulous right now because they hadn't so much as laid eyes on one another for a month. And as Jake kissed her neck and Kate trailed her fingers down his freckled brown back, she forgot about the underwhelmingness, and about the note he'd written to her, telling her that it was over because he had nothing left to give; she'd even forgotten that it was Jake's fault that she was living in her boss's garden shed. Well, not strictly his fault, but she and Jake had been saving for a place together and she'd agreed to give up her overpriced studio flat so that they could buy somewhere quicker and be together. But Kate forgot all these things and bit hard into Jake's shoulder and let bygones be bygones. Until Mirabelle Moncur walked in and ruined everything.

"Kate Disney?" she demanded, without so much as a knock on the door or a polite cough to announce herself first. Jake, who was submerged somewhere in the vicinity of Kate's left breast at that moment, completely lost his stride and practically gave himself whiplash as he turned to see who was behind him. Kate gave a cry of pain as Jake crushed her right leg.

"Who the bloody hell are you?" Jake asked the intruder as he ungraciously wrestled the sheet from Kate's grasp to cover himself up. Kate suddenly remembered why he was her ex. Apart from the fact that he'd dumped her. He always put himself first. He was completely self-absorbed, not to mention, she noticed in the late-afternoon sunlight streaming in through the shed window, a bit on the fat side.

"Oh, you don't need to cover up." At the foot of Kate's bed stood a strikingly attractive woman, possibly in her late fifties, with disheveled blond hair, the sort of cheekbones that hold a beauty together no matter how far south her face gravitates, and deep green eyes that at this moment in time were locked on Jake's crotch. "You have absolutely *nothing* to hide." And with that she glanced the tip of her Gitane cigarette with a lighter and raised an unimpressed eyebrow. Jake turned beet red and looked uncomfortable.

"Yes, who the bloody hell are you?" Kate demanded as she reached for an old nightdress that was lying on the floor to cover herself with and clambered from her bed.

"I'm Mirabelle Moncur," the woman said in a French accent as thick as nightclub smoke as she looked around the shed. "Do you actually live here?"

"I'm sorry, do I know you?" Kate demanded crossly. Knowing full well that she didn't. Though there was something familiar about Mirabelle Moncur.

"I want you to come and work for me," the woman said and watched unabashed while Jake stumbled into his boxer shorts, one leg at a time. Kate had never seen him so ruffled.

"Well, you could have knocked first," he muttered under his breath.

"Look, I don't know who you are, or how you got in, but this is actually a private residence and if you want me to work for you then you'll have to make an appointment and come back."

Mirabelle sniffed the air in a way that told Kate that she didn't believe this to be a residence of any sort. Let alone a private one worth knocking at. She walked over to where a few of Kate's canvases were stacked up against the wall and began glancing through them. "These are your paintings?"

"Yes, and as I've said, you can make an appointment to come back later and see them. But right now, as you can probably see, I'm busy."

"They're a little old-fashioned but I suppose you'll do," the woman said. "I want you to paint Bébé for me. He's very beautiful, so I suppose it'll be easy to do. Even for someone like you."

"Who the hell is Bébé?" Jake asked, not, Kate noticed, leaping to defend her work, which he'd never complained about when it was funding his cigarette habit, paying for recording studio time, and keeping him in whiskey and the cashmere socks he absolutely had to wear or his feet got too hot, for the past three years.

"Bébé is my pussy. He arrives tomorrow morning from Mozambique and you can begin work in the afternoon," Mirabelle Moncur filled in. Jake looked staggered.

"Right, well, I'm sure we can discuss my old-fashioned paintings later. And whether I'm prepared to paint your . . . pussy. But for now would you mind leaving me and my . . ." Kate always hesitated to call Jake her boyfriend, even before they'd split up, lest he get nervous and feel like she was trying to tie him down and put him under pressure. She turned to look at the man who was sitting on the corner of her bed waiting for her to deal with their intruder so that he could get on with the birthday treat. ". . . my friend alone."

"I'll come back later, if you prefer," Mirabelle Moncur said as she dropped a glowing cigarette butt on top of a yellow canister of fertilizer with a skull and crossbones on the lid. "There's nothing worth hanging around here for." She looked at Jake with a sneer and walked out the door, without closing it behind her, leaving Kate to pick up the burning Gitane or risk being blown up.

"Who on earth was she?" Kate asked as she went to the window and watched the woman disappear down the garden path.

"Mirabelle Moncur. Rings a bell," Jake said. "Now, sweetheart, cute as you look in that little nightie, I prefer you without it."

"You do?" Kate laughed girlishly and went in a pair of old sneakers to Jake's side. He pulled the white cotton slip over her head and began to kiss her stomach.

"Mmmhhhmmm," he said. "I'd forgotten what a great body you had." Kate smiled inside and ran her hands through Jake's hair. She, in her turn, forgot how ungracious he'd been with the sheet when that weird woman had barged through the door. Amnesia was a requirement with Jake as a boyfriend. If you remembered all the bad stuff, you'd have to wonder what had happened to your mind. Because you certainly weren't in possession of it. Kate chose to concentrate on her body instead, and how good it was feeling right now.

Chapter Two

Kate made her way toward the enormous, rambling house at the end of the garden path. If you followed it from the shed, past the cherry trees, and over the patio, you landed at Leonard's back door. Leonard, as his name might suggest to even the most obtuse of strangers, was a raving queen. He was also Kate's boss who owned both the house and the shed. Leonard was one of the smoothest, kindest, and most successful antiques dealers in London, and Kate was widely regarded (well, at least by the *London Evening Standard*) as one of the best young painters of animals in the country. And as Leonard had at least a hundred clients with animals whose whiskers and wet noses and tabby stripes they wanted to preserve for posterity, Leonard and Kate had teamed up to become a match made in heaven. Or at least Primrose Hill.

Kate had known Leonard since she was five years old when her father and he had been friends and business acquaintances. Harry Disney had been a taxidermist—where Kate painted live animals, Harry stuffed dead ones. He'd been one of the last practitioners of this dying art—"no pun intended," he used to cheerfully say as often as possible when asked about his unusual line of work—and their home was always filled with stuffed Pekingese and Manx cats and the usual parade of pets taken on commission to pay for the school fees. There was also a sideline of distinctly uncommon creatures that, when Kate was growing up, were as familiar to her as coffee tables and porcelain shepherdesses were to other children. These included Ernest the eleven-foot-long crocodile who greeted guests in the hallway of their Georgian town house; Cecilia the wild boar, named after Harry's mother-in-law, who occupied a seat by the window of their drawing room; not to mention a brown bear at the foot of the stairs, a penguin on the mantelpiece, and an ever-rotating zoo of zebras on the landing, stoats on armchairs, and bison on the top floor, which had officially been Harry's workshop before it ceased to be big enough to accommodate more wildlife than the Serengeti Plain.

It was this exposure to fur at such a young age that helped fuel Kate's passion for animals, both living and dead. And with her first packet of color crayons she drew yellow squiggles of otters and scrawls of Ernest, which would mature into the vast, vivid canvases that now hung in smart private collections in country houses and old ladies' bedrooms; one had even put in an appearance at an exhibition at the Royal Academy last winter. All of which made Kate Disney a fairly successful artist at the age of twenty-eight.

She, however, saw things rather differently—she thought her work was pedestrian, uninspired, and dull. She believed that anyone could capture a likeness of an animal. The real challenge, which she never attempted for fear of failure, were portraits of people. So whenever she was fêted by Leonard or her clients for miraculously conveying the haughtiness of a pony or the curmudgeonly nature of a Yorkshire terrier, she simply thought it nonsense. People projected what they wanted to see onto an image; it had nothing to do with her talent, in Kate's opinion. Still, her commissions paid the bills, and they helped add to her house-buying fund, which had been occasionally laid low when she'd had to dip into it and hand out a thousand pounds for Jake's costs.

Jake was a musician, and studio time didn't come as cheap as paintbrushes, unfortunately. In Kate's eyes Jake's career was much more important than her own. He was the one with the genius, the one on track for fame and glory. Jake's songs were going to be the soundtrack for a whole generation, just as soon as they got heard. His lyrics were heartbreakingly beautiful, his voice raw and anguished. Kate could listen to him all day, if only one of his songs would be playlisted on the radio—that was all it would take to break him. Kate knew the day would come. Just as she knew that the day would come when he'd settle down and they would be together properly—have a house and babies and a recording studio in the basement and Kate wouldn't have to wonder every time she saw Jake whether it was going to be the last. Whether she'd scared him away by being too conventional, too needy, too difficult. Luckily for Jake she never stopped to wonder what *she* saw in him. She was too busy wondering what he could possibly see in her. Still, this late-spring morning, as she made her way in a pair of old sneakers and combat pants past the beds of white flowers humming with bees, over the dewy grass toward Leonard's house, Kate wasn't burdened by anything much. Jake had left last night with a promise to call her this morning to fix up a proper reconciliation dinner, so she was as close to euphoric as she had been for as long as she could remember. She'd even taken the bold step of putting her box of tissues back in the bathroom cabinet, safe in the knowledge that she'd be dry-eyed for a while to come.

As Kate wandered down the side of the house and out into the front garden on her way to buy a pint of milk and the newspaper, she didn't even mind the fact that she lived in a shed. It was spring, she was back together with the man she loved, and she got to hang out with Leonard, who had become as close to her as a father since Harry Disney died six years ago. It had been Leonard who had persuaded her to leave her job as a gallery girl in Cork Street and pursue the marginally more lucrative path of painting. And when she'd come to him a few months ago and explained that she wanted to rent his, admittedly very smart, garden shed because she was saving up to move in with Jake, Leonard hadn't bleated a word about the fact that Jake was still living in a plush flat belonging to his aunt in

Chelsea so why should she downsize—he'd simply handed over the keys; helped her move out the lawn mower, build a shower, and install a sink; and filled the place with ancient rugs and a fairy-tale iron bed when she wasn't there to protest that he was spoiling her. Similarly Kate was always happy to be roped in to hand around canapés at his swish champagne parties. And since Leonard had no children of his own and his long-term lover, Phillippe, had died around the same time as Kate's dad, Leonard and Kate were as inseparable a pair as a couple of Ming vases.

Kate looked out for the canary-yellow corduroy trousers that were Leonard's trademark as she wandered through the overgrown front garden toward the gate. But Leonard wasn't anywhere to be seen. He was probably in some auction room in Sussex already, outbidding everyone on a Biedermeier dresser. But there was nothing that couldn't wait. She could tell him all about Jake's return later this afternoon over tea.

"There's someone coming out," a man called out as Kate unlocked the tall, wooden garden gate.

"It'll be her," someone else said, and there was a flurry of noise and scurrying feet in the street outside. Kate pushed open the gate and put her head around, only to be greeted by what appeared to be a firework display of popping, exploding lights. As a crowd of about twenty men came crashing toward her wielding enormous, cumbersome cameras, she slammed the gate shut again and caught her breath.

"Mirri. Oy Mirri," they were shouting, in a chorus of cockney accents. "Just one picture, come on, love." Kate peeked through a crack in the wood and saw the men, roused into action, poised on the other side of the gate with cameras obscuring their faces. All of them pointing in Kate's direction. What on earth was going on? She looked back toward the house to see if there was any sign of Leonard. But nobody was stirring. The only thing that could be construed as out of the ordinary was that the curtains were drawn on the third story of the house and the windows were closed. Normally on a bright spring morning they'd be open—Leonard was a stickler for fresh air. Kate slid the latch on the gate and hid behind the wall as the men hammered away.

"Come on, darlin'," she could hear an out-of-breath man heaving on the street, "just one picture and we'll leave you alone. That's all we want."

"Who do you want?" Kate asked, convinced that these men, who must be paparazzi, were at the wrong gate. They must have been here to capture an off-guard snap of one of the countless hip young actors or rock stars who lived in Primrose Hill. Though Kate never saw any of them—not the boys from Oasis, not the cool supermodels, not Jude Law—she had read in the Sunday supplements that this leafy, expensive, and pretty part of London was the only place for any self-respecting superstar to settle with his or her Egyptian cotton sheets and pool tables.

"Mirri, is that you?" the heavy-breathing paparazzo asked through the slats in the wood.

"Who are you trying to photograph?" Kate asked, and remained glued to the mossy garden wall, which she hoped they wouldn't be bold enough to climb.

"Mirri Moncur," he said. "We only want one picture."

"Wrong house," Kate said, "sorry." And she hurried back down the side of the house. She'd have to nip into Leonard's kitchen and pinch a pint of milk from his fridge. She didn't feel up to facing twenty paparazzi, even if they were after some ancient movie star whom Kate had presumed was long dead of an overdose or something. Mirri Moncur. It was only as Kate pushed open the kitchen door that it dawned on her that Mirri Moncur could easily have been the woman who had come into her shed yesterday. Mirabelle. Mirabelle Moncur. Kate stopped and gazed into the fridge for a long moment, forgetting totally about the milk and wondering how such a weird chain of events might be related. The woman yesterday had looked familiar. *Mirabelle* could easily be shortened to *Mirri.* And wasn't that old actress—Kate struggled to remember her story, knowing only that it involved being very beautiful once and then either dead or reclusive—wasn't she a famous French film star? But even so, why were the press outside Leonard's house, even if it had been Mirri Moncur in her shed yesterday?

"Got me." Kate gave up the conundrum and pulled a pint of milk from Leonard's fridge to pour into a jug. Enough for a day's tea and a drop to spare in case . . . well, in case Jake came around this evening and wanted milk in his coffee tomorrow morning. As Kate helped herself to half the pint—she drank a lot of tea; it alleviated thirst, boredom, loneliness, and provided a welcome respite from trying to get the color of a blue whippet she'd been painting just right—she noticed a pile of post on the table in front of her and glanced through to see whether any of it was hers. For once none of the envelopes looked brown. In fact it was her favorite kind of post—the stiff, white, square-enveloped sort that heralded weddings, parties, christenings, or other excuses to spend money on a new dress that she could ill afford. But Kate quickly noticed that most of the envelopes had already been opened, so it clearly wasn't her post after all. She thought it odd that Leonard hadn't, as he usually did, opened his letters in his office several hours ago and already responded before she could drag her lazy behind out of bed.

Kate was just about to pick up the milk jug and leave when she spotted a very, very grand-looking crest at the top of one of the stiff cards. Now, Kate wasn't accustomed to getting letters from dukes and barons, but she did recognize a very important coat of arms when she saw one—working in the gallery, she'd become familiar with the clout of a title, even if it was vaunted by someone whose wallet was as empty as his often mesmerizingly inbred brain. And as she ran her finger over the embossed crest, it bumped along like a very uncomfortable road. Up down, up down. Maybe this was Leonard's invitation to the queen's garden party, Kate thought. If it was, she'd have to do something to get him out of the canary cords; there was no way they were appropriate attire for meeting Her Majesty. But as she looked closely at the card, trying to get the gist of what it said without officially prying, Kate was surprised to see that it started with *My darling lady* . . .

Surely not from the queen to Leonard then? Perhaps from

Leonard to a queen, but that was a different matter. Kate couldn't help herself. Her curiosity got the better of her, so she read on.

> *My darling lady,*
>   *It has been such a very long time! I have missed your charming ways enormously. I have missed your wickedness and laughter and I very much hope that if you are in England, as a little bird tells me you are, you will come and have tea with me at the palace.*
>
> *With much love*

And the letter was finished off with a signature of such grandness that Kate found it impossible to read. Though she imagined that it was written by no less a person than the heir to the throne. She wondered if perhaps Leonard had robbed a museum and taken some ancient artifact—until she noted that it had been written only two days ago. But who was the darling lady in question?

"Ah, good. I was going to come and find you if you didn't arrive soon." Kate looked up and saw, not Mirabelle Moncur actually, but a bunch of lilies so vast that the bearer was obscured. Kate bristled and hastily averted her prying eyes from the letter, but it was too late. "Oh, you've seen my letter. Isn't it sweet to be remembered by an old friend? We had a liaison, but that was many years ago." The bunch of lilies was laid on the table, and Kate saw the equally exotic Mirabelle Moncur where they had been.

"I was looking for my post, actually. I didn't expect to find someone else's here," Kate said defensively as she took in Mirabelle's penetrating green eyes, which exactly matched the color of her silk robe, which was only just managing to conceal her extraordinary breasts.

"Oh, I'm living here now," the woman said as she went to the fridge and pulled out a bottle of champagne. "Leonard and I used to be lovers."

"You did?" Kate said incredulously. For all the obvious reasons. Like Leonard's being gay.

"I liked his eyes," Mirri mused, suggesting to Kate that this alone was enough. That liking a man's eyes meant that no matter how married he might be, what his sexual orientation was, and regardless of whether he liked *your* eyes or not, you got to sleep with him. Not in Kate's world, that was for sure. Kate generally had to talk herself into liking abstract bits of a man such as his wrists, or the way he laughed loudly at jokes or had once read a book. Men with nice eyes were generally reserved for girls who spent their days with their nails in a manicure bowl rather than painting biscuit-colored dog fur.

"I see," said Kate as she watched this stranger pour herself a generous glass of Leonard's finest vintage champagne and then put a slice of bread in the toaster.

"So when will you be able to make a start?" she said, resting against the counter and appraising Kate carefully.

"Start?"

"Painting Bébé. He's caught up on all his sleep now, after his dreadful time in quarantine, so we want to start as soon as possible."

"I'm sorry but I'm a bit lost," Kate said as she tried to piece everything together. "You're a friend, sorry, ex-lover of Leonard's, and you've moved in and you'd like me to paint your cat. Is that correct?"

"Yes yes, really you are very slow, aren't you?" Mirabelle Moncur said as she slathered her toast in at least an inch of butter. "Come and see us at four o'clock on the top floor and we'll see whether Bébé likes you or not. After all, it's really up to him."

"I see . . . well . . ." But before Kate could protest about the absurdity of being interviewed by a rude woman and her cat, Mirabelle Moncur had picked up the ringing telephone.

"Ah, my darling Charles, so sweet of you to invite me for tea. Of course I'd love to come, though it will have to be next week, I'm so terribly busy right now, in fact I'm just dashing out, but call back later and we'll arrange it, *d'accord*?" And with that the woman hung up, on whom Kate dreaded to think. But one thing was for sure, she was lying through her teeth. She wasn't dashing anywhere. She was settling herself down at Leonard's kitchen table as casually as you like, with a copy of *Le Monde,* some toast and marmalade, and a glass of champagne. Kate was just about to turn on her heel and leave when she felt something tap her ankle. She glanced down but there was nothing there, though she knew that she hadn't been imagining it. So she leaned down to see what it was; maybe the famous Bébé. But just as she put her face under the table, a very un-cat-sized paw shot out and batted her hair. Kate screamed and shot up, which served only to make the animal barrel out from under the table and pounce on her feet.

"Holy shit," Kate yelled, and backed herself into a corner of the room. "That's not a cat, it's a tiger," she went on breathlessly as she tried to keep the animal at bay.

Mirri, who didn't lift her head from the front page of her newspaper, simply hissed, "Bébé, leave her alone. Come here." She clicked her fingers near the ground and the cub bounded back on himself and toward the clicking fingers, which he proceeded to lick. "And he is a lion, not a tiger. Which you should remember when you paint him. Or he will be very upset. Won't you?" Bébé was then scooped up by Mirabelle and kissed as if he were a relative arriving at an airport after twenty years abroad.

"Well, I think perhaps you should have warned me," Kate said crossly. She was slightly shocked but in truth she was much more embarrassed. She'd reacted like a complete idiot. And now, as she watched the adorable and unutterably beautiful animal rub noses with his owner, she felt a bit jealous. She wanted to stay and play but she'd made a fool of herself. Perhaps if Mirabelle were a more gracious human being, she would have stayed. And she had clearly forgotten that Kate even existed, because seconds later she lowered Bébé back onto the floor, lit up a cigarette, and proceeded to blow the smoke right in Kate's face with a force that could have lifted the rooftops off houses. Hurricane Mirabelle, it seemed, had arrived!

"Okay, I've found it. Here she is. 'Mirabelle Moncur. Otherwise known as Mirri Moncur. Goddess of the Silver Screen. The most beautiful woman in the world,' " Kate read aloud from the slick white computer screen in front of her. " 'Mirabelle, onetime sex kitten, 1960s icon, and lover of every man she tossed her blond mane at, was married three times, appeared in fourteen movies, and retired at the age of forty. The woman who was reputed to have slept with over two hundred men, whose garden was once showered with a million roses from a lover's helicopter, finally decided that she preferred wildcats to wild oats and went to live in Africa on a wildlife reserve, where she still resides in seclusion from the world's media.' "

"So she's definitely not dead then?" Tanya, who was sitting next to Kate at the computer, asked.

"Unfortunately not," Kate said as she clicked onto a stunning black-and-white photograph of the legendary beauty. "She's sitting in my kitchen eating the marmalade I bought from Fortnum at Christmas." Kate had finally fled the smoke-filled kitchen when it became apparent that Mirabelle had said all she intended to say to her. She'd then braved the doorstepping paparazzi—who now appeared to have the correct house after all, and were clearly not going to go away until they'd had the first shot in twenty years of Mirabelle Moncur—and gone to her friend Tanya's house across the park.

Tanya was Kate's greatest and oldest friend. She was also so pretty, it was wrong. Not just morally wrong that one person should lay claim to the prettiness jackpot quite so unequivocally, but wrong because it just wasn't right to be that pretty anymore. It wasn't very *now,* to be quite honest. To be a true modern beauty required a delicately broken nose, the grainy skin of a party girl, the breasts of a showgirl, and lips so swollen, they looked as if they'd been attacked by a swarm of Japanese killer hornets. But Tanya was truly flawless. She looked like a digitally enhanced Grace Kelly— blue of eye, pink of lip, and hair so softly, wavily blond that people,

not just men either, often got the urge to bury their faces in it. Most
of them resisted. When they didn't, her equally beautiful husband,
Robbie, would appear by her side and look down on them from his
six foot three in threadbare socks and smile until the offender realized that this wasn't a dream, and then he or she would skulk back
to ordinary life in a bit of a daze. Naturally, Robbie was as rich as
chocolate mousse.

They were also the happiest couple that Kate knew. He was the
publisher of a deeply worthy website devoted to all issues green and
unpleasant—if it involved offshore dumping of chemical waste,
pesticides in cucumbers, or genetically modified anything, Robbie
was the man to take an interest. Not only was he brilliant and
handsome, he wanted to save the world. Kate would have hated
them if she didn't know them. But thankfully she and Tanya had
met way back when—one summer when both girls were working
for peanuts in galleries in Cork Street. They'd both just left art college, and they used to hover outside the back doors of their respec-
tive galleries having a sneaky fag beneath the shadow of the
dustbins.

One day Kate threw her cigarette butt over her shoulder. It soared
up, up, and away over the mountains of rubbish in the Dumpsters
and landed in Tanya's hair, thankfully only singeing a few locks.
Thus began a summer of sore feet, stroppy heiresses, indecent pro-
posals from married oil magnates, and—most significantly—a new
friendship. The girls would sit on a bench in Bond Street, share
sandwiches, and invent shopping lists so grand and jewel-encrusted
from the windows of Asprey and Bulgari that they were invariably
late back into their galleries and got filthy stares all afternoon from
their bosses. Still, in Tanya's case at least, the filthy stares were replaced by obsequious (and bewildered) smiles when the most eligi-
ble and sought-after bachelor in just about every hemisphere you'd
care to mention slouched casually into Tanya's gallery one rainy
summer afternoon in search of a small Picasso. And the moment he
set foot on the shiny parquet floor, it was obvious that Tanya wasn't

long for the sore-feet, gallery-girl business. Instead a whirlwind of long dinners, weekends of being whisked off down winding country roads to grand houses, and giggly evenings of getting to know one another gave way to snap snap in the newspapers, horror horror that Robbie Hirst was marrying the daughter of a schoolteacher and a doctor's receptionist (albeit a pretty one), and the pop pop of corks at their low-key but exclusive Chelsea registry office, then on to the Ritz wedding. And nobody had looked back since. The only dark specter looming in the background of the fairy tale was that thus far, and not for want of trying, the Hirsts had not had a baby. But as everyone reassured them, often protesting a little too much for the couple's liking—there was plenty of time yet.

"But it's good, isn't it, if she wants to commission you?" Tanya reasoned with Kate. "I mean, if you paint one cat well, there's a whole bunch more animals to do out in Africa or wherever."

"I just don't like her," Kate said as the girls left Tanya's study and headed for the kitchen. Which was a brisk three-minute walk away through the vast, Belsize Park house. Because not only were the girls' love lives a world apart, but their homes were so incomprehensible to the other that each time one of them visited the other's place, it felt like an adventure to a strange, undiscovered land. Tanya, cushioned by riches and love, was deprived of the disaster that for many people is everyday life. And she was always riveted to hear what life was like in Kate's world of boyfriends and living in sheds and getting dumped and having a drawer stuffed with unopened bank statements. So her trips to Kate's world were filled with wide-eyed, grass-is-always-greener-type admiration for her friend's fabulously bohemian existence.

"Is that a snail?" Tanya would try not to sound too impressed as she watched one of the many creatures that inhabited Kate's shed amble leisurely across the floorboards. Equally, when Kate came to Tanya's house she would run her fingers over the smooth granite surfaces, slide her hands along curved glass walls, and marvel at the five stories of light-infused, vaulting-ceilinged rooms filled with spectacular art, and long for marriage and a future of never having to worry again about not having someone to spend New Year's Eve with.

"Kate, what are you talking about? You're never fussy about what work you take on. And it's not like you'd have to paint *her*. It's her cat."

"I don't know, she's just not particularly nice. In fact, she's a rude old cow and if she ever comes into my home again without knocking, I'll put her and Bébé on the first banana boat back to Mozambique."

"She's that bad?"

"She walked in on me and Jake having sex yesterday."

"What?" Tanya froze in midair as she was handing Kate her drink.

"Oh yeah. That," Kate replied sheepishly. She'd been meaning to get around to telling Tanya about her and Jake being back together, but she'd been waiting for the right moment. Like one when Tanya wasn't listening so she couldn't be disapproving and disappointed and worried about Kate. "I didn't mention it, did I?"

"You had sex with Jake?" Tanya put the glass back on the counter and looked incredulously at Kate. "Wait a minute, you *saw* Jake? You *spoke* to Jake? You had *sex* with Jake?"

"Did you make this barley water yourself?" Kate asked, picking up her drink and hiding her shame behind the rim of the glass.

"Tell me. Everything." Tanya glared at Kate.

"Not much to tell," Kate said, trying to make light of the incident but unable to prevent a thrilled grin from spreading slowly across her face when she remembered that she and Jake were on-again.

"I can't believe you slept with him." Tanya shook her head as she navigated her way through the French doors, out onto the terrace, and into a garden chair without once taking her eyes off her friend.

"Nor can I, really," said Kate, who followed obediently in her wake. "I haven't had a second to think about it. I've been too preoccupied with Mirabelle Moncur and the parade of Louis Vuitton steamer trunks that were arriving on Leonard's doorstep when I left. Honestly, it's like Rose Dawson in *Titanic*." Kate followed Tanya's lead and sat down. "I hope she's not planning on staying too long."

"So Jake," Tanya reminded her. "What happened? Did he call? Did he show up unannounced? Do you think one of your spells worked?"

Kate looked a bit embarrassed by the last suggestion. When she and Jake had first broken up, Kate visited a psychic who told her that they were two sides of the jagged heart who'd been together in a past life. Which actually made her stop crying for thirty-seven hours. Then she'd had her tarot cards read and they told her that she was currently experiencing widowhood, female sadness, embarrassment, absence, sterility, mourning, and separation. Which was such an impressive list of bad things that even in a spectacularly pessimistic moment, Kate might have struggled to dream up such curses. But she learned her bitter lesson. He who lives by the Harrow Road dies by the Harrow Road. Meaning if you go to cheap, nasty fortune-tellers in run-down parts of town, you can't expect them to speak of untold riches and love everlasting.

And finally, in a desperate moment, Kate bought a love spell from a witchcraft website. She had burned a candle every day and night on an altar that consisted of Jake's guitar plectrum and a photograph of him in a pub in Scotland. So now, as she looked at Tanya's expectant face, Kate felt her toes curl a bit because although she was still in love with Jake, she was no longer in the insane phase of mourning. That shameless period where the only way to get by is to believe in the supernatural and focus on your chakras. Men, in the same phase of mourning, simply have sex a lot. With other women. But straight after the breakup with Jake, Kate had been prepared to try anything. She had also gone to Harvey Nichols, where the shop assistant had handed her a bag with an eight-hundred-pound dress in it. Which wasn't witchcraft but felt so good that it should have been.

"I don't really think that it was one of the spells working," Kate conceded. "I think it was more because it was his birthday and the idea of not having sex would have made him a monumental failure in his own eyes," she added pragmatically. If there was one thing that she had learned during her relationship with Jake, it was pragmatism. Which is not the same as good things like learning to give unconditionally or learning to share your deepest dreams with another person. But it was something, she supposed.

"A sympathy fuck?" Tanya asked, horrified.

"No, I think he really wanted to do it," Kate reasoned.

"Good God, Kate, I meant you gave *him* a sympathy fuck."

"Oh, right." Kate nodded. Though she wasn't sure that it was the case. She had been just as in need of last night's exchange as Jake had. If not more. After all, it had been Jake who had walked out of her life. Not the other way around.

"So, what, you guys went out to dinner and then . . . ?" Tanya prompted.

"We didn't go out to dinner at all. Actually." Kate began to look sheepish. "Not dinner. No. He called by on his way home the next morning. Just to say hello." Read *have sex* for "say hello."

"And then he invited you to dinner? Right?"

"Why are you so obsessed with dinner, Tan?" Kate asked disingenuously.

"It's a euphemism for Jake taking you seriously. To prove he wasn't just calling back so he could scratch his birthday itch. See?" Tanya was reluctant to make Kate suffer any more than necessary. It would probably take about two days, she estimated, for Kate to realize she'd made a huge mistake in backpedaling with Jake to a time when she was vulnerable, at his mercy, and unspeakably unhappy.

"Tanya, I'm still in love with him."

"I know, sweetie." Tanya let out a deep sigh. "And everyone's allowed to slip up once in a while. But you know that if you got back together with him, it wouldn't be any different from before."

"Before was okay." Kate thought of the way Jake had kissed her face all over last night. At least thirty times. She knew that he loved her. He was just confused.

"He was mean to you," Tanya reminded her.

"That was just his sense of humor."

"Except it wasn't funny."

"He made *me* laugh."

"He would go for days without calling you. Then freak out if you complained."

"He wrote songs for me."

"He never once told you he loved you."

"His parents were divorced. He has a hard time with emotions. It doesn't mean he doesn't feel it," Kate persevered.

"He said he was emotionally incapable of buying you flowers."

"The sex was amazing."

"That's a moot point. We're talking about love." Tanya focused her wide blue gaze on Kate.

"It didn't feel like a moot point last night. In fact, it felt like the whole point."

"Except, Kate, you're not the sort of girl who's capable of detaching. Sex love love sex. It's all mixed up like a pint of sick where you're concerned."

"Thanks for equating my love life with vomit." Kate bit her lip and looked down at her cell phone, which she knew would be viewed as closely and regularly as the *Mona Lisa* hanging in the Louvre in the next few days until Jake called.

"Jake's a lovable tosser." Tanya drained her coffee cup. "Leave him for someone who can't do any better. What about Joss Armstrong? I really think that if Robbie and I invited you both over to dinner, you'd get on like a house on fire."

"He's not my type."

"Meaning he might make you happy."

"Meaning he'd never make me smile."

"The offer stands. I know he fancies you. After Robbie's birthday party he asked who you were." Tanya nodded cheerily.

"I have a cat to paint. I don't think I've got time for a relationship."

"I'm talking about dinner."

"Thanks for trying, Tan."

"You've got an eyelash on your cheek." Tanya leaned forward and gently flicked the lash onto the back of her hand for Kate to blow and make a wish.

"Here goes." Kate blew the eyelash away and closed her eyes. She should have wished that she could be like Tanya. Happy with a good man. Someone like Joss Armstrong who had almost-sandy hair, brown eyes, athletic parts, and a degree in philosophy. She knew that Joss was very good news. But instead she wished for what she knew. She wished that she'd be having hot sex with Jake again very soon. That they'd be knocking back vodka shots together at his local bar until she couldn't feel her legs. That sometime in the near future she'd be lounging on his sofa painting her toenails silver while he played records for her. Because that was all Kate was interested in. Career? Money? Joss Armstrong? Third World debt? Important art? No, just Jake.

"So what's this Mirabelle Moncur character doing here anyway?" Tanya asked. "Did she come all this way to have her cat painted by you?"

"Oh, yeah, didn't you know, people travel far and wide to have their pets put in oils by Kate Disney?" She laughed. "Truly, I've no idea. But Leonard's never mentioned her before and she claims to have been his lover. So your guess is as good as mine."

Chapter Three

"Darling, I came to tell you that we have a visitor." Leonard, dressed today in a lilac sweater and tweed trousers, stood awkwardly in the doorway of Kate's shed as she scrubbed her hands clean. Since she'd arrived back from Tanya's her phone hadn't so much as winked at her with a text message, let alone heralded a call from Jake, so she'd immersed herself in a brush-cleaning scheme of such epic proportions that she was now out of turps, and, it seemed, most of the skin on her knuckles. Still, as she laid her brushes out to dry on the windowsill of the shed, the sable bristles gleamed in the late-afternoon sunlight and she felt a sense of satisfaction that lifted her spirits at least an inch off the floor.

"Ah yes, Madame Moncur. We've already met. I met her lion as well. In the kitchen this morning."

"I feared you might have." Leonard walked over to the stuffed zebra in the corner and stroked him. "Sorry I wasn't here to warn you and make the introductions—only she didn't really tell me that she was coming at all."

"She just showed up?" Clearly Kate and Jake weren't the only victims of Mirabelle's unannounced arrivals.

"I mentioned to her in a letter a month ago that you were living with me and that you painted animals and she sent a reply suggesting that she might like a portrait done and, lo and behold, I come home this morning and there she is, on my lounge chair without her top on." Leonard still bore the look of surprise, but he was too much of a gentleman to ever complain. "Anyway, it's a delight to see her. She really is a very dear old friend."

"How dear, exactly?" Kate rubbed a ton of lotion into her hands and raised a cheeky eyebrow at Leonard.

"What do you mean?" Leonard sat back in Kate's armchair and looked a little uncomfortable.

"Were you really lovers?" she asked, not for a moment expecting him to say that they were. She just thought that Mirabelle was the kind of woman who lied unconscionably about anything that came to mind.

"Is that what she told you?" Leonard looked serious.

"Yup."

"Actually we were."

"Oh, you were not." At which point Kate stopped rubbing cream into her hands.

"I was." As far as Kate knew, Leonard had never so much as held hands with a woman. That he might have had sex with one of the greatest female icons of all time, next to Helen of Troy, was incomprehensible. He liked only very hirsute, very dark, very handsome men. And never a hair under six feet tall. "Did she drug you?" Kate giggled as she pulled on her sneakers.

"The year was nineteen hundred and sixty-seven. Biarritz. I'd had three glasses of red wine and she began to squeeze my knee beneath the dinner table. At first I thought it was her second husband feeling me up. He was a terribly attractive Italian gentleman." Kate pretended to organize her canvases. She knew that if she paid too much attention to Leonard's story he'd become self-conscious and cut it short. So she feigned nonchalance as his very proper English tones clipped around the edges of the tale of his seduction by Mirabelle Moncur. "Then she began purring something in French in my ear and her hand moved upward, as it were."

"Poor Leonard." Kate turned and bit her lip to stop herself from laughing.

"Precisely. Well, she insisted that if I were an English gentleman as I seemed, I would walk her home. I don't know what became of the Italian film director husband. I think perhaps he was having it away with a young novelist who was at dinner, too. Not that Mirri cared. She'd set her cap at me." Leonard looked up and scowled at Kate, warning her not to laugh.

"She told me it was your eyes that did it."

"Unfortunately it wasn't only my eyes she wanted." Leonard shook his head. "So I walked her home. As I'd been brought up to do. And when I got to her gate she began walking a few paces ahead of me. Half dancing, half walking. She used to be a dancer when she was younger. She still has a very haughty demeanor."

"I'd noticed," Kate muttered, nodding for Leonard to continue.

"Well, first she took off her scarf and draped it around my neck. Then off came her skirt." Leonard pulled a handkerchief from his pocket and dabbed at his brow. "She did have absolutely splendid legs. Rather like Michelangelo's *David,* you know. Muscular. Rather boyish hips. Well, I was beginning to find the whole thing rather intriguing. Then she began to tug at my tie. In the manner of a kitten, cheeky but rather charming."

"Leonard, you fancied her."

"She had a certain charm."

"Wow." Kate was impressed. This was a miracle of biblical proportions.

"Anyway she pawed at my tie. Dropped it to the ground. Then she proceeded to unbutton her blouse. Needless to say she wasn't wearing a brassiere."

"Needless to say," Kate echoed.

"And then, well, before you know it we're standing naked beside her kitchen table and she's, well . . . perched on the table and she's got her legs wrapped around me and, well, what could I do?"

"You could have told her that she wasn't your type. To put it mildly," Kate suggested.

"She did smell rather wonderful, too. Rather feral. If that's not too crass a word." Leonard was back in 1967 and quite enjoying the trip down memory lane, Kate suspected.

"Woo hoo!"

"Indeed. There was a lot of woo hoo for the next two days, as a matter of fact. Mirabelle Moncur was not known for letting her conquests escape until she had drunk the cup dry. Then she used to toss them carelessly back into the real world. Often they were found stumbling around the streets of Biarritz days later. Spent and bewildered."

"Holy moley." Kate whistled. She'd heard of man-eaters but this should have been a wildlife documentary all on its own. "So what happened to you?" she asked, wondering how it was that Leonard had emerged not only alive but also as a friend of this woman.

"Well, as I was gathering up my trousers and tie on the third day and she was sitting looking very bored on her veranda painting her toenails, I thanked her for having me to stay."

"Ever the gentleman," Kate interrupted fondly.

"Indeed. And then I said it had been a most novel experience as I'd never been with a woman before."

"And?"

"She said, 'You are 'omosexual?' And I replied, *'Mais oui, madame.'* At which point she let forth a peal of laughter, spilled nail polish all over her dress, and hugged me like a long-lost brother. And we've been firm friends ever since." Leonard took a deep breath and uncrossed his legs, signaling the end of the story. "I think she was enormously flattered and amused. As I said, she has a great sense of humor."

"I'll take your word for it." Kate leaned down and planted a kiss on Leonard's forehead. "That completely cheered me up. Thank you."

"Were you miserable, my dear?" Leonard stood up and made for the door. It was five o'clock and no word from Jake.

"I don't seem to have the same effect on men I sleep with as Mirabelle Moncur."

"Beauty is a terrible curse, Kate. It usually comes in inverse proportion to happiness." Leonard let himself out of the shed. "I've spoken to Mirri and she'd love to have supper with us this evening. If you're available, so you two can get to know one another properly and talk about the painting."

"All right," Kate agreed, "I'll give her another chance. I'm sure we just got off on the wrong foot."

"Good, good. Come up at about seven, then. I'll rustle up something special."

In agreeing to dinner Kate had also officially buried the hope that Jake would call today. He probably slept all day, or felt hungover, or had to be at a band rehearsal, or something. He'd call tomorrow. And if not then, definitely by Wednesday, no matter what. Then Kate thought over Leonard's comment about beauty and happiness as she watched him walk down the garden path. Did he mean that Kate should be grateful she wasn't beautiful? Or that she was unhappy because she was so damned attractive? She suspected rather miserably that he meant the former.

———

As Leonard hummed at the chopping board, arranging sprigs of rosemary for the lamb shanks that he was preparing for the welcome supper, on the top floor of his house Mirabelle Moncur was languishing in her bath, the vetiver mists enveloping her, her disheveled blond hair piled on top of her head and her breasts, still showstoppingly spectacular, submerged beneath the warm, fragrant water. She looked around the room—at the ancient blue carpet on the bathroom floor, the huge, dusty pot of geraniums on the windowsill, and the stack of crossword books by the loo—and realized how much she'd missed England. It had been at least twenty years since she'd been here. She liked the big shabby houses with overstuffed furniture and civilized rituals—like afternoon tea and gin and tonic before dinner and taking walks. In Africa she might get in her Land Rover at sunset and set out for a hair-raising drive—she was, after all, a Parisian, and no amount of living abroad or dating race drivers had ever divested her of the appalling habits of her native city—around her property to check that there weren't a bunch of poachers lurking or an injured rhino beneath a baobab tree. But nothing, in Mirri's book, came close to a walk in England. So she decided to reacquaint herself with that ritual and take a stroll before supper. In fact, she'd even take Bébé; the poor thing needed some fresh air and exercise.

Mirri had thought very carefully about bringing the cub away so soon after the death of his mother last month. Although she'd kept wildcats since she was in her twenties, she'd never removed one from his native environment before. All her cats had been found looking dejected in zoos or in circuses on the outskirts of industrial French towns. When she heard any story of ill treatment or brutality or cramped, dirty cages, she would jump in her car, get out her map, and race to the scene. Once there she would offer the zookeepers or circus owners so much money for the animal that they couldn't refuse her. And if that failed, she was, quite simply, Mirabelle Moncur—the very sight of her, even in civilian clothes of jeans and a half-unbuttoned man's shirt, would often be all that was needed to persuade them to unlock the poor animal's cage and help her put the creature in the back of her Citroën estate. She'd then take them back to the house in Biarritz, where they'd join the other strays and refugees—in the eyes of the world she was fast becoming a pampered eccentric, but in reality she was much more St. Francis of Assisi.

But with Bébé it was different. He'd never known a world outside the game reserve and she wasn't sure that it was wise to bring him with her to England, but she had consulted the vet at home and grilled him exhaustively before she decided that, on balance, the trauma of being in a city and of enduring the flight from Africa was actually not so great as the trauma of being without her, his surrogate mother, for what might end up being rather a long time. Depending, of course, on how long it was going to take her to complete the business she'd really come to London for. And now she had Bébé here, safely through customs and happily rolling on the damp bath mat beside her, she was determined to make him feel as happy and secure as possible. So just as soon as she got out of the bath, she was going to take him with her for a walk. Just down the road. Not too far, but enough for him to stretch his legs. She knew that she might encounter a bit of curiosity from people, but she would just have to handle that. She'd spent years dealing with un-wanted attention, but if you just avoided eye contact you were fine. She'd bypass the paparazzi by going out of the back gate and straight onto Primrose Hill and she'd keep Bébé on the leash she'd ordered from Paris. He'd soon get used to it. And after all, when she was younger she'd rarely left home without Shiva, her first-ever lion cub, prancing fabulously beside her. So where was the harm?

After her bath Mirri pulled on one of the strappy sundresses that were her trademark in the 1960s and which she still looked a mil-lion dollars in, locked Bébé onto his navy-blue Hermès leash, and headed for Primrose Hill. It was a struggle for anyone walking by to make up his mind where to stare. If he was heading home from a nasty day at work or was adding up how much money he owed in bills this month, then he was invariably looking down at the pave-ment and catching sight of Bébé first. He'd have a second of think-ing he was hallucinating, look again, and then, when he realized it was in fact a lion cub on a leash, he'd look up to see if this was part of some circus procession striding down the High Street or whether the zookeeper from nearby Regents Park Zoo was taking his work home to meet the wife and kids.

If, on the other hand, the passerby was one of the straight-shouldered, soft-cheeked yogic beauties emerging from Triyoga after a heart-opening pranayama session, then she'd be looking straight ahead and catch sight of the legendary visage of Mirabelle Moncur first. This would cause a blink, a fear that all the alternate-nostril breathing she'd just done was more than mildly intoxicating as her teacher had suggested, and she had actually lost her mind. Mira-belle Moncur seen in public for the first time in years. The yoga princess would at once check out Mirri from head to toe—to see whether she was in as great shape as herself—and as she was doing so, she'd catch sight of Bébé and know that it was in fact Mirri Moncur, as nobody else would have the bottle, or style, to take a lion cub for a walk at six thirty on a Wednesday evening in the city. But whichever sight you saw first—Mirri or Bébé—it was still pretty remarkable. And certainly contributed to the three-car pileup at the junction of Regents Park Road and the argument between a married couple outside the fish-and-chip shop when the husband clocked the onetime goddess strolling with her snub nose in the air and without a care in the world.

Among the heads that Mirri caused to swivel that evening was that of Jonah Sinclair, an Academy Award–winning young actor who lived in an ivy-covered house in nearby Chalcot Square. Jonah had a pretty, makeup-artist wife and what seemed like several hundred children, but was in reality only about four. He was always pictured very sexily in the newspapers as part of a supercool, white-toothed, impenetrable family unit. But to those in the film industry he was known as Shagger Sinclair. It was often said that he was having affairs not just with every single woman on his particular film set but also the actress on the set of the movie that was shooting down the road. Fortunately for him and his wife, the press had him pegged as a family man, which was probably just to save Fleet Street from the exhausting task of taking seedy photographs and running stories on all his infidelities. Because even the usually insatiable British media would have limped home in second place with the energy it required to report even half of Jonah's peccadilloes.

At thirty-two years old Jonah was one of those actors who look fabulous on screen but in real life is so scruffy you wouldn't necessarily want to wipe the floor with him, let alone brave his treacherously unshaven face to kiss him. But he had spied Mirri Moncur and, as an avid movie-head, recognized her immediately. So lion by her side or no lion by her side, he was not going to let something as dangerous as a killer species come between him and sex with possibly the only woman in the world who could rival him in the Notches on Bedposts open heat. In fact, as he watched Mirri walk by the park bench where he was sitting, Jonah's rather crusty trousers sprang to life for the first time since his lunch with a flirty journalist all of four hours ago.

Jonah had been reading the newspaper with a can of McEwan's Export by his side—the lager was favored by tramps for its strength and cheapness—but he stopped as Mirri Moncur prowled past in her pretty dress and sandals with her chin high and her bottom seemingly even higher.

"Oy," he shouted out. Naturally she ignored him.

" 'Scuse me." He coughed and put down his newspaper. Mirri pranced on, her balletic steps just as elegant as the feline paces of Bébé. She had spent a lifetime sneering down her nose at unwanted attention and occasionally slapping its face. She was hardly about to stop and give the time of day to some disgusting bum. Until there was a tap on her shoulder. Mirri swung around and gave Jonah Sinclair a hatchet stare so tough, it could have felled acres of forest.

"I'm Jonah Sinclair." He moved his can of beer into his left hand and freed up his right one to shake Mirri's. He even wiped it thoughtfully down his trouser leg before he proffered it. Mirri glared at his hand, his revolting can of beer, and his matted hair and turned her back on him, setting off again on her evening walk across the narrow paths of Primrose Hill.

"Nice arse," he murmured as she walked away. At which point Mirri stopped in her tracks and turned to face him again. This time she took him in properly. She could tell by his audacity that he was probably worth a second look. Her appraisal began with his feet: sneakers, which she thought lazy style-wise but definitely youthful. And she liked a young man. They had stamina. Then his trousers: grubby, for sure, but well cut. She paused and, in the way an antiques dealer might appraise a fine piece of porcelain, she looked at the discernible bulge in his expensive pants. She pursed her lips, giving nothing away. Then she took in his shirt in a cursory way, little of interest to her there; checked out his arms with a little more care, she liked a well-shaped wrist. She noted the watch. The man wasn't a tramp. He wasn't even a banker on his day off. This man was much, much wealthier than that.

Having been the recipient of expensive jewelry and fine watches from men since the day she cast off her spectacles and dental braces at the age of seventeen, Mirri could distinguish between a run-of-the-mill Cartier or Patek Philippe and the Superwatch, the type of which only nine are made every year by a decaying Swiss gentleman in a garret. They cost as much as a small castle in the Scottish Highlands. Jonah was wearing a Superwatch. Intrigued, Mirri raised her eyelashes and looked him square in the eyes. Which, despite his mucky appearance, were clear and sharply focused on hers.

"You're whom?" she said, betraying not a whit of interest in the answer.

"Jonah Sinclair." He was smiling now, and Mirri suspected at once that he was an actor. He had a mouth that was created for the big screen: symmetrical and generous and made for uttering lines that you wanted to hear whispered in your ear when the lights went down.

"Would you like to buy me dinner?" Mirri offered charitably, but still without a smile or a handshake.

"Sure." Jonah nodded, relieved that this particular ship had come in. And so easily, too, as it turned out. He'd thought for one awful moment that the hottest woman he'd seen all day, hell if not all week, was going to turn him down. "So what you doing in this neck of the woods?" he asked as he walked by her side, a respectful distance away, back toward the High Street.

"Neck of the woods?" Mirri looked puzzled, for even though she'd dated Michael Caine for a few months when she was twenty-five she had never really spoken to him enough to get the hang of cockney accents.

"You live in Africa, don't you?" Jonah asked reverentially.

"How you know this?" Mirri always pretended to know less English than she really did when she was being chatted up. As well as being great for seduction, her heavy French accent also meant she didn't have to speak any more than was absolutely necessary and could get on with the business at hand. Which for Mirri was crucial, it was the whole point.

"Mirabelle Moncur. I'm a huge fan of yours," he told her. "I've seen all your films."

"Ah, and I assume you're an actor, too. Though I've seen none of your films and never heard of you."

"Actually I am, you're right," replied Jonah, not even slightly perturbed, only turned on by the fact that she was the only person in the Coca-Cola-drinking world who wasn't aware that not only could Jonah Sinclair convincingly act his way out of a paper bag, but he was also the highest-grossing box-office actor. Ever. "Now, I was thinking we could go to this restaurant called Manna. They do great vegetarian." Years of being a total dog automatically stopped him from adding *so my wife tells me* at the end of such sentences.

"Vegetables?" Mirri scowled.

"You love animals, right?" Jonah looked down at Bébé, from whom he'd carefully stood as far away as possible.

"And I love to eat them." Mirri looked at Jonah and wished he'd behave as carelessly as his clothing; she wasn't in the mood for an overly solicitous man tonight. She'd hoped from his "nice arse" remark that he'd be rougher than he now seemed. She groaned to herself. She usually made a point of not dating actors for this very reason. You thought you were getting one thing and ended up with whatever it was they thought you wanted, rather than what you really wanted. She decided to nip the niceties in the bud.

"We'll go to Lemonia and then maybe we'll fuck," Mirri decided. And Jonah, after a second of openmouthed shock, relaxed visibly.

"Cool." He smiled and began to swagger a bit. "So do we take the cat, too, or do you want to drop it off home first?"

"The owner of the restaurant will look after him for me. She's very nice. Well, she was twenty years ago, I suppose things are still the same. That's the thing about England, *plus ça change*. You can go away for twenty years and when you come back all is just the same as when you left."

Mirri smiled for the first time, pleased that Jonah had relaxed enough to drape his arm around her neck and brush her face with stubble as he muttered, "I meant what I said about your arse, y'know? But your tits are fucking unbelievable, too."

"So what about you and Jake?" Leonard was laying out wineglasses on the pale yellow linen tablecloth in his orangery. The old glass-and-stone room was one of Kate's favorite parts of Leonard's amazing house, but thanks to the generally useless nature of the English weather it was only a viable place to be for about three weeks of the year—on a clear, crisp, warm summer's night. The rest of the time it was damp, smelled of mold, and was freezing cold. But this evening it had the air of a favorite old dress that had been brought out of mothballs and tissue paper for a special occasion—the mossy bricks were warmed from a day of sun, the light of the sunset cast an apricot glow over the flaking paint, and the Victorian pineapple tree, the palms, and the cascading ferns lent a smell of dewy greenness to the air. Kate bunched her damp, newly washed hair into a ponytail and helped Leonard lay the silver out next to the place mats.

"Oh, I think possibly it was a red herring," she said, not giving away the black depths of disappointment she felt in the pit of her stomach about Jake not having called. "It was his birthday. I thought things had changed . . ." She responded to Leonard's gentle look of disbelief by adding, "He told me that he loved me, Leonard. He'd never done that before. That's why I thought it was different this time . . ." Kate needlessly rearranged the already perfect flowers on the table. "Anyway, it was obviously a one-off. I won't call him. I promise."

"Darling, as you know, you can do whatever you wish. But just be careful. Jake is a very charming and alluring man . . . but he is also what I would call a cad. And for want of a more original expression, a leopard doesn't change his spots."

"I know, I know. But no harm done, hey? I'm still in one piece." Kate shook back her ponytail and smiled, to prove her bravery to Leonard. But really she knew that this wasn't the end of it. Sure, she'd pretend to the others—to Tanya and Leonard—that she'd washed her hands of him, but really how could she? Jake loved her more than he loved anyone or anything; he just loved differently from other people. But she knew there would come a day when he was worn out. When he wanted to settle down. And Kate was all he knew and all he trusted—he'd be with her. Eventually. In the meantime she just had to ensure that when Jake was stepping all over her, it was because she was his rock and not his doormat. At times she wasn't sure that he understood the difference.

To tell the truth, when Mirri asked Jonah to take her to dinner she had clean forgotten that Leonard was making supper for her and that she was supposed to be meeting the rather charmless painter girl who lived in the shed. And to be even more truthful, even if she had remembered, it probably wouldn't have made a scrap of difference. Mirri hadn't been in such a glorious position as this for a long time and she wasn't going to throw it away just because she'd made an arrangement. Leonard had known her for years—he was used to her vanishing into the night. After all, that had been how they'd met. And when she did remember, somewhere toward the end of the main course, that he was cooking lamb shanks back at the house, she simply vowed to take him to the opera to make up for it. There was just no way she was going to let Jonah Sinclair disappear down the road now she'd found him. She was in the mood for him, and like all appetites, hers may have disappeared by tomorrow. Besides which, it had been years since she'd met a man in this way. Of course, she'd had her lovers in Africa—even though she lived hundreds of miles from anywhere, there had always been a handsome twenty-two-year-old on sabbatical from his American university or a passing journalist who came to interview her for his drab magazine about endangered species. She'd even had an affair with the vet last year, which was not as much fun as she'd hoped, because his wife had found out, but needs must be met, even in the African bush. Consequently the frisson of her encounter with Jonah was deliciously appealing to Mirri, and though she had originally intended their dinner to be a mere formality, not much more than a precursor to the fingers-on-lips and hands-on-zips routine of later, they were actually enjoying themselves.

Unsurprisingly they discovered that in many ways they were very similar: Both had experienced the adulation of millions, were possessed of similar sexual appetites, and also exhibited flashes of such pampered wickedness that to most people they would have seemed amoral. To each other it was amusing. So a bottle of wine down and after much talk of film directors they'd worked with and how nauseating they found the paparazzi, they still hadn't even gotten onto the subjects that interested them most—namely themselves.

"So, Mirri, why aren't you married?" Jonah leaned across the table and fed Mirri a golden ring of calamari. She took a very well-practiced bite, which had half the men in the restaurant distractedly putting forkfuls of aubergine in their ears instead of their mouths.

"Why are you married?" Mirri asked Jonah. "I can't imagine why you would want to. Unless you want a housekeeper and mother for your children."

"Well, sure, she does those things. But really . . ." Jonah leaned over and confided theatrically in Mirri's ear, "being married makes it easier when it comes to other women—they don't get as heavy, they don't expect as much, they know where they stand. It's neater."

"I suppose. But if you're honest you don't need to hide behind anything. That is the neatest way possible," Mirri told Jonah, who hadn't enjoyed himself this much for a long time. Here was a woman who was completely unintimidated by him, perhaps even a little bored by him, and he found that enormously sexy.

"So you're always honest?" he asked her.

"Of course. Life's too short not to be." She took a mouthful of red wine.

"I think we should start." Kate said as she drained the last drop of what was probably her third glass of wine. She'd been picking at the bread for the past half hour and was in danger of not having the appetite for even an olive if she ate any more. The sun had set and the garden had all but sunk into darkness; the only light now came from the flickering candles dotted around the still-pristine table.

Leonard looked at his watch. "I hope she's okay. That she's not hiding in an alleyway somewhere from the paparazzi."

"She doesn't strike me as a woman who would hide in an alleyway from anything." Hunger always made Kate irritable. "Besides which, she has a lion with her. I don't think she'll come to much harm."

"Yes, yes. You're probably right." Leonard finally picked up his fork and hesitantly skewered a piece of poached salmon. "Who knows, she may still make it in time for the lamb."

"She might," Kate said, not caring whether Mirri Moncur even made it for cornflakes in the morning. As far as Kate was concerned she'd let Leonard down and welshed on a meeting with her, and that was neither kind nor professional. And until Kate had polished off a decent supper, she wasn't likely to feel any different. "But then again maybe she's gone to visit her smart friends at the palace. In which case we may never see her again," she added.

"No need to be catty, my dear. Mirri has nothing against you."

"I'm sorry, she just seemed a bit full of herself. But then if you're an actress I suppose that's your job description."

"Indeed. But she does terribly good things for animals, you know. She's made millions with that wildlife trust of hers. So she can't be all that bad at heart." Finally Leonard had managed to shame Kate into silence.

"So how were the auctions this morning?" she asked as she tucked into her dinner. "Any good finds?"

"Very nice set of Regency chairs and a bookcase." Leonard nodded. "A little overpriced but worth it, I think." As Leonard discussed the hellish drive back into London from Sussex, Kate stole a peep at her cell phone, which had been nestling in her jacket pocket. If Jake had been asleep with a hangover all day he had to be up by now—it was ten o'clock, after all, and that would have been the longest lie-in in history. But no, the phone wasn't blinking with a message for her. It was plunged into darkness. *Like my heart,* she thought morosely and wanted to stab herself with a fork for being such an idiot last night and believing him.

———

Meanwhile Mirri and Jonah held hands as they collected a much-admired and well-fed Bébé from the restaurant owner and headed back across the park toward Leonard's place. Mirri, who was in no way interested in a head-on collision with the paparazzi, led her handsome prey through the back gate and onto Primrose Hill. Together with Bébé they stalked through the undergrowth of nettles, over the dried-up grass cuttings and neglected garden canes, and emerged beside Kate's shed. Mirri noted that no lights were on—the girl was probably still at dinner with Leonard, she thought, with a barely there pang of guilt.

"You have the bottle of wine?" Mirri asked Jonah in a hushed voice.

"Sure do." He waved the bottle that they'd brought from the restaurant in the air and reached a hand out for Mirri's irresistibly apple-shaped bottom.

"Okay, come with me. I can see them having dinner in the house, so be as quiet as possible and stay in the shadows, okay?"

"Terrific, I go home with an older woman and we behave like teenagers. I love it," Jonah said, moving his hand up and hooking it into the awesome curve of Mirri's waist. God, they didn't make women like this anymore, he thought. They were all skinny and sinewy these days, with muscles where only men were supposed to have muscles and hard little tummies that seemed to be made for keeping men at bay, not tracing a lazy finger over. No, Mirri was like a piece of soft, slightly overripe fruit, he thought longingly.

"You sit over there," Mirri said, breaking free from his hold and taking Bébé by the leash up toward the house. "I'm going to sneak in and put him to bed. I'll be back soon." She disappeared stealthily into the dark and headed for the house, bypassing the orangery, where clinking sounds of china were mingling with chatter as Kate and Leonard cleared away the table. She held her breath and hoped they didn't suddenly appear in the kitchen as she was tiptoeing through it.

Moments later, after Mirri had deposited Bébé in her bedroom, she reappeared with a packet of Gauloise and no shoes. She found an old hammock hanging in a far corner of the garden and sat down in it.

"Here, you must be very careful not to fall out of it," she instructed him. "And if you do then you must not scream."

"How come you're so afraid of being caught?" Jonah asked as he lowered himself carefully down beside her.

"I'm not afraid. But if I am caught then I will have to join in and talk when really I just want to be here." She lit up a cigarette and inhaled as if her life depended on it. "I hope you are as good as you look."

"Well, so do I," said Jonah, taking Mirri's half-smoked Gauloise from her and dropping it to the ground. "I'd hate to disappoint, madame."

As Kate wandered back toward her shed she was sure that she could smell cigarette smoke and decided that it must be coming from the camp of photographers who seemed to have taken up permanent residence on the pavement outside the house. She even felt a little sorry for the woman who had stood her up for dinner. It must be pretty hellish having twenty men baying for your photograph. Men who would be particularly pleased if she were to show up looking raddled and ancient—because that way they'd be able to sell their photos to the newspapers for so much more. A glimpse of cellulite or a turkey neck, even if it was just a trick of the light or a bad angle, was so much more to the general public's taste.

"Sshhhh." Kate heard a thud and then a low-pitched male laugh somewhere in the bushes to her right. She stopped in her tracks and was about to launch herself into the house and inform the police that some gentlemen of the press were trespassing in her garden—when she heard the inimitable sound of Mirabelle Moncur.

"Oh that is very good. I like *that*," she was saying in her husky voice. Kate stood stock-still and peered in the direction of the voices. There, beneath the cherry tree, where Kate had hung her hammock only last week, she saw something glowing in the pitch dark. She crept in closer and noticed that it was a lit cigarette butt that somebody hadn't extinguished. God, Kate hated people who discarded their cigarettes all over the place. But just as she was about to march over to Mirri and ask her to pick it up, she heard another sound that suggested she might not want to march anywhere other than the opposite direction at the moment. It was the satisfied groan of a man. So instead of taking a step closer, Kate crept away, making a mental note to ensure in the morning that the cigarette butt had gone. And if not she'd take up the matter with Leonard. It was a filthy habit.

Once back in her shed, Kate went to shut the window that she'd left open before she'd gone out. But as she approached it she realized that not only were the noises of Mirabelle Moncur and her lover being carried very efficiently on the breeze—right into her shed—but she also had top-dollar, ringside seats for the show.

"Oh, hell," she said as the light from the neighbor's bathroom, which overlooked the garden, perfectly illuminated the scene in the hammock.

"Oh baby, that is great," the man, who was lying back on the hammock, with his trousers in the nearby herbaceous border, was saying. Mirri, rather unsurprisingly, was kneeling on the grass and had her head planted firmly in his lap. Facedown. Kate, who was squeamish even about couples who made out on escalators in the tube station, almost let out a yell of disgust, but managed at the last moment to suppress it. She wasn't quick enough, however, to prevent a startled "Fucking hell" from flying out of her mouth when she saw the face of Jonah Sinclair bob up for air. She knew instantly that it was him because not only was he more famous than the prime minister, but his was also the same face she had seen on a movie poster at the bus stop only yesterday as she wandered through Primrose Hill. It was indeed the face she gazed at every time she went to the loo. It peered out at her from the cover of *Heat* magazine, which lay on the floor of her bathroom. But though Kate did her best to duck down beneath the windowsill so that she couldn't be seen, it was too late.

"Oh, Kate, hi there. I'm glad you're home," Mirri said loudly, barely looking around, and without stopping doing that thing she was doing to Jonah. "I want you to start on Bébé early tomorrow. I have to go shopping in the afternoon."

"Okay," Kate said in alarm as she turned her head away from the spectacle before her and darted toward the bed, where she sat down with a thud. "Sure."

"Okay, eight o'clock," Mirri confirmed. "Good night." And without another word she got back to business, leaving Kate hyperventilating at the trauma of being busted. Watching someone, and an old person at that, have sex.

She wondered whether she ought to turn on the light. Or whether she should draw the curtains. Certainly she ought to draw the curtains, she decided, and twitched as silently as possible back over to the window.

"I'm so glad that some things you read in the press are true," Jonah Sinclair was murmuring as he slipped his tongue into Mirri's ear.

"You like?" Mirri laughed as she pulled her skirt up to her waist and, with perfect sleight of hand, removed Jonah's boxer shorts.

"I bloody well love," Jonah groaned just beyond her window.

"Oh no," Kate breathed to herself as she gathered a curtain in either hand. But before she could pull them together and put an end to the sight, the human pretzel that was Mirri and Jonah had spilled out of the hammock and onto the ground. And horrifyingly for Kate it was compelling viewing on a par with suddenly realizing that you've been allocated a porn site on cable by mistake. You would never order it yourself but you can't help having a sneaky peek. Especially if the stars are two of the most sexually desirable, and probably sexually experienced, human beings on the planet. Albeit one might be just a bit past her use-by date.

"Yuck," Kate said, as she bent down a bit so she could see more clearly just which leg belonged to which sex. What she was witnessing was like a how-to lesson in carnality. Mirri and Jonah were now standing against the cherry tree, Jonah going hard at it as Mirri licked his armpits. Kate thought this a bit gross, but it certainly seemed to be doing the trick for Jonah, whose buttocks were pumping up and down as enthusiastically as a toddler on a trampoline. And when Mirri then slithered down the tree with a satisfied series of gasps and decided to pay a little more attention to Jonah's indefatigable erection, Kate had an overwhelming urge to make notes.

But she didn't. Instead she just watched very carefully as if studying for a biology paper, and vowed to practice every lick and stroke on Jake one day, possibly in another lifetime, but hey, even if they came back as ants she'd be sure to blow his mind. She watched and learned, before realizing that the glass was steamed up and she was probably a pervert. At which point she snatched the curtains shut and tiptoed to the sink to brush her teeth in the dark.

Chapter Four

The next morning Kate was woken by a colossal thudding on her shed door. It didn't take more than a split second for her to fathom that it was Mirri Moncur and that Kate had overslept. But not by accident. Just before she had fallen asleep last night, Kate had rather belligerently decided that she was not going to abide by orders issued in flagrante delicto from a hammock containing a handsome, naked young actor. She simply didn't see any reason why she should kowtow to Mirabelle Moncur's needs. Especially when she hadn't turned up for dinner last night and had failed to let Leonard know.

Kate was also just a bit peevish about the fact that Mirri was having great, tree-banging sex, and that she herself had gone to bed in a pair of earplugs and a bra. The earplugs because the "wow"s and the "again, again"s were not conducive to sleep, and the bra because as she'd pulled on her nightie she had suddenly noticed that her boobs were a bit farther down her chest from where she usually found them. In a panic she remembered that Marilyn Monroe slept in a bra to avoid such a horrifying eventuality as this. So Kate followed suit. She supposed she could ask Mirri, whose tits seemed, like time and tide, to wait for no man, for some tips in the keeping-your-breasts-aloft department, but that would have entailed talking to the oversexed old tart.

"Bugger off," Kate shouted at the pounding outside.

"It is eight twenty-five. I waited twenty-five minutes before I came to find you." Mirri's voice rang out like a French foghorn.

"Well, you can wait even longer. I don't open until nine," Kate barked and pulled the duvet over her head.

"I say to you last night, eight o'clock. You say fine. This is unprofessional."

"Well, you crossed the boundaries of professional behavior when you decided to remove your dress on my doorstep and reenact the bloody Kama Sutra," Kate yelled back. But instead of a brick through the window she was met by sounds of merriment behind the door. Kate ignored it for all of five seconds, then couldn't contain herself any longer. "What's so funny?" she snapped, and sat up in bed.

"You watched us." Mirri had sat down on the doorstep and lit a cigarette. "It was a good performance, *non*?"

"Don't be so disgusting," Kate spat, with the disapproval of a Sunday school teacher at a wife-swapping party.

"No wonder you are tired. You lay awake all night thinking about it." Mirri laughed. At which point Kate got out of bed, stomped toward her door, and threw it open.

"Would you please put that thing out? It stinks." Kate glared at Mirri and her cigarette. "And for your information I would rather have burned my hair than watch that pathetic display outside my window last night. Next time I'll call the police."

Mirri casually stubbed out her cigarette and stood up. "Then I shall return to my room until nine, when you prefer to begin working. But you must stop being so English about making love. It is too boring," Mirri said, before she pushed off back to the house without a hint of emotion. Leaving Kate looking like a rhinoceros about to charge—all dust and fury. *The only difference being that rhinos don't wear bras under their nightdresses,* Kate thought with a cringe as she looked down.

Eventually Kate pried herself from bed and made her way to the house with her sketch pad and pencils—but only for Leonard. She didn't care a bit about Mirri Moncur or her lion cub. In fact, this morning she cared about very little. She had slumped into one of those black pits of despair that seemed to be part of the landscape of life with Jake. They were the times when he vanished from her life for days on end. And these were the days that she barely survived. The days she wished that she could just sleep through and not have to feel. She knew that the sensible thing to do would be to resolve, quite simply, never to see him again. But she also knew that it was the time she was least likely to make the break—she was weak and diminished and she knew that when he did finally reemerge, she'd be so relieved that she would forget the misery. She often wondered, as she did this morning, how she had become involved in such a dysfunctional relationship. She'd never have believed herself capable of it before she met Jake. It was something that insecure, idiotic women in magazines or television talk shows did. It wasn't something that an attractive woman with a job and friends should have given the time of day to. But what she'd never understood before was how you could actually love someone who behaved so carelessly toward you. She didn't understand it now, either; she just knew that she didn't want to spend another minute without Jake in her life. But for Leonard's sake and for the sake of not allowing her life to be completely governed by Jake, she got up and, tucking her cell phone into her jeans pocket, went to find Mirri Moncur.

Kate arrived at Leonard's kitchen door and rapped out a perfunctory knock before pushing it open and letting herself in. She and Leonard had lived this way for a while now. His house was open day and night to Kate, and he was very fond of saying, "*Mi casa, su casa,* my dear." Actually he applied this expression to everything from cornflakes to friends. What was Leonard's was, by extension, Kate's. Similarly she'd have been delighted to share everything she owned with Leonard. Though it hadn't come to that yet—he had little need for either combat pants or pencils, and

though he had taken a queeny shine to a pair of Janis Joplin's cowboy boots that Jake had bought for her on eBay, they would never
have fit him. So Kate merely shared her tales of youthful mis-
spending and occasionally her magazines with Leonard. And one
day, when she had a palazzo in Venice and caskets of jewels, she'd
share those with him, too. Though jewels weren't really his thing.
Leonard was not camp in an Elton John way; rather he was discreetly appreciative of all beautiful things and had exquisite taste.
There was nothing of the rhinestone poof about him.

"Leonard? It's me." Kate poked her head into the kitchen. The
house was deserted.

"Through here," Leonard called out from his study across the
hall. Kate looked about slightly cautiously in case Bébé was off his
leash and prowling the corridors. Or indeed to see if Mirri was off
her leash. Though in fairness it was Kate who had been unreason-
able and pathetic this morning. Kate had been practicing a bit of an
apology and planned to deliver it with as much grace as she could
muster.

"Come in, come in." Leonard was sitting behind his desk and
stood up when Kate walked in. "Tea? Coffee? Sherry?" he inquired
as Kate gave him a small hug and then perched on the edge of a
leather library chair.

"Thanks, but I've got to speak to Mirabelle about this portrait,"
she explained as Leonard seized the moment and poured himself a
small sherry.

"Ah, yes, the poor thing was very apologetic about not making it
to dinner last night. She ran into an old friend and got carried
away."

"I'll say," said Kate when Leonard's back was turned.

"Sorry?"

"That's a shame." Kate smiled. "Still, we had a lovely time."

"Absolutely we did." Leonard settled back down to do his work.
"Can't possibly look my accounts in the eye without one of these,"
he said as he raised his sherry glass.

"Quite right, too." Kate stood up. "Have fun with your accounts." And with that she went out into the hall and up the stairs to the top floor.

"Ah, come in, come in." Mirri opened the door with a flourish as Kate waited hesitantly. It wasn't the reception she'd expected. Mirri was smiling, warm, and dressed in a flowing sky-blue caftan. Kate had imagined that the only thing that would be blue would be the air—with a stream of abuse for Kate's rudeness this morning. But Mirri seemed not to even remember, let alone mind. "We've been waiting for you."

"Good, well, here I am," Kate said, somewhat disarmed. "The thing is, Miss Moncur, about this morning, I'm sorry. It was unprofessional of me not to turn up on time. You're right."

"Oh, this is fine." Mirri swept Kate into a chair in the corner next to where Bébé was sleeping on the carpet. "I understand that you are just jealous of what happened last night."

"Jealous?" Kate wondered if she'd misunderstood Mirri's French accent.

"It was not diplomatic of me to make love near your house." Mirri sat down on the bed and waved her hand dismissively. "I understand."

"I wasn't jealous," Kate said.

"Darling, of course you must be. You were with a slug of a man when I came in the other day. Quite charmless."

"I'm sorry?" Kate asked, not able to believe that Mirri was serious for a moment.

"Don't be sorry. I felt sorry for you."

"What?"

"You could do better." Mirri smiled at Kate. "But enough of that. Let's discuss my *petit chat*. He is after all why we are here."

"You just called my boyfriend a slug."

"He was your boyfriend?" Mirri scowled. "Then why didn't he behave as if he was? He took the sheet from you. He didn't defend you when I said your paintings were average, and he didn't throw me out. This is not the kind of man you want for a boyfriend."

"I really don't think that it's any of your business." Kate's cheeks had begun to glow pink with anger. Who on earth did this old cow think she was? And what was she doing noticing all those things about the way Jake behaved? If Kate spent her whole time not noticing them, then why should anyone else?

"No, you're right. The sex must be amazing. For you to put up with this slug. Am I right?" Mirri wandered over to the mirror and began piling her hair on top of her head. More as an act of vanity than hairstyling.

"I refuse to talk about this any longer." Kate got up from the chair and went to sit beside the lion cub on the floor. She was shaking with fury. "So were you thinking oil or watercolor?"

"I was thinking that you shouldn't put up with a man like that. You're not unattractive. Although your clothes are wrong."

"My clothes?"

"Those trousers? You were perhaps going to repair a drain?" Mirri asked.

"It's called fashion. It's something *young* people tend to enjoy." Kate sucked air in through her mouth and looked pointedly at Mirri Moncur's slightly turkeyish neck.

"Oh, I'm not criticizing you." Mirri smiled. "I just find it amusing that so many young women complain of not finding a husband yet they dress as if they don't need one. See? If you look as if you can unblock your own drain, a man will not feel wanted or needed."

"That's an interesting view of the casual clothing phenomenon. I'll be sure to alert the Gap to the implications of the mass production of cargo pants on the institution of marriage."

"Oh, you're too serious. I just think there's nothing wrong with looking pretty." Mirri eased her long blond mermaid hair back over her shoulder.

"Nor do I. But I think the connection between trousers and husbands is tenuous. And it didn't do Jennifer Aniston's chances any harm when it came to nabbing Brad Pitt."

"This Pitt is not a man. He's a girl with facial hair. No substance."

"I think a lot of women would disagree with you." Kate was losing her patience now; the woman was clearly mad. "If you don't want to discuss the painting, then I really ought to go and do some work."

"I think oils." Mirri bent down to kiss her pet on the nose. "Women may disagree with me about this Brad Pitt but this is why there is no romance left in the world. What has he to offer that a lesbian lover doesn't?" Mirri argued in her perfectly irrational, perfectly confident French way.

"Well, I think maybe . . ." Kate shook her head impatiently.

"Oh, apart from the cock. They all have the cock. But do they know what to do with it?" This was a rhetorical question. And one look at Kate told Mirri Moncur that her visitor was not qualified to answer it. Kate suspected as much herself, too. Much as she hated to admit it. "No, because women are all fair and good and charming and dying to fix their own drains and take responsibility for their own orgasms so there's no point in the man even trying to be a man anymore. See?" Mirri lit up a cigarette with her omnipresent lighter. "We have castrated them. It's too sad."

"I love men." Kate tried to sound liberal and on top of the argument.

"No, you love the wrong man. You love a slug who isn't capable of loving you back," Mirri pronounced.

"He's my boyfriend," Kate lied. "And I really take exception to you commenting on something you know absolutely nothing about." She knew that was becoming irritatingly bolshy but there was something about Mirri Moncur that brought this side out in her.

"I'll tell you everything you need to know about . . . what's his name?"

"Jake."

"Jake." Mirri took a long drag on her cigarette. "He is weak. Maybe because he has the small cock. Maybe because he doesn't like his mother. Really it's irrelevant. He's weak and he thinks that because you love him, you are even weaker. So he is mean to you. He won't call you. He doesn't care whether you call him. But if you do, he thinks you're foolish."

"You don't know the first thing about Jake," Kate said, not able to look Mirri in the eye. "He loved me. He wrote songs for me . . ."

"He's not good enough for you." Mirri stubbed her cigarette out on an ashtray on her bedside table.

"I see" was all that Kate could manage. She knew it was true. It was so close to the bone that she thought she might be sick. At which point Mirri Moncur abandoned her perfectly executed *tour de Jake* and changed the subject. "So how long will it take you to paint this picture?"

"About a month," Kate said blankly. Then, with her blood boiling, she added, "Which should give you just long enough to hang out with Jonah Sinclair."

"Ah. Mr. Sinclair." Mirri smiled and nodded at the memory.

"You might think that my judgment's bad. But yours isn't much better. He's married, you know?" Kate had decided that an eye for and eye and a tooth for a tooth was the best way forward.

"Oh, yes yes, of course I know," Mirri said in a blasé way as she flipped through Kate's sketches.

"Don't you think that's a bit off?" Kate asked.

"Off?" Mirri didn't understand the implication.

"Off color. Wrong. He's got children, too. A few, I think."

"Darling, I'm not the one cheating on my wife." Mirri shrugged.

"I know, but isn't it bad karma or something? I mean, I always think that if I were married and some tart—" Kate checked herself. "—some other woman came along and had an affair with my husband I'd be miserable. I wouldn't necessarily want to make anyone else that miserable."

"And you would blame the single, unattached woman who had never made a vow to be faithful to anyone? Rather than the married man who was cheating on his wife who had made that vow?" Mirri was rearranging a vase of antique lilac roses she'd picked from the garden yesterday afternoon.

"No, but I'd just be worried that if I ran off with someone else's husband then someday my karma would come back and bite me on the bum and some woman would run off with my husband."

"Oh, I see." Mirri turned and looked at Kate quite seriously, then in a light way, like a young girl who's just realized that Santa Claus does exist after all, added, "But I'm not married. And I don't want a husband. So that's fine."

"Yes, but . . ." Kate was about to expand on her objections when she realized she was wasting her breath. Mirri was as likely to feel guilty about her fling with Jonah as she was to become a Carmelite nun. "I just feel sorry for his poor wife."

"Then she should take a lover, too. Everyone would be happy."

"Typical French," Kate mumbled to her pencil and carried on sketching. "So we're decided on oils, are we? I can do watercolor. And we haven't even discussed the background."

"Oh, oils, oils. I was once painted by Picasso, you know." Mirri pressed her nose into Bébé's neck. "He said, 'I paint objects as I think them, not as I see them.' This is beautiful, *non*?"

"Isn't it," Kate said, wondering what would happen if she painted Bébé as a spoiled fat cat and Mirri as a black-hearted Jezebel. "Did you sleep with Picasso?"

"Of course," Mirri said, and turned languorously onto her back on the bed. "Short men don't have as far to go down." She laughed throatily and pulled a packet of cigarettes from her nearby handbag. "Have you ever slept with a short man?"

"No, I don't think I have." Kate didn't add, though, that almost every other physical shortcoming in a man was represented on her list of conquests.

"They are very good. They have a lot to prove so they try very hard." She sat up and looked at Kate carefully. "You need good sex, my darling. It will make you happy."

"So how was Picasso. I mean the important stuff. Like his art. Not his dick. How was the portrait?" Kate decided that if she got involved in a debate with Mirri about her sorely lacking sex life she would skewer someone with a sharp pencil. It was like being told by a bossy shop assistant that you look great in a sweater you can't afford. Highly annoying.

"The painting sucked. Wow, it was bad." Mirri laughed. "He was in his bad phase."

"Is it in a gallery?"

"No, it's in my kitchen in Mozambique."

"Shouldn't it be preserved? In a gallery?" Kate asked, concerned.

"No, *I* should be preserved. The painting should be thrown out. But one day I'll sell it to save an elephant. I tell you, *ma choux,* you would stop worrying about such things if you were having good sex. People who are angry and resentful and full of judgment of others, they are simply not getting enough sex. I see it time and time again. If we all had good sex there would be no wars, no divorce, no sadness."

"Mirri, please, can we just not discuss this anymore. It's distracting. And like I said, quite unprofessional." Kate was now bored of the subject. Jesus, this woman needed to go to Sex Addicts Anonymous.

"Did The Slug give you orgasms?" Mirri asked.

"If by 'The Slug' you mean Jake—" Kate looked inquiringly at Mirri, who nodded yes, she meant Jake.

"Yes, actually. All the time. Every time," Kate blurted out.

"Good. Then it was just love he didn't give you?" Mirri shook her head disapprovingly, and Kate chewed incredulously on her pencil and tried not to cry.

"I'll be back at eleven tomorrow morning to paint your pet," she choked out as she stood up and gathered her things together. "If I haven't killed myself."

Chapter Five

"Dad, have you seen my Sex Pistols CD?" Ella asked. She was nine but Nick had let her have the album for Christmas because she was mad about the song "Who Killed Bambi?" He made a conscious effort to be as liberal a father as possible so that his daughters would always feel that they could tell him anything. Though at twelve Jasmine was pushing the boundaries of his laissez faire approach to parenting—she had gone to a birthday party last week and had her ears pierced despite a very firm edict that demanded she wait until she was thirteen. She also insisted on wearing a bra despite him yelling at her, "Take that thing off and don't put it back on until you've got tits." He'd wondered afterward if he'd been too harsh. But she'd taken it off for a few hours, at least.

"Dad?" Ella came into the room with dripping black hair and a sodden bubblegum-pink bathing suit.

"Have you looked in my car?" he asked, without glancing up from the newspaper.

"Yes," she said, as though he were the slowest, most stupid human being she'd ever come across.

"Have you asked your sister?" He tore his eyes from *The Times* and smiled at the desperation on his youngest daughter's face.

"Dad," she groaned.

"Okay, come on, let's look in your room." Nick put down his paper, picked up the wet little hand, and led her out of the drawing room into the hallway. "And where's your towel? I thought I told you not to come into the house dripping water like that. Look at your lips, they're blue."

"I'm not cold. I'm really warm," the shivering little body that was trotting beside him promised.

"You're mad," he said, and chased Ella up the stairs, shrieking her head off.

Sometimes Nick felt too old to have such lively young children. He was sixty-one and looked it. He'd married Jessica, their mother, when he suddenly found himself hurtling toward the fifty mark with nothing to show for his life except for the spectacular buildings he'd designed all over the world and a large cellar of extremely fine wines. He'd only bought this place, his beautiful house in Oxfordshire, with its swimming pool and paddocks for the ponies and walled vegetable gardens, because a family was supposed to have a place to live, right? Before Jessica came along it had never occurred to him that he might want a home. But now he was glad he had one. He had his library of architectural books, his friends came to stay for weekends with their children, and he had begun to see the point of something other than work.

"Here it is." Ella turned around and waved the CD in the air as if it were buried treasure.

"Terrific," Nick said, leaving his daughter to her music. "Now, ten minutes, and then it's lunch, okay? Don't go getting back in the pool."

" 'Kay," she said absentmindedly as her father carefully negotiated the minefield of Barbie dolls and Groovy Girls on the way out of her bedroom.

While Nick waited for their lunch guests to arrive, he returned to the drawing room and his newspapers for one last moment of peace and quiet. He settled down in an armchair and picked up

The Times from the floor, hoping he'd at least make it through the financial pages. Underneath it, though, was something that caught his eye, a headline in the *Daily Mail* that read:

MIRABELLE RINGS THE CHANGES

He lifted the paper carefully off the floor and squinted closely at the picture beneath it. Mirabelle Moncur clambering over a garden fence, her sundress bunched up in her hands, with a lion cub beside her. Nick's heart stopped in his chest. He could no longer hear its beat. Hollow and still, he became able only to move his eyes down the thick black lines of words.

> Reclusive star of the silver screen Mirabelle Moncur was sighted in public for the first time in many years yesterday—scaling a fence in London's Primrose Hill with a lion cub on a lead. The eccentric wildlife campaigner and former actress is not thought to have visited Britain for twenty-five years. She is staying with old friend Leonard Ross in his luxury London home. When asked about his exotic houseguest, Mr Ross declined to comment. Miss Moncur, who was married three times, is thought to be in London on business.

Nick held the picture in his hand and looked again at the photograph. It could have been taken twenty-five years ago. Mirri's hair cascaded over her shoulders, and her legs looked as lithe as they always did.

"Dad, they're here. Can we just have one last swim before lunch?" Jasmine had shoved her head around the door and was waiting for a reply. Actually she was waiting for a yes. "Dad, are you deaf?"

"What?" Nick looked up at his daughter and found himself propelled headlong down the decades back into the present. His daughter wanted to go for a swim. Before lunch. "Yes," he said.

Jasmine stared at him for a moment, certain that she'd misheard. She was never allowed to go for a swim this close to lunch because her hair always dripped on the table. "Really?" she asked.

Nick didn't answer this time. He was somewhere else entirely. Different place. Different time. And the way it felt when he looked down at the familiar woman in the newspaper on his knee, he'd been a different person then, too.

"All-righty," Jasmine said under her breath, in case he changed his mind, then bolted from the room and back out into the garden in delight.

Kate almost ran from Mirri's room. In fact, if she'd had in mind a place to run to, she would have. But the worst part about this whole thing was that she couldn't run from what was in her head.

You can't run from the truth, you see. Kate heard the voice of Mirri Moncur in her mind. Smug and yet horribly unsettling as she hurried down the stairs and into the hallway.

"Ouch!" She crashed shin-first into a vast steamer trunk and two men in blue overalls who were looking gravely at it.

"Careful, love, you'll hurt yourself tearing around like that."

"Bit late now," she said bitterly as she clutched her shin and hobbled back down the garden. Behind the trunk had been another three of the things that Kate could see. How many more things could one woman own, Kate wondered. Unless of course Mirri had simply had Africa covered in Bubble Wrap and shipped over. "Most likely has," Kate mumbled. Her shins hurt even more when she realized that there was no way that the ghastly woman upstairs, with her out-of-control libido and deep love of her own hair, was going anywhere soon. It'd take her a week to repack her underwear drawer, for heaven's sake. No, the fact of the matter was that Mirri Moncur was most likely staying for a while, whether Kate painted her stupid cat's portrait or not. So she'd better get used to the idea. Or move out.

Kate went back to her shed and pulled her phone out of her

pocket to see whether maybe it had vibrated with Jake's call at the precise moment she was bashing into Mirri's luggage, in which case she would have missed it. It hadn't. Kate picked it up and dialed.

"Hi, Kate," Tanya answered.

"Do you think that I'm delusional?"

"What?"

"Do you think that I'm delusional? About Jake?" Kate sat on her bed and waited for her friend to refute her wild notion.

"Well . . ."

"Well?" Kate sat up a little straighter. A direct no from Tanya would be enough.

"Darling, I'm actually just at lunch with Robbie's parents. Can I call you back later?"

"Just say yes or no. Please," Kate pleaded.

"Kate," Tanya said uncomfortably.

"Yes or no, Tanny?"

"Yes."

"No?"

"I'll call you later, darling, I promise, we'll talk then." And Tanya hung up and resumed her lunch with Robbie's mother and stepfather and, as usual, Lady Hirst was clunkily attempting to steer the topic of conversation around to babies.

"You have to put them down for Eton terribly early these days," Lady Hirst was saying while topping up her glass. "Practically before they're conceived." She laughed at her biting wit and looked pointedly at Tanya over the rim of her glass. Tanya glared at Robbie, who flew to her rescue.

"Mother, are you still using that wretched weed killer on your tomatoes? I can taste it. Why can't you use manure like a civilized person?"

Kate meanwhile was still on the edge of her bed, blinking in the cold, harsh light of the truth. Not only did Mirri Moncur think that Jake was a waste of space, but apparently so did Kate's best friend. And really, who was Kate to argue. It wasn't as if the evidence pointed to any other possibility—her phone was hardly ring-

ing off the hook, and Jake wasn't exactly prostrate on the grass outside her door. No, sadly the facts seemed to bear out these opinions.
Nor was it such a revelation to Kate; it was simply that she'd never
heard the truth spoken quite so unequivocally before. Probably because she'd never asked. And the strange thing was that once a truth
is spoken, it has, well, the ring of truth about it.

"Right." Kate stood up and without putting down her pad and
pencils, which she'd had in her lap this whole time, grabbed her
purse and left the shed. She needed to think, and she knew that
the only place she could do that was away from the bed she'd slept
in with Jake and the garden shed that her love for him had landed
her in.

Ten minutes later Kate was sitting on the top deck of a bus.
There was something about motion, she found, that always made
you feel better. Once, when she and Jake had split up before, she
and Tanya had gone on a road trip to Scotland. Granted, it wasn't
Thelma and Louise in the Arizona desert, but there was something
about the fields flashing by, the clumps of trees, the vast gray skies,
and finally the heather-quilted Highlands that soothed her. That
sense of time and things flying by was like time travel into a future
without Jake. Of course when she got home to London she had
found him asleep in her sitting room with a bunch of dying carna-
tions on the coffee table by way of an apology and the Scottish
Highlands ceased to matter. But she tried to remember that they
were always there if ever she needed them. As was Arizona, if the
going ever got really tough. The bus to Regents Park, though, was
barely one stop, let alone a road trip. Still, it was high above the
street, and the people below looked small enough to give life a similar sense of perspective.

Kate watched Londoners shedding their clothes in the afternoon
heat. From here she could see everything. On building sites shoulders were turning lurid shades of pink, and out-for-a-stroll-at-
lunchtime businessmen were rolling up their sleeves. Kate clutched
her pencils and stood up to ring the bell. The next stop was the zoo.

"Thanks," she called out to the driver as she hopped off the bus and onto the soft pavement. Kate hadn't been to the zoo in months, which only served to remind her how miserable she must have been. She used to come here all the time and laugh at the monkeys or marvel at how sinister and prehistoric the crocodiles looked. But to be honest she couldn't even remember the last time she'd felt joyful at a normal thing—like laughing at a stupid newspaper headline or seeing a seagull in the city—those sweet, *Sound of Music* moments like dewdrops on roses. She was a painter, for heaven's sake, she loved stuff like that. But it really had been ages since she'd been properly happy, she realized with a wave of depression. God, with or without Jake, she didn't see the good in life anymore. Which was about as bad as it got. Once upon a time Kate would have laughed and called all her friends to tell them that Mirri Moncur and Jonah Sinclair were shagging in her hammock outside her window. Last night she'd simply been a belligerent cow.

Kate took a ticket from the man in the booth at the entrance to the zoo and made a point of smiling at him. Granted, underneath her smile she felt wretched and fearful of what all this thinking was going to mean, but she had to start putting her life right somehow.

"Which way are the polar bears?" she asked. "Only I think it's all changed since I was last here."

"Polar bears is still in the same place they always was," the ticket man said, and bared his crumbling teeth at her in what she took to be a smile. The zoo smelled even more pungent than usual in the heat but was eerily quiet; there wasn't even a school party of bored teenagers or a huddle of Japanese tourists today. Kate pretty much had the place to herself. As she wandered through the cool darkness of the reptile house, she couldn't hear even the faintest squeal of a monkey outside, only her sandals tripping on the concrete floor. She stopped and watched as a snake drew his dry scales against the glass of his tank and felt glad that she'd come here. Not only did the zoo remind her of home and the inanimate creatures that had roamed her parents' house, but she also managed to justify being here to herself as work. Because even though she'd drawn and painted every single animal, reptile, and bird in the whole place at least six times, she never ceased to come away with a sketch that she was happy with.

She'd decided to start with the polar bears because they were the most robust and, she imagined, well adjusted of the animals. The gorillas would have made her sad with their lonely eyes; the monkeys, with all their showing off and flirting, would have made her wish for companionship; and she wasn't in the mood for docile elephants and their mooning ways. No, she definitely wanted to hang with the polar bears today. She loved their vast size, their elegant walk, and the way they somehow seemed incredibly friendly. Though she wasn't convinced that if she landed in their den at mealtime this theory would hold much water. When she arrived at the polar bear enclosure she rolled up her cardigan beneath her, placed it on the hard grass, and sat down. She also arranged her pencils in a row next to her and pulled out her sketch pad.

She must have stared at the polar bears for ten minutes with her pencil scratching away at her page before she really noticed that she hadn't produced anything vaguely resembling a polar bear, and had instead simply been doodling. Not, thankfully, anything as inane as Jake's name, but rather words like LIFE and LOVE and HOPE and, a little less obviously, FISH and FLASH. She had also been thinking about whether she was a masochist for having hung around Jake for this long. There were, she imagined, all sorts of very lovely men out there who would allow her to use the term *boyfriend* in relation to them without calling their lawyers to sue her. She remembered when Tanya and Robbie had first gotten together. Not only was he her boyfriend after three dates, he was her fiancé after seven and her husband six months later. When Kate had first gone and had coffee with Tanya and her fabulous new man, Tanya had said, "Oh, Robbie and I don't mind whether we live in his flat or mine. We just want to be together." She'd said that in front of him, too. Kate contemplated what Jake would do if she said the same thing in front of him—three years down the line and for a joke. And while she couldn't be completely certain, she knew that it would involve cardiac arrest and an ambulance.

"Okay, guys, enough of that," she said out loud and stood up so she could get closer to the bears for a bit. She walked over to where they were lolling on the wet rocks beside the arctic-cold water. "I love him, you know. Do you think I'm mad?" she asked a bear who was looking directly at her.

"No, you're not mad. It's perfectly normal to speak to polar bears about your emotions." Kate heard a man's voice behind her. She'd assumed, of course, that she was alone in the zoo apart from a few sweeping keepers.

She spun around. "I was just—"

"It's okay. I just wanted to let you know I was here before you went any further." Behind her, standing on the grass next to her dumb doodles, was a man with a gray cotton hat over his head and a huge baggy sweater on, dressed as if he was oblivious to the soaring mercury of the afternoon. She took a couple of steps back, not able to ascertain at this close a proximity whether she should run and scream blue murder or not. "Kate, it's me, Louis," the man said.

"Louis?" Kate reappraised the sinister figure and then rushed toward him and gave him a huge hug. "What are you doing here?" she said with a broad grin on her face.

"I've got a few issues with intimacy that I wanted to work out in therapy. I thought I'd take the next appointment after yours." He pulled the hat off his head, and thick blue-black hair spilled down over his face as he pointed in the direction of the polar bears. Kate had known Louis Alcott for years. Well, eight years to be precise. They'd met at art college when they were on the same bench in metalwork class. One day a shard of iron filing from the horse she'd been sculpting had flown up and caught him in the eye, and an unseemly amount of blood had gushed through his fingers as he'd clutched his palm against his face and turned the color of putty. Terrified that he'd been blinded, Kate had refused to wait for an ambulance as the tutor demanded and had instead thrust him into the front seat of her car and driven him on what he still referred to as the most nerve-racking ride of his life, to the local hospital. Then she'd sat with him in the emergency room for four hours while they waited to be seen by a doctor. Kate had tried to distract him by telling him about her father's taxidermy—about the processes of stuffing and embalming rare species. It was only when he rushed to the nearest rubbish bin and threw up that she realized that she might have chosen a better subject matter to preach to a bleeding man with pending stitches in his eye area. Still, afterward, when it was revealed that he wasn't blinded, only cut in a gangsterlike way through his eyebrow, and would need only five stitches and an eye patch, Kate took him home and fed him noodles and Ribena. Louis had been slightly baffled by all the attention from Kate, and they'd become firm friends.

She'd encouraged him in his career as a conceptual sculptor even though she didn't understand the first thing about it, and he always showed up for her private views with one of a string of gorgeous girlfriends who made Kate feel like a frumpy suburbanite with a penchant for paint-by-numbers art. They invariably had golden legs, knee-high boots, and whiplash wit; were ominously intellectual and flashed their wares as a columnist for a national newspaper with a sultry photograph at the top of their page; or appeared on stage as the latest, diaphanously clad Ophelia in a hip North London production of *Hamlet*. At least that's how it had felt to Kate. She had never quite understood how Louis, who was painfully shy even with her and hid behind his admittedly very sexy devilish black hair most of the time, was so successful with women. And as she was too intimidated by the hothouse orchids he dated to dig them in the ribs and giggle about what it was they saw in her old pal, she was never likely to find out, either.

"Still in love with that loser boyfriend of yours, I take it?" Louis asked through tightened lips. He'd always hated Jake. Well, not always, just since the day he'd bumped into a sobbing Kate in the car park of Sainsbury's in Notting Hill after Jake had delivered one of his early flesh wounds over the phone. Louis had picked her up off the pavement she was crying on and taken her to the circus. They'd

eaten cotton candy and they'd had a laugh, but the next day, when
Kate called Louis to say thank you and announced that she was
okay now because Jake had seen the light and was on his way over
with a bottle of wine and takeout, he was less than amused. In fact,
Kate hadn't seen much of Louis outside gallery openings for the
past couple of years. But she was thrilled to see him now, and in-
dulged his crossness over Jake.

"Unfortunately yes. And for the record, you and the polar bears
aren't the only ones who think I'm mad. *I* think that I'm mad, too.
But it doesn't seem to change things."

"Yeah, well. I'm prepared to overlook your terrible taste in men
for the moment." He smiled. "So what are you up to, kitten?" He
always called her kitten because there had been two Kates in their
year at art college. And even though it was only Louis saying it, she
always had a feeling of loveliness when he did.

"This and that. Actually I'm doing a portrait of a lion cub, believe it or not." She shrugged. "Oh, and I'm miserable, broke, and
living in a shed. How about you?" she said blithely.

"A shed?" Louis looked genuinely alarmed. "You're serious?"

"It's okay. It's Leonard's shed so it's very high end," she reassured
him. "What about you? Shouldn't you be having some amazing exhibition soon? It's been a while. Well, that is, unless I've fallen off
your invitation list."

"What, for keeping bad company?" He smiled wanly. "No, I'm
just a slow worker. I've got a show opening at Tate Modern next
month, though. It's a retrospective with a couple of new pieces, too.
That's why I'm here. Looking for inspiration." He nodded at the
polar bears.

"God, Louis, don't tell me that you're going to take up animal
portraits. I'm not sure that there's room for both of us in the mar-
ketplace and as living in a shed's about as rock bottom as I can
stand . . . ," she pleaded with a smile.

"Don't worry, I'm just thinking of doing a big piece. Not sure
yet, though, what it'll be. I wanted to look at huge things. I'm into

messing with perspective at the moment." He gestured to the polar bears, who were sunning themselves on a rock in the blazing afternoon.

"So are you, you know, married yet or anything?" Kate asked, in what she thought would pass for an adult tone. But just as Louis pulled off his sunglasses, clearly preparing an answer for her, there was a fantastic crashing sound behind Kate as one of the bears, in a bid for attention, stood up and dived into the water. Kate felt an enormous splash crash over her and then water seep through the back of her T-shirt. She screamed as the cold hit her warm skin, then laughed and pulled at her wet top to investigate just how soaking she was.

"Holy shit. I'm drenched." She laughed, then looked up and saw that Louis was smiling shyly, trying to look at his feet but clearly unable to resist the lure of her translucent top. He was swinging his sunglasses in his hand, and through the slivers of bangs she could see his deep, bottle-green eyes flicker to hers as he finally managed to avert his gaze.

"Can I help?" he asked.

"I think I'll survive," Kate told him. "It's quite refreshing actually. "

"Damned right it is." He winked at her then hastily added, "So where were we? Oh, yeah, me. No, I'm not married. Only to work. You know how it is."

"I wish I did," Kate said, as she was forced to recall her financial woes, which always made her stomach lurch as surely as hurling herself from a moving train might. "Still, at least I've got this big commission for the lion cub. Could be worse." She forced a cheerful face.

"Come on, kitten, it can't be that bad. You were the most talented painter in our year."

Louis was looking intently at her. She'd forgotten how penetrating he could be when he looked at her. It had been so long since she'd been alone with him. She felt slightly uncomfortable, because even though Louis was sweet he wasn't the easiest person in the world to get along with. It wasn't as though conversation just flowed.

"It's not at all bad." She batted the black cloud away. "So why don't you come by and have a cup of tea one day soon. We ought to catch up properly. When I'm not wet," she added, and tugged at her T-shirt to make it dry out more quickly.

"Sure," Louis said, and was about to shuffle from one foot to the other when he noticed Kate's sketch pad at his feet. "So, you've been sketching today. Can I have a look?"

"No." Kate jostled past him and dived onto the book. If he saw FISH and FLASH and her lunatic scribblings he'd think she'd really lost her mind. Then she noticed, as she hugged the incriminating page guiltily to her chest, that he looked slightly hurt. "Well, what I mean is, best not look as they're not all that great." She tried to smooth over the crack she'd just driven through their conversation.

"Sorry, I shouldn't have asked," Louis said shakily.

"Actually, Louis, they're hardly sketches. They're the musings of a half-wit," she confessed.

"No problem," Louis said gently. "Well, I'd better head off. Leave you and Percy the Polar Bear to your important discussion." He shrugged and gave her the trace of a smile.

"It was great to see you, Louis," Kate said overeagerly. "You will come around for coffee, won't you?"

"Yeah, 'course I will," he promised. Though Kate suspected that he wouldn't. He waved and walked away.

" 'Bye, then," Kate said to herself as she sat back down on the grass. Once again she picked up her pencil, but still she didn't draw anything. And she was so distracted by guilt and how messily her chat with Louis had gone that it was a whole fifteen minutes before she remembered to check her phone for missed calls.

Chapter Six

"Okay, I'll do it." Kate sat down heavily on Tanya's sofa and tossed her sketch pad on the coffee table.

"You'll do what?" Tanya and Robbie had just gotten back from Robbie's parents when Kate had rung their doorbell and demanded entry. She'd come straight from the zoo to tell them about her decision.

"We finally get to adopt you?" Robbie asked as he put his jacket over the arm of a chair and made for the drinks cabinet. It had long been a joke among the three of them that if Kate never found a husband, she would just come and live with Robbie and Tanya. They would keep a spare room and en suite bathroom for her, she'd bring them cups of tea and newspapers every morning for the rest of their lives, and they'd all get to lounge around on the duvet gossiping until Robbie went to work and the girls went to yoga. Any babies born would be communal, and Kate's lovers would be welcome on the understanding that they were quiet and didn't waste water. Sharing baths was very much encouraged in the Hirst household.

"Actually, no. You might finally get to marry me off, though," Kate said as Tanya sat down wearily in the chair opposite.

"Has this got to do with the phone call earlier?" Tanya asked guiltily. "Only if it does I'm really sorry. I didn't mean that you were delusional, only that, well, Jake isn't always as nice to you as he should be."

"You're not getting married to him, are you?" Robbie suddenly stopped pouring gin into a glass and turned to Kate.

"Don't be ridiculous," Kate said sadly. If she were she'd be shouting from rooftops and pole-dancing around chimneys rather than calmly imparting her news like this. Then she quickly added, "I've decided to take you up on your offer to set me up on a date."

"Oh, darling, I'm sorry. I'm already married." Robbie handed Kate a generous gin and tonic with a slice of lemon.

"With your friend Joss. You know, the guy who's kind and sweet and clever and good at cooking."

"The one you think is dull," Robbie teased.

"I don't think he's dull. I just think he's . . ."

"Great news. I'll call him." Tanya said, reaching for her phone. "He's so kind and sweet and clever and . . ."

"Good at cooking," Robbie and Kate said at the same time.

"But what about Jake?" Tanya suddenly remembered that this was Kate she was talking to, not some normal person who was longing to meet a Joss.

"I went to the zoo and I'm over him," Kate declared theatrically.

"I see," Robbie said. "Nice work."

"What happened?" Tanya said as she sipped at her tonic and abandoned her phone for the moment.

"Well, I had this conversation with the madwoman in the attic and she told me that she thought Jake was a slug and treated me like dirt and then, even though I hate her and thought she was talking out of her overexposed backside, I called you and you said that I was delusional, too. Anyway, I went to the zoo, realized that I didn't get excited by the smell of cut grass anymore, and then I bumped into Louis Alcott in the polar bear enclosure and I realized that by persisting in living the same nightmare over and over with Jake that I've lost the sympathy of a lot of people I love . . . so I decided that I ought to at least try to get over Jake because while he's still around I'm not open to good things."

"Darling, do you think you ought to have that G and T?" Tanya asked, a little concerned by her friend's flagrantly mad behavior.

"Hang on a minute. Can we start again?" Robbie asked. "Who's the madwoman in the attic?"

"Oh, she's some decrepit film star called Mirri Moncur who's staying with Leonard. If she stays another day I'm moving out," Kate said bitterly. "Does Joss have his own place, by the way? That would be a distinct bonus."

"Mirri Moncur. My God, what's she doing staying with Leonard?" Robbie was suddenly much less laconic than usual. In fact, he was positively overexcited.

"They had sex in the sixties," Tanya informed him.

"Everyone had sex in the sixties," Robbie said. "Is that the real Mirabelle Moncur?"

"Well, if she were only a hologram I'd be much happier," Kate said. "But unfortunately yes, she's real."

"Can I meet her?" Robbie was sitting on the edge of his chair. "I can't believe you're both being so cool about this. Kate, Mirri Moncur is staying with you. Why did nobody tell me?"

"Why would we? She's just some washed-up actress." Tanya sat back in her chair and picked up her phone. "So, Kate, you really want to go on a date with Joss? Because I'll call him right now if you do."

"Yes I do," Kate said decisively. "I have to break the Jake habit sooner or later, don't I? And it's not that I was paying any attention whatsoever to Mirri's advice, but when *you* said that I was being stupid . . ."

"I said delusional, Kate, not stupid," Tanya said guiltily.

"Same thing, anyway . . ."

"Would you two just stop talking a minute please?" The girls looked up at Robbie, who was standing in his long jeans and lilac rugby socks in the middle of the room, holding a remote control in his hand. They stopped talking at once.

"Watch this," he said with unusual authority for such a mild man, sliding a DVD into the player and clicking a button on the remote. Then he pulled down the blinds on the sitting room windows and plunged the room into darkness. Moments later Kate and Tanya watched as a black-and-white movie began.

"What is this?" Tanya whispered loudly to her husband, who had perched himself importantly on the arm of her chair, his eyes riveted to the screen.

"Ssshhhh. You'll see," he said. And they did. As the credits began to roll, the words

MIRABELLE MONCUR

came up on the screen in large white letters and were followed by the flash of what seemed like several hundred exotic and implausible names of French actors. Then, just as the girls were about to go to sleep, the film began. With a young woman lying naked on a bed fast asleep.

"Wow, look at that cinematography." Robbie leaned back on Tanya's chair.

"Ssssh," said Tanya, who was trying to concentrate on the subtitles flashing across the screen.

"Look at that body," said Kate, who had curled her legs underneath her in a bid to get comfortable.

The woman on the screen was quite simply the most stunning creature that any of them had ever seen. She couldn't have been any more than nineteen years old, but she literally steamed with sexuality, and as she stalked about the bedroom in the movie, the camera clinging to her naked curves more closely than any underwear could have done, Kate, Tanya, and Robbie watched in awed silence. They continued to be mesmerized for the next three hours and ten minutes as the naked girl acquired clothes and lovers and experienced heartbreak and isolation and just about every sort of misery that the French could dream up. And boy, were they good at that. By the end of the film, when it was definitely twilight beyond the curtains, the three of them were totally wrung out emotionally. When the screen finally flashed to black and Robbie reached for his remote control and pressed STOP, Kate rubbed her eyes.

"Oh my God," she said as she stretched her legs out in front of her. "That was incredible."

"She's amazing," Tanya said as she went to the window and pulled back the curtains.

"And you think she's some washed-up old starlet?" Robbie asked.

"I'd have slept with her," Tanya said. Robbie raised his eyebrows.

"Well, just because she was the most beautiful woman ever doesn't mean that she's not really annoying to live with," Kate said. "But I will admit she's pretty impressive. She was an amazing actress, too."

"Sure was." Robbie looked very pleased with himself. "So when can I come around for dinner and meet her?"

"Oh, you'll have to get to the back of the queue. Behind Jonah Sinclair and the Royals," Kate told Robbie.

"I'm more than happy to stand in line. I'd have to be pretty inventive to get noticed, though. One of her lovers used to shower her garden in red roses every day from his helicopter."

"Yes, but that kind of thing would never happen in real life," Kate said wistfully. Right now she'd settle for a bunch of the things in some cheap cellophane wrapping.

"It might, but I'm not sure Jake's your man." Robbie guided Kate down the corridor toward the kitchen where Tanya was.

"Now, darling, are you staying for supper?" Tanya called out. "Only I think that we should brief you on Joss a bit. Before your date." Robbie and Kate, who were just walking in the kitchen door, looked at one another suspiciously.

"Isn't it better if Kate's a bit more spontaneous?" Robbie asked, and kissed Tanya on the back of the head as she unloaded some celery and bacon from the fridge. "If she gets to know him herself?"

"Oh, you're such a spoilsport, Rob," Tanya moaned. "We can tell her that he prefers women to be quite conservatively dressed, though, can't we? I mean, it's only fair."

"Well, I'm hardly the miniskirt type, am I?" Kate said as she pulled at her combat pants to demonstrate her point.

"That's true," Robbie said grimly, but before Kate could leap to attack him for the implied criticism, he'd moved on. "And by the way, do you still mean to tell me that Mirabelle Moncur doesn't know what she's talking about when it comes to men?"

"Yeah, Rob might be right about that," Tanya said as she heaped the vegetables into a saucepan to make the only thing she could cook—soup.

"Just because she's had loads of experience doesn't mean she's an expert," Kate argued. Even though she had to admit to herself that Mirri had been depressingly accurate about Jake. "Anyway, where do you think that Joss will take me? I haven't been taken out since . . . Well, actually I don't think I've ever been taken out. Jake and I just *went* out. And before him the men I dated couldn't *afford* to take women out. So this is a whole new thing for me," Kate said with forced optimism while Rob and Tanya looked at her with what they hoped was affection but was really ill-concealed pity.

Mirabelle Moncur was not feeling like the most beautiful, experienced woman in world when she looked in the mirror that evening. She was too busy pulling her hair back from her face with the palm of her hand to examine the gray roots beneath the blond. She'd have to find a bottle of bleach soon or things would get ugly. Because quite aside from the possibility of the world (and that included her cats and friends as well as the paparazzi and the curious millions) noticing her gray hair, Mirri was much more concerned that she *herself* would have to face up to the irreversible onset of old age. She hadn't quite come to terms with the possibility that there hadn't been a single naturally blond hair left on her head for years.

Strangely enough, she'd begun to go gray at thirty-five, which isn't old age by anyone's standards, but at that time it had been only the odd hair here and there and she'd just pulled them out by the roots with irritation and asked her hairdresser to make her blonder.

There had, though, come a point somewhere around her forty-fifth birthday, just after she'd moved to Africa, when she'd made what she considered "the decision"—either to grow old gracefully as God intended, to embrace the graying and the fading and the widening of herself as being as much a part of nature as the seasons, the rain, the elephants who pulled up the lettuce that she persisted in trying to grow in her garden, or—and the alternative required almost as much courage and certainly more commitment—to fight it. To fill her life with the bottles and facialists and creams and exercise regimes that would hold it all together until the day the embalmer came and let her off the hook. Thankfully the effort paid off, and by the time she was bleached and tinted and taken her daily walk and applied the lipstick, she looked pretty stunning. And not just "for her age." She looked stunning by anyone's standards. Her top secret, though, the trick she never let anyone in on, was smoking and eating butter. By doing these things that she loved and could never have the discipline to give up, she also fooled everyone into thinking that she was oblivious to vanity. That she didn't spare a second thought about her looks, and it was this, above all other things, that she believed made her an attractive woman at the age of sixty. Certainly attractive enough to cause Jonah Sinclair to call her four times today and beg her to go to dinner with him.

"I can't, I have dinner with a friend tonight," she had said unapologetically. Jonah was sweet and they'd had a perfectly nice time in the hammock, but when you'd been wined and dined and made love to by as many Jonahs as Mirri had, it barely seemed worth putting on your lipstick for. But Jonah, to whose ears such words were music, was charmingly, amusingly persistent. Eventually she gave in because he made her laugh with his outrageous begging.

"No matter what happens to me in the rest of my life, if I don't get to take you out to dinner tonight and kiss your cheek—just your cheek, by the way—one last time, well, then I'll die an unfulfilled man. I'll sit in my armchair smoking my pipe, looking out the window at the age of eighty, and remember the woman I never had," he had complained down the phone.

"You had me last night." Mirri had taken a drag on her cigarette and smiled as she wandered around her room, stroked Bébé, and caressed the rug with her toes.

"Ah, but last night I didn't know that I was going to have you. It wasn't the same. I need to know beforehand. That way I can commit it to memory and play it over and over again for the rest of my days."

"Maybe you should just bring a video camera," Mirri joked.

"You're so cynical. Don't you understand that these things are once in a lifetime?" he said, with an edge of humor in his voice. Mirri laughed and resisted telling him that on the contrary, they'd happened many times in her life and she'd forgotten most of them, even the ones that had been videotaped.

"Okay, if you must. I need to eat, I suppose."

"Darling, you're so romantic and you make me feel so good about myself." Jonah laughed loudly. "I'll pick you up at eight."

"Okay." Mirri feigned indifference and was suddenly glad that she'd be seeing him again. She liked to dress up and be flirted with.

"Thank you, by the way," Jonah said, and hung up.

So now Mirri had to find a headscarf for the evening. She'd find a hairdresser tomorrow. Thankfully she'd been famed for her pioneering fashion in her day, so whatever she wore was seen as a style statement rather the desperate remedy it really was. In fact, she'd been amused yesterday to find herself wandering down Bond Street and noticing the sundresses and capri pants and hot pants of her youth in all the store windows. And she wasn't wrong in thinking that forty years later she was still influencing what women wore. Even though the world was an entirely different place and she'd been vilified for some of her outfits, now there seemed to be nothing you could do to shock. Which rather disappointed her if she thought about it for too long. No wonder girls like Kate who lived in the shed were so dull. They had nothing to rebel against.

"Tonight you'll stay at home, my darling," Mirri said to Bébé as she nuzzled into his neck. "Mummy is going to have a little fun."

Chapter Seven

Kate's evening had started out so promisingly. Well, certainly in the respect that she had enjoyed a lovely shower, and the sky had glowed with the pale pink of the setting sun above her. She'd even bothered to slather on a slick of body lotion in case her shins got lucky later and collided with Joss's caressing hands. To boot she was also doing an admirable job of keeping the memory of Jake at bay. And she wore a very nice, clean denim skirt, a rather neat pink cashmere sweater, and even conceded to some beaded flip-flops instead of her usual sneakers, bearing in mind what Tanya had said about Joss liking his dates on the conservative side. She was doing all she could to promote goodwill.

"Are you going to church?" Leonard had asked when she emerged from her shed carrying a fake Kelly bag that she'd picked up at Camden Market years ago.

"No," she said quite huffily; she'd been quite impressed with her respectability when she'd checked out her reflection in the glass panes of her shed. "I have a date." Leonard was sitting with Mirri drinking Pimm's on the lawn. They had polished off half a pitcher and were smiling inanely at her. Mirri was very done up and was looking Kate up and down with her usual expression of incomprehension.

"Is he a vicar, then?" Leonard grinned cheekily.

"Get lost." Kate smoothed down her skirt primly and made for Leonard's glass, which was on the table. She took a slug of Pimm's and replaced it. "He's a banker and he likes art and Tanya thinks that we'll get on like a house on fire. He's husband material apparently," Kate informed him.

"Why would you want a husband?" Mirri, whose snooty French gaze Kate had been trying to avoid, asked. "They're very passé."

"Because I don't really want to end up a lonely old woman." Kate claimed victory for herself.

Mirri was undaunted. "Ah, you need a man to take care of you financially. You just want to marry for money," she said disingenuously.

"Absolutely not. In fact, in the past *I've* been the one to support my boyfriend financially, if you must know." But Kate instantly regretted saying this when she saw the pitying look on Mirri's face. And for once she seemed genuine. Kate hurried to sound less pathetic. "What I'm saying is that I'm an independent woman but I still want a husband. I want companionship."

"I find lovers to be very good companions. And animals and friends, too. But I always found husbands to be the poorest company." Mirri cast her mind back over the decades and thought how dull her lovers had become as soon as she married them. They suddenly expected her to know where their socks were and what they wanted for dinner. In short, they wanted her to be their mother. "I would never marry again."

"Well, I intend to choose mine well," Kate said pointedly.

"I think maybe Kate wants babies," Leonard, whose face was blushing from the excess of alcohol, blurted out. He was usually much more restrained, but Mirri's influence seemed to be making him reckless.

"She has years before the babies have to be born," Mirri said, and pulled a piece of apple from her glass with her fingers. "I just don't understand why all these young women are interested in is finding husbands and having children. It's an obsession. My niece in France is the same. It was different when I was young. I had to be married; otherwise I'd have had to live with my parents forever. But now you can live where you like, travel where you like, shave your head, wear no clothes, swim with dolphins, and live in a castle and have babies with your best girlfriends if you want to, but all you all want to do is what my generation fought tooth and nail *not* to do—think about men's socks and babies' nappies." Mirri shook her head.

Kate was silenced for a moment. She couldn't deny that what the old tart was saying was true. The one thing that kept her awake with knots in her stomach at four o'clock in the morning was the fear that she might never meet a man who would want to marry her. In fact, she'd officially given herself another two years before she dropped her standards. Then she would settle for someone who didn't excite her as much as Jake. Someone like Joss, for instance.

"Well, I don't see what's so wrong with wanting stability," Kate said and was about to leave when Mirri had the last word.

"Nothing, I suppose." She sucked a mouthful of her drink through a straw. "Just as long as it's not at the expense of love. Because that would be stupid. And you may be lots of things, Kate, but you're not stupid." Mirri smiled knowingly and Kate thought how beautiful she looked. She understood for a moment how men must feel to be on the receiving end of her attention. Because when she said something even vaguely flattering it made you want to jump up and down with delight.

"Thanks. I think," Kate said disarmed. "Though I'm still keeping my fingers crossed that he'll be husband material rather than just a shag-on-the-hammock. See you both later."

" 'Bye, darling," Leonard slurred, raising his glass as Kate turned and left.

"She'll learn." Mirri smiled to herself. "But she's got a long way to go."

Kate had arranged to meet Joss at Brooks. It was a very smart Gentleman's Club in St. James's, and she was glad that she'd decided on the conservative route. She put on her best Queen's English voice for the concierge and smiled like Julie Andrews.

"I'm here to meet Joss Armstrong," she said.

"Follow me, miss," the man said without looking at her, but also, rather cleverly, without condescension. That was what was so brilliant about these lovely old English institutions, Kate realized: You really could get away with almost anything because the staff were so unerringly well mannered. Quickie on the sweeping staircase? Not a flicker of interest from the gentlemen in black suits. Leonard was always boasting about the outrageous and debauched behavior that went on in his club. But then Leonard's club didn't admit women, so Kate had no way of knowing whether he was telling the truth.

"Kate, hello, lovely to see you." Joss rose from the chair where he was reading *The Times,* placed his hands carefully on Kate's shoulders, and kissed each cheek methodically.

"Joss. Hi." Kate smiled and sat in a leather armchair, carefully tugging her skirt down.

"Well, this is very nice. Would you like a drink?" he asked as he put his newspaper to one side.

"I'd love a G and T," she said breezily as the waiter mysteriously appeared before them, seemingly out of thin air.

"And I'd love another sparkling mineral water," Joss added.

"Oh, in which case maybe I'll just have an orange juice," Kate chipped in. She always felt like a complete lush ordering a large cocktail when everyone else was on the soft stuff.

"Oh, well, if you like," Joss agreed hastily. "An orange juice instead of the gin." The way he said *"the gin"* made Kate glad she'd changed her mind. He made it sound as though she'd just requested three lines of cocaine and a rock star's bottom to snort it off. Very disapproving.

"So, Kate, how is the painting?" he asked.

"Oh, you know, all over the place. I'm doing a cat. Well, a lion cub actually."

"And you work in oils, don't you?" he said grandly, as though she were Vermeer.

"Yeah." She took the orange juice that the waiter had carefully set down. "I do. And charcoal sometimes. Whatever I'm asked to do, really. I'm a bit of a whore for cash that way." She laughed lightly. And Joss looked a bit taken aback. He did, though, also look very handsome. He had lovely straw-colored hair, greeny-gray eyes that matched the elegant eau de nil of his silk tie, and a dark gray suit that made him look very authoritative and commanding. He was nicely tall, too, Kate had noted when he stood up. And smelled of citrus. He was definitely not a man you would want to hide behind the sofa whenever your friends came around. And he looked as though he'd also do casual quite well; a well-chosen pair of loafers and a pristine white T-shirt and you'd have yourself a perfect accessory for a weekend in a soft-topped sports car. In short, he was the sort of man you saw in restaurants with beautiful women and wondered where you found such perfect specimens and what otherworldy attributes a woman had to have to attract such perfection. Kate felt happy for a moment. If she played her cards right she might at least have a chance to win him for a weekend. A sort of luxury-break-for-two offer that you might get with a new pair of Armani sunglasses.

"So tell me what you do, Joss." Kate smiled as she imagined the beautiful woman with perfect attributes might smile. "I know it's banking, but what exactly?" And he proceeded to tell her. Very little of which Kate understood but it sounded impressive and involved hedge funds and pharmaceutical companies and she knew that far from being a boring job as she'd thought it might be, it was actually fascinating and much, much more demanding and stimulating than splodging paint on canvas for a living whenever the bank demanded it or the mood took you. Eventually they ordered another round of almost-drinks and Kate told Joss all about her love of taxidermy. He seemed a bit squeamish and mistrustful of the idea at first, but eventually she managed to convince him that a dead, stuffed zebra in the bedroom was actually a bit of fun, and not a weird perversion. Well, he was nodding understandingly at least, whatever *that* meant.

"I thought that what we might do next is go to the launch of this magazine around the corner, it's an arts monthly and some friends of mine run it. Does that appeal to you at all?" Joss asked when Kate had drained her glass and was wondering where their pleasant conversation might meander to after dead animals.

"That sounds great," Kate said, sitting up a bit too hurriedly. This place was interesting for a while but then she could have sworn that the liver-spotty, yellow-faced old man in the corner had not moved so much as an eyelash for at least forty-five minutes and she suspected he could well have just died. Plus she was dying for a sip of champagne or something on a silver tray with a bit of a kick.

"I'd kill for a proper drink, too," she said as she pulled her cardigan over her arms, which were getting just a bit goose-bumpy in the cool, dark room.

"Ah, I see," Joss said and, rather than standing as she'd expected, sank back a bit into the sofa and made a serious steeple of his hands, with his forefingers joined beneath his chin.

"If you know what I mean." Kate smiled sweetly.

"Well, I do actually. Or rather I did. But all that's behind me now." Joss was looking very intently into Kate's eyes, and she quickly put her handbag back down onto the floor and plastered on her best listening face. Though already she suspected that she wasn't really going to be delighted by what he was about to say. "You see, Kate, I feel that really, before we go any further, I ought to tell you about something . . ."

Before we go any further, Kate thought, *What, like down the road to a party? Out of the door? Into a taxi?* She couldn't imagine how far he was planning to get with her tonight, which might mean that nothing short of complete disclosure of all his deepest, darkest secrets might be necessary. She always imagined that skeletons were only dusted down and brought out of closets when an introduction to the parents or a fortnight's holiday together were imminent. This seemed very premature to her.

"Well, if you want to . . . ," Kate said, hoping to stall him. For the look on his face didn't exactly smack of parties and glitter-balls before dawn. More like Confessions of a Troubled Mind.

"I'm a programmer," Joss said earnestly. "Do you know what that means?"

"Well, it's not your job. 'Cause I already know you're a hedge fund wizard." Kate laughed a bit.

"It means I'm a recovering alcoholic. It means that I had a very bad drink and drug problem and that before I came here tonight, as I do every night and twice on weekends, I attended a meeting for people like me." He hadn't liked Kate's attempt at wit. Obviously.

"Right," Kate said, chastened.

"When I was twenty-two I woke up in a gutter in Ibiza with half my hair missing," Joss said without blinking. "I had been on a six-month binge of cocaine and alcohol, which left my liver in ruins and my life in shreds."

"How terrible," Kate said. Without too much sympathy. *Only very rich people can afford such indulgences,* she thought. Most people had to work in boring offices and make coffee for a bullying boss at that age. Not much flouncing around party islands in the Mediterranean for most people.

"I struggled for years with my demons and thankfully now, well today at least, I'm free of most of them. Though I'm still in therapy."

"As well as the eight meetings a week?" Kate asked. Joss nodded. "Can't leave much time for tennis and stuff then, hey?"

"Actually I'm rather good at tennis. My coach said that I have the strongest backhand he's ever seen and I ought to compete. But my therapist thinks that it wouldn't be good for my self-esteem to partake in competitive sports."

"Poor you," Kate said, rather genuinely this time. Because whatever Joss's crimes were, however many drugs he had taken, it was a bit unfortunate that he was such a world-class bore.

Kate proceeded to listen to Joss for at least another half hour. She sat with her cardigan on her shoulders and a sympathetic look etched on her face and listened as he told her all about his sobriety. He even had the audacity to tell her that if she was attracted to him, then it probably meant that some form of alcohol abuse had taken place in her own family.

"Well, my mum does like a sneak of the cooking sherry now and then," she volunteered.

"It's the sneaking that's the problem, you see," Joss told her gravely. "If she can't be open about it, then that suggests abuse."

"Gosh, I'll have to have a word with her," Kate said, quite enjoying the idea of how much her mother would howl with laughter to be told that she was a closet alcoholic.

"And don't neglect your own needs, either, Kate," Joss told her with a lot of seriousness but not a huge amount of compassion, she decided, given that he'd just broken to her the devastating news of her dysfunctional family. "I can give you my therapist's number. And if you and I are going to have a relationship, then I'd be more comfortable if you were attending Al-Anon meetings. For families of recovering addicts."

"Actually, Joss, I think I went a bit mad with the orange juice. I've got to dash to the loo. Would you mind?" Kate smiled and fled for cover to the ladies', where she sat for a startled moment or two wondering whether she could face going back or whether he'd have a brigade of counselors waiting to cart her off to Farm Place or some rehab joint because she'd confessed to having a bit of a craving for the hard stuff earlier.

Eventually she had managed to convince herself to head back out into the club and give Joss one more chance. He was so handsome, and maybe she had been a little bit hasty to condemn him as a spoiled, bossy bore. She decided she'd try a bit more compassion. And thankfully when they arrived at the magazine launch they barely had to speak to one another at all. They said hi to people, Kate had a sneaky cocktail behind a pillar, and Joss seemed almost normal among the people he knew. Kate picked up a copy of the glossy magazine to take home, found herself a goodie bag with a bottle of scent in it, a ticket to a spa, and a miniature of Absolut vodka (*Save that for later,* she thought). So all in all it hadn't turned out to be a bad evening. And every date was an experience, she told herself as Joss climbed into a taxi beside her and invited her back to his place for a fine green tea.

"My teas are my Bordeaux these days," he said. And though Kate thought this mildly hilarious, it was quite sweet, so she agreed to a nightcap.

Unfortunately, as Kate and Joss sat next to one another on his smooth leather sofa and talked about modern art, she began to feel miserably depressed. The whole situation was so sterile, so unsexy, so unlovely. It wasn't the easy fun time she'd had with Jake. (There, she'd said it, she hadn't meant to but his name just popped up.) And Joss, while not such a bad person, was absolutely no fun at all to be with. His sense of humor, if he'd ever had one, had probably been left behind in the gutter in Ibiza along with half of his hair.

"Can I kiss you?" he'd asked, and Kate felt just a bit as though he was simply being polite and kissing her as a favor to Robbie and Tanya, like bringing a box of Bendicks Bittermints along to a dinner party.

"If you like," Kate said sweetly, because even if he was being polite, it was still more flattering than not being asked. So she sat with her hands in her lap until Joss finally closed in on her, clasped his hands carefully and dispassionately around her cheeks as though she were a hot dish of stew he was removing from the oven, and kissed her. Kate moved her hands from her lap and returned the gesture. At first she thought how pleasant the citrus smell of his cheeks was and she was even feeling a butterfly or two in her stomach, until Joss finally settled into a rhythm and she realized that it was not the kind of kiss she was used to at all. And not the kind she wanted to get used to, either. This was not a slow, sexy, playful moment that she wanted to last for hours—it was a sort of dry washing-machine motion—round and round one way for a bit.

Oh, and then the cycle changed to a wools-and-silks cycle—slower, with less power and certainly not as much heat. Kate put a hand on his chest and held Joss at bay for a second.

"Just getting a sip of my lovely green tea." She smiled and grabbed her mug. God, something had to warm up the proceedings. She took a deep breath and decided that it had to be her. *He's handsome, he's clever, he's kind,* she told herself as she plunged back in for the rematch. *Show a bit of enthusiasm, Kate,* she told herself. *The guy's probably just nervous.*

"I love your lips," she said, and began to slowly kiss them, while simultaneously reaching down with her hand. She felt for the sign of life in his pants, but nothing much seemed to be happening. Ah, well, she continued the kissing, and ran her hand along his chin, taking the lead, kissing him in what she thought was a sexy way. She even contemplated doing a Mirri-on-the-hammock and making for his zipper with her teeth, but thought maybe she wouldn't terrify him with the full repertoire just yet, and the prospect of failing and biting the wrong thing or breaking a tooth was more worry than she could deal with just this minute. So instead she just made a few hot and heavy noises and pulled his head close into her face.

"You're quite bossy, aren't you?" Joss suddenly said as she was sucking softly on his earlobe.

"I'm sorry?" Kate wasn't sure what he'd said. Or really whether she'd heard right.

"Well, much as I hate to say this," he began, with his nose ever so slightly in the air, "I really don't like aggressively sexual women." Clearly he didn't hate to say it or he wouldn't have, because Kate didn't see any thumbscrews or torture implements forcing him to tell the brutal truth.

"I see." Kate felt as though she'd been punched in the ribs.

"God, don't take it personally." He rolled his eyes as though she was overreacting as she sat back on the sofa and wiped her dry lips.

"Well, how would you like me to take it, Joss?" She stood up and was about to button up her skirt but she realized that he had never actually unbuttoned it. "It wasn't the girl in the flat next door who was kissing you. It was me. So really I have no choice but to take it personally."

"Christ, you're so sensitive." He groaned irritably.

"I am actually, Joss." Kate, quite uncharacteristically, took a deep breath and decided to speak up. "I'm so sensitive that I sat for three hours this evening and listened to your tedious stories about drug taking. I'm so sensitive that I actually pretended to care. And you couldn't even muster up enough gentlemanliness to pretend for a second to fancy me."

"I did fancy you a bit." He remained seated on the sofa as Kate made her way to the door. "I just really can't bear it when women try on that sexy shit."

" 'Bye, Joss," Kate said with her hand on the door before turning around and adding, "And by the way, my mother is a really nice woman and a sip of cooking sherry before Sunday lunch does not make her a dysfunctional freak like yourself. Okay?" With which she closed the door of Joss's flat behind her and ran down the stairs from his building, her heart beating furiously in her chest.

As Kate stood outside on the pavement, hoping against hope that she might find a taxi on its way back from a drop-off in South Kensington, she felt a tear slip down her cheek. She wiped it away, furious with herself.

"Don't you dare," she snapped, and pulled her cardigan tightly across her chest. She pulled off her shoes, which were rubbing the back of her heel, and walked from Joss's flat toward the lights of a busy intersection. She fought back the thoughts of Jake and she fought back her humiliation. She told herself that Joss didn't matter and that it wasn't her he hated, it was just women. But it didn't make her feel a whole lot better. Finally a taxi came by and picked her up.

"Primrose Hill, please," she said to the driver as she sat in the backseat and rummaged through her purse to make sure she had enough cash. She saw that her phone was blinking and pulled it out. ONE MISSED CALL. Her heart did the dance of the stupid people for a moment until she saw that it was from Tanya's home number. She looked at the phone long and hard, as though it were the I Ching or an ancient prophet sitting on a throne of lotus leaves, and might tell her what she must do next. Then she flicked down the list of names until she stopped at the number she had hoped to see and took a deep breath. And a sensible person would have pressed the OFF button and put the phone back in her bag, but Kate wasn't thinking like a sensible person. She was worried. Worried that if Joss was someone who was supposed to be nice, clever, considerate, and came highly recommended by good friends, then God only knew what would happen if she went out on a date with a man she'd met at a bus stop. It was as if someone had cauterized her soul. She felt like Woody Allen in *Annie Hall* when he tried to re-create the magic of his and Annie's lobster moment with another woman. She felt as if she'd never have fun with anybody again, as if nobody else in the world *got* her. Apart from the man whose number she was dialing.

"Kate." Jake sounded pleased to hear from her. And not at all surprised.

"I've had a terrible evening, do you want to go get a drink?" She closed her eyes, laid her one card on the table, and waited for him to reply.

"I always want to get a drink, angel."

"Then I'll see you in ten minutes. Are you in Bernie's?" she asked.

"Sure am," Jake said.

"See you soon." Kate hung up.

Kate leaned back on the seat and was besieged by a sense of euphoria. "Excuse me, do you think we could do a detour to Chelsea?" she asked the cabdriver apologetically. "Slight change of plan." And as the cab swung around in the middle of the street Kate slid to the other side of the leather seat and grappled with the contents of her makeup bag at the same time. Lipstick, comb, and a mint. Well, she still had revolting Joss's dirty washing swilling around in her mouth so that was a must.

Kate hadn't been to Bernie's for months and she felt her legs

begin to weaken slightly as she stepped from the cab onto the pavement outside the door to the bar. She swallowed the remains of her
mint and pushed the door open. There at the bar, in his usual place,
sat Jake. As he heard the door he turned to her, his familiar brown
eyes taking in her smart but shoeless look.

"Scotch for the lady." Jake winked at the barmaid as Kate walked
in the door and made her way toward her familiar stool. This was
Jake's place. He ate supper here almost every night and smoked his
last cigarette of the day here. It was a dark and very average bar but
to Kate it was like returning to the only place she'd ever been truly
happy. She and Jake had spent entire Sunday afternoons here reading the newspapers together, arguing madly over politics, poring
over horoscopes, deciding which movies to go and see. He'd brought
her here on their first date and yet for some reason she couldn't remember the last time they'd been here together. Probably near the
end. She suspected that she'd blocked it out along with a hundred
and one other miserable moments that she and Jake had experienced in the last few weeks of being together, when he stopped
looking her in the eye, when she had known by the rash that always
broke out on the back of her hands when she was deeply unhappy
that it was all over.

"Hi, Jake." Kate raised herself onto the bar stool and gave Jake a
kiss on the cheek. She pulled her shoes back on and then sat up and
looked at him. She was still a little unsure of postrelationship eti-
quette, but one thing she knew for sure: She didn't want to make it
too easy for him. Even though she knew she'd been criminally available when she rang him, it didn't mean she had to roll over and
concede defeat now that she was here. In front of him and as good
as on a plate with goddamned garnish on top.

"You're looking like a million dollars." Jake smiled at her over his
drink. She looked away.

"I went on a date from hell. I came to wind down a bit before
bed," she said by way of an excuse. She had also hoped that Jake
might be taken aback or even upset by the fact that she was dating
again so soon after him. If he was upset he didn't show it.

"We both know why you came." He leaned in close and breathed on her neck, near the back where her hair was hot and sticky.

"I wanted a drink and, frankly, Jake, you're the only person in London I know who would be available for a stiff one at this hour."

"No pun intended." He wouldn't let her drop his gaze.

"None at all." Kate picked up the Scotch that had been placed in front of her and took a pinch between her lips. It melted the back of her throat and tasted awful. She took another sip. "Just too much work and then terrible men." She looked down into her glass, through the deep amber liquid to the heavy bottom.

"Nothing changes, then." Jake smiled.

"You got it," Kate said. "Anyway I didn't come here to discuss that. I came to escape it. So what's new in your life, Jake? Since we didn't get a chance to talk much last week."

"I very much enjoyed our not talking last week," Jake said as he took a drag of his cigarette and leaned forward onto the bar. And Kate knew that this was why she had come back. Because when you were sitting next to Jake it didn't matter what he'd done or what you knew he wouldn't do next, like not call you or not fall in love with you, it just felt like the only place she could ever imagine wanting to stay for the rest of her life. And she felt this so acutely that her eyes stung with the Scotch and tears.

"Shame you only have one birthday a year then, hey?" Kate ignored the hand he'd placed on her knee. Not on her thigh where there was a protective layer of skirt, but on the pale brown skin of her knee. This wasn't actually why she'd come. She hadn't come so that she and Jake could abscond to his flat, do the whole great-sex thing all over again, and then she could be politely evicted at nine o'clock tomorrow morning when he remembered he had to meet some producer on the other side of town. Kate had no idea why she'd really come other than to remind herself that there was at least one man in the world whom she could love.

"So if there's no birthday to celebrate, how about we bring Christmas forward?" Jake put his hand over Kate's as she held the glass between her fingers.

"I don't know why I'm here, Jake." She looked him in the eye and let out a sigh.

"I want to play you this new record I bought." He picked the keys to his flat up off the bar and stood up. "Will you come?" Kate looked up at Jake and stayed seated in a feeble gesture of defiance. Jake put a twenty-pound note on the bar to pay for the drinks and looked down at her. "I'd like you to." And every fiber of her brain screamed not to and every inch of her flesh ignored it. She tipped the last drops of her drink into her mouth and stood up.

"Sure." But she refused to hold his hand. She knew that she was going to go home with him and have sex, but she didn't want to encourage any superfluous intimacy that might confuse her even further.

Jake's room was its usual mess, but the smell was so evocative of all the great times they'd had that it nearly floored her. She sat down quickly on the sofa as Jake kicked off his shoes and went to his music corner.

"It's this really sweet reggae record," Jake announced with his back to her as he carefully placed the black vinyl onto the record player and set it playing with a faint crackle from the needle. Jake was obsessed by music. He'd spend hours online tracking down old recordings by obscure Jamaican artists or heartbreaking country-and-western songs. He had the soul of a DJ and he loved playing to an audience. It used to be Kate. She'd sit for hours on his sofa painting her toenails silver, reading a book, or she'd be in the kitchen cooking supper and with all the sweet simplicity of a teenager Jake would call out what he was putting on next, imploring her to listen to the lyrics or the cute voice of the female singer. Or he'd tell her how the artist had killed himself not long after or some other piece of trivia. And though most of it had gone over her head when they were going out together it was one of the things she missed most about Jake: his music, the hours chilling and just being in the same space as him.

The song started and Jake went into his own world, dancing a bit as he put the record sleeve back on the table. "You like, baby?" he said in a singsong Jamaican accent.

"I like." Kate smiled at him from the sofa. She'd taken off her shoes and had her knees curled up to her chest on the sofa in a pointlessly defensive pose. The room, Jake's scruffy but somehow immensely comfortable bedroom with the old guitars and the books, filled with the airy sound of a summer evening. Kate rested her head on the arm of the chair.

"Listen to this bit . . ." He hummed along and crossed the room with his hips swaying and his holey gray socks peering out from beneath his too-long jeans. Jake had great limbs, Kate remembered as she watched him meander toward her. He sat down on the sofa next to her and gently sang along to the music as he took her face in his hand and looked at her lips. Kate closed her eyes. Oh shit. It wasn't that she was a fool. She wasn't one of those women who can't resist a bastard and brag about it. She *wanted* Jake to love her. She *wanted* him to be good to her. She wasn't out for some man who would treat her badly. She just wanted him to settle down and appreciate her a bit.

"You like this?" He closed his eyes and sealed Kate's misery for the next few weeks. He kissed her. And so instead of hating herself Kate succumbed. She took the stray curls at the back of his neck in her fist and pulled gently as she kissed him back. And this was just what she'd needed because this wasn't Joss. This wasn't paint-by-numbers sexiness with the right sort of man. This was the real thing. Definitely with the wrong man, but then, everything has its price.

Before long Kate was lying in Jake's familiar bed, with her underwear kicked off and Jake above her, his eyes closed in ecstatic concentration. She hated him. But there was no winning, she thought, as he collapsed beside her and kissed her forehead over and over. And she was back where she'd started.

Chapter Eight

When Kate woke the next morning Jake wasn't there. But he'd left her a can of Coke and a peanut butter sandwich by the bed along with a note saying that he had to go to rehearsals and he'd see her later. Kate smiled as she pulled the ring on the can. She was glad she had come by last night. Sometimes she just needed to take the initiative, and Jake was perfectly happy. She took a bite of the sandwich and went across the room to find her phone. She knew that Tanya would be dying to find out about her date with Joss Armstrong and was actually a bit worried that he'd have called first and complained what a psychopathic nightmare Kate was. But for once there was no message from Tanya—but there was one from Jake.

That was a blast. Have a good day. Jxx

Kate smiled and wondered how long the goodwill might last between her and Jake this time. Then she remembered that tomorrow was her birthday; maybe she would invite him along to the party she had only just decided that she would throw. Just so she got to see him sooner rather than later. Also it might put an end to everyone's cynical eye rolling every time Kate mentioned Jake's name if he was actually by her side on a day that mattered. She pressed REPLY on her phone and tapped out

My birthday tomorrow. Dinner at Lemonia at 8 if you're up for it. Kxx

And by the time Kate emerged from Jake's shower with her hair in wet strands around her face, her phone was winking at her again. The red light flashed as she opened an envelope.

Happy Birthday for tomorrow, beautiful. See you there. xx

Kate smiled and rubbed her hair with a towel. Twenty-nine years old tomorrow and the happiest girl alive. Suddenly living in a shed felt fine. Her animal paintings seemed quite promising, the sun was out, and she suddenly had a party to organize.

"Tanya, I'm having a party." She called Tanya and left a message. "Come, and bring Robbie."

"Leonard, it's my birthday tomorrow," she said when she finally made it home. Leonard was at the kitchen table eating his scrambled egg and summer truffles.

"And you thought I needed reminding of that fact?" Leonard smiled and looked decidedly worse for wear after his Pimm's session with Mirri on the lawn.

"I'm having a party at Lemonia. If you can get me a table, that is." Kate added. She'd suddenly realized that they would be extremely lucky to get a large table at short notice and she had absolutely zero power to alter that.

"Well, I'll try, my dear, but I'm not sure that I'll be able to. You know how busy they get, especially on a Thursday night." Leonard grimaced apologetically.

"*I'll* get you a table at Lemonia, *pas de probleme.*" Mirri sauntered into the kitchen, a cigarette hanging out of the corner of her mouth, pulling the belt of her dressing gown in a knot about her waist as she shuffled toward the kettle. Looking not dissimilar to any old suburban housewife.

"Really?" Kate's good mood was pretty unsquashable today, and she wasn't cross or stupid enough to look a gift horse in the mouth. "That'd be great. Of course you're invited, too, if you're around."

"Okay," Mirri said as she stubbed her cigarette butt out in the sink. Leonard smiled and rolled his eyes discreetly at Kate. He was enormously house-proud but he was also a very stylish host; he would never have chided Mirri for her slatternly ways. "I'll come. How many do you want the table for?"

"Well, there's me and Leonard and Robbie and Tanya and you"—Kate nodded toward Mirri and counted on her fingers— "and Jake," she added without looking up to take the temperature of the room. Not that she needed to look up, because Mirri always spoke up.

"The Slug?" She gasped in horror. "I thought you were dating a vicar."

"I went on a date with a banker and he was dreadful. I spent the night with Jake."

"Ah, well, at least that's interesting." Mirri shrugged. "How old will you be tomorrow?"

"Twenty-nine," Leonard said proudly. "With her whole life before her."

"Ah, when I was twenty-nine I went to Las Vegas and married my lover. Then we made love in his airplane all the way to Mexico, where we stayed for a month until we got bored and divorced. The ring is quite beautiful." She held out a hand in front of her, as a canary diamond at least as big as the Ritz, if not the whole of Piccadilly, cast shafts of light around the room. "He was an Italian playboy. Fun, but once you stop making love they want you to make pasta."

"Thank God times have changed." Kate buttered a piece of toast. "I couldn't make pasta to save my life."

"I liked twenty-nine, though." Mirri smiled. "At that age one is old enough to know what one is doing and young enough to do it all the same. Well, I was, anyway." She looked at Kate. "And will The Slug be putting rose petals on your pillow? Will you be drinking champagne and making love all day?"

"Well, I don't expect so." Kate scowled at the notion. "I'm not sure that I'd really want him to, either. But he is coming to dinner," she said smugly, and waited for Mirri to make some remark about it not counting as a birthday if you didn't make love seventeen times with a count from Medici.

But she didn't, she just smiled, raised her coffee cup at Kate, and said, "I shall call the restaurant after lunch and book for six then."

"Thanks, Mirri. That'd be amazing," Kate said as she flicked through her post, which was sitting on the table. No cards yet, but maybe tomorrow.

"Oh, by the way"—Leonard tapped Kate on the arm—"I had a telephone call this morning from a gentleman inquiring about you."

"Really?" Kate said. "That sounds promising."

"He wants to employ you, darling, not marry you." Leonard stirred his tea.

"Oh, well, never mind. What did he want then?" Kate was undeterred.

"He said he'd heard that you were one of the more accomplished animal painters in London and how did he go about hiring you?"

"Well, a commission's a commission, I suppose," Kate said, thinking that it would take her at least a small distance closer to her deposit for the flat. "But I've got to get to work on Bébé, too, you know." Kate looked at Mirri. She was feeling a pang of guilt because she always seemed to be walking out the door and not painting the portrait even though Mirri had paid a check into her bank two days ago.

"De rien," said Mirri with a sweep of her hand, which, even though Kate didn't speak French, she imagined meant something like "what the hell" or "don't worry your silly head about that."

"I told him that you'd be in your workshop this afternoon if he wanted to call around and see your work."

"Great, I'd better go and hide my underwear then." Kate stood up from the table. "It shouldn't take long. I imagine he'll just want to look at a few of the dog pictures, ask whether I have a problem with temperamental whippets, and go away to think about it."

"Oh, no, it sounded a good deal more than that," Leonard interrupted as Kate made for the door. "He was talking about life-sized. He asked what the largest thing you'd ever done was."

"Oh, well, a Great Dane then. Not a whippet. Do you think he'll be long?" Kate asked. "Because I've really got to get some sketches of Bébé done this afternoon."

"He said he'd be here before two." Leonard picked up *The Times* and began the crossword.

"Okay. Mirri, I'll be up just as soon as he's gone if that's okay," Kate said. Once again Mirri shrugged and didn't look up from *Le Monde*. Well, at least Kate had made an effort.

Kate jumped when she caught sight of a figure outside her shed. It was the back of what she assumed was a man wearing an olive-green parka coat with the hood up. At best he looked like a worshipful Druid; at worst a demented murderer from a teen-scream movie.

"Hello?" Kate asked tentatively as she slowed down her approach a little. She thought he was probably her new client, but then again he might be a lunatic fanboy of Mirri's or a lurking paparazzo. Things had certainly changed around here since Mirri arrived. And not all for the better where the litany of lurking strangers was concerned.

"Oh, hi." The figure turned around and pulled down his hood. Well, it was a glorious summer day, Kate thought, why would anyone be wearing such a thing?

"Hi, I'm Kate." She took a couple of steps closer and instantly recognized the thick black hair and the elegant hand that was extended toward her. "Louis. It's you," she squealed. "What are you doing here?" She hugged him and he kissed the top of her head.

"Ah, so Leonard managed not to let on that it was me." Louis seemed pleased. "Good. I wanted it to be a surprise."

"I'd have preferred a cake," she said. He raked the hair out of his eyes and Kate thought maybe she spotted a deep blush creeping up his cheeks. "No, of course I wouldn't. I'd love to work for you. What do you want? Your sheepdog or goldfish painted?" She walked down the path toward the shed, and he followed.

"I need a life-sized painting of a polar bear."

"You do not, " Kate said with disbelief.

"It's for an exhibition I'm doing in a couple of months."

"And you want me to do it?" Kate could understand strangers wanting to hire her. But Louis? "You're a professional artist," she reminded him.

"So are you, Kate," he said quite seriously. Kate took a look at her shed and realized that self-deprecation was not going to pay for a deposit on a home. Well, certainly not one that didn't have a lawn mower for a roommate. So she straightened up her shoulders and smiled in as professional a manner as she could manage.

"Well, Mr. Alcott. If you want to come in, then maybe we can discuss this." She opened the shed door and stepped inside.

"Is this your studio, then?" he asked as he stepped into the shed.

"It's where I live, Louis." She gave him a friendly push.

"I don't believe . . ." But before he could finish his sentence he looked up at the room and fell silent. "You live here?"

Kate wasn't sure whether he was horrified or plain amazed. She drew her lips back over her teeth in a wince; God, she hated having to admit this part. But it did sort the snobs from the good guys. People who thought she was poor and freaky tended to vanish; those who saw the novelty, or at least the necessity, of where she lived were awarded secret gold stars in Kate's head. And if she ever married George Clooney she'd invite them to the wedding. "I do," she cheerfully announced. "It's only temporary, I'm looking for a flat at the moment," she lied, "but actually I quite like it."

"Cool." Louis had unzipped his coat all the way and stood beside an old pitchfork, nodding approvingly.

"Would you like a bit of a tour?" she asked. "It doesn't take long."

"I'd love one." Louis looked around and around the room, and Kate noticed she'd left a sketch pad on her bed with very poor drawings of Jake in the nude on it. She ushered him toward the bathroom, scooping up the book as she went.

"The woodlice are very good neighbors, and I have a very sophisticated garden shovel alarm system in case of break-ins.

"The shower's actually pretty great," she went on proudly, because Louis, despite his silence, was making her feel as though she were showing him around the Hanging Gardens of Babylon. She could tell he thought this place was the greatest.

"Fantastic," he muttered when he stepped behind her bamboo shower curtain. "Did you do this yourself?"

"I did actually," Kate replied.

"I love it," Louis proclaimed and made his way around her, steering about six feet clear, and out into the main part of the shed, where he was confronted with the overwhelming choice of sitting on the bed or sitting on the floor. "And I know that you think that I'm hiring you out of some sense of loyalty or something, but you're wrong. You know how much I've always loved your work."

"Really?"

"I nearly bought Arthur at the Appleyard gallery." He nodded. "But I was broke."

"You liked Arthur?" Kate was surprised. It was the one achievement that she was actually proud of. She'd won a competition a few years ago with a painting of her dad's dog Arthur. Her dad had been determined to live out his cancer long enough to make it to the opening of the exhibition but had died only three days before. Kate had never been sure whether the work was actually good or whether she was just sentimentally attached to the piece because her dad loved it so much.

"It had huge range and freedom of movement." Louis was almost spinning in circles in the middle of the room.

"But they're animals, Louis. It's not exactly art."

"It's completely art. Compared to so much of the stuff I see it is." He didn't look at her, he looked at the canvases in the corner and, without asking, as most people did, began flipping through them, stopping at some and staring as though trying to commit every stroke to memory. Kate kept quiet. She always pretended she didn't notice people were looking at her work. It was too embarrassing.

"Kate, you've got so much better. Not that I ever doubted your talent. But this stuff's great." Louis was standing at arm's length from a picture of a stallion that she'd done in the style of an old Stubbs. "He's so beautiful." He moved his head slowly from side to side, taking in the glossy oils, the horse's sinewy flanks and gleaming coat.

"His name was Aeneas. He belonged to Leonard actually. I keep meaning to get it framed and give it to him for a present but I always forget." Kate stole a glance at Louis from the side. He looked quite formidable as he continued to gaze at Aeneas, but maybe it was just because he was looking at her work that she felt vulnerable.

"So the polar bear?" She coughed lightly. She really had to get back to Bébé soon, and she wasn't convinced that Louis could really be serious.

"Oh God, yeah. That." Louis broke off and began pacing a little across the shed floor. He had his sleeves pulled far down over his hands and was looking at the worn carpet, which Kate wished he wouldn't because it hadn't seen a vacuum cleaner ever and was covered not only in snail slime but also, she imagined, hairballs of hers and maybe a few of Jake's toenail clippings.

"Thing is, like I said, I'm doing this piece and that's why I was at the zoo. To check out the polar bears. And as you know I can't paint for toffee so I want to hire you." He returned to the canvases and stroked the top of one of them absentmindedly. "To paint. For me. Please." He stopped and took a breath.

"Great," Kate agreed.

"Great, well, I'll call you in the next day or two. I've got to go now. I've got a meeting. Thanks, Kate, you're a star." With which he threw a kiss on her cheek and practically bolted out of the shed door. She watched through the window as he hared through the side gate and vanished.

Chapter Nine

Later, as she meticulously applied her birthday lip gloss, Kate wondered what Jake would get her for her birthday. He always bought her great gifts—certainly not great by Mirri's standards, but Kate always treasured them. He'd once bought her a great little gramophone player from the sixties, which was impeccable and shiny despite its years. And with it were a bunch of old 45s. And when she played them she could hear the faint crackle of dust and age. Another time he'd bought her an antique Chinese wedding coat that he'd found somewhere at the top of Portobello Road. Kate had worn it until one of the sleeves hung off; it was still sitting under her bed waiting to be repaired, she thought guiltily. Kate was interrupted as her phone vibrated in her pocket. She flipped it open.

"What are you wearing?" Tanya demanded from the other end.

"Cream frothy skirt and a tank top," Kate replied as she fastened her gold sandals.

"Perfect." Tanya, who always restricted herself to sugared-almond-colored cashmere sweaters and a pair of pants that perfectly displayed her impeccable bottom, approved.

"Oh, and darling?" Kate knew something was up because usually Tanya didn't really care a whit what Kate wore. "If you're going to tell me off about Jake then don't. We're back together and despite what might have happened you're not allowed to be rude. He's my boyfriend and he's coming tonight. Okay?" When Kate had called Tanya earlier and filled her in on the date hate with Joss and told her about creeping back to Jake's afterward, Tanya hadn't been able to disapprove, because Kate had made her feel so terrible about setting her best friend up with a whingeing teetotaling misogynist.

"Chippy." Tanya laughed.

"Just defending my corner. That's all."

"Actually, Robbie asked if you'd do him a favor."

"Robbie did?" What Kate could possibly do for Robbie was a mystery to her. *Fabulous handsome businessman with pots of money asks pitiful artist with patchy love life for favor.* Implausible.

"He wondered if you'd invite Mirri along tonight."

"Oh, he did not."

"You know he loves her and I told him how much you hate but *hate* her. But he said it'd mean the world to him. Make his week. Or something."

"Well, it is Robbie. And I do love him. But wouldn't a different favor do? A little bloodletting? Put my eye out with a knitting needle?"

"Okay, don't worry. I'll tell him she couldn't make it." Tanya didn't care either way.

"Oh, I'm kidding. She's coming anyway because she booked the table and she's actually not in my worst books today. That place is reserved for Joss. So I'll make sure Robbie gets to sit next to her," Kate said, before adding, "But I won't be held responsible if she ends up shagging the waiter in full view of the restaurant before the main course has been served. Okay?"

"Fine. See you there." Tanya hung up and Kate filed the nail on her ring finger and wondered what Mirri's diamond, or one very similar to it anyway, would look like on her hand. The answer was actually plain ridiculous with her dirty nails and too-long fingers, but she wasn't going to let that put her off dreaming of Jake and a padded box.

Kate had hoped that at the last minute Mirri would develop other plans for tonight that might include aiding and abetting Shagger Sinclair with his latest foray into adultery. But when she arrived at the house she felt guilty for ever letting this cross her mind because Mirri had not only dressed up specially for Kate's birthday, but also shouted *"Bonne anniversaire"* out of the window at the top of the house and ran down to the kitchen, where she squealed and kissed Kate on the cheek and become all warm and sweet about friendship and family. Kate, thinking that her mother would have probably told her if she was adopted, and if she was, it wasn't likely that she was the love child of a famous French movie star—and besides, she didn't have Mirri's boobs—decided that this was simply Continental overfamiliarity and smiled magnanimously, genuinely pleased that a twenty-ninth birthday could make anyone so disproportionately happy.

While Mirri whizzed off to settle Bébé down for the night, Kate turned to Leonard, who was just finishing up on a business call. "That was odd," she said with a frown.

"What, the fact that she was happy to be invited to your birthday party?" Leonard replaced the receiver and stretched his arms out in front of him.

"Yeah. I mean my sketches of Bébé this afternoon were fine but they weren't *that* good," Kate said suspiciously.

"She likes you, Kate. And she's a very generous woman. You're the only one who can't seem to see that."

"Oh, Leonard, do me a favor. She walked into my life, told me I had bad taste in men, then proceeded to call me repressed and frigid, implied that I didn't get enough sex, that when I did it was very poor quality, and that I dressed badly and would never find a husband even though she couldn't understand why I'd want one anyway because they were passé and made you cook pasta." Kate drew breath. "How can you possibly imagine that she likes me?"

"She does. But she's just being honest."

"Are you saying that you agree with her?" Kate's voice was growing more shrill by the second. "That all those things are true?"

"I'm saying that Mirri isn't unkind. She's just very very different from you. And despite what you think, she is very fond of you."

"Yeah, well, I don't see how she can be, because she barely knows me, and I think she's just coming along tonight so she can score herself a date. And so she won't have to stay in and watch television on her own."

"Darlings, I am ready," Mirri called down merrily from the upstairs landing. "Shall we go?" And with that, Kate and Leonard shut up and simply marveled as she glided down the stairs in her Pucci caftan. She then hooked one arm through Kate's and one through Leonard's, and led them out into the garden. Kate winced guiltily and prayed she hadn't overheard.

London had that magical feeling that happens only a few evenings a year. Summer had arrived and the air smelled as though it had been steeped all day in jasmine and roses and sunshine. Everywhere people displayed as much warm, pink skin as they could get away with. The shops were closing up but the owners lingered on the pavement chatting to one another. Occasionally a car would thud by with its bass-pumping music and its windows open.

"London isn't so bad," Mirri proclaimed above the ecstatic birdsong on Primrose Hill. As they took a shortcut over the nettles and grass, Kate looked across and saw the Post Office Tower on the other side of the city, then caught sight of the London Eye, imperceptibly turning as the tourists and natives within its seemingly minuscule glass carriages marveled at the clear evening views across the river. This hill was probably the best place to see the whole of London unfolding before you, and it seemed only a hop, skip, and jump across town to the overbooked restaurants in the West End where girls in flimsy dresses were spreading foie gras onto toast as they talked unashamedly about shoes and not politics. To the right the painfully style-conscious inhabitants of Notting Hill would be behind their stuccoed housefronts, carefully considering their shabbiness and lack of grooming before stepping out to a pub to meet friends who were drinking Guinness standing on the pavement. Meanwhile in Soho crowds of gonnabe filmmakers and young features editors would be crammed into the stifling clubs, where even though the windows were open they would fail to catch a breeze.

"London's great," Kate agreed. The trio walked arm in arm, looking forward to the first glass of chardonnay.

Kate and her unlikely crew were ushered to a long wooden table by the windows, which had been thrown open all day—pointlessly, it seemed, as there wasn't even a hint of a breeze. The waiters distributed bottles of wine across the table and small plates of olives flecked with bitter herbs.

"To Kate," Mirri toasted as she sloshed wine into three large glasses.

Leonard raised his glass and seconded the motion: "To my dear Kate."

"Cheers." Kate raised her glass, which was duly clinked on either side by the others. And no sooner had they taken their first sips than Tanya and Robbie walked through the door, hand in hand. Robbie, as always, commanded the attention of most of the room. It may have had something to do with his well-scrubbed blond good looks and rangy frame, but it was also due to the fact that he was manna to the gossip columns and society magazines that everyone pretended not to read but devoured in the dentist's waiting room. He was instantly recognizable, at least to the media-savvy clientele of Lemonia.

Robbie's father, who had died five years ago, had been a charming, fantastically wealthy industrialist who had a series of ever-more beautiful and tragic wives, and even more mistresses. The press were much given to speculation that Robbie might go the same way as his father—something that Kate considered well-nigh impossible. Robbie Hirst would rather have his teeth pulled than cheat on Tanya with one of the saucy young eco-babes who made it their business in life to try to lead him astray.

"Happy birthday, Katie." Robbie leaned toward Kate and kissed her cheek as she stood to greet her guests. He also gave her an unnecessarily large hug and handed her a small box.

"I love tall men with small boxes," Kate giggled flirtatiously, as most people in the restaurant, except for the really smitten women, stopped staring and went back to their supper.

"And we love *you*," Robbie reassured her, before casting his eyes over Kate's shoulder to catch a glimpse of Mirabelle Moncur.

"Tanya and Robbie Hirst, this is Mirabelle Moncur. And you've both met Leonard before." There was a general shaking of hands and kissing of cheeks and Mirri, who was almost telepathically programmed to pick out a fan in a crowd of thousands, presented Robbie with exactly what he wanted. He wanted Mirabelle Moncur and he got her—pout, hair, and smoldering eyes.

"So good to meet you." Robbie rose to the occasion and kissed Mirri's hand.

"Oh, but my goodness, it is you," Mirri said with surprise.

"I'm sorry?" Robbie began to blush.

"Peter Hirst's son?" Mirri asked with a look of pure delight on her face.

"You knew my father?" Robbie was thrilled.

"Oh, I'll *bet* she did," Tanya said under her breath to Kate. Kate and Tanya exchanged a brief look of *oh-how-predictable* before giving in to laughter. Kate picked up her present from Robbie and Tanya and the large one that Leonard had given her earlier and wondered whether she ought to open them or wait to find out from Mirri just how well she had known Robbie's father. But the pair were already deeply engrossed in conversation and wine, so she sat back down and looked at her watch. She was used to Jake being the last one to arrive. He'd doubtless stroll in just as they were all cursing him because it was rude to order before he arrived, but he was forty-five minutes late and everyone was starving. And then he'd be forgiven by all and sundry because he'd regale them with a tale of how he got caught talking to a couple of East End gangsters in a betting shop and they'd given him a tip on a horse who had romped home, so the champagne was on him. Jake had charm, and style, there was no denying that.

"He'll be held up on some harebrained scheme or other. I

promise." Leonard caught the look of anxiety that must have flashed across Kate's face.

"Oh, I know he will." Kate smiled, aware that everyone was now looking at the birthday girl to see if she was going to open her presents. "Typical Jake."

"I'm not even hungry anyway." Tanya took off her cardigan and put it over the back of her chair. "It's far too hot to eat."

"I'll open my presents in a bit," Kate said. Which everyone correctly interpreted as *I'll open my presents when Jake gets here.*

But sometime later, as Leonard poured the last drops of yet another bottle of wine into Tanya's glass, it became miserably apparent that Jake probably wasn't waylaid. He simply wasn't going to turn up. Kate, who was checking her phone for a blinking red light an average of once every seventeen seconds, was beginning to feel sick to her stomach.

"I think we should all order." Kate tried to put on a brave face. She motioned to the waiter to come over to their table.

"I'll have the fish, please. And potatoes." She smiled and then, when everyone else was ordering, stole away from the table and out onto the street to call Jake. Her friends politely pretended not to notice and nobody exchanged sympathetic glances. Her hand was shaking as she dialed. How on earth could she be here. Again? And on her birthday.

"Hi this is Jake. Leave a message." His phone went directly to voice mail. Kate snapped it shut and took a few breaths of the balmy evening air. The sky was a vivid cobalt blue, and the sun had only just set. As she leaned her back against a lamppost and contemplated kicking a nearby car wheel in bitter frustration, she felt a hand on her shoulder.

"He is not coming?" It was Mirri. Kate instinctively thrust the phone into her pocket and plastered a smile to her face.

"No, he can't make it." She looked Mirri in the eye and defied her to be nice. "Which is a shame but never mind, the party must go on."

"You're right, a girl gets only one birthday a year," Mirri said softly. And as Kate positively flounced back into the restaurant with a determination that ought to have won her a medal of honor, Mirri watched her and looked sad. She really had been there, she really had done that. And she knew how painful it was.

Kate's fish was on the bone, which made life even more awful. Every time she took a mouthful she was skewered in the windpipe by a sharp sliver. She gave up and dallied halfheartedly with her potatoes.

"You know this waiter we have?" Mirri leaned into the assembled company and asked in a theatrical whisper. Everyone except Kate looked at the waiter and nodded. "Well, he looks exactly like a man I knew when I was younger." Kate wiped butter off her lips with her napkin and looked one more time at her phone. The nasty bastard. She barely had words harsh enough for Jake right now, but she knew, simply knew, that this time it had to be over. Someone had once told her that the areas of the brain that govern pain and love are right next to one another and sometimes the signals get crossed. Kate certainly knew that there was a fine line between the two—but she had truly crossed over into masochistic territory now, and unless she ditched Jake once and for all, really walked away, she would quite literally have to go and have her head examined. And she couldn't afford a shrink so she'd have to just quit now.

"He was called Tyler, which is a terrible name, and I should have known that he was trouble. But, *non,* off I tripped after this Tyler." Mirri loaded the name with such melodramatic disdain that Kate was momentarily distracted by her story.

"He would have been incredibly handsome if he looked like that waiter," Tanya, who was clearly also warming to Mirri, chipped in.

"He was okay. I've had better. I've had worse." *Ugh, here we go.* Kate couldn't believe that Mirri was about to turn her burned-out wreck of a birthday into an opportunity to gloat. That was just about beyond the pale. Even for a thoughtless, pampered pain-in-the-ass French movie star.

"Anyway, for some reason I loved Tyler. And he didn't love me. And the more he didn't love me, the more I tripped after him and changed my hair and read books so that I could impress him with my knowledge of early French novels and invited him to come on expensive holidays with me. And sometimes he would come and I'd want to have his babies and sometimes he'd leave. And then one day, when I realized that he had told all my friends that I was a pest—after he stole money from my purse to take another woman out to dinner—when he had told me that I dressed badly and ate noisily and after he had brought some girl back to my house and made love to her in my swimming pool and she had worn my robe . . . well, then I thought, you know, Mirabelle—" Mirri paused and the table was still. "—this man is a piece of shit."

"Absolutely right." Leonard broke the silence and guffawed.

"And what happened then?" Tanya asked.

"I have no idea. I never saw him again." Mirri shrugged and fleetingly looked over at Kate.

"And the moral of the story is, at least I'm not going out with Tyler," Kate said miserably to Mirri.

"There is no moral, darling. Just immoral men who take beautiful, sweet women for granted."

"Let's have a toast . . . to Kate." Leonard raised his glass and stood up. "To a beautiful and sweet woman whom I have known for a very long time now, and who, like the finest of clarets, simply gets better and better and more and more delicious with age."

"Hear hear." Robbie leaned over and kissed Kate on the cheek, then stood up himself. Much to the delight of the women in the room, who hadn't quite managed to tear their eyes away from him entirely. "To my gorgeous friend Kate. I hope you have the fabulous, successful year you deserve and I hope all your wishes come true, darling."

Kate looked up appreciatively at Robbie and felt a sudden surge of anger. How the fuck dare Jake ruin her birthday like this? Here she was surrounded by wonderful friends saying amazing things about her, a once-in-a-lifetime moment, and he was spoiling it for her. Like he'd spoiled too many days. Days when the sun was shining yet Kate couldn't be happy. Days when she'd been given a great commission but was miserable to the core because he'd behaved badly toward her.

Kate looked at Robbie and her friends. "Thanks, guys," she whispered almost inaudibly and then stood up and made her slightly jagged way to the bathroom, where she stumbled into a cubicle and closed the door behind her.

Kate sat down on the loo seat and a huge, stupid tear rolled down her cheek. She must not cry. She had all those people out there smiling at her, her friends rallying around. And she could not bear for them to feel sorry for her. The role of abused, pathetic girlfriend was wearing thin even by her standards. Everyone else must be bored to the back teeth of her. But she couldn't help it. She pulled a tissue out of her bag and wiped her eyes. The roller coaster of life with Jake had taken her from yesterday morning when she was singing in the shower to now, with her head in her hands at her own birthday party. She had to get off this bloody ride.

"Darling." There was a gentle tap on the door of her cubicle. Kate contemplated not responding. It came again.

"Tanya?" Kate sniffed.

"It's me. Mirabelle," the voice came back.

"I'm fine, thanks." Kate was beyond rudeness. Besides, why should she punish poor Mirri, who really only seemed to be being kind to her.

"I have a present for you."

"I'll be out in a minute. I promise. I just have to . . . get myself together." Kate rubbed her eyes with the crumbling, surprisingly wet tissue.

"Then I'll come in. Please." Mirri wasn't going anywhere, Kate deduced, so she slid back the lock of the door.

"Here, darling. I was going to give it to you this afternoon when you were being so sweet with Bébé in my bedroom but I couldn't find it. I think it will bring you luck." And Mirri took Kate's hand and pressed something small and hard into her fist. Kate opened her palm and through her tears saw a ring. Not the great canary diamond that Mirri had been wearing this morning but a tiny little shiny ring with a perfect, glinting little stone on the top.

"Mirri, don't be ridiculous. I couldn't. It's too generous," Kate began.

Mirri simply folded her arms and refused to be drawn. "It was given to me by my favorite husband. He had a very kind heart and not as much money as many of the others. And I'm giving it to you because I thought that if you had something sparkling to wear on your finger then you won't be so desperate to find yourself a husband and then . . . and only then . . . can you begin to enjoy yourself like a charming girl like you should."

"Mirri, you can't. Really that's amazing but I think that—"

"I've told you before that you think too much. Now put it on."

Kate looked down at the diamond on her finger. A beautiful, sparkling movie star's diamond. "It's beautiful."

"It's not the Hope Diamond but it will give you hope. I promise." Mirri looked approvingly at Kate's finger. "Now, look at your face. You have red eyes and your hair . . ."

"God is it a mess?" Kate smoothed down her hair with her palm.

"A mess? Heavens no. Not a mess at all." And with that Mirri took Kate's hand and led her out of the cubicle toward the large mirrors in the bathroom. "Let me look at you." She swiftly extracted a black eyeliner pencil from her handbag and took Kate's face between her hands. "They say that every woman is preserved in her heyday. I know that I wear too much eyeliner and too many jewels but it makes me feel young and sexy. And you, my dear, have not had your heyday yet."

"I don't think I'm the heyday type." Kate sighed defeatedly.

"You are very silly sometimes." Mirri began drawing dark rims around Kate's pretty amber eyes with satisfaction. "And you are also very pretty. And for tonight, and until you find the man who lights up your heart and your life and you find your own heyday, you are going to borrow mine. Okay?"

"What do you mean?" Kate asked as she patiently allowed Mirri to run her fingers through her hair and gently shove her under the hand dryer until she looked as though she had been sitting on the wing of a jumbo jet in midflight. Or—and Kate thought this was probably the point—she'd been kissed to within an inch of her life, had sex for six hours without pause for breath, and hadn't been near a mirror for a week at least. "Just fucked." Kate smiled sadly. "Then chucked?"

"No no no. This Slug. He loves you. But his love is not enough. He loves you in his way but you deserve so much more. You deserve a man who will want to die for you." Mirri assured Kate, "He probably won't be required to do this, you understand. But you need to feel that he would if you asked him to."

"But why should anyone die for me? Why should anyone die for anyone else? Really, Mirri, I just don't believe that any human being should ever rely on someone else so completely."

"That is because you don't know what it's like to really be loved." Mirri looked almost sad.

"Don't feel sorry for me. I'm okay. I like my life this way," Kate said. "I'm independent, I'm strong. Despite all the Jake stuff. I'll be okay." Clearly the hair was beginning to work its magic.

"I wasn't sorry for you. I was sad for me," Mirri said unexpectedly.

"Really?" Kate looked in the mirror and though she didn't look a bit like herself, she did look pretty hot.

"Life isn't simple for anyone, Kate. I tell you. Whether you are alone or with a man you love. It's never without problems." And Mirri checked her own reflection in the mirror and turned to her new charge. "Now I want you to come out there with me, not give another thought to that man all night, and have some fun. And I don't mean just eating olives and being polite. We are going to enjoy ourselves. Okay?" She looked at Kate, who nodded resolutely and checked her phone one last time. No Jake. No more Jake ever, she decided, as Mirri took her hand, with her new, first-ever diamond on her finger, and led her out into the restaurant.

"We have a birthday over here, darling." Mirri called the Tyler look-alike waiter over as she and Kate settled back down into their seats, "And we'd like to celebrate." She looked intently into his eyes,

and doubtless his lungs were being scorched with the scent of Shalimar, which was the MM signature scent. Well, at least she could
commit to something, Kate thought, even if it was only a fragrance.

"You would maybe like some champagne?" The waiter was shaking just a little bit.

"And some music. We would like a little music."

"I'm afraid that as it's a residential neighborhood we're not really
allowed to play music . . ."

"Pah." Mirri scoffed and stood up. She marched toward the bar
and sought out the manager, returning moments later with her hips
swaying to the beat of what could only be described as jungle
drums. The lights of the restaurant had been mysteriously dimmed.
Mirri was followed moments later by a procession of slim young
men bearing in turn a bucket of champagne on ice, a birthday cake
ablaze with candles, and, at the end of the line, the ultimate conjur-
ing trick of all time, Jonah Sinclair.

"Now we dance," she said as she shook off her shoes and began
pouring out overflowing, foaming glasses of champagne. "Jonah,
this is my great friend Kate."

"Ah, the birthday girl." Jonah took Kate's hand, rather satisfacto-
rily, the one with the diamond on it, and kissed it. "May I have the
pleasure?"

"Well, I usually only dance when I'm drunk or alone," Kate
began to stammer. Not only was she knocked out by how sexy
Jonah was in real life, close up, but she also felt a creeping sense of
embarrassment in case he knew that she was the peeping pervert
from the other night at the house.

"Ah, no, you're not getting out of it that easily." He grinned and
pulled Kate to her feet. His voice was lilting and gorgeous, and she
was about to humiliate herself by not being able to dance with him.
She snatched up one of the now diminished glasses of champagne
and felled the lot in one swallow. "That-a-girl," he whispered in her
ear as he led her to the dance floor. They were followed moments
later by Mirri, whose dress was already swishing around her thighs
like a gypsy queen, and Leonard, who had Tanya's hand and was

ballroom whirling her around. Mirri then proceeded to lure the famously undancing Robbie Hirst to the floor with one come-hither curl of her finger.

At first Kate could not get her feet to beat in time to anything. Not her heart, not her thudding head, and certainly not the music. She was hopelessly off beat, and her shoes seemed to stick awkwardly to the floor. Everyone else looked as though they were gliding around on crushed velvet. But Jonah knew exactly what he was doing, and when he stood opposite her, with both his hands resting on her hips, there was little she could do but get in time with him. Or evaporate, of course. But that would have seemed a little ungrateful.

"You've got pretty lips." He breathed his warm, champagne-sour breath onto her neck.

"So have you," Kate replied. What else to say? Mirri sidled over and Jonah, try as he might to be polite to the birthday girl, clearly couldn't stop himself from reacting to the musk in Mirri's scent. Or something, because seconds later his pretty lips were having a party all of their own with Mirri's neck.

"My turn." No sooner had Kate sidled over to where Robbie was dancing than Leonard whisked her off to spin the light fantastic. "Are you having fun?" he asked.

"A ball." Kate laughed. Having genuinely forgotten all about whatshisname. "I love being twenty-nine."

And so, in the words of Leonard Cohen, Kate was danced to the end of love. Well, not the end, exactly. But certainly the end until the morning, when she would undoubtedly remember all about Jake. But for tonight she was lovely. She was adored by her fantastic friends and she had a whole new friendship with Mirri.

"Thank you," she called out to Mirri as she was flung, inexpertly, by Robbie across the restaurant-cum-dance-floor.

"My pleasure." Mirri laughed, then whispered something into Jonah's ear. Moments later Kate found herself on the receiving end of a true screen kiss. It was sweet and sexy and just like the movies. And it was delivered with a twinkle by Jonah Sinclair. As his hands settled on the back of her neck and his lips sank into hers, Kate was aware only that this was very, very nice. This blew whatshisname out of the water. Until tomorrow. But then, in the words of another song, Kate had tonight, who needed tomorrow?

As Mirri and Kate walked home, arm in stumbling arm, the weather broke for the first time in days. At first there was a light misting of rain; then, as they walked barefoot, shoes in hand, along the street, drinking in the heavenly smell of newly damp earth and revived grass and moistened air, it began to rain more heavily. They had been the last to leave the restaurant. Jonah had finally given in, after Mirri had made it clear that there would be no hammock action tonight, and Leonard and Robbie had drifted off home when they realized that they had blisters on their feet and meetings to attend in the morning. Tanya reluctantly went with her husband when he mentioned for the fifth time that he had to work tomorrow. The only person left, after the music was finally turned off, was the manager, who had wearily nudged Kate and Mirri out of the door before he bolted it. It was late and his wife would be furious enough when she heard who had been dancing on his tables past midnight. He couldn't have had Mirri and Kate falling asleep on one of the banquettes. As wonderful as that might have been for all concerned.

"Did you ask Jonah to kiss me?" Kate asked Mirri, who had paused momentarily to remove a sharp pebble from between her toes.

"Only so that he might have the pleasure." Mirri held Kate up so she wouldn't topple over. "And a little bit so that you might see how a real man kisses."

"He is so unbelievably sexy," Kate tried to whisper, but her judgment was shot to pieces with all the champagne so it was more of a husky yell.

"That is just the tip of the iceberg, as they say." Mirri put her arm through Kate's and they continued their halting progress home.

"Is he amazing in bed? Or in a hammock, I mean?"

"He is pretty good, yes." Mirri laughed. "Would you like me to arrange something?"

"What you mean . . . ?" Kate's mind was bubbling over with the possibilities.

"In France the young men do this often. They take a wonderful, older lover so that they might learn. I think this would be useful for you. Have a competent, handsome lover so that you set yourself a standard, so that you learn to appreciate good lovemaking with a man who also appreciates you," Mirri continued.

"Oh my God, I couldn't." Kate giggled excitedly as the rain poured harder on them and they were forced to quicken their pace just a little so as not to be swept away into a storm drain.

"The thing is, darling, you think that this is all about sex. You think to yourself, *Oh that Mirabelle Moncur, she is a sex maniac and all she thinks about is cock.*"

"Well no, I don't think that. I mean not very much," Kate blustered. Just when she thought she was on Mirri's wavelength, the woman had a way of catching her off guard with her candor.

"You don't?" Mirri sounded surprised.

"Yes, actually, I do. Well, I did. Now I know there's more to you." Kate hugged her new friend closer.

"But it's not about sex. It's about being appreciated. The Slug, he doesn't see you. He doesn't know how beautiful you are."

"He's often said that he thinks I'm pretty." Kate remembered fondly, and thanks to the emotional Bubble Wrap that the drink had afforded her, she didn't feel the pain.

"Pretty is no good." Mirri sat Kate down on the bench at the top of the hill and looked intently at her. Thankfully the rain had eased off a little, and though they were distinctly damp and both women's hair hung in rat's tails about their faces it was warm, summer rain. "A lover will see the real beauty. A lover will look at your breasts and if they are like tiny apples he will adore them. Or if they are enormous and resting on your stomach he will think that they are remarkable. If you have a mole on your shoulder he will notice it and take time to kiss it. He will feel the rough skin on your elbow and imagine you resting on it as you gaze out a window from your desk. He will bury his face in your hair and will be in heaven at your scent. This man will really see you. And every woman is a work of art. Every woman is beautiful and should be seen." Mirri sat back and looked out at the lights across London.

"That sounds very . . . well, very French, I suppose," said Kate, whose English blood ran thick enough to ensure that whenever someone spoke about *things like that,* in a way that was very straight-faced and earnest, she wanted to hide behind a pillow or take a large sip of Earl Grey to disguise her embarrassment.

"You don't think this is true?" Mirri asked, slightly disappointed in Kate's response.

"I just think that if a man told me I had boobs like apples I'd probably laugh," Kate said apologetically.

"You would not."

"I would, you know." One of the reasons Kate liked Jake was that he could laugh. At Kate. At himself. At the whole thing.

"So English." Mirri waved her hand dismissively. "What are we to do with you?"

"I'll be fine," Kate promised. "Although if you were offering a sampler of Jonah Sinclair then I don't think I'd say no."

"You would fall in love with him and this would be a disaster."

"You're right. I'd definitely fall in love with him," Kate agreed. "In fact, I'm already a bit in love with him."

"Is there anybody else?" Mirri asked as they walked back through Leonard's garden gate.

"Not even slightly."

"Oh dear." Mirri was completely dispirited now.

"It's okay. I have a lot of work to do. I'll just keep away from men and focus on my pictures. That way you'll get a much better portrait of Bébé, that's for sure."

"Yes, maybe you are right. Good night, my darling." Mirri kissed Kate on both cheeks and looked at her closely. "So young and lovely. It is such a waste."

"God, less of the young," Kate pleaded, "I'm twenty-nine." She walked toward her shed door as Mirri sat down on the hammock to have her last cigarette of the day. "Thanks, Mirri, you're a star." Then Kate laughed. "Really."

Chapter Ten

Kate was flung out of her dreams with such violence that for a few moments she had no notion where she was or what was happening. And when, seconds later, she realized that the calamitous, terrifying noise that had woken her seemed to be right outside her shed she merely froze. Something was in the garden. And it wasn't any mower or pneumatic drill or leaf blower on the face of this earth. It was entirely alien, and she was petrified. She listened for distant screams but heard none. Finally she wrested herself from the grip of fear and her sheets, which were wrapped around her body like a mummy, and tiptoed nervously across the shed, stubbing her toe on a discarded gold sandal. But as she leaned down to clutch her throbbing foot the noise began to fade. It seemed to lift and drift away until it was just a distant whir.

Kate approached the door with trepidation. And finally, relieved that the noise had all but vanished, she unlocked the door and put her head outside, unsure what kind of carnage or alteration would greet her. Her first thought was that it was snowing. For the air was filled with fluttering whiteness. She couldn't see Leonard's house because the sky was alive with snowflakes. Then she realized that they weren't snowflakes; it was the blossom from the apple trees and it was scattering madly and slowly drifting to the ground. Above it was still sky. A breathtaking cerulean sky that promised another day of sundresses and laziness. And when Kate looked down at the grass, at the snowfall, or blossom petals, settling, she saw only roses. Hundreds, maybe thousands of long-stemmed red roses. It was the oddest and most magical sight she'd ever witnessed. And for a moment or two she stood stock-still in her nightdress at her door and gazed at the scene without making any sense of it. It was quite simply sublimely beautiful and she couldn't tear her eyes away.

Then she noticed, at an upstairs window of Leonard's house, which came into view as the blossom dissolved into a pale carpet on the lawn, Mirri leaning out and laughing delightedly.

"Katie, isn't it marvelous?" she yelled across, waving an arm at Kate.

"What on earth is it?" Kate called back, as she took her first footstep out onto the snowscape, careful to avoid stepping on the roses.

"Pick them up. Take a hundred," Mirri offered. So Kate bent down and began to pick up the exquisite, elegant stems and collect them into a bunch. "I'll be down in a moment." Mirri vanished from the window and Kate picked up a few more before realizing that she'd be here for several days if she were to gather the whole lot. Where on earth had they come from? What had that apocalyptic sound been that had woken her up? She took her bunch of flowers and sat down on the grass. She looked up to the blossom trees to see whether they were now bare and mean looking since they'd shed so many flowers. But no; miraculously they seemed to be as snowy white and frothy as ever.

"He hasn't done this for years. But I think when he heard that I was in London he couldn't help himself. For old times' sake." Mirri was crossing the garden with two mugs in her hand and her satin dressing gown tightly done up for once.

"Who did this? How?" Kate asked as she raked her fingers through the petals and sniffed one of the wildly scented red roses.

"Tony. An old lover of mine." Mirri settled down on the grass next to Kate and deposited the mugs on the ground. "Early Grey for you, builders' tea for me."

"An old lover. Why doesn't that surprise me?" Kate said, for once without any rancor.

"When we were together he would do it every day." Mirri picked up a rose and carelessly pulled off a velvety red petal to smell.

"But how did it happen?"

"You didn't hear the helicopter?" Mirri laughed.

"I had no idea that's what it was."

"Ah yes. He would make my gardener at home crazy by swooping down over my breakfast table in his noisy helicopter and flinging a thousand red roses everywhere. It took hours to clear up and we never had enough vases. Too too much." She shook her head with resignation. "But a lot of fun. No?"

"It's incredible. Do you think he's still in love with you?" Kate asked, wondering how two people's lives could be so very different. Quite apart from the fact that Mirri was stunningly beautiful. It was more than that, Kate realized. It was about joy and expectation. Mirri expected magical things to happen to her, things beyond the realms of most women's wildest imaginings, and she got them. Kate expected nothing of the sort. And guess what? Here she was sitting on the rose petals of another woman's dreams.

"He's not in the least in love with me," Mirri proclaimed. "He has a beautiful wife and grown-up children. But he's generous and he loves to do nice things. I shall have him to lunch later and you'll meet the man who lost me the best gardener I ever had. Since then my rhododendrons were never the same."

"You're very lucky," Kate said pensively, sipping her tea and inhaling the glorious fragrance, which was beginning to fill the air as the morning sun warmed the petals of a thousand flowers.

"I know. I have been blessed. Now, how about you work on Bébé today and I make us a picnic? We must escape Leonard because he'll behead me when he sees what has happened to his poor garden. And I heard one of the neighbors yelling that her tulips were flattened."

"Great idea," Kate said. "As I said last night, I'm ready to throw myself into work. Lose myself."

"Then we'll take Bébé with us. You sharpen your pencils and I'll prepare."

"It's a deal," Kate said, tipping the last of her tea back and standing up. "Would you mind if I took some for the shed?" She held out her handful of rose stems.

Mirri looked at Kate as though she were mad. "What do *you* think?" she asked, so Kate took her flowers and retreated to her shed.

———

Kate was gathering together her pencils and a wedge of paper large enough to really get to grips with Bébé's ears and whiskers and all the details she needed to master before she got to work on the portrait itself. But just as she was about to bring along a packet of biscuits she realized that she didn't know the first thing about her subject. In fact, she'd been so involved with her whole Jake crisis since Mirri arrived that she'd barely noticed Bébé at all.

"He's a cat, Kate. Not a Labrador," she chided herself and so instead of taking the biscuits picked up her purse. She was about to step into her combat pants when she noticed at the back of her wardrobe an old satin slip dress that Tanya had once left behind when she'd stayed the night at Leonard's. It was technically a nightdress and it was definitely made for seduction and not fixing drains, but Kate thought she'd give it a trial run anyway. Then she slipped on her sparkling flip-flops, in the daytime no less, ruffled up her hair à la Mirri, and ran out of her shed. She felt odd but she was only slipping down to the shops, so if she felt exposed or too slutty she could always hide in a doorway or dash home again, she figured. She would just run to the fishmonger's and then back. She usually made a concerted effort to befriend her subjects, and she was great with animals; they loved her. With cats she had a canny way of letting them come to her, being just a little bit cool, catching their eye and looking away. But with the Bébé sitting she'd been so ridiculously distracted that she hadn't tried to win his affection at all. It was time to change all that.

Kate locked the shed behind her and went out the side gate of the garden, hoping to avoid the paparazzi who would be drinking from Styrofoam cups of coffee on Leonard's front wall. She sneaked a peek around over the back gate and then, certain that the coast was clear, unbolted the gate.

"Going somewhere, beautiful?" From behind one of the trees on the avenue, coming toward her across the road, was Jake.

Kate paused for a second and then, closing the gate behind her, proceeded to walk down the street toward Regents Park Road. "I've got to run an errand," she said matter-of-factly.

"Baby, I'm sorry." Jake jogged to catch up with her and walked alongside her.

"What on earth for?" She looked ahead and thought about whether she should get prawns or whitebait for Bébé.

"For not coming to your birthday," he said in a really saccharine voice. Which was incredibly helpful to Kate. One thing she hated on men was cutesy voices. Especially when they intended to be contrite. *Why not be a man and face up to what you've done in a grown-up voice?* she thought.

"Kate, I'm sorry. Truly. Will you give me the chance to explain?"

"I'm actually in a bit of a hurry, Jake." She was a little shocked at her own lack of emotion, she had to admit, but it felt amazing. Slightly out-of-body and as though she were acting, but still incredibly empowering.

"Angel, don't be like this. Can we talk? Can we go for a coffee?"

"Jake, if you want to talk then call me up like normal people and ask me. Don't sneak around in the street outside my house assuming that I'll be in."

"You're always in." Jake laughed. Clearly her social life was a joke to him. He wasn't wrong, either, which was the galling part. Kate rarely went out without Jake.

"Well, now I'm out."

"Where are you going? I can come with you." He was breathing a little heavily as he struggled to keep up with her practically sprinting pace. *Ha, all those cigarettes,* she thought. She hadn't turned to look at him once.

"The fishmonger's," she snapped. She wished she hadn't had to say that. She wished she were leaving the house to do something other than buy seafood. But someday soon she would be, she vowed. It had been nobody's fault but hers that she had subjugated her life and fun to Jake's for three years.

"I see." Jake laughed jovially. He was beginning to annoy her, shuffling and panting at her side like this. And she hadn't even begun to remember his crimes of last night, or she might have thwacked him over the head with her purse. Which was full of small change and gratifyingly heavy.

"Listen, Jake." She finally stopped and turned to look at him. Mistake. He looked sexy. Done in. Rumpled. With a smile about his lips. Kate steeled herself and looked at his shoulder. "There was a place for you at dinner last night. You didn't show up. Regardless of whether you were my friend, my lover, or some person on the street that I'd invited, it was incredibly bad-mannered of you not to call and say you couldn't make it. This isn't about us. There is no us. There really never has been. If there had then I would have been able to ask you to have dinner with me without being terrified that I might scare you off. You wouldn't have flinched and gone into a filthy mood every time I forgot myself and called you my boyfriend. If there had been an us you might have once, just once in three years, given a damn about my feelings. But you didn't. So there is no us. And I am fine with that concept. But you were simply rude last night for not calling to say you couldn't make it. Though if that's what you're trying to apologize for, then fine. Apology accepted. See you around."

Kate looked into his eyes and nearly burst into weird, hysterical laughter because he was so completely shocked. But instead she took advantage of the moment to break free and disappear very melodramatically around the corner onto the next street. She listened for footsteps or panting behind her, but she could hear nothing. She was a bit disappointed that she didn't hear some low-pitched keening as if from a wounded animal, but ah well, it was Jake after all, and she hadn't really expected that. She'd never expected anything from him before, so keening and wailing now might have been too much to handle anyway.

"I got Bébé some prawns." Kate breezed into Leonard's kitchen, where Mirri was reaching to the back of the fridge and pulling out a bottle of wine for the lunch. "Does he like them?" She put two white containers down onto the kitchen table.

"Oh, he loves them. I'll put them in the icebox and bring them along to the picnic." Mirri was being unnaturally domesticated, and the entire kitchen smelled of delicious garlic and onions.

"Mirri, you didn't have to go to all this trouble," Kate said as she spotted about six saucepans bubbling away.

"Don't worry," Mirri assured her, "I didn't. Most of this was just delivered from my friend who's the chef at Saint Quentin in Knightsbridge. I'm just adding a few bits and pieces." Mirri licked a wooden spoon and closed her eyes with pleasure.

"I've just had Lady Hamilton on the phone." Leonard wandered into the kitchen with his pipe between his teeth, looking cross. "I gather there was a little contretemps with some flora this morning."

"I beg your pardon?" Mirri looked puzzled.

"So do I," Kate added.

"The flowers, Mirabelle. The helicopter? The damage to Lady Hamilton's prize tulips, not to mention the fact that her Chihuahua won't come out from under the bridge table, he's so petrified."

"Oh la." Mirri pushed her nose far into the fridge and foraged for an imaginary jar of chutney.

"Leonard, that was the most romantic thing I've ever seen. How can the old bag be so mean?" Kate said defensively.

"Because the Chelsea Flower Show is in a month's time and the tulips were due to be harvested this week."

"Perfect, then now she doesn't need to bend down and pick them up herself." Mirri emerged from the fridge empty-handed and looked sheepishly at Leonard.

"Mirabelle," Leonard reproached.

"It's not Mirri's fault if a man is so in love with her that he decides to scatter the garden with roses, is it?" Kate ventured.

"Well well well." Leonard nodded meaningfully. "I see."

"What do you see?" both Mirri and Kate asked in perfect unison.

"I see that I am probably going to have to move out of my own house because the idea of having two women on the same side against me is frankly unspeakable. And I'm sorry that I ever dreamed you two would become friends. Good Lord, I should go and pack my bags for Morocco at once." Leonard drew laconically on his pipe and shook his head.

Kate and Mirri began to laugh.

"Oh, Leonard, please stay. If you don't who shall we have to laugh at?" Mirri kissed the old man's cheek and Kate smiled.

"We'll apologize to Lady Hamilton and send her around some fudge or whatever one does when one's offended the aristocracy," Kate promised.

"I should think it'll take a darned sight more than fudge to fix her," Leonard remarked.

"Fine, then we send around Jonah Sinclair," Mirri decreed. "He will remove the tulip from her ass and she'll forget all about this flower show."

"Oh, that should definitely do the trick," Kate remarked. "Mirri, are you sure that I can't help?"

"Not a thing to be done. But you might take Leonard outside to get him out from under my feet."

"No problem. Leonard, bring your newspapers and we'll go outside," Kate said bossily.

"Oh, God, this is like living in a nursing home," Leonard groaned as he picked up a pile of newspapers and removed himself to the patio.

"Well, what a bloody mess Tony has made of my garden," Leonard continued as he and Kate settled themselves in the shade.

"Have you met him?" Kate asked.

"Handsome brute." Leonard said, "But frankly a little vulgar. I mean, honestly, look at that." And Kate did. The garden still looked like the floor of Scheherezade's tent—ready for a thousand and one Arabian nights.

"You have no soul, Leonard," Kate said, and picked up the *Evening Standard* magazine to flick through. She looked grimly at an advertisement for Tiffany engagement rings, which were about as far-out a thought as Kate moving to the moon right now. But hey, even though she was still a bit shaken by what she'd said to Jake, she really felt that there was no going back. There was a whole future waiting for her out there. Everyone met someone eventually—that was the beauty of love. Even the strangest people fell in love. People who collect clothes pegs and breed dogs met their perfect match. Hard-boiled career women who didn't have time for breakfast and went to the gym at five A.M. managed to find husbands. *That's the law of the jungle,* Kate reassured herself. Then she stopped thinking suddenly and squinted hard at the page before her, where a face had caught her eye. Actually it wasn't a face, it was a name: Louis Alcott.

Louis? she wondered. *My Louis?* It couldn't be. There was a photograph of this Louis and it wasn't her Louis. This Louis had a face that she would have bowed down before and worshipped. Really, he looked like he ought to be commanding armies in the ancient world. His nose slightly Roman and noble; *aquiline* was the word, she thought. And his eyes were black. Even though the picture was in black and white she could tell this. There was no distinction between pupil and iris. All black, as if you looked in them and would be turned to stone or vapor. And his skin was like marble and his lips wide and yet not generous. Quite hardened in fact. Good God, Louis, razing cities to the ground, in a laurel crown, his profile on a gold coin, would take no prisoners. Kate moved her face closer to the picture but then pulled away. She checked the photo credit:

LOUIS ATWOOD, CONCEPTUAL ARTIST.
BY PHILIP BERRYMAN

Was this really Louis? Kate felt a sort of shiver down her spine. In the photo Louis was standing against a wall. More stone. His legs were long in black jeans, and his shoulders surprisingly broad under his T-shirt. The way he loped around in real life, Kate assumed he'd be quite scrawny under his layers. But he didn't look that way in this picture. Kate looked at the rest of the article on Britain's Most Promising. She bypassed a series of brilliant young historians and musicians—no Jake—and sat up cross-legged on her bed to contemplate the revelation. Deeply, wildly sexy, he looked. But then she knew how photos could lie. And the Louis whom she had known for almost a third of her life, the Louis who had flicked through her canvases yesterday, wasn't the same man. Which was just as well. She was intimidated enough by his clearly brilliant reputation in the art world, she didn't need to be reduced to a monosyllabic twit because she had a crush on him. And funnily enough, as she put the magazine on one side to take back to her shed later, she didn't feel half so unsettled about what had happened with Jake as she had ten minutes ago.

Chapter Eleven

"Have you really never had your portrait done since Picasso?" Kate asked Mirri as she timidly fed Bébé his prawns from her fingers.

"Not a photograph or a portrait. Barely a paparazzo picture, really." Mirri was working through some financial statements for her wildlife charities, which Kate had been impressed to learn she handled personally; not a penny that was meant for a lion went astray. "It's not that I care, simply that I don't have time for such vanities."

"Would you mind if I did some sketches of you. While you worked?" Kate asked.

"Not at all. As long as Bébé is completed before the summer you can do whatever you like," Mirri said without lifting her eyes from the morass of figures. Certainly the image of Mirri with her half-moon reading glasses on and a slight frown on her face was a world removed from the iconic woman the world had known more than twenty years ago. In this light, as she sat on the edge of her bed, wearing a gold-colored caftan with one foot perched beneath her, she was a different woman entirely from the parted-lipped, heavy-lidded creature that she had been in her goddess years. Gone was the lush cleavage, momentarily at least, and in its place was a serious-hearted campaigner for animal welfare.

"How much money does the trust make in a year, say?" Kate asked as she won Bébé's momentary acceptance with a final, juicy prawn and then tentatively allowed him to lick her fingers clean with his pink sandpaper tongue.

"Last year it was seventeen million worldwide." Mirri scratched some sums into the margin of her sheet, and Kate couldn't resist making a lightning-swift impression of her engrossed face on her notebook.

"That's a huge amount," Kate replied as she captured a wayward lock escaping from the hastily bunched ponytail, which Mirri had secured with a chewed ballpoint pen.

"We need more. The animals are dying. The poachers are still out there. I buy more land, they find new ways to invade it. Bigger guns."

"So it's basically a wildlife reserve." Kate hadn't really understood the magnitude of Mirri's commitment to her cause before now. She had just assumed that she was some eccentric old star who preferred cats to people and slept with the odd, glamorous big kitten on her bed. It was part of the general look, she'd assumed. Merely an inevitable and slightly hackneyed fate for a onetime legend. You either got a bad face-lift and carried on acting and showing off until your eyes grew so tight with surgery that you couldn't see and everyone assumed that you had died years ago anyway, or you did cats. But this was quite serious business.

"I also have concerns in Asia and Sri Lanka, but I cannot run these, too. I have people I trust there who take care of the whole thing. Once a year we have a conference in Mozambique. I don't like to leave too often."

"But you came all this way just so that Bébé could be painted?" Kate inquired. It didn't seem to add up particularly neatly.

"Leonard is my friend. I have lots of other friends in London. You're a good painter. I decided to come," Mirri said, with a note of irritation in her voice.

But I'm not that good a painter, Kate thought. *I'm okay but that story seems a little far-fetched and implausible.* Kate also reckoned that if Mirri had simply wanted Bébé's portrait she would have flown the painter to Africa. Certainly Kate would have gone in a heartbeat. As would a hundred others. No, there was some other reason why Mirri was here, but she had no clue what that might be.

After about twenty minutes of sketching Mirri, Kate knew that she had to get on with Bébé. Besides which, Mirri had finally put down her pencil and was now on the telephone, making calls in French at breakneck speed. Shouting, laughing, with lots of *"Merde"* and *"Non?"* thrown in. So Kate worked laboriously on Bébé's eyes, which she had to admit were sheer perfection. So ferocious and yet with moments of complete sweetness.

"Oh, now, darling, don't fall asleep on me," Kate said, plucking up the courage to hand Bébé a toy mouse that she'd picked up at the pet shop last week. It had catnip in it and worked like a charm. He was roused from his sleep, and though Kate suffered a left hand covered in scratches and nips, with just enough blood drawn to be stingingly uncomfortable, she and Bébé were actually having fun together.

"So when is your next date?" Mirri hung up the phone and released her hair from the pen. She was no longer the international woman of business as she began to paint her fingernails. "I am seeing Jonah tonight and it would be such fun if you had a date, too."

"I'm not sure. I gave Jake short shrift earlier. He came around and tried to apologize but I wouldn't listen. You'd have been proud." Kate stroked Bébé's ears.

"Très bien," Mirri said, "Now what about that vicar the other night who was clearly homosexual?"

"Blew him off, too." Kate puffed out her chest. "But really, I'm pretty busy, so unless someone comes knocking I'm going to concentrate on work for a while."

"You are creative. You need passion in your life." Mirri was letting Bébé play with her hair, which she was dangling in his face, much to his delight.

"But do you know what's so strange?" Kate asked.

"Non."

"Well, I was looking at this magazine at lunch when I saw a photograph of the guy who actually did come knocking on my shed door. *You know, the one Leonard sent?*"

"With the nice black hair?"

"Louis."

"A French name."

"He's very, very odd, though," Kate said, "not my type at all. I mean he barely speaks."

"I always like a man who doesn't say too much." Mirri laughed and buried her face in Bébé's fur.

"Speak for yourself. I happen to like a conversation from time to time."

"Invite him to dinner," Mirri ordered. "I'd like to meet him."

"I can't invite him to dinner to be vetted by a woman who isn't even my mother," Kate complained. "Besides which, I told you. He's not my type."

"Oh, he's handsome, is that what you mean?" Mirri laughed sarcastically.

"Well he didn't look especially handsome in real life, if that's what you mean. He's just a bit hunched and terrified."

"But he looked good in the photograph?"

"He looked great in the photograph." Kate shrugged, as if it made no difference at all. "So you and Jonah are getting quite serious."

"Jonah is very keen to please. I like him. I am not in love with him."

"How do you stop yourself from falling in love?" Kate asked, because whatever the secret was, she'd like to buy a couple of bagfuls of it.

"Practice," Mirri said. "So you had better get going."

"The only thing I'm going to get going on is my work." And with that Kate got to her feet, shook out her legs—which were heavy with pins and needles—and patted Bébé goodbye. He didn't exactly growl at her, just stared a bit witheringly.

"Have fun with Jonah. Don't do anything I would," Kate said, and made her way back to her shed, armed with enough sketches of Bébé to keep her employed, and enough of Mirri to keep her stimulated. She'd always wanted to do what she thought of as "proper portraits"—that is, pictures of people. People with expressions, emotions, tragedies etched onto their faces. She'd mastered animals a long time ago. She'd managed to capture mischief in their faces; she was able to give them a haunting sadness, even, if they had that air about them. But it was a limited range of emotion that she was required to capture in pets. Much to her dismay, she'd never met a dog who had left his wife for a homosexual affair, or a cat who had shot her lover, or even a jealous rabbit. Though if she did, she imagined that she'd know straight away and be able to portray it perfectly in oils.

Jake sat on his sofa with the Manchester United versus Everton on the television set and his guitar on his knee. He strummed through a few chords of "You Can't Always Get What You Want" and then put his instrument to one side, deciding that as it was four o'clock in the afternoon it was perfectly fine for him to have his first drink of the day. He picked up the bottle of Glenfiddich and then put it back when he saw that there was only a fine layer of golden liquid left on the bottom. Clearly he'd polished that off last night when he'd been watching *Unforgiven*. The film had left him depressed and when it had finished at three A.M. he hadn't really wanted to even make his way upstairs to bed. Instead he'd put out his cigarette, pulled his jacket over him, and fallen asleep on the sofa. And today he had a pain in his stomach and one in his neck and he hadn't been able to shake off the stupid funk that Clint Eastwood had left him in.

"Bollocks," he moaned, as he realized that he'd have to go out and buy some more fags and another bottle of Scotch if he was going to make it through the evening.

"Hey man, we're going to see a band in Kilburn. Coming?" a friend had called up and asked him half an hour ago.

"Thanks, buddy, but I'm feeling lousy. Maybe I'll come up later, but can't promise anything."

"There's a poker game at Seb's tomorrow, too," his friend had persisted.

"Yeah, yeah, let me know." Jake was similarly unenthused. Which was saying something. Whatever virus he had, whatever Clint had done to him, it was pretty tough if it meant that he'd have to miss a poker game.

———

When Kate walked in the door of her shed, she noticed that her phone was blinking. She picked it up and, with a lurch of her stomach that was more Pavlovian than real, wondered if Jake had called. Though she knew logically that he was gone from her life, the old habits died hard. There were certainly moments when she found herself wondering which pub he was at, whose party he had been to last night, and she'd long to be sitting on his knee in the Groucho Club, laughing and drinking red wine and listening to one of his ridiculous stories as he had everyone in fits of laughter. She let out a deep sigh and pressed the button for her voice mail.

"You have two new messages. First message sent at eleven twenty-three A.M." There followed a long pause. Not a murmur. Clearly it was a hang-up. Kate clicked forward to the next message, but it was the same buzzing silence. Oh, well. She checked the number but it wasn't Jake, out of his mind with love and calling just to hear her voice. It was a number she didn't recognize. A West London number by the look of it. Oh, well. She put the phone down and went to wash her hands, which were still a bit fishy and catty from her session with Bébé and the prawns. As she hunted for a hand towel in the old cupboard in the corner of the shed, there was a knock at the door.

"Hang on," Kate called out. "Just coming." As she couldn't find a towel, she flicked her hands dry and went to answer the door.

"Hi there." It was Louis, with his olive-green parka on again. This time, though, with a nod to the weather—which was so scorching that Leonard's lawn was turning yellow and mottled in places—he had it unzipped to reveal a baggy black T-shirt. His hair was all over his face.

"Louis." Kate dried her hand on her skirt and kissed him on both cheeks. He didn't look very at ease standing on her doorstep. "Come in. Come in."

"Oh, I erm . . . well I can't really stop . . . I was just passing and I thought I'd call by and bring you . . ." He struggled for a moment with his hand in his pocket and then produced a slightly balding square of white fur. Kate looked down at it, clasped between his dirty but very slim fingers. "This."

"Your nails are as filthy as mine," Kate remarked.

"Yeah, yeah they are." He turned his hand palm up and hid his grotty digits. "Occupational hazard." Still he held out a hand, proffering the square of fur to Kate, who didn't know whether to admire it, run from it, or take it from his slightly shaky grip.

"It's ummm . . . it's a piece of fur." Kate settled for the obvious.

"It's for you," he said with the simplicity of a child. Louis then flicked his hair back and for a second she caught a glimpse of his eyes, which were the same olive green as his parka, only a bit more dangerous. There was a slightly demonic look about Louis sometimes, she thought as he stood before her with this strange gift. This man was so unlike Jake, who was always at ease, was never lost for a glib aside, and sadly never once shook in her presence.

"Thanks." She took it tentatively, and he nearly dropped it as he pulled his hand away in haste. "I'll, erm . . . well . . . what exactly *is* it, Louis?"

"Oh, Christ, didn't I say?" He pulled the zip up on his coat until his chin vanished. "It's polar bear fur."

"Oh, I love it." Kate cried as she realized what the whole past two and a half minutes of foot shuffling had been about. "That's great. So when do you want to start?" she asked, because despite their conversation he still hadn't called her to confirm the commission.

"God, yeah, well, I suppose we need to discuss that," he said as if it had just occurred to him.

"Well, you could come in now if you like," she offered. Then suddenly hoped that she'd removed the magazine with Louis in it from her bedside table, where she had put it down after lunch.

"Oh, no thanks. I've got to get going."

"Well, maybe we should have a meeting sometime this week?" she said, realizing that if this painting was ever going to get done she'd have to be the proactive party in the deal.

"Yeah. Come around. I'm at Two Twenty-five Ladbroke Grove now. Just down from the canal."

"Tuesday? Wednesday? Thursday?" She guided him gently.

"Tomorrow," he said hastily. "Well, unless you can't. In which case . . . well, then we won't."

"That sounds perfect. I'll see you tomorrow. Two-ish?"

"Cool." Louis nodded and was about to turn away but hastily grabbed her shoulders and gave her a kiss on either cheek.

"And thanks for the fur," Kate added. "It'll be really useful."

She smiled and closed the shed door behind her. She loved Louis but God he could be hard work when his work was involved. Probably because he was a proper artist.

By the time Kate had finally transposed her sketches of Bébé onto canvas, by the time she'd gotten just the outline of his beautiful little head right, the sky had imperceptibly left behind the brilliant blue of the afternoon and taken on a rained-on inky hue of night. The sun had sunk behind Leonard's house several hours ago and when she looked at her watch it was ten o'clock. Kate put her pencil to one side and stretched her arms in front of her, letting out a quiet squeal and then a yawn. The room was practically dark and she'd barely noticed. That was what she called a good day's work. No matter how much she pretended that she hated what she did, a few hours at the canvas was the best way she could ever find to chase away the black dog of depression, as her father had called it. Man was made to work. As was woman. And it always left Kate feeling elated and invulnerable when she did finally get down to it. She turned on the light, poured herself a glass of orange juice from the fridge, and walked around the shed for a couple of minutes, stretching out her legs and feeling very pleased with herself.

"Yoohooo." There was a call from the garden, Mirri no doubt, Kate thought, and went to the door and poked her head out.

"Hello?" she replied to the dark garden, for she couldn't see anyone in the blackness of the trees.

"We thought you were out. Or asleep. But we saw your light just come on, so if you're not busy then come join us." As Kate's eyes adjusted to the dark she spotted the silhouettes of two people on the hammock. One of whom was obviously Mirri; the other, more than likely, Jonah.

"I'm only coming if you've got your clothes on," Kate said, laughing, as she went toward the voice.

"Hi there, gorgeous." A deep sexy voice came from the shadowy figure next to Mirri, and as Kate approached she saw that it was indeed Jonah and Mirri. Not, thankfully, naked, but Jonah had his arm slung over Mirri's shoulder and she was looking cozy and happy, tucked in close to his side.

"Hi, Jonah." Kate settled onto the grass by their feet with her orange juice. "Did you both have a fun evening?"

"We've had quite a mellow time, haven't we?" Jonah said to Mirri. "Just dinner and then back here. I nearly came to blows with some photographer outside the restaurant so we decided to retreat back here. Paparazzo-free zone."

"Good idea," Kate said.

"What have you been doing, darling?" Mirri asked as she gently stroked Jonah's knee. If Kate hadn't known better she would have thought that Mirri was smitten with her young suitor.

"Believe it or not, I've been working. I think I've got Bébé's eyes perfectly. Well, one of them at least. It makes me happy."

"Oh, and speaking of work." Mirri leaned forward excitedly toward Kate. "I saw your young man."

"That doesn't sound much like work." Jonah laughed. Then he paused. "Sweetheart, aren't you a bit cold down there. It's bloody damp on that grass."

"Oh, I'm fine," Kate scoffed. "It's summer."

"Get your arse over here," Jonah demanded, shoving over on the hammock a bit and gesturing for Kate to come and sit next to him. "And besides, I'm always happier with two birds." He grinned. "In fact, you might say that two birds in the hammock's worth one in the bed. Eh?" Then he hastily added, "Unless that bird's called Mirabelle Moncur." Kate did as Jonah asked, getting to her feet and making her way over to the hammock. For some reason she felt comfortable with Jonah. It wasn't because she was so used to hanging out with movie stars or found it easy to get on with sexy men usually, though. She put it down to the fact that Jonah was so besotted with Mirri that she didn't need to even attempt the compulsory flirt-and-rejection scenario she might have otherwise. Jonah was like insta-brother to her. And she liked that.

"That's much better." He laughed as Kate snuggled in under his other arm. "Aren't I a lucky bastard?"

"So I thought your man was divine," Mirri said as the three got comfy on the hammock.

"You don't mean Louis, do you?" asked Kate.

"Louis." Mirri said the name as though it were a poem. "So charming, and so handsome, darling. Do you think maybe he is in love with you?"

"Are you sure you don't mean Jake?" Kate was puzzled.

"Not The Slug, no. This Louis who came calling for you earlier—I was in the kitchen gutting the fish for Bébé's supper and in he came through the kitchen. Like a very young Lord Byron."

"No way." Kate could barely control her mirth.

"Why do you laugh?"

"Because we cannot be talking about the same person. I mean, granted, he looked good in the photo. But wasn't he wearing his parka this afternoon?" Kate was completely disbelieving. Then she cottoned on to the joke. "Oh hang on, I get it. You think that if you say you think he's charming and handsome, then you'll persuade me of it and I might find myself a boyfriend. But to be honest, Mirri, I'm not that desperate."

"The man was beautiful. He had a coat slung over one arm and we talked very intelligently about African art for some time."

"Sounds like a bit of a tosser to me," Jonah said, and began to play with Mirri's knee.

"What would you know?" Mirri snapped, and pulled away.

"Okay, guys, I'm going to head for my bed," Kate said, sensing a fight in the making, or, worse, a making-up session, which would be even more embarrassing to witness. "I have a ton of work to do tomorrow. I'll come around at ten. Is that okay, Mirri?" Kate asked as she kissed Jonah, and then Mirri, good night on the cheek.

"Make it eleven, would you?" Jonah asked, and winked at her. "Good night, sweetheart, you smell all sexily of turpentine."

"Make it ten," Mirri said pointedly. "We're meeting Tony for a picnic at lunchtime. I also happen to think that if you're going to be so choosy with men, then you'll never find the right lover."

"Good night." Kate felt secure enough in Mirri's affections now to take a bit of her evil temper from time to time. "See you soon, Jonah."

And as Kate wandered back to her shed she could hear only the cooing, placating tones of Jonah and the sharp hiss of Mirri's crossness. If Jonah didn't watch it, he'd end up having to crawl home to his wife tonight, Kate thought. And it was only when she was back in her shed and spotted the ripped-out pages of Louis that she remembered what Mirri had said about him. But Kate knew what she was playing at. Louis was perfectly fine, there was no denying that. But no woman in her right mind would even try to get beyond his crippling shyness. It'd take an eternity just to ascertain if he was even remotely interested in you. And that was before you thought about scaring him away with a little light flirting. The whole thing was just too enormous a project. Even for an almost desperate girl like Kate. She decided to wait until she'd been on at least one more date, before she declared herself officially that close to the bottom of the barrel.

Chapter Twelve

"I'm not going to be a gooseberry, am I?" Kate was lying on her stomach with her head buried in her hands so that the glaring sun didn't cause a constellation of freckles to erupt across her face. She and Mirri had found a quiet but sun-drenched glade in Regents Park and laid out their rug and picnic hamper in anticipation of Tony's arrival.

"Of course you're not gooseberry. I haven't had sex with Tony for hundreds of years. He's quite different now. Not at all irresponsible or sexy anymore."

"Okay, but you know that I'll happily make myself scarce if you want me to, don't you?"

"Well, so will Tony and I if you want us to." Mirri grinned slyly.

"You and Tony? Why would you?" Kate lifted her face from her hands and turned to Mirri, who was obscured by an enormous straw sun hat. She had the straps on her dress pulled down for a more even tan.

"Well, Tony said he might bring Felix with him." As Mirri spoke, Kate had a dawning sense of something being up.

"I want Felix to be Tony's dog but I have a nasty feeling that he isn't going to be." Kate instinctively began to smooth down her hair and sat up straight instead of slouching on the rug as if she were watching Friday-night TV alone with her sweats on. If they were expecting company, she had to be ready.

"You're right, he's not a dog. He's Tony's son." Mirri refused to meet Kate's nagging gaze.

"You're setting me up and you didn't warn me?" Kate said in slightly cross but hushed tones in case Tony and Son appeared from behind a hedge.

"I'm introducing you to a handsome young man. Don't be so ungrateful." Mirri waved her hand dismissively but not without a trace of guilt.

"I'd have put on some makeup at least if I'd known."

"And you would have been stiff and formal and not pretty and freckly and relaxed as you really are."

"I haven't got freckles." Kate was mortified.

"Have a drink and stop fussing." Mirri handed Kate a glass of rosé and lay back on the grass. Kate scrubbed a finger beneath her eyes to make sure that she didn't have ancient smudges of mascara lurking in the cracks.

"What does he look like?" Kate attempted to be nonchalant.

"I don't know. He was very cute when he was six. I'm his god-mother, apparently. Though I think he's become a financier so I'm not sure how good I can have been at spiritual guidance."

"Shit, Mirri. Does he know that he's supposed to fancy me? What if he's not remotely interested? Oh, God, you're turning out to be the pushy mother I never had."

"I prefer to think of myself more as a sister." Mirri scowled and pulled her hat back over her face. Clearly Kate had hit a nerve and would have to suffer for it now.

Fortunately before Mirri's sulk could set in irreversibly the sound of voices emerged from the bushes. A man in a khaki linen suit with snow-white hair and the palest blue eyes Kate had ever seen stepped forward. "Mirri, sweetheart, is that you under there?"

"Tony." Mirri pulled off her hat and sat up. Without bothering to reinstate the straps on her dress she leapt to her feet and squeezed the life out of the man.

"Oh, look how handsome you are. I have not seen you for years and you are more, more beautiful than ever. And thank you so much for the flowers." Mirri kissed him all over his face in a puppyish manner and he grinned wildly. "And is this Felix, my longlost godson?" Everyone turned to check out Felix at the same moment and Kate knew that the second Mirri saw how remarkably good looking he was, she regretted being quite so generous in her introductions. She wouldn't have minded an ungodly moment alone with her godson, that was for sure.

"I am," he said in a halting French accent as both Kate and Mirri stared with practically open mouths at the suntanned young man with cropped black hair and his father's slightly unnerving blue eyes.

"Très bien," Mirri said with a slow inhale as she leaned forward and hugged him. "And this"—she turned and gestured toward Kate—"is my good friend Kate."

Kate climbed to her feet, straightened her skirt, and held out her hand with a lead-weight feeling in her heart. She may as well go home now and spare everyone the politeness and effort that would be involved in trying to get Kate and Felix together. Forget that she wasn't his type; he wasn't her type, either. Impossibly handsome, well educated, charming Frenchmen just weren't her cup of tea. It was simply too taxing to even contemplate the paranoia and insecurities and wardrobe catastrophes and books she hadn't read that would result from even a pint of beer in the pub with such a man.

"Hi there." She smiled shyly, first at Tony, averting her eyes from Felix as if he were the sun.

"Hi there, sweetheart." Tony shook her hand.

Before she could compose herself Felix said, "Pleased to meet you." And held out his hand.

"Hello," Kate replied, barely looking at him, until she caught sight of Mirri over his shoulder.

Mirri's look was like a mirror telling her how lame and pathetic and self-pitying she was being. Mirri's look despaired at how impossible it was for Kate to understand that the guy in front of her was just that—a guy. *Every woman,* Mirabelle Moncur was saying, *has something that a man wants.* Aside from the obvious, too. And though he may not necessarily want it for all time, he will certainly want it for the duration of an encounter, which is just fine. Every woman can have her scene in the movie. But in order to get a man to understand what he wants from her, a woman first has to know what it is she has to offer. Then, as she read this in Mirri's look, in that brief moment, Kate was transformed. She forgot that she had a spot on her cheek and that her hair wasn't washed and that there were a million things she'd change or obsess over given a chance, and instead she saw herself from another point of view. She knew that the sun would be shining in her eyes and making them the color of liquid amber; she knew that her freckles would make her nose look, if not perfect, then at least adorable; she imagined her creased skirt looking careless, as if she had better things to do than stay home doing the ironing. And as she glanced down and caught sight of her muddy knees from where she'd knelt in the grass earlier she hoped that instead of looking as though she'd been dragged through a plowed field behind a tractor, it might seem as though she'd been having a bit of fun in the plowed field.

She looked at Mirri for confirmation—yes, there she stood, the goddess—a model of imperfection, her hair was a veritable bird's nest, her long peasant skirt was ripped on the hem, and one of her earrings missing. In short, she looked as though she'd just spent a very happy hour or six with Jonah Sinclair on the hammock. And she was fantastically sexy. Kate blinked and looked up at Felix.

"Nice to meet you." She smiled. And it wasn't the most scintillating line of all time, but Felix didn't notice. He was too busy checking her out in that slightly hungry way that Frenchmen have.

"Right, well, who wants a drink?" Mirri clapped her hands together before anyone could linger and before Kate could collapse in an exhausted heap from the exertion of her epiphany. Because as selfish and wrapped up in herself as Mirri Moncur appeared to the world, she had observed precisely what had just happened to her protégée. And she was filled with pride, even if she was a bit peevish about the fact that Felix was so delicious looking that she wouldn't have minded him for herself. She also wondered whether she hadn't presented Kate with a challenge more on a par with an Everest than a Himalayan foothill, but still, she was sure that her young charge was up to the job.

"Oh, not for me, thanks, doll," Tony demurred. "I'm pure."

"Of course you are, that's why I look like an old handbag and you don't." Mirri laughed, then translated for Kate from Tony's sixties-speak: "He doesn't drink or smoke or take drugs or any of the things I love."

"I see," Kate said. "Well, I'll have some more rosé."

"*C'est parfait,*" Felix said. Mirri poured the drinks as everyone settled down onto the picnic rug. Kate tried not to be self-conscious and stopped herself from shuffling in the opposite direction when Felix stretched out his legs beside her. Anyway, with Mirri and Tony in one another's orbit for the first time in years it soon became apparent that Felix and Kate weren't going to have the monopoly on flirting.

"Oh, how can you say I didn't do any of the things you like. I did a few things that you loved if you remember." Tony looked at Mirri as if he wanted to eat her up while she handed him a glass of sparkling water.

"Papa, please, this is too much to deal with," Felix said with a grin at his flirtatious father. But it was clear that Tony was another satisfied customer of the Mirri Moncur Academy of Mind-Blowing Sex. There was going to be nothing else for it but to ask Mirri for tips, Kate decided. *I mean, why look a gift horse in the mouth?*

"So, Kate, tell me, what about you?" Felix asked in his absurdly cute broken English as Mirri and Tony drifted off on a tangent about the time they had accidentally boarded a brothel ship at the Cannes Film Festival.

"What *about* me?" Kate asked, ripping the crust off her sandwich in the hope that it might unlock some fascinating secret about herself, which she could then share with Felix. "Well, I met Mirri when she commissioned me to paint Bébé, her lion cub. I live at the bottom of the garden of the house where she's staying and . . . well, that's me," she finished hastily. Kate hated rambling on aimlessly about herself. She was okay with a specific topic but that was just a bad question, she told herself.

"That is you? All of you?" Felix asked with a grin. Kate had never been informed that French men had senses of humor. It wasn't in any of the guidebooks, that was for sure. But it made her a bit more relaxed than she would have been if he'd wanted to discuss Baudelaire.

"Yes, I don't think there's anything more to me," Kate said with a straight face.

"I think you are lying." Felix looked at her defiantly. "I think there is an awful lot to you, Kate." Ah, this was more like it. The textbook Frenchman with the intense gaze and cheeseball lines. Kate couldn't help but smile.

"If you mean my enormous bottom, then fine. But I'm never going to agree with you," Kate said. "I never admit my faults to strangers." With which she took another bite of her sandwich. She couldn't bear to be stuck in this ridiculous conversation where she was supposed to be getting seduced. It just wasn't her style. She saw him draw breath, about to deliver another line, and suddenly felt compelled to stop him. "And if you're about to tell me that I'm perfect and that I have no faults, then . . . well, then I'll have to put my sandwich crusts up your nose."

Felix's brown eyes blinked uncomprehendingly, and at the same moment Mirri and Tony's conversation came to an abrupt halt. Everyone was looking at Kate, and her ridiculous comment hung in the air. Mirri looked puzzled by her protégée, as did Felix.

She relented. "I'm sorry, Felix. I was just joking, and, really, I'm sure you weren't going to tell me I was perfect. In fact, I'm positive of it. And I wasn't really going to put anything up your nose." Kate stumbled at their bewildered expressions, until there was a huge snort.

"Bloody hell, you two, anyone would think someone had died." Tony snorted again. It was obviously his laugh. "Quite right, too, love. The boy's just used to chatting up dolly birds who fall for that crap. This one's not a supermodel, Felix. She's a normal bird who likes a laugh." Tony patted Kate on the back. Oh, how right he was. She wasn't a supermodel. She was Kate and the French didn't find her funny.

"Ah, I see. This is funny?" Mirri asked.

"I suppose you're right," Felix said, and pondered the so-called joke that Kate now wished she'd never made as if it were a medieval text. Or a supermodel's vital statistics. Then he began to giggle in a snorty way, like his father. Which made him much more charming than his perfect looks.

"Kate, you are right. I was going to be . . . how you say? Smooth?"

"Smooth is great. But the thing is, I don't really believe in it." Kate tried to look kind and not like a lunatic. "Though I think I would if I were a supermodel." She shrugged.

"Felix, you like the models?" Mirri asked.

"Sometimes. But I like the normal women, too." He looked at Kate with admiration.

"He's a bit of a playboy," Tony said. "Gets it from his mother. She knows all these princes and geezers with yachts and I don't mind just as long as they've got somewhere on board I can do me yoga."

"I like to race speedboats and I like to ski and I am often in beautiful places. But I am not a playboy," Felix informed his father.

"In my day that's exactly what you'd have been." Tony took a bite of a sandwich. "This bread organic, Mirri, love?"

"It's bread," Mirri said. "And I think that we will go for a walk. I have the pain in my legs."

" 'Cause you don't do any exercise, isn't it?" Tony told her.

"I don't really care why it is. I just want to see the ducks," Mirri said sternly. Tony cottoned on fairly quickly that they were supposed to leave Felix and Kate alone. "Yeah, right. The ducks. You're not going to shoot them, though, are you? Because I know you like duck à l'orange, but those birds there aren't ducks. They're swans. And they belong to the queen." He stood up and pulled Mirri to her feet.

"Ah, yes, I remember, all swans belong to the queen in this country. How wonderful. Perhaps I made the wrong decision when I turned down Charles. I would have liked to own all the swans in England."

"Well, I came along didn't I? Swept you off your feet?" Tony said. Mirri took his arm. "We'll be back in a bit, kids. Just got a bit of catching up to do."

"See you soon," Kate said. Suddenly a bit alarmed at the idea of being alone with Felix. She didn't really have anything to say to him, and it was clear that their lifestyles differed wildly—yacht boy meets shed girl. All they had in common was wood.

"So, Felix, you must be very fit."

"Fit?"

"Skiing."

"Ah, well, I only ski a little during the season," Felix said. "Do you ski?"

"I did once on a school trip but I couldn't stay up." There was an awkward pause.

Felix looked around the park as if fascinated. "The swans are beautiful. No?" he asked as he rested back on his elbows.

"They are. I used to have one in my bedroom," Kate informed him.

"Your mother is the queen?" He smiled warmly. Clearly he wasn't holding the lack of scintillating conversation against her.

"My father was a taxidermist, actually. I still have a zebra by my bed."

"It's not creepy?" he asked.

"I'm pretty used to it. Men sometimes get a bit freaked out by it, though," Kate said, aware that it made her sound like a multi-lovered woman. But what the hell. *Nothing wrong with a little embellishment,* Mirri would have said.

"These English men are pussies," Felix said. "A Frenchman would never be afraid."

"So that's where I've been going wrong all these years," Kate said. "Wrong nationality."

"Most definitely." He looked at her for a long second before closing his eyes and letting the sun fall full on his face. Kate was relieved that he'd relaxed. Following his example, she lay back, sighed, and resisted saying anything about the weather. Sometimes it was better to say nothing. But just a moment after Kate had settled back, letting the long blades of grass tickle her ear, she felt a similar sensation on her leg—an ant, possibly. She twitched her leg but it didn't go away. It was only when she moved her hand down to brush the insect off that she suspected that it wasn't an ant at all. It was larger than that. And furrier.

"Shit!" Kate leapt up and screamed as she felt a stabbing sensation above her knee. "Ow ow." She pulled up her skirt to see what had happened.

"Kate, what is it, what's the matter?" Felix pulled off his sunglasses and looked at her leg.

"I think I've been stung," she said as she noticed a half-crushed bee staggering on the ground beside her. "It hurt."

"They can be nasty," Felix said seriously. "Are you allergic?"

"I'm not sure," Kate said, quite honestly. She'd never been stung before. And it bloody throbbed. She breathed—to see whether she still could. "Am I swelling up?" she asked him.

"Let me see." Felix leaned into her and looked closely at her leg. It was just above her knee, practically on the inside of her thigh, she noted with a wince that was part pain and part embarrassment. He touched what was now a swollen red lump on her skin.

"I can see the sting." He looked at her face, which paled. "Do you have a credit card?"

"It got swallowed by the machine the other day," Kate said, slightly bemused. "Why? Are you going to call an air ambulance?"

"We have to take the top off the stinger or it'll pump in more venom."

"Oh." Kate was impressed by his ability to survive in the wild. She was even more impressed when he produced a black credit card from his jacket pocket and lanced it across the red lump on her leg.

"Ouch," she yelled. "Fuck."

"I'm sorry, but it needed to be done. It should be fine now." And with that he reached into the picnic hamper.

"Thanks," Kate said with relief as she pulled her skirt back down over her knee. "That's much better."

"Not yet." Felix pulled a handful of ice out of the hamper and with the other hand lifted Kate's skirt back above her knee. In fact, way back above her knee. Practically to her knicker line, she noticed. He saw her surprised look. "I don't want to make your skirt wet," he said.

"Right," Kate said quietly, as his brown fingers clutched the ice and placed it gently on her sting.

"Ah, it's cold," she said, trying not to sound hysterical.

"It will be." Felix looked at her, and at first she assumed that he was just checking that her glands weren't swelling up and slowly murdering her, but he wasn't. He was looking at her face. And he wasn't turning away.

"Oh, that's much better," Kate said briskly, avoiding his gaze and looking at his hand on her thigh. "Thanks, I'm sure it'll be fine now."

"I think it needs more time," Felix told her. And he carried on looking at her. Then he pulled the icy hand away and examined the place where the sting had been, which was now just a big goose-bumped red patch. "Yes, just a bit more."

"Okay," Kate agreed. Hoping that he wouldn't notice how much her breathing had deepened, and how, despite trying to remain practical, this was just about the sexiest thing that had happened to her in decades. Having a proper man lift her skirt and run ice into her thigh. Even in the name of first aid.

"You have very pretty legs" was the next thing he said.

"I ride a bike. Everywhere," Kate told him, trying to ignore the way he was looking at both her legs, not just the stung patch anymore.

"I like them."

"Right." Kate swallowed hard and tried to focus on the sting. But the pain had gone. All she could feel now was Felix's hand on her thigh. Then he caught the look on her face, which was flushed pink, and that was all the encouragement he needed to swing into seduction mode.

"I think that's enough ice," he said. Before Kate could register disappointment he had bent his head into her lap and kissed the sting. "But it's never better without a kiss."

"Oh," Kate said, as Felix repeated the kiss. This time without removing his lips from her skin. "Well it certainly feels much better now," she added cheerfully. She didn't want him to think that she was enjoying herself too much—in case what he was doing was simply saving her life, rather than giving her a thrill.

"Good," he said softly as he changed his position and knelt between her legs, from where he began to slowly kiss his way up her thigh, dotting her leg with small, lingering kisses. Oh, so he wasn't saving her life anymore. At least not in the technical sense. "Do you like this?" he asked.

"Sure," Kate said. She wished that she could lose herself in the moment but it was difficult. She didn't know the guy, she was in the open air in Regents Park, his father would be coming back any second, and the scene, though sexy, felt slightly contrived. Which, when you put it like that, actually sounded like the hottest way to spend an afternoon that Kate could ever have dreamed up. She'd often had fantasies about sex outdoors, but Jake had always scoffed. But then Jake didn't have the body that Felix had, she noted, as he removed his shirt and lifted her skirt up over her knickers, now. She was torn, at that moment, between trying to remember which underwear she'd put on this morning and wondering what Mirri would have done in her position.

Forget about your underwear and enjoy the fact that there's a handsome man kissing the inside of your thigh in the afternoon sunshine.

That was exactly what Mirri would have done. So seconds later Kate moved her legs just a fraction farther apart and began to smile as Felix pulled back her cotton knickers and began to do such incredible things to her that she closed her eyes, lay back, and stopped thinking anything at all.

Until what felt like years later, when she felt Felix's breath by her lips.

"Can I kiss you?" he asked.

"I think you already did." Kate moved her lips toward his. Her first truly French kiss. Okay, she was patriotic and stuff but she had to concede that it beat every other kiss she'd ever had, hands down. She tried to analyze why—his lips were soft and beautiful, his skin smelled of warm sun and sandalwood, his hair felt so incredibly thick and short between her fingers, and whatever he was doing to her breasts, she didn't ever want him to stop.

"I love the feel of your skin," Felix said as he stroked a finger over her cheek. "And your eyes, did you know that they are like amber?"

"Thank you," she said and pulled his head gently back toward hers so that she could have another one of those things that she had mistakenly spent her life, until now, referring to as kisses. When really what she'd been getting until about ten minutes ago were cheap imitations of the real thing. She wanted to tell him that she loved him. But really she just loved what he was doing to her.

"Ah, I'm glad that you have found something in common." With an overwhelming sense of déjà vu, Kate heard Mirri's voice hovering above her.

"Mirri." Kate pulled her skirt back around her knees and tried to sit up, but Felix's arm was slung around her shoulder and though he'd stopped kissing her, he was playing with her hair, twisting it around his finger, hugging her close.

"Did you have a nice walk, Mirabelle?" he asked. He was stretched out beside Kate, his voice low and relaxed in her ear. He wasn't flapping about having been discovered shirtless, kissing a strange girl in the park.

Kate sadly wasn't that cool. "I got stung." She sounded shrill. "Felix was helping me. He put some ice on it. And used a credit card. Did you know that you should use credit cards? I always thought it was tweezers but apparently that just sends the venom deeper."

"We saw the swans." Mirri judiciously avoided Kate's near hysteria. Well, somebody had to.

"Mirri, love. Can I have some of that avocado salad you were telling me about?" Tony said as he sat down. "I still can't believe you can cook."

"Will you come home with me?" Felix whispered in Kate's ear as Mirri searched for the salad and Tony poured himself another glass of water.

"What? Now?" Kate asked. And she did for one fleeting second wonder whether perhaps Felix was being paid by Mirri to bury his head between Kate's thighs and take her home.

"Yes." He smiled and sat up. "We can call by your house and get your passport?"

"My passport?"

"If we leave soon we will be there for cocktails," he said.

"Be where?" Kate noticed that Mirri was looking on with a huge smirk on her face. If she could have gotten away with it she would also have clapped and waved pom-poms. But that might have blown Kate's cover.

"Capri," he said. "Don't worry about a bikini, you can buy one tomorrow."

"*Capri* Capri?" Kate asked. "I mean it sounds great but it's not London, is it?"

"No, it's an island near Italy." Felix laughed and then kissed her on the lips. "Did you have something else planned?" Kate shook her head. She decided not to tell him that she'd been planning on spending the evening cleaning jam jars.

Chapter Thirteen

"So you're what they call a playboy?" Kate warbled happily as she dangled her feet in the milky blue, moonlit water of the swimming pool and took another sip of the most delicious white wine she'd ever tasted.

"I suppose so," Felix said as he swam a few slow strokes toward her and stopped at her feet. They had arrived on the island three hours ago in Tony's helicopter, just in time to see the sun set over the rocks where the Sirens of myth were supposed to sit and lure sailors to their death with their irresistible song. Kate had wondered how many times Felix had told this story to different women—but hadn't been even faintly bothered by her conclusion that it must be in the hundreds. The sky above Capri was pale—the moon was almost full—and from the clifftop where Felix's house was perched, you could see for miles out to sea, until the point where the sea became as dark as the sky and the horizon vanished. Then they'd eaten dinner on his deck—just a bowl of fresh pasta and tomato sauce, because the cook, not expecting Felix back, had taken off to Naples for the afternoon. But it was perfect nonetheless. And after they'd talked a bit, about Mirri and Felix's work in Paris and Kate's painting—nothing that was going to set the world on fire but pleasant enough—Felix had put Kate on the back of his moped and sped down through the unlit, narrow streets and alleyways to the local square where the gelateria was just closing. They hopped off onto the dusty ground and Kate insisted on buying him a pistachio ice cream until she realized that she didn't have a euro to her name, only a five-pound note in her purse. Felix had laughed, bought her the ice cream, and they'd sat for a while on the steps of the local church, where they watched the dogs scrabbling for scraps in the gutter and listened to a young couple arguing in a house across the square. They'd sat there and eaten their ice creams until their hands were sticky and she was longing to get back to the house where she hoped he'd kiss her again. Because despite their racy start in Regents Park earlier that afternoon, Felix hadn't so much as held Kate's hand since then.

But now, back at his villa, as he swam toward her, Kate knew that the hiatus was thankfully over. She was still wearing the same dress she'd had on in the park, her hair hanging grubbily over her shoulders now. She'd only had time to run into the shed and collect her passport as they were leaving, and had no time to preen herself for one of the most unimaginably romantic things that was ever likely to happen to her. They had dashed to Battersea heliport and then hopped to Capri so quickly she had nothing but her purse and the clothes she was standing in. But Felix didn't seem to notice her disarray, because it was obvious that the sparkle in her eyes was so dazzling. Hell, it had to be blinding if Felix the Frenchman was tugging gently at her feet the way he was.

"I like beautiful women." He shrugged. Here, in his own home, Felix was entirely different from the quiet, reserved way he'd been in the park. He was confident, at ease, and couldn't seem to take his eyes off Kate.

"I like your pool," she told him. She was learning quickly that it didn't really matter what you said in a situation like this. You could be as moronic as you liked and talk the most uninteresting nonsense—just as long as the attraction was there. Which was a huge relief to her. She'd always thought that she needed to be unendingly fascinating for a man to fancy her. But she was discovering that some things were much more important—like going with the moment.

"Have you ever made love underwater?" he asked, not taking his eyes off her. And though part of Kate wanted to roll her eyes to heaven and write Felix off as a cliché with a suntan, she also wanted to do just that—make love underwater.

"No. I haven't," she told him as he took hold of her hands and helped her down into the water, fully clothed.

"Perfect," he said as she stood on the bottom of the pool on tiptoes and put her hands on his tight, muscular waist under the water. "I'll show you how to."

"Perfect," Kate echoed, as she tried to suppress the triumphant voice in her head that wanted to call up Jake and tell him how great sex in a swimming pool in Capri with an international playboy with a helicopter and a suntan was. She'd left her phone behind, however, and, though she didn't ever believe it would be so easy, when Felix took off her T-shirt under the water, when it billowed out and drifted away, and when Felix touched her nipples with his fingertips and edged his knee between her legs as he kissed her— she left Jake behind, too. And there was no way he was ever going to be able to catch up again, she realized, not knowing whether it was her heart that was sinking, or her that was floating.

———

"So did you have fun?" Mirri asked when Kate wandered into the kitchen two days later wearing a man's pale blue Turnbull & Asser shirt with the sleeves rolled up, and her denim skirt, which Felix had laid out to dry all day yesterday on a rock in the sun. A new gingham bikini they'd bought in a hotel foyer yesterday morning was scrunched up in her handbag.

"I'm shattered," Kate said as she collapsed into a chair and smiled.

"I'm so happy." Mirri put her hair into a ponytail and leaned toward Kate conspiratorially. "Was he fabulous?"

"Yes, he was fabulous." Kate stretched her legs out and hooked one ankle over the other. "We made love underwater, which I've always wanted to do. We made love on a coastal path overlooking the sea and nearly got caught by a couple walking their dog. He taught me how to ride a moped and when I woke up this morning he told me that I was beautiful."

"Wonderful." Mirri grinned. Then she looked concerned for a second as she scrutinized Kate's face. "You're not in love, are you?"

"God no. Of course I'm not." Kate emerged from her reverie. "That's the best thing about it. For the first time ever, I slept with a man and felt nothing but warmth and . . . well, pleasure."

"It's very liberating." Mirri nodded.

"And it's really thanks to you," Kate said.

"Oh, nothing to do with me. He found you very attractive. I could see that. But then, who wouldn't? You have removed the stick from your ass." She winked.

"Really? Was I that bad before?"

"You weren't bad at all. You were good. Unbearably, boringly good. You were good to that Slug and you were pleased with yourself for being good. Now you're just . . . well, you're just being."

"That's very zen."

"It's very selfish. But it's also very honest. If you can't please yourself you'll just get angry and the stick will remain in your ass for ever and you'll never be really happy." Mirri was opening her usual reams of post. She seemed to give meaning to the Royal Mail.

"Mirri, how do you know all this stuff?" Kate asked as she sniffed the cuff of Felix's shirt and smelled sandalwood.

"I had to learn it or I'd have gone mad. I was brought up at a time when they thought you were possessed by the devil if you didn't want to please a man. I was lucky. I married a man who let me have a career and so I escaped my parents. But they still thought I was a black-hearted Jezebel. When I left my husband, when I had affairs, when I behaved like a man by sleeping with men I didn't care about I was spat at in the street by strangers. Newspapers wrote about how I must be a witch. I had to fight to have my freedom.

Because I was never going to just wash some man's socks. I liked sex. I liked adventure."

"You were a pioneer, weren't you?" Kate said, understanding for the first time the significance of Mirri on the progress of women. And not just the sexual revolution, either.

"Not because I was great. Just because I wanted to have my own way. But even though I was doing what I wanted to do, I sometimes wished I were a better person. That's why I ended up with the animals. Because I can love them in a way I could never love men."

"Why couldn't you love men?" Kate asked. Mirri had stopped opening her post. Instead she was rubbing the edges of an envelope with her fingernails.

"Because they just wanted me as a trophy in those days. They wanted to be the one who tamed me. It was too boring to give them what they wanted."

"So you've never been in love?" Kate asked, bewildered by the fact that this incredible woman could have done just about everything in her life but be in love.

"Never," she said, and looked down at the envelope.

"That's awful," Kate said, then became aware of how judgmental she sounded. "Well, I suppose you don't miss what you never had?"

"You know, I'm not sure," Mirri suddenly said, in a voice that had become very distant. Kate remained quiet. "I think that maybe once I did have it."

"Love?" Kate asked gently.

"I met a man. In England actually. But it was just a weekend. It couldn't have been love because love can't happen in two days. Right? That would be ludicrous." Mirri seemed suddenly to be completely uncertain. She looked at Kate fleetingly, then quickly back down at the envelope. As if she didn't want to know the answer.

"That depends whether you believe in love at first sight or not," Kate replied.

"Well, I'm not sure if I believe in love at all. So I suppose I'll never know," Mirri said. "And anyway it doesn't matter one bit. It was thirty years ago and I've lived without knowing all this time. So it can't have been love."

Kate was at a loss as to what to say. Mirri seemed frailer than she'd ever seen her. She looked entirely lost. "Who was it?" she asked. But the very moment she spoke the kitchen door opened and Leonard walked in, carrying an Indonesian statue in front of him. He couldn't see the anguish on Mirri's face around the bulky statue, so he bulldozed in regardless. "Goodness me, the wanderer returns," he said cheerfully, and deposited the statue on the counter with a groan. "How was Capri? Did you see the Tiberian villas?"

"Leonard. Are you mad?" Mirri asked as the color returned to her face and she flung the envelope aside. "She was making love day and night."

And then in unison both Kate and Leonard shouted, "Mirri!" in horror, because this was not the sort of information either of them wanted to share.

"Boffe, so English." Mirri giggled and once again set about tearing open the pile of fantastically heavy, watermarked envelopes, discarding most of them into the kitchen bin on top of the potato peelings and sodden tea bags.

"I didn't make it to the ruins, Leonard, no," Kate said. Then in a bid to reestablish some decorum, she added, "But I did go to a church."

"Really, which one?" Leonard asked. Mirri looked up in vague alarm.

"Oh, well, I don't remember but it was white and pretty and in a square."

"You went sightseeing?" Mirri sounded disappointed.

"Acutally we ate ice cream on the steps. But it was pretty. Really pretty. And the bell rang," Kate said defensively.

"Well, it sounds very jolly. Now I've got to get this chap into my office so I can see whether he is fifteenth century or whether I've been robbed blind. I'll see you ladies soonest."

"Good luck," Mirri chimed as the door to Leonard's office banged shut.

"Mirri . . . about what you were saying?" Kate uttered, after a moment of silence.

"I think that it's the perfect moment for you to do a little more sketching of Bébé, don't you? He will have woken from his nap and you said you want some time with him outdoors." Mirri stood up hastily and in doing so consigned Kate's question to the rubbish bin, along with the discarded envelopes and unappealing party invitations.

"Sure, I'll go and have a quick shower, then I'll get my pencils," Kate agreed, because she felt guilty, not only for haring off to Capri at the tweak of a nipple, but also for pressing Mirri on the subject of her lost love. For it was clear to Kate from Mirri's total unwillingness to continue with the conversation that she had been in love thirty years ago. What had happened since then she had no idea. But it didn't stop Kate wondering very hard indeed about the matter.

Chapter Fourteen

By Tuesday Kate had made a considerable amount of progress on her secret portrait of Mirri. She had taken her sketches to her shed and was transposing them onto canvas. When she was finished she would turn it toward the wall to dry, and on more than one occasion she'd slid it behind the wardrobe when she'd heard footsteps outside the shed, or Mirri and Jonah chatting in the garden. She didn't know exactly why she was keeping it a secret, but somewhere she felt that she was transgressing a trust by actually beginning a full-blown portrait when Mirri had only granted her permission to sketch her. She also suspected that if and when Mirri saw the very honest job that Kate was making of her, she might have heart failure. Because even though in Kate's eyes Mirri just became more and more beautiful by the day, as Kate began to realize what a remarkable person she was, Kate knew that her subject wouldn't want to be confronted with the graphic vision of lines and living that Kate saw in her face.

"You keep on drawing me with this terrible frown on my face," Mirri had complained as she continued to run the Moncur Trust from Leonard's guest bedroom. Most mornings she sat at the kidney-shaped dressing table, her pencils and calculator mingling with the antique silver hairbrushes and strings of pearls in porcelain bowls, and scribbled away.

"I thought you said you weren't vain," Kate retorted as she positioned her chair by the wall where she could catch Mirri in profile.

"But neither am I stupid." Mirri rolled her eyes and put down her pen. "I have no desire to look like a hag. Are you finished with Bébé?"

"Yup, I'm finished for today. He's getting agitated with being stared at so much. He's got sitter's fatigue."

"Very well then." Mirri sat up straight and pretended to be beaten into submission. "I will sit for you for a short time. Okay?"

"Oh, Mirri, thank you, thank you." Kate leapt up and began arranging the eiderdown on the bed so that she'd get Mirri at just the right angle. "Now, could you just sit here? And look as natural as possible. What I was thinking was that I'd keep a couple of the trademark sex symbol characteristics, like the hair and the dark, heavy eyes, but that in between I'd allow the years to show, the living, the caring . . ."

"The lines?" Mirri scowled.

"They're just laugh lines." Kate perched on her chair close to the end of the bed and waited for Mirri to feel at ease.

"My lines are very deep. Nothing's *that* funny," Mirri said with a deadpan look at Kate.

"Maybe you want to think about Africa or something," Kate said helpfully. "You know, something that means a lot to you. Something you love." What Kate really wanted was for the expression that had registered on Mirri's face that day when she was talking about the time she'd been in love, to surface again.

"I try not to think too hard, I don't believe that it's very good for you," Mirri said, and looked out the bedroom window, onto the garden, as Kate made mark after mark on the paper, furiously trying to convey the essence of Mirri on her page.

For twenty minutes or so Kate was lost in the picture. She was lost in Mirri's face. Then her neck began to ache so she rested her pencil for a moment and pushed her chin into her chest, stretching out her shoulders. But when she looked up again she caught the look. The one that wasn't about Africa or Bébé or even Mirri being mournful about lost youth and fading beauty. It was a much more distant look than that, and Kate knew what she was thinking about. For a moment she was taken aback because it was such a haunted expression that all Kate could think of was that this woman's life was going to slip by without her ever being truly happy. Then, out of some sense of guilt at having partially unearthed the secret, Kate gently coughed to let Mirri know that they were done and that she could stop dwelling on whatever thoughts she'd been having. Though later, when Kate thought more about it, she wondered if this wasn't just what happened when you painted portraits of people instead of animals. She'd never really done it before, she'd only ever attempted life drawing at art school when she was pretty callow. In those days she'd also been much more concerned with getting a limb right than conveying the personality through her drawing. Perhaps this was simply how it was when it came to painting people.

"I'm done, thanks," Kate said quietly to Mirri, who snapped back to herself and shook her hair back over her shoulders.

"Thank goodness, it made me feel like an actress again. All the staring, the prying. If it weren't you, I wouldn't do it. Ugh."

"It is amazing of you to do this for me," Kate said gratefully. "I mean, it's one thing I've never had the courage to do. Draw a person. And I'm not sure I'll be good at it, but I'm glad you trust me."

"It's fine," Mirri said. "Now I have to get on with work and phone calls, if you don't mind."

"Oh sure. I'm going. I've got to go and meet Louis. Remember?"

"I know Louis." Mirri smiled teasingly, but she wasn't her usual boisterous self, berating Kate for not being attracted to him. "I hope it goes well, darling."

"See you later." Kate stroked the fur under Bébé's collar and left.

She closed the door quietly on Mirri's room and went down the stairs.

"Good morning's work?" Lenoard was at the bottom of the stairs opening a vast cardboard box with a Stanley knife.

"Really good, thanks," Kate said, wondering if she ought to ask Leonard if he knew anything about some man Mirri had met thirty years ago, but thinking better of it. What would she do anyway? Go and confront Mirri about it? Hardly. And what would be the point now? He could even be dead. God, that'd be terrible. Maybe he had died tragically and that's why Mirri never found out if she was in love with him. Kate decided that letting sleeping dogs lie was the best thing she could do. Though it didn't quell her curiosity much.

"What've you got there?" Kate asked as she held back the edges of the box so that Leonard could begin removing the Styrofoam squiggles that were spilling from the sides.

"A wonderful Henry Moore." Leonard dug deep with a look of sheer joy on his face, and Kate thought just how blessed they both were to do what they loved. She with her painting—which, granted, she thought was a bit tacky and not exactly the last word in artistic brilliance, but she did enjoy it when she was actually doing it—and Leonard with his passion for his collecting and selling. "Want to stay and have a peep?" he asked with the excitement of a child with a new bicycle.

"I'd love to but I've got to be somewhere." Kate pushed a hand through the Styrofoam and felt the top of the sculpture. "Actually I'm meeting Louis," Kate said as she made her way past the mess on the stairway.

"Oh, yes," Leonard said distractedly, "Sounds like it might be a fun project."

"Maybe." Kate sounded dubious. "Though I think what he wants is pretty huge. I'm not sure that he's not overestimating my talent." Then, pointing to a smaller box, she asked, "Is that another Henry Moore?"

"That? No, that's some old Super Eight footage that I just had transferred to DVD," Leonard replied while knee-deep in fake snow. "Some funny ones from the sixties and seventies. I thought that Mirri and I might have a look later."

"Cool," Kate said, thinking that she might check them out herself. "Is Dad in any of them?"

"I honestly don't know, dear. If he is I'll tell you."

"Great. See you later, Leonard. I'll come and look at the sculptures," Kate said, and glanced at her watch. Twenty-five minutes to make it to Louis's.

It wasn't until she was on her bike, cycling through Regents Park, that it dawned on Kate that she was nervous about the Louis project. Sure, they'd been at art college together and he knew her talents, but he was in a different league now. He sold work to international collectors and he was fêted by both the critics and the public, and even if he claimed that what he was after was perfectly simple, Kate still wasn't convinced that he wasn't just hiring her out of sympathy. Plus, things felt awkward between them. It was as if he'd moved from their shared past, and they didn't really have much in common anymore. He had these glossy girlfriends and while Kate knew everything there was to know about portraiture—she'd gone to the Rembrandt exhibition at the National Gallery at least once a week the whole time it was on; she was also very well versed in Scottish colorists, Victorian painters, and could probably write a book on Augustus John—she wasn't exactly Miss Tate Modern. In fact, she barely knew a thing that had happened to art since 1940. It had just never been her scene. Whereas Louis was now the poster boy of the modern art scene. They were worlds apart these days.

So Kate vowed to herself to keep it simple with Louis. He had his life and she had hers and she'd let him know that he wasn't obliged to hire her for old times' sake. It was perfectly natural that people grew apart; it happened every day. There are just some friends whom you can't move forward with—the ones you can reminisce with for an hour or so and then you had to make your excuses and leave. Kate suspected that Louis and she had become friends like this. Anyway, it didn't matter, she didn't need to hang out with anybody right now—she had so much work to do. And though she hadn't had any pangs for Felix since their wonderful two days away, despite his having left her a very sweet text message a couple of days ago, what their fling had made her think about was that maybe she wasn't going to be getting married anytime soon. She'd always imagined in the back of her mind, even if she'd never quite admitted it to herself, that when the man came so would the house and the car and the school fees. They'd magically be part of the package. But since she'd put Jake out her mind and begun to see the point of casual sex—not to mention the fact that there wasn't a suitable knight on a thundering-hooved charger to be spied anywhere on the horizon—then she was going to be just fine on her own. She would have to make enough money to support herself and also to move out of the shed by the end of the summer, when it would cease to be an eccentric place to live and instead become a one-way ticket to pneumonia and rheumatism.

Kate hadn't really fathomed just how far it was to get to Louis's new place. It wasn't exactly a skip and a jump. By the time she got to Notting Hill she was more than a bit damp around the edges: Her skirt was sticking to her legs, and the back of her neck was sweating madly. God only knew what she looked like. She'd also gotten oil all the way up one leg because the chain had caught on her shin as she stopped sharply at a traffic light in Camden. She hoped, with her new faith in not trying too hard, that she might look like Mirri's proverbial dirty girl. Then she caught sight of herself in the window of a shop and noticed she looked more like a demented mechanic with a bad female wig. Oh, well, in and out. She'd get her instructions from Louis, find out how much he was planning to pay her, and then leave. But as she began to count up her savings in her head and do the math as to how much money she could make by September, she heard someone call out her name.

"Kate?" She sailed dangerously out of control down Ladbroke Grove as she tried to look over her shoulder. It was a man's voice. She thought maybe she'd ignore it—she was late enough as it was without stopping for some vague acquaintance—but the man

shouted out louder this time, "Kate, it's me." She turned and saw
Jake, standing outside Rough Trade Records with a cigarette hanging out of the corner of his mouth. She waved a hand in the air and
contemplated not stopping, but his face was full of expectation.
"Hey, how are you, angel?" Damn it. Now she had to stop. She
slowed down and did a U-turn in the middle of the road.

"Hi, Jake," she said, a little irritated by having her stride broken
like this. She was supposed to be at Louis's three minutes ago. God
it was typical, wasn't it. She'd spent the past three years walking by
places where she might casually bump into her so-called boyfriend
and now, when she was trying very hard to make him her ex, he'd
apparently turned into a bloody leprechaun, popping up with a
daft grin on his face wherever she turned.

"You look wild." Jake was staring at her in a slightly disconcerting way. She kept her distance, though and didn't attempt to shuffle close enough on her bike to give him even a polite kiss. But she
did try to flatten her hair with one hand and hold the handlebar
with the other.

"Ha. Well I'm a bit late actually. "

"About the other day, angel—"

"Jake, you really don't have to go through that again. You apologized. I accepted your apology. We broke up. Again. Not much
more to it, is there?" She smiled a bit sadly. It wasn't as though seeing Jake was easy. Just because she was moving on, didn't mean
whatever it was about Jake that had made a fool of her for the past
few years had gone away completely. She still felt shaky as she
looked at him and she still felt the pain in her heart—whether it
was vestigial or not. Neither did it help that he looked like he always looked. Handsome and louche and relaxed with his sunglasses
on and the gentle thud of reggae music all around him. But, thankfully, her fright, fight, or flight hormones were racing around inside
her body with all that cycling and her lateness for her appointment
with Louis, so it was easy for her to just keep going. "I'd better be
off," she said before he could reach for her hand and hold it gently
or brush her hair back from her face or something killing like that.

"I'll call you," Jake said.

" 'Bye, Jake." Kate put her foot on the pedal and negotiated her way back across Ladbroke Grove.

"I miss you," she thought he said, but she couldn't be sure because a white van and a Citroën were both blasting her with their horns as she narrowly escaped unscathed from the middle of the road.

When Kate finally arrived at Louis's she hopped off her bike, locked it up on the lamppost outside, and looked at her watch. She was only ten and a half minutes late. She rang the doorbell and pulled her underwear, which had twisted itself all around her body, back into place. As she looked up at the house she saw that it was painted a drab gray color and looked like an old firehouse or bakery. Certainly it had once served some purpose and was the only stand-alone house as far as Kate could see. The others were run-down warehouses or terraces of flats and peeling stucco-fronted buildings.

"Kate?" The buzzer came to life and she tried to look human in case Louis's entry phone actually worked and he could see her.

"It's me." She coughed. She wondered if there was some proper thing to say into those machines that everybody else knew and she didn't. Some snappy phrase she wasn't party to.

"Come up." Kate heaved open the heavy front door and made her way up Louis's shabby staircase. The carpet was worn; mildew was making its way up the wall. Pieces of a motorbike littered the carpet. This wasn't exactly what she'd expected. Kate found it surprising how few people really had the lifestyle you imagined they would. She always thought she was the only one who hadn't gotten it together by her late twenties. The only one who didn't yet own the hell pad she wanted—the bath she could lure lovers into, the chandeliers, the light, airy rooms dotted with occasional pieces of her work, definitely her zebra. It was a dream but it kept her going. And she knew that someday it had to happen, or she'd end up raising her fantasy family of three children in Leonard's shed. Which simply wasn't practical, and was probably barely legal.

So all in all it was always a relief to discover that nobody really seemed to have life as sorted as she envisaged. Louis, despite his achingly hip status, still lived the life of the student she'd known—in a run-down house in the wrong part of Ladbroke Grove with a bad carpet. Well, at least they still had something in common, she thought with relief. That was, until she walked through the door at the top of the staircase and clocked all the swirling neon lights on the walls, the twisted and sinister wooden sculptures, and an enormous table completely covered in shavings of metal, planks of wood, blowtorches, and an electronic sander. She wasn't Larry Gagosian but she imagined this was Louis's workbench and not another piece of art. Though to her eye it looked good enough to exhibit. Kate loved mess and paraphernalia. She loved the bottles and brushes and scalpels and lacquers. It made her heart soften to just be in a studio among tools.

"Louis, I love your workshop," was the first thing she said as Louis stood back and let her in the door, a welder's mask over his face.

He lifted it and grinned. "Me, too."

Kate turned away from the magnificent workbench toward him and remembered herself. "Sorry I'm a bit late. I ran into Jake outside Rough Trade."

"Sounds about right," he said sourly.

"Oh, no, you'd have been proud. I told him where to get off actually," she said as she lifted an old mallet with a rusting orange head and looked lovingly at it. "God, I'm jealous you get to do all this."

"Yeah, just like the old days in metalwork, eh?" he said as he dumped his mask on the table and wiped his hands down his wrecked blue overalls. "Only without the nutty chick at the next bench trying to maim me all the time."

"Oh, you can't just forgive and forget, can you, Louis Alcott?" Kate said as she ran her fingers over his chipped, abused wooden bench.

"It's hard when you're scarred for life." He raised a mischievous eyebrow.

"You are not," she shrieked. "Show me." And with that she moved closer to him and stood on her tiptoes to examine the offending brow. "Can't see a thing," she declared before taking a step back to the bench, hoisting herself up, and sitting on it, her feet dangling above the floor.

"Well, if you bothered to look properly, in the light, I think you'd see your evil handiwork pretty clearly," he said with mock pomposity.

"Rubbish," Kate said. Louis then positioned himself in front of her face with the light full on his face. Kate finally conceded and looked at him.

"Am I right?" he demanded. Kate squinted at his dark eyebrow as he held his bangs back with his hand, and she saw that there was a definite balding patch and a white slice of scar through the outside corner of his eyebrow.

"Oh," she said.

"So you admit it now, do you?" He dropped his hair back and looked at Kate, but neither of them seemed to realize how close they were to one another, because each instantly pulled away. Then, as Kate tried to banish the overwhelming thought she'd just had—that Louis's skin was the smoothest golden color she'd ever seen, that his nose was so much finer close up, and that his eyes were green as uncut emeralds—she shoved him in the ribs with her elbow.

"Okay, I admit it. You're hideously scarred. It's very unfortunate, but there's nothing I can do about it. Apart from offer you the use of my shed so you can go and live like Quasimodo for the rest of your life." She jumped down off the workbench and went over to the sink where Louis's grubby kettle stood, covered in big, inky black fingerprints. "Now, if you're not going to be a good host then I'll make *myself* a cup of tea."

"Well, Esmeralda, as you're making one, mine's two sugars," he said, moving toward an ornate, limed-oak French door at the end of the workshop. "But you might want to use the other kitchen, unless you like great big chunks of lime scale in your tea and mugs with indelible black rings inside."

"Yeah, I was wondering whether the health and safety officer had been around lately." Kate lifted a stained teaspoon from a moldy saucer.

"Through here." Louis held open the door and Kate ducked under his arm to enter. "We can get this polar bear thing straight, too, without all those tools tempting you to ruin my looks again in a jealous rage."

"Yeah, right." Kate laughed as she stood in the hallway of what was clearly the rest of Louis's house. "Wow, Louis. This is yours?" she said, staggered at the vast and beautiful corridor that lay before her.

"Where did you think I lived?" he asked as he led her through to the kitchen. "Oh, yeah, I forgot, the bell tower."

"Go to hell, Louis." She laughed and followed him. She wondered why she'd been so convinced that she and Louis hadn't really much of a friendship left anymore. They still laughed at one another's dumb jokes like old mates; there wasn't a hint of awkwardness really.

"So you want me to lace your tea with arsenic, do you?" he asked.

"Perfect," Kate said. "Then I can poke around your flat first, discover all your dark secrets, and you can kill me. Does that work?"

"Help yourself," Louis said as he filled the slick silver kettle from the tap and waved a hand at the rest of the flat. "Leave no drawer left unturned."

"Fantastic," Kate said, "license to snoop. Thanks." She shot Louis an excited look and headed out of the kitchen and into the corridor. Unlike the fluorescently lit studio, this part of the house was darker and cavernous and was essentially a row of rooms strung together like a beaded necklace—one room led to another, all linked by adjoining wide doorways with no door. So that as Kate stood at the top of the corridor she could see all the way through to the bedroom at the end—albeit very distantly, as it was a pretty enormous flat. First was the sitting room whose walls were lined with disturbing but very important-looking paintings and rich damson-colored velvet sofas and chairs; a bowl of sweetpeas on a low coffee table gave the room a friendly air, and dark cherrywood floorboards ran throughout the flat. The air smelled of darkly exotic white flowers. Light flooded through the vast bay windows and from a balcony at the end of the corridor, off the bedroom. *This* was a house. A grown-up's house, no less. Kate realized that she alone did live a stunted life. Leonard had a great place. Tanya and Robbie had a great place. Louis had a great place. She had a shed.

Kate leaned forward and peered through into the next room, calling out as she went, "Louis, I love it. I never realized that you had any taste." She heard a snort in the kitchen and moved through into a dining room with a newspaper strewn across the large, imposing table and the remnants of some toast. The table could easily have seated ten, and Kate wondered whether Louis ever actually entertained here—certainly she and Jake had never been invited to dine chez Louis, though she wasn't about to ask why. She already knew the answer. Next came a sage-green room that was like a library, with leather-bound red volumes lining the walls and an ancient writing desk covered in invitations and what she thought of as gentleman's notepaper—thick cream sheets with Louis's name and address at the top, bordered in olive green. It was all so seductively male that for a moment Kate yearned to be a man and read *The Times* and play poker in the evenings and smoke cigars.

In fact, for a moment she wanted to be Louis. She looked over her shoulder to see if he might be following her but there was no sign of him, just the clatter of cups in the kitchen. She took another step into the office, vaguely conscious that she was looking for some giveaway as to Louis's private life—a photograph in a heavy silver frame perhaps, showing one of the hothouse girls. But though she peered keenly, she found nothing. Eventually, when she had spent a suspiciously long time in the office, she wandered into the next room, which was covered in silver swimming pool tiles. A giant Victorian bathtub sat in the middle of the floor complete with claw feet. Little else cluttered the room apart from some dusty apothecary jars filled with colored liquids. Then, just as Kate was about to lift the lid off one of the potions, she realized that the room beyond was the bedroom—a brilliantly light room with a huge bed strewn with cushions, pillows, and stone gray linen. The paintings here were beautiful and serene, not like the disturbing ones in the sitting room, and the bed, out of keeping with the rest of the flat, was unmade. Kate looked past it onto a small deck, which was home to pots of lavender and camellias. It was overhung by an ancient lilac tree in full bloom. She turned back and looked through the flat with a sense of complete awe. She had never imagined this of Louis. He was a scruffy, nail-biting, mumbling guy who happened to have a phenomenal talent for contemporary art and who got her jokes. But this was something else. She couldn't help but wonder whether Louis ever had women back to his gray linen bed. As her mind began to wander and she thought of him bringing one of the short-skirted media darlings back here to spend the night, she heard his footsteps in the hallway outside the kitchen.

"Kate?" he called out. For some reason Kate felt embarrassed to be in his bedroom, even though she'd been very blunt about her intentions to snoop shamelessly. Suddenly, with the place being so tasteful and with Louis not quite being the person she thought she knew, she felt slightly gauche. She was about to dart through to the bathroom, but then she'd have to make a sudden move and it might look as though she really had been poking around in his underwear drawer.

"Here," she said, and dashed out onto the balcony where there were no underpants to incriminate her. "Just admiring the view," she added dreamily. But then she looked down and noticed that the view was in fact quite a rank one of the canal, with its filthy brown water and bicycle wheels strewing the banks.

"It only smells when the wind's blowing." Louis gave her a

slightly puzzled look as he put two cups of coffee onto a dilapidated garden table and sat down.

"Did you do the flat yourself?"

"Yeah, mostly. I got a bit of help with the towels and stuff. I think you have to unless you're truly gay," he said, voicing a thought that had occurred to Kate only a split second before—that any man with such fabulous taste must be gay.

"Yeah, right." Kate hastily picked up her coffee and took a sip, burning her lips in the process. "From a designer?" She winced.

"From a girlfriend actually," Louis said calmly. For some reason Kate was surprised—she hadn't expected Louis to have a girlfriend and she certainly hadn't expected him to be open about the fact. That wasn't the point of Louis. He was someone who was interested in her life but who generally kept his own under wraps. She didn't really want to ask him about it but she felt she ought to, now he'd mentioned it.

"So tell me about your girlfriend," she said as lightly as she could muster.

"Oh, we're not together anymore." He looked awkwardly into his coffee. "She was a florist."

Of course she was, Kate wanted to say, *with pretty petal skin and rosebud lips, slightly bohemian but in a sweet way.* Kate felt a twinge of something in her stomach. How easy other girls seemed to have it—they didn't struggle with men who couldn't love them like Jake, they undoubtedly lived in normal houses and they dated funny men like Louis and tied bunches of tulips together with colored braid and polka-dot tissue paper for a living. Kate felt a stab of envy.

"That's nice," she said, wondering whether the sweetpeas in the sitting room had come from her. Probably. "So what about the piece, Louis. What is it that you want me to do exactly?"

"Right, the piece." Louis tore his thoughts away from the sweet-pea girl and looked out at the canal for inspiration. "I'll need the sketched piece by a week on Tuesday, if that's okay. And what I really wanted to talk to you about was working in the gallery on it. It's going to be at least twenty feet wide and eight feet high. I think maybe you should paint it on site. How do you feel about that?"

"Well, I mean it sounds fine. I suppose. It's Tate Modern isn't it?" Kate asked.

"Yeah, it's at Millbank. We'd actually be working in a space next door but close enough that we're virtually on site for the purposes of installation," he said. "In fact, I was thinking that maybe we could go down there this afternoon and look at the space. Give you a feel for it," he finished, slightly uneasily. Kate wanted to say yes, because he'd clearly been a bit embarrassed to ask, but she simply couldn't.

"I'm really sorry, but I just can't do it this afternoon." She bit her lip apologetically. "It's a friend who I've promised to help out . . . with . . . with something . . ." She sounded unconvinced even to herself but she couldn't exactly give him full details about having promised to go with Tanya to the hospital for her laparoscopy to see if there was any medical reason why she was failing to conceive. It was just a bit too much information.

"Sure, okay. Of course," Louis said. "Well, maybe another time then."

"I can do it tomorrow afternoon," Kate said hurriedly, to prove that she wasn't unwilling, just unable. "I have a session with Mirri and Bébé first thing and then I'm all yours."

"Okay, great." Louis said. "Shall I meet you there? At the Tate?"

"Perfect. About two?" Kate stood up with her cup in her hand. Even though she hadn't quite finished her coffee, it was clear that their meeting was at an end. They'd fallen back into behaving with the awkwardness of strangers, and all the silliness from earlier had vanished. Kate couldn't wait to get out.

"Great." Louis stood and ushered her through the rooms and back into his studio. "Tomorrow it is then." He stood at the top of the staircase, with his glossy black bangs falling in his eyes and his loose jeans hanging frayed over bare feet. Kate suddenly felt like the least cool girl in school. Louis was this hip, forward-thinking conceptual artist with an entrée to every party or club he couldn't be bothered to attend who hung out with beautiful, interesting girls. She was the hangover from his college days. The friend you couldn't quite bear to take to Goodwill. Like the great aunt who painted pictures of bulldogs and kittens, which you hung on your wall only when she was coming around to visit. Try as she might to reassure herself that she made people happy with her paintings of their pets, Kate felt like a huge nerd right now.

"Yeah, see you tomorrow," she said dumbly. When she closed the front door she unclenched her knuckles to reveal four red crescents printed on either palm where her fingernails had dug in. Something about Louis made her nervous. She wondered if his not speaking very much was actually a tactic, a way of making people think he was deep and enigmatic. Unlike Kate, whose chatter seemed to bulge from her conversation like an overstuffed sofa most of the time. She closed her mind off to the thought that tomorrow she'd have to find something to talk to him about once their banter went into remission. Perhaps tonight she'd read up on postmodernism for some pointers.

Chapter Fifteen

Thankfully for Kate she had no time to dwell on her inadequacies. She had to make it back to Tanya's in Belsize Park or she'd miss the appointment. So without so much as a thought for her personal safety, she hared out into the chaos of Ladbroke Grove traffic once more and set off back through the park. Thankfully Jake was no longer propping up the doorway of Rough Trade, but Kate kept her head down anyway, in case he emerged from a bar or car or petrol station.

"Darling, I'm on my way," Kate yelled down her phone once she was out of harm's way and in the relative quiet of the park.

"You're not cycling and talking are you, Kate?" Tanya asked disapprovingly.

"I can't hear you, there's wind in my earpiece," Kate shouted, in order to avoid a telling-off. "I'll be there in fifteen. I might need to borrow a T-shirt, though, I'm a bit sweaty."

"Lovely," Tanya said. "I'll dig one out." Kate hoped for a Chloe piece or maybe even Balenciaga.

"Gotta dash or I'll get killed." She put her phone in the back pocket of her skirt as a policeman looked fit to arrest her. She smiled at him and pedaled off madly.

Tanya was waiting by the large front window of her house with a nervous smile on her face. She rushed to the door when Kate sped up the drive on her bike and chained it to the drainpipe.

"I've got you a top out. It ought to fit." Tanya ushered Kate in the front door and into her hallway, which was practically bursting with sunlight filtering through the stained-glass window above the door.

"Thanks. Are you driving?" Kate said as she pulled off her grubby T-shirt and screwed it into a ball.

"I thought we'd take a cab. I've got one coming in a minute or so." Tanya was shifting her weight from foot to foot.

"Don't be nervous, it's just routine, right?" Kate asked as she pulled Tanya's T-shirt—a very understatedly beautiful Dries Van Noten, she noted with delight—over her head. She could actually use a new bra, too, she thought as she caught sight of her rather dubious number in the mirror. It was the old rule of thumb that dictated that once you painted the baseboard, the rest of the room looked rather shabby. Kate simply had to look at an item of Tanya's clothing to realize that she was a nonsensical sartorial mess. And despite her new subscription to Mirri's way of doing things—the disheveled, careless messy way—she suspected that tatty, graying underwear did not fall into even Mirri's category.

"Well, yes. But God, Kate, I'm petrified. What if something really terrible is wrong with me? What if they say there's no hope of me ever conceiving?" Tanya closed her eyes miserably and Kate went to hug her. "I didn't sleep a wink last night. Robbie had a meeting at seven this morning. God knows how he got up."

"Sweetheart, there's always hope. They're just doctors. And if they say that all's fine, then great. It just may take a bit more time before you and Robbie have a child. And even if they say that there is something wrong. Well, what do they know? They make mistakes all the time." Kate stroked her friend's hair gently and then looked at her face.

"Do you promise?" Tanya, who was always so indomitable, so

practical, was so desperate for reassurance that Kate was overcome with the urge to take away her pain.

"Darling, it's never the end of the road with these things. We both know of a million people who've been told that they can never have babies and then by some miracle they do. It happens every day. I had a friend who went away on holiday right after the doctors told her that she was infertile—she and her husband got drunk, went skydiving, and had the wildest time and guess what? She got pregnant. Good God, look at Cherie Blair. She got pregnant at forty-five. Madonna did it at forty-two. You've got an absolute age to go yet even if there is something wrong. Science will catch up with you or something like that."

"I hope so." Tanya looked defeated for a moment and then jumped when the cab honked loudly in the street outside. "Better get going."

"Tell you what, in no time you're going to be cursing the afternoons you spent worrying about silly things like this," Kate said brightly. "Because you won't have a moment to spare between nappies and bottles and sore nipples."

"God, I hope you're right." Tanya smiled weakly.

"Just don't come complaining to me," Kate said drily as she climbed into the cab beside her friend. "Because I'll be off raging like a rock star with one of my many lovers. Or more likely on my yacht in Saint-Tropez with an indecently young boyfriend."

"Really?" Tanya asked, still too tense to be completely with it.

"Hardly, considering that when I woke up this morning I discovered new lines down the side of my nose." Kate groaned. "I've discovered this whole new place to have wrinkles. Nobody I've ever met has them there. But look, I do."

"No you do not." Tanya smiled as Kate forced her new wrinkles into her friend's line of vision. Then she added, "Oh, God, you're right. You do. How weird. I've never seen lines there before."

"Thank you," Kate said matter-of-factly. "Now I do have to fill you in on a couple of minor happenings in my life," she went on coyly, trying her best to take her friend's mind off the tube-in-the-belly-button ordeal that they were hurtling toward.

"I wondered why I hadn't heard from you for a few days. I thought you were engrossed in the portrait," Tanya said as she fastened her seat belt.

"Capri, darling," Kate said excitedly. Tanya gave the requisite look of surprise, and Kate's tale of making love in swimming pools was the perfect device to stop Tanya from noticing the angry lanes of stationary traffic making them late for her appointment. When they finally pulled up outside the hospital, it was too late to worry.

"Eleven pounds forty, please, love," the cabbie said to Tanya, who looked up at the imposing red brick of the hospital with dread on her face.

"Thanks." Tanya paid and the girls got out. "Promise it'll be okay, Kate?" she said as she pressed Kate's hand hard between her hot, pale fingers.

"How can it not be, sweetheart? You're going to be the best mother in the world. I know it," Kate promised.

———

When Kate arrived home, having left Tanya at the hospital when Robbie arrived to sit with her, she went inside to lie down and cool off. The air was thick and muggy and she felt as though she'd spent the entire day in traffic, inhaling blue hazy fumes, her skin getting stickier and grimier by the second. She had no plans for the evening except to take a cool shower and maybe do a bit of work on one of the portraits. Suddenly she had more work to do than she could handle, which was not something she was going to complain about in a hurry. As she glanced at the floor she noticed that there was an envelope lying there behind the door. She wasn't sure she could muster the energy to pick it up, but eventually she unpeeled herself and practically crawled toward it. She saw immediately that it was Jake's handwriting. With surprisingly little curiosity she tore it open and found a CD with a pale blue Post-it note attached. It read:

Have dinner with me tomorrow, angel?

Kate hadn't fostered enough cynicism toward Jake yet to think how predictable it was for him to be making more moves on her than he'd done in as long as she could remember. In fact, more moves than he'd ever made on her. Instead she turned over the CD case, which he'd scratched three large xxxs on, extracted the CD, and slid it into her stereo. She climbed apathetically back onto the bed, thinking that it'd be one of Jake's compilations that he made for his friends every so often. But instantly she recognized the voice that drifted out as Jake's. He was singing softly and sweetly the words of a song she loved, "Magnolia" by J. J. Cale. She closed her eyes and listened as he filled the room with words of love.

Magnolia you sweet thing . . .
Got to get back to you, babe. . . .

Inexplicably a tear coursed its way heavily from the outside corner of her eye down into her hair. This song reminded her of how much she had yearned for Jake not so long ago. In fact, not so long ago it would have been simply too achingly painful for her to listen to. Now it was just incredibly sad. The man who had opened so many doors in her life—and slammed so many in her face—was gone for good. Because this time she'd shown him the way out. But now as she cried it was different from the other times. This time there was a faint pleasure in the feeling of loss. She'd loved Jake but now she was free. Though clearly he wasn't aware of that fact. She picked up her phone and sent him a heavyhearted text.

You know that I can't. Kxx

Then she fell asleep on the bed, clutching her phone as Jake's voice spun endlessly in her stereo.

"Darling, would you mind babysitting for me?" Kate was wrenched from sleep by Mirri, who was standing above her. She had learned that hammering on Kate's door wasn't polite, but she hadn't quite grasped that standing over someone with your hands on your hips while she slept was equally alarming.

"Agh, Mirri." Kate's head almost collided with Mirri's as she sat up. "What?"

"Will you babysit for me? I have to go out tonight," she said as she sat down on the edge of the bed. Kate rubbed her eyes and leaned over to turn Jake off.

"Yeah. Okay," she murmured sleepily. "What time is it? Have I been asleep for hours?"

"I saw you come back about an hour ago," Mirri said. "It'll just be for a couple of hours in the house while I'm out. I'm not planning to stay long."

"Where are you going?" Kate rubbed her eyes and wriggled herself up into sitting position. "Anywhere exciting?"

"I have to tell Jonah that he must not leave his wife," she said matter-of-factly.

"Wow. He's going to leave her?" Kate was impressed. Much as she didn't agree with the breaking up of families and such, it was a real coup for a sixty-year-old woman with a bad temper to lure a man away from his wife. Without even trying or wanting to.

"I'm not going to let him. Honestly, I don't know what he thinks we'll do together for the rest of the week, let alone our lives. But he's very sweet and I don't want to hurt him so I have to try to be, how do you say it? *Diplomatique.*"

"Poor Jonah." Kate smiled. "It's quite miserable, really, isn't it, breaking hearts?"

"It is not so much fun as everyone thinks." Mirri was dressed in a pair of navy sailor's pants and a tight T-shirt with her hair tied back in a simple ponytail; she looked more elegant than Kate had ever seen her. Kate guessed it was because she had serious business to attend to. "So whose heart have you been breaking, my dear?" she asked.

"Only The Slug's. I'm not sure it counts since he's already shattered mine into a million pieces several times over."

"How quickly hearts heal." Mirri smiled knowingly. "Especially when you only *thought* you loved the person."

"I did love him," Kate said. Though she wasn't so sure anymore that the whole thing hadn't been some absurd and warped game, rather than love. Love was supposed to be so much more. And it was also supposed to be loving, actually, now she came to think of it. "But I saw him in the street today and I really think I'm over him. I told him so but of course he's decided that he can't live without me." This wasn't strictly true but it was the least Kate deserved after all the rejection. "He wants me to go to dinner tomorrow but I couldn't even if I was tempted to, because I'm seeing Louis."

"Louis?" Mirri's eyes lit up.

"I've told you before. I've known Louis forever and we're friends."

"It's good to begin as friends."

"Mirri, even if I did have a crush on him—which I don't, though he makes me laugh sometimes—we're not very relaxed around one another."

"It's the sexual tension. How can you be relaxed when all you want to do is fuck?" Mirri said excitedly.

Kate made a point of ignoring her. "Even if I did have a crush on him, he always goes out with these gorgeous, high-achieving women. I'm just like a sister to him." Kate improvised furiously.

"You're gorgeous, too," Mirri said impatiently, "or do you need to have another man suck the bee sting out of your leg to remind you?"

"I'm not Louis material. And Felix didn't suck me, he swiped me with a credit card," Kate said flatly. "Now, please be careful with Jonah, won't you? I like him."

"He's cheating on his wife," Mirri reminded Kate sanctimoniously.

"I know—how about you get rid of Jake for me and I'll let Jonah down gently? That'd be much more appropriate."

"But not nearly so much fun," Mirri said as she hopped down from the bed in her bare feet. "Come to the house soon. I've left you a bottle of champagne out and some oven chips. Bébé will be thrilled to have the company."

"Me, too." Kate huffed. "For all the helicopters and star-crossed exes I'm still the only girl in London alone on a Thursday night."

A few minutes after Mirri had gone, Kate bundled together her pencils in case the mood took her later, which it never did—the TV was always much more interesting. Hell, the wallpaper was always much more interesting than doing work. Her cell rang and Robbie's number came up.

"Just wanted to let you know that all's well," he said.

"Really?" Kate asked. Her stomach had dive-bombed when she saw the number. Because even though she'd made a point of being positive for Tanya, she was terrified that she might not be okay. And she couldn't imagine the impact that would have on her best friend's life.

"Well, they couldn't find anything wrong. Which is great, but it doesn't really solve our problem. Basically they told us to go away and think about fertility treatment," Robbie said. It was strange discussing something so intimate with Robbie, but Kate supposed that this kind of situation forced people to open up in ways they would never have before. Kate also hoped that it'd just make them stronger as a couple—forging an even greater bond in adversity.

"Well, tell her I'm so pleased that nothing's wrong," Kate said with relief. "And fertility treatment is so common these days that I don't think there's anything to worry about apart from a few injections in the bum," she added in what she hoped was a casual and reassuring voice.

"You're right," said Robbie, clutching at the idea that it couldn't be so bad if so many people endured it. "Everyone's at it, aren't they?"

"Sure are," Kate said.

When Kate arrived at Leonard's later, Mirri was adding hoop earrings to her sailor's outfit.

"I may not want him to leave his wife," she said, checking herself in the mirror, "but I still want him to want to be in love with me."

"You're a terrible woman, Mirabelle Moncur. You can't just make it easy on the poor chap, can you?" Leonard said as he finished his supper for one.

"Men hate things to be easy." She added lipstick. "Kate, my dear, Bébé has had his supper and he's in his bed in the television room. You just need to nuzzle him occasionally. The champagne is in the fridge." She kissed first Kate and then Leonard on the top of their heads as though they were a pair of children being left by their mother for the evening. Then she disappeared, leaving only Shalimar where she once was.

"Are you staying in tonight?" Kate asked Leonard in surprise. She'd assumed that she'd been called in to babysit because he was out.

"I had a drinks party but I decided that my bookkeeping couldn't wait another day, so I'm going to lock myself away in my office. Though I will have a glass of something with you first." He twinkled. "It'd be churlish not to."

"Oh good." Kate raided the fridge for the champagne and pulled two glasses from the cupboard. "Now, what's on telly? I'm dying for a good soap opera." She shamelessly left her pencils and sketch pad behind on the kitchen table and made her way into the television room with Leonard in tow.

"Forget soap operas," he said as he sank down into his armchair, "I have home movies."

"Ah," said Kate as she spied the neat mountain of DVDs he'd shown her earlier on the table. "Which is the silliest?"

"Well, we have Verbier in 1967. That will be very silly. We have Onassis's yacht in 1973. Which will be deranged."

"My taxi is late." They both turned around to see Mirri standing in the doorway with a face as black as thunder. "So I stand around by the gate like an idiot while the photographers go crazy and try to make me smile or hit them and still he doesn't come. So I have come back in and told Jonah that if he wants to take me to dinner he must come and collect me. These men today really have no manners. I should never have had to go to the restaurant alone in the first place." She came and sat on the edge of Kate's sofa.

"Well, the paparazzi are going to love Jonah Sinclair turning up to take you to dinner, aren't they?" Kate said, and tucked her legs in so that Mirri could sit down.

"He wants his wife to find out. Well, now she will," she said sourly. "So what are you watching?"

"We were just wondering whether we should feast our eyes on Ari's yacht, or Christmas the year you divorced Christian."

"You were not going to be such sad people to sit at home and watch such things?" Mirri couldn't help but smile, despite her vile temper.

"There's always Verbier 1967. Or Jimmy Hendrix in the Isle of Wight." Leonard read the labels. It sounded to Kate like a very glamorous history book.

"Let's look at Christmas." Mirri managed a wry smile and settled herself into the sofa. "I think I was happy then."

"You certainly were," Leonard said as he slid in the tape. The first shot was of Mirri in a Santa Claus hat and bikini. "Good Lord, you look like Playmate of the Year."

"I think I was." Mirri winked. And within seconds she and Leonard were on the floor laughing at themselves, Leonard with his fabulous porn-star mustache and a shirt open to his waist and Mirri on the lap of a man who looked like every matinee idol who'd ever smoldered rolled into one perfect *homme*.

"Oh my God, you were both so beautiful," Kate said as she scooped Bébé up off the floor into her lap and tickled his tummy. Because they were. They were dancing by the swimming pool, they were smoking Gauloises in the sun, they were kissing and diving into water, and in every scene they looked like ancient gods and goddesses of youth and beauty.

"We were, weren't we?" Mirri had tears on her cheeks. "Darling, do you remember that ghastly boyfriend you had. The one who cut his toenails at the breakfast table."

"Frederico." Leonard erupted into a fresh fit of mirth. "He was my bit of rough. I fancied him as a lorry driver."

"And there is poor Yves Saint Laurent in the corner, too shy to speak to anyone." Mirri pointed to the screen.

"And Jean Paul and Talitha." Leonard added. Kate assumed that they meant the fabulous Gettys. And as they laughed and reminisced, Kate found herself feeling just the tiniest bit bluesy. She doubted that when she was sixty a friend would ever bring out a home movie and they'd split their sides with laughter at the fun they'd had. Mirri was certainly right about one thing: Nobody knew how to have a good time anymore. They were all dying to move on to the next installment of success—better car, high-flying job, bigger flat, ideal husband, perfect number of children in the right schools. Did anyone really stop and smell the roses anymore, let alone drop a thousand of them from a helicopter? Well, Kate certainly didn't. All the same it made her determined to find a few movie moments in her own life from now on. If she spent a second more worrying about what she wasn't doing, then she'd never do anything anyway. If that made any sense.

As Leonard and Mirri cried their way laughing through Verbier, Kate sneaked out to unearth a packet of cheesy Wotsits and a few olives. When she crept back into the room Leonard pulled out Verbier and slipped in another.

"I don't know what this one is, it just says June 1971," he said and sat back as the screen once again flickered to life.

"Oh, I hope it's that birthday party that you all had for me at the Chelsea Arts Club," Mirri said, sitting forward in her seat, "the one where the future king of England put his hand up the skirt of a French harlot. Or so the newspapers said." Mirri clapped her hands together delightedly. And then stopped abruptly when what appeared on screen instead was the outside of a church, the doorway framed with white roses and an impossibly glamorous couple locked into a kiss.

"It's Tony's wedding," Leonard remarked. "He was a handsome bugger, wasn't he?"

"Stop it," Mirri suddenly said, almost inaudibly.

"What's that, darling?" Leonard asked, not having heard her hushed order properly.

"Please stop the thing. Now," she said, and reached for the remote control from Leonard's hand. "I have to leave." And with that Mirri flicked off the television, handed the remote back to Leonard, and walked from the room with a look of abject misery on her face. "I will wait outside for my lift. *Bonne nuit.*" Kate and Leonard were left in shocked silence for a moment or two. Just watching the space where she'd been sitting.

"What on earth's the matter with her?" Kate asked.

"Well, it's Tony's wedding . . . but I can't think why it upset her like that." Leonard looked shocked.

"Maybe she's still in love with him. She's let slip that there's someone she's been in love with for years, but I didn't think it was Tony. She's definitely hiding some real sadness, you know. I've noticed," Kate said quietly, once she'd heard the front door close.

"Oh, she probably just looked fat in her frock at Tony's wedding and didn't want us to see." Leonard said. "Which is just as well because I must get down to my figures." That said, he handed the remote control to Kate and went back to his office.

Kate ate an olive and flicked through the TV guide. But as she was about to switch on some crummy documentary, she couldn't resist pressing the PLAY button again. She turned down the volume in case Leonard overheard and sat close to the telly, her finger hovering above the STOP button, and watched the tape. At first it was just Tony's wedding and lots of amazing people in short skirts and men in floppy velvet suits. Really it was like a *Vogue* shoot. Or an avant garde movie of the Swinging Sixties. Lots more laughter and a whole heap of cigarettes, as on the other tapes, and no sign of

Mirri or Leonard. But then, as the camera drifted by a small crowd of people leaning on a Mini Cooper in the street, she saw Mirri, wearing a knit dress that barely skimmed the top of her thighs, with her hair hanging golden and hippieish around her shoulders. She looked about as un-made-up as Kate had ever seen her from that era, and more beautiful than ever, too. And beside her, talking intently, focusing every bit of his attention on her, was a man with curly dark hair and almond-shaped, dark eyes. Mirri was giggling like a schoolgirl at whatever he was saying; the pair looked seventeen. Though really, they would have been in their early thirties, Kate worked out. But why Mirri didn't want to watch this particular piece of footage was beyond her. She looked great, her frock didn't make her look fat, and she was having fun. And then, on screen, a pretty, neat girl with a Jackie O bouclé suit came over to Mirri and the man and hooked her arm proprietarily through the man's arm. Mirri looked the girl up and down for a moment or two and then turned to another man next to her and said something to him. And then the camera drifted away again. On to a cluster of elderly guests in ridiculous hats, who were clearly the parents of the piece—the outsiders.

Kate watched a moment or two more of the film and then flicked it off. She suspected that she'd seen all she needed to of Mirri. Certainly she'd seen enough to get an inkling of what might be causing her faraway looks. It was undoubtedly a man, and very likely the man in the film, but what had happened, or not happened, between them was still very much a mystery.

Chapter Sixteen

Jake hated to lose. If he lost a hand in poker, his eyebrows would knit together and the players on either side of him would edge away. If he lost an entire game, he would go into a deep funk for days. Losing was something that didn't happen to him very often, and he wasn't good at it. When he got his text message back from Kate saying that she wouldn't have dinner with him, he'd been at rehearsals with the new keyboard player for his band. She was a New Yorker called Simone and she looked like Nico. She had white-blond hair in thick bangs, and her thighs were reassuringly sturdy beneath her small kilt.

"Jake, do you mind if I get out my tambourine and play on a couple of the tracks?" She strode over to where he was sitting, chatting to the drummer.

"Yeah, whatever you like, Simone." He gave her a wink intended as a friendly dismissal and watched her as she walked away, tapping her tambourine occasionally and filling her skirt perfectly. Ordinarily he would have given her more time. In fact, ordinarily he'd have given her one, probably, but he was still smarting from Kate's message. Yesterday when he'd seen her cycling like a demented fairy down Ladbroke Grove, he'd assumed she really was just in a hurry and that she'd call him later. But now, as he slid his phone into the back pocket of his jeans, he wondered whether there really was something wrong. She had never once turned down an invitation to dinner with him. And the idea that she might have done it after he'd sent her J. J. Cale was unimaginable to him.

For the first week after Kate had told him to get lost and he'd felt like shit, he assumed that he'd been partying too hard. Then, when he still didn't want to get out of bed a week later and he couldn't find any enthusiasm for anything, he'd begun to think that he had a mystery virus. He contemplated going to the doctors until his aunt suggested that maybe he was sickening for something—or someone. Someone with toffee-brown hair, gold-flecked eyes, and a penchant for painting. Someone who had picked Jake up every single time he was down. Who had laughed at his jokes, told him he was sexy when he didn't feel it, and listened to his every moan and paranoia as if it mattered more than anything else in the world.

"Come on, Catherine," Jake told his aunt, who was just a bit fed up with coming home from lunch and having to unearth her nephew from beneath the ashtrays and booze bottles that littered her sitting room. "You know how things are with me and Kate. I like her and in my own way I probably love her. But she's not The One." Aunt Catherine, who knew a thing or two about love even though many years had passed since she'd last been in love, kept her mouth shut and said nothing.

She did, though, give Jake a look that said it all. It said, *Oh please, Jake, you can't be so stupid that you still talk about The One? How about the greatest girl you're ever going to meet, who has untold patience for your pathetic, selfish ways and still wants to be with you. If you don't think she's The One then you'd better hotfoot it to Selfridges right now and grab yourself one of those mannequins from the window who have perfect bodies and faces, no personality and will be whatever you want them to be.* Jake had glared at Aunt Catherine after she'd given him this look and gone to the pub.

But a few days later, when the mystery virus, which he was now convinced he'd picked up in India last summer and it had been lying dormant in his system since then, was still making him tired, irritable, and gloomy, he had seen Kate come flying over the hill out of nowhere. And he'd felt momentarily better. He'd said hello to her then gone back into Rough Trade and bought a bunch of new vinyl. He'd even cleared up his ashtrays and thrown a few whiskey bottles into the recycling bin when he got back to Catherine's. And though he was fantastically lacking in self-awareness, even Jake had to admit that it was looking more and more likely that Kate might just be The One.

Any suspicions he had were confirmed later that night when he and the band were hanging out in Catherine's flat and Jake went to his room to find the lyrics he'd been working on during a bout of insomnia. He was rummaging on the bedside table when he heard the door open. He glanced up and saw Simone standing in the doorway. Naked. She was dangling her panties on the end of her little finger and smiling like Eve might have done as she plucked the apple from the Tree of Knowledge. Her bangs fell heavily over her eyelashes and Jake had to admit that she looked every bit as succulent in the flesh as she did in that kilt.

"Hey, Jake," she said, and rested against the closed door. "The boys were boring me."

"Yeah, I know what that's like," Jake said with a faint grin.

"We could amuse each other." She pouted.

"We could." His look told her that he wanted her. She walked slowly toward him, her round thighs and fruity breasts swaying irresistibly.

But fifteen minutes later, Simone was less seductive. She was a bit bored, a bit offended, and, more than anything, confused. She knew what a hot little number she was, so what was the deal with Jake? She'd heard he was a rocket in bed and she'd heard that he was available. But right now his goddamned rocket was still on the launching pad. She huffed and sat up.

"It's fine. Probably shouldn't get involved with someone I work with anyway," she drawled in her sultry New York accent.

"What can I say?" Jake ran a hand through his hair and gave her an apologetic shrug. "I think you're fucking gorgeous. I guess I've just got other things on my mind," he said as he cursed Kate's fucking text message. What the fuck was she playing at anyway? If she wanted him to come crawling around she was going the wrong way about it, because right now he was just pissed off.

Kate stopped shuffling from foot to foot as she waited in the foyer of Tate Modern because she was afraid that if she didn't, she might look like a line dancer. She'd put on her cowboy boots—well, Janis Joplin's cowboy boots, to be precise, the ones that Jake had bought for her—because she'd left her only pair of gallery-worthy sandals under Leonard's coffee table last night. She hadn't wanted to go and collect them this morning lest she run into Mirri. Kate had been asleep on the sofa when Mirri came home last night and their paths hadn't crossed but she'd heard on the house grapevine—that is, Leonard—that all was not well with Mirri. Whether it was a Jonah thing or a video nasty thing, they couldn't tell.

Whatever it was, Mirri had been sitting on her windowsill chain-smoking all morning. When Leonard had approached with black coffee, she had just blown smoke in his face; she was still there when Kate stole out the side gate at lunchtime. Which was how Kate came to look so inappropriate for her meeting with Louis. She was wearing a too-short denim skirt and an old gingham shirt because all her clean, decent clothes were sitting in the ironing basket in Leonard's laundry room and she hadn't dared risk the dash indoors. An encounter with the temperamental goddess would leave her either bruised or extremely late for Louis. Still, when Leonard had come down to the shed to cower for a moment or two, Kate couldn't resist delving a little deeper.

"Leonard?" she had asked as casually as possible as she cleaned her teeth.

"Yes, my dear." Leonard was on his hands and knees on the floor and appeared to be examining the rug. "Gracious, did you know that this rug is eighteenth-century Persian?" he asked excitedly.

"Yes." Kate hoped he didn't get snail slime on his best tartan trousers. "You told me that when you gave it to me."

"Did I? Good heavens." He lay the corner of the carpet back down. "How generous of me."

"Leonard, how well do you remember Tony's wedding?" Kate asked as he creaked to his feet and parked himself in the armchair to catch his breath.

"Very well indeed. I was an usher, you know," he said proudly.

"And Mirri?" Kate stood over the sink and rinsed her mouth out. "Did she have a boyfriend at the time?"

"Darling, that's like asking me to remember the runners in the Derby of the same year. She always had boyfriends. Hundreds of them. Oxford practically gave out degrees in keeping up with Mirabelle Moncur's love life."

"Okay, well, was there someone special? Maybe someone she had an affair with who was . . . unavailable or turned her down?"

"Nobody turned her down. Ever," Leonard said emphatically. "Not even me. What are you trying to get at, my dear?"

"Was there ever a man who broke her heart?" Kate wiped toothpaste from around her mouth with a towel and sat on the bed. No point in trying to be discreet anymore; Leonard was sublimely unhelpful even when he was trying his best. Trying to worm secrets out of him would have left her more clueless and confused than when she'd begun. "Or maybe someone who turned her down?"

"There was Nicholas. But I'm not sure he turned her down. I think he was engaged to be married to somebody else when they met. Just one of those things. Though I think she was rather fond of him."

"Nicholas?" Kate leaned forward on the edge of the mattress.

"Nicholas Sheridan," Leonard said as he squinted his eyes with the effort of remembrance. "Not her usual type. Very quiet. I liked him but it would never have worked, she'd have tired of him before breakfast."

"Why didn't it work out?" Kate asked.

"Darling, you'll have to ask her yourself. I really can't remember."

"Do you remember what he did? For a living?"

"He was a terribly good architect, now that I come to think of it. Built some wonderfully clever thing in Madrid. But like the best Englishmen, he was much more successful abroad," Leonard said wistfully.

"And he was engaged to someone else?" Kate looked at her watch and realized she had to leave right now for her meeting with Louis. She grabbed her purse, messed with her hair, and tracked down her cell phone.

"No idea what happened. Only that I wasn't invited to the wedding, if there was one," Leonard said. Kate often thought that he measured out his life in parties and antiques—anything that didn't slide neatly into one of those categories was likely to fall by the wayside.

"Oh well . . . feel free to hang out here as long as you like, by the way," Kate told him as she made her way out the door. "Just don't kill my snails. It's bad luck."

———

"Sorry I'm late." Louis rushed through the door at the Tate Modern and gave Kate a fleeting peck on the cheek. "I got stuck with a journalist from the *Telegraph* who wanted to know all about my show. I told her we had something very striking up our sleeves."

"We?" Kate asked.

"You're not going to turn me down, are you?" Louis looked concerned.

"No, of course not. Only I'm just the worker bee," Kate said.

"Couldn't do it without you." He touched her elbow and guided her through into the main room. "I'll show you where the piece is going to be."

Kate followed Louis up to the second level of the gallery. The space was huge, and walking with Louis—who had a special pass around his neck and cut through the crowds with authority and ease—made her feel just as she had at his flat yesterday. She felt distant from him—as she had when she'd seen him in the magazine and was somehow intimidated by him. There was something about him that made her feel slightly in awe. Which was ridiculous. He was Louis. But as she strode past the works of art and installations by his side she saw him as other people seemed to see him—a tall, strikingly attractive man with his naughty-boy black hair over his eyes, jeans that were slightly too dirty, and a scruffy, gray T-shirt. He looked bigger than usual, that was it, Kate decided. He had real presence. From his wrist hung a silver chain bracelet that she'd never noticed before. Maybe he'd been given it by one of the over-achievers. Though on second thought maybe he'd always had it and she'd never noticed before. Still, there was something about the way it hung at the top of his hand that made him look magnificently in charge.

"What do you think?" Suddenly they seemed to have arrived. Kate had to back up and take notice of the room.

"Wow," she said as she focused her attention and saw instantly what an incredibly huge, important thing it was that he . . . they . . . were going to be doing. "Fuck."

"Exactly," Louis said, moving deeper into the room, with its north-facing window. "In fact, now I know why I got you here." He turned to Kate and looked earnestly at her.

"Really?" she asked. Completely and utterly unsure what he was about to say. And of course it didn't occur to her for any more than a microsecond that he was going to say something unfeasible like *to tell you I love you.*

"I'm afraid," he said.

"Of?" Kate remained rooted to the spot.

"Of the piece. I think maybe that's why it's so important to me that you do it with me. I don't want to do it alone." Kate saw instantly that he needed her. "It's the biggest thing I've ever done, Kate. It's the Tate. Do you think I can do it?" He walked toward the window and looked out over London. Kate followed him. So much for the swaggering artist—Louis was petrified. She put her hand on his arm.

"Of course you can. They wouldn't have given you the exhibition if you couldn't," she said quietly. "I'll help you. I'll do all I can to help you. But I suppose if I'm going to, then you're going to have to explain to me all you can about conceptual art and what the hell it is we're supposed to be doing together. If you don't mind." Louis turned his head just enough to read the look on Kate's face. Which was one of baffled optimism. Clearly she'd said the right thing, though, because just a few moments later Louis had forgotten all about his stage fright and was instead leading Kate back down the stairs into the Turbine Room, describing in exuberant detail, with the occasional tap on Kate's arm to emphasize his point, the beginnings of postmodernism.

———

". . . This is Rebecca Horn. It's called *The Blind Conductor*. Can't you sense the desperate, frantic feeling of being blind by watching that wooden stick tap on the ground and then stop?" He turned and looked at Kate, who nodded. She could actually see exactly what he meant. They'd now been navigating the gallery for the past two hours and rather than beginning to flag, Kate felt as though she was just picking up pace. Each piece meant slightly more to her than the last, and with each artist she felt she not only understood, but also liked most of what Louis was showing her. Instead of being pretentious rubbish, as she'd imagined so much conceptual art was, the work here not only was mentally challenging but also moved her.

"You're really not bored yet?" Louis asked her as she gazed intently at the cane.

"No," she said truthfully. Then added tentatively, "But I am hungry."

"Oh God, you must be." Louis looked mortified. "You have to

eat." He looked around as if a sandwich might be lurking in the ether.

"No, let's wait a bit longer," Kate insisted. "At least until teatime. While we're here you have to finish my education."

"Are you sure?" He looked at her as if for signs of faintness or malnutrition.

"Completely. Come on." And so they toured the Tate Modern until Kate felt as if she might have taken LSD. What had previously been a tarted-up old building full of meaningless junk and strange contraptions was now meaningful. Granted, she still didn't have a clue why Louis wanted her to paint a life-sized polar bear for him, but in time it was entirely possible that she might.

Finally they ground to a halt back in the Turbine Room. Well, Kate didn't so much grind as collapse. Her stomach was wailing to be fed and she was dizzy. Not only had she not had lunch but because the house had been out of bounds, she'd had to make do with two triangles of Toblerone from her bedside drawer for breakfast as well.

"Do you think maybe we can find a packet of crisps or something?" she asked Louis as he stood back and surveyed the gallery optimistically. Doubtless he was imagining the private view and all the people who would be praising his work with glasses of warmish champagne in their hands. Well, *Kate* was anyway. When she wasn't thinking of her grumbling stomach. Louis was actually thinking of the dimensions of the piece and how they would be able to fit each one into the square footage of the room.

"Kate!" he said, as if he hadn't noticed her by his side for the past three hours. "I am so sorry." Then his attention snapped away from his work and back to Kate, who was leaning against a wall looking feeble. "And there's no way I'm going to let you off with a packet of crisps." He looked at her sternly.

"Oh no, crisps would be amazing. I'd give my kingdom for a packet of crisps to be honest," she pleaded.

"No way. I have a plan." He confidently pulled off his Tate Mod-

ern VIP pass and stuffed it in his pocket. "Come with me." But
Kate was not quite so swift off the mark. She remained pasted to
the wall, summoning the energy to move, until Louis noticed and
then came back for her. "I said come on." He took her hand and
gently tugged her away from the wall, back down through the galleries, and then out into the street. "Taxi!" He threw his other hand
in the air and a black cab sailed to a standstill right beside them.

"Wow," Kate said as she clambered in the back, "you're quite impressive when you want to be."

"Just you wait," he promised, "I'm about to get a lot more
impressive."

Louis, as it happened, unlike most of the men of Kate's acquaintance, was completely true to his word. For fifteen minutes later
they wandered past the doormen in bowler hats and into the foyer
of Claridge's. Standing there with the soothing sepia light enveloping them, they looked as if they'd just wandered off the stage of *Ok-
lahoma!* Kate was in her cowboy boots, gingham, and denim skirt,
and Louis looked as though he could have been riding bareback all
afternoon. They stood in the middle of the checkerboard floor in a
daze until one of the doormen began his approach.

"I think maybe we'd be better off in the canteen at St. Martins,"
Kate whispered to Louis. She would definitely have had more of a
sense of belonging around the corner at their old art college grab-
bing some macaroni and cheese.

"Mr. Alcott." The doorman gripped Louis's hand in his. "Very
nice to have you back. Are you well?"

"I'm great, thanks," Louis replied warmly. "And what I would
love to do is to take my friend here to tea. Are we too late?"

The doorman looked at his watch and nodded conspiratorially.
"Just wait here for one moment, Mr. Alcott, and I'll see what I can
do." He vanished like the Mad Hatter in *Alice in Wonderland.*

"They do crisps here," Louis reassured Kate, who was admiring
the Medusa-like chandelier that seemed to squirm in a serpentine
manner on the ceiling.

"Perfect."

"Mr. Alcott, this way please." The Mad Hatter returned with the flush of victory and led Louis and Kate through to the café, where a few ladies were just finishing their afternoon tea.

"Thank you," Louis told him as he helped Kate into her chair. "Good to see you again, Charlie."

"And you, sir," the Mad Hatter said, leaving them in the capable hands of a waitress.

Unbeknownst to Kate, one man of her acquaintance who was never as good as his word was at this precise moment just around the corner in New Bond Street. Jake had been standing outside the small casement windows of S. J. Phillips for what felt like an eternity. He'd been staring for so long at the canary diamonds, sapphires circa 1910, and ruby rings that had belonged to duchesses that his eyes were beginning to hurt. But not as much as his stomach, which felt like a butterfly house on a summer's day. He kept glancing beyond the displays of jewelry, gold snuffboxes, and *objets de vertu* to the men in dark suits who were sitting behind desks inside. When he'd left home this morning he'd known exactly what it was he wanted to buy. Now he wasn't so certain. Though knowing Jake, if he could have seen Kate tucked cozily into a booth with Louis in the silver-leaf, art deco haven of Claridge's right now he would have plumped for the most sparkling, dazzling diamond that his money could buy. As it was he couldn't see Kate, so he had gone for a short walk to the nearest bookmaker's, just to be sure that their love was meant to be.

When the four-tiered silver cake stand had first arrived on their table, laced with delicate egg-and-cress sandwiches, fondant fancies, and miniature éclairs, Kate had estimated that it would take her about six minutes to devour the lot. Now, as she took a sip of her Earl Grey and came up for air, she wasn't so sure.

"Okay, not only does this place look like something out of a fairy tale, but the food is magic, too." Kate leaned across the table to Louis. "This is the never-ending plate of sandwiches."

"You said you were starving."

"I was but this is ridiculous. Why don't you have another?" Kate inched the cake stand toward Louis. She hadn't even touched the crisps that had come in an accompanying silver bowl as if they were a rare delicacy from Jaipur. "Please."

"You don't have to finish them," he said.

"It looks as if I haven't even begun." She sat back in her chair and glanced down at her stomach, which was snugly nuzzling up to her waistband.

"That's the magic, like you said."

"So, come on, Louis. Tell me, how come everyone here knows you?" Kate had been dying to ask since they arrived. Every member of staff had practically hung out bunting when they saw him. "Did you live here as a child or something?" She wanted to make an E-louis-e joke but wasn't sure that a man would understand.

"I worked on some pieces here. A few bits of furniture, some of the glass. I spent a lot of time here. Just kind of got to know everyone." He added, "They were like family for a while."

"Now you just come here to impress girls." She winced almost as soon as she'd said this. She didn't really want to know whether Louis brought girls here, or anywhere else for that matter. Did she?

"Only the pretty ones," he said in a surprisingly smooth manner. Suddenly Kate couldn't seem to make Louis out anymore. Where was the shy man she knew? Perhaps he was suffering from a multiple personality disorder, she decided. "The least I can do is buy you a cocktail for listening to me harp on about modern art all afternoon."

"Okay," Kate agreed. "But I warn you. I'm going through my dancing-on-tables phase so you might want to keep me away from anything too pink or too strong."

"Caipirinha it is, then." Louis grinned and stood up. "After you."

There was nowhere in the world as reassuring as the bar at Claridge's, Kate decided as she sipped her way through her second caipirinha. Which was both pink and strong. The dimly lit room was coated in silver and sleek wood, and if there was ever an alien invasion Kate would feel safest here.

"Louis," she ventured, feeling truly relaxed for the first time all day. "Why did you hate Jake so much?"

"Ah." Louis tried to sound amused, but she'd caught him off guard.

"I'm sorry. You don't have to answer that." She backtracked. She'd been tipsy enough to ask the question but not drunk enough to be insensitive to how it made Louis feel.

"No, I think maybe I should," he said, and proceeded not to say anything. Kate looked at him closely as he peered down into his glass as if hoping to find the answer to her question. As he gazed into his drink and Kate gazed at him, however, she suddenly saw everything very clearly indeed. It wasn't that Louis was bipolar at all. He *was* shy and awkward and tongue-tied, certainly, but—she realized with the resounding thud of truth—only when he was talking to *her.* Immediately Kate wished that she'd never asked Louis why he hated Jake. Because the thing was, she already knew the answer.

"Because . . ." He took a deep breath and she saw his chest inflate slightly beneath the gray sweater that he'd pulled on over his T-shirt earlier.

"Because he was mean to me. Because you had to scrape me up from the ground of Sainsbury's car park. Because he was a faithless idiot who didn't deserve me." Kate leapt in so that he didn't have a chance to say what she'd just forced him to pluck up the courage to say. He looked at her very hard for a moment and she watched his chest deflate. The flare of honesty went out of his eyes.

"Exactly," he said, and stared at the melting ice in his whiskey sour.

If Jake had been looking for a sign that he had to marry Kate, he would have found it in the black cab that hared around the corner of New Bond Street and onto Conduit Street. He would have seen the sign pretty quickly if he'd witnessed his former girlfriend looking with new eyes at an old friend. He would have sensed he was in danger of being left out in the cold. But Jake was looking the other way.

"Come on, you beauty," he screamed at the television screen on the wall of Ladbrokes. "Come on Mickey Mouse." Okay, it wasn't as if the horse was called Love of My Life or Run for Your Wife or anything supersignificant, but Mickey Mouse was about as close to Kate Disney as he was likely to get. And she—the horse, not Kate—was flying into first place in the six thirty at Sandown. Jake launched his fist into the air victoriously and then went to collect his winnings. So while he hadn't seen Kate and Louis—God had given him a different sign.

"If Mickey Mouse wins I go straight back to S. J. Phillips tomorrow morning and buy her a ring."

He'd gambled with fate and Kate had won. At least that was how he saw it.

"Come on, Louis. This isn't some magical mystery tour. I have to go home. I have cress stuck to my skirt and I'm drunk." Kate giggled as Louis refused to break his silence. He was sitting opposite her in the backseat of the cab, defiantly looking out the window. "Where are you taking me?" she pleaded. He'd whispered his instructions to the cabbie as they got in. "Please not back to the Tate." She knit her fingers together in prayer and begged. "And not to dinner somewhere. I still have chocolate éclairs up to here." She slammed her hand on her breastbone to show how full she was. "Speak to me, Louis. Please. And if you won't then take me home." Louis turned around. Kate was looking imploringly at him. "Are you trying to kidnap me? Did you just offer the driver twenty quid to take me to Balham?" she asked as they made their way down The Strand and on to Aldwych.

"We're here." He smiled as the driver pulled up in the middle of

Waterloo Bridge. Louis handed him a note and he handed back a bottle that had been on his passenger seat. Clearly Louis had slipped it in when Kate wasn't looking.

"Okay, you're throwing me off London Bridge," Kate said as the muggy evening air wrapped itself around her. Instinctively she went and stood at the railings to see if there was a cool breeze coming off the river.

"It's Waterloo Bridge, you twit," Louis said as the cab pulled away into the traffic.

"I missed you, Louis," she said, and leaned her head over the edge of the bridge so she could see the water. She'd completely forgotten how much they used to see of one another before Jake had appeared on the scene. They'd go to galleries together; they even went on the London Eye for the first time together. Kate turned and looked at the giant wheel as it cast a shadow onto the water. Louis was looking at it, too. "You thinking what I'm thinking?" she asked quietly. The fresh air had taken away her shrill edge and she felt unexpectedly calm being here with him. Calm for the first time in ages—for the first time since she'd split up with Jake, since Mirri had arrived, since her interlude with Felix. It suddenly dawned on Kate that she'd been through so much stretching and pulling and molding lately that she'd barely been in her own skin. And now, as she looked down the river at the most heartrending view in all of London, with Louis by her side, she felt settled.

"We were miserable all those years ago." She laughed. "And I can't even remember why now. I was getting over some guy whose name I've forgotten and you were down in the dumps for some reason and we called it the Millennium Wheel of Hope."

"Yeah, we came for a walk here every Sunday before they'd raised the wheel and we'd promise that by the time it was spinning we'd be okay."

"And we were," Kate said. She really had rewritten history in her own head—she and Louis had been great pals for a while. Until Jake happened.

"Here's to being okay." Louis had been holding on to the bottle he'd brought from Claridge's. Now he lifted it up, and Kate saw that it was champagne. "I thought it was an auspicious way to start our new project together. Like naming a ship."

"Let's name our ship *Hope*," Kate said dreamily as she looked at St. Paul's and Big Ben in the fading twilight.

"Oh, right, 'cause that's original." Louis popped the cork on the champagne and gave her a teasing sidelong glance. Then, before she could protest or hit him, he thrust the foaming bottle in her direction. "Cheers," he said. Kate put her mouth over the bottle and gulped it down, trying not to choke. When all the foam had given way to fizzing liquid she caught Louis's eye.

"If you make one suggestive remark I'll push you in," she warned. He gave her a butter-wouldn't-melt look and took a swig himself. Then he leaned back against the railings.

"Are you still going through your phase?" Louis moved his head close to her head as they both watched a riverboat in the distance. She could feel his hair brushing against hers.

"Which phase is that?"

"The dancing one?"

"Oh, the tables!" She moved her head a fraction nearer. Any more and she would have been resting on his shoulder. "No, that was weeks ago. I think I've grown up since then."

"My loss," he said.

"Sorry."

"I'm used to it." He took another mouthful of champagne and passed the bottle to her. "Day late and a dollar short. That's me."

"Louis." She tried to sound stern but it came out wrong. Instead she sounded pitying.

"You know why I hate Jake so much, don't you?" He turned his body to hers. Kate only turned her face.

"Yes."

"Really?" He looked surprised.

"I only worked it out today. About an hour ago, in fact." Kate looked at her watch. It was nine o'clock. "A few hours ago, then . . . time flies, doesn't it?"

"I don't mind anymore," Louis said, and his dark eyes held hers. She gave him a quizzical look. "I don't mind being in love with you and not having you. I'm used to it."

"I never knew." His face was close to hers again, but unlike yesterday Kate didn't pull away. She looked at his lips, which were wide with a sharp Cupid's bow that looked like it had been carved out of marble. She remembered how she'd felt when she saw the picture of him in the magazine. As if she were seeing him for the first time and as if he were her secret and it was weird having to share him with the world. She felt like that now—he looked so strange and yet so familiar.

"Would it have made a difference?" he asked, and then looked away, knowing that she was going to say that it probably wouldn't have.

"I have no idea." She tried to see him objectively but she couldn't. He was Louis, he was indistinguishable from herself. "Hand on heart I have never, ever thought of you in that way."

"So all the times I thought you were undressing me with your eyes . . ." He laughed, and the tension between them vanished.

"You probably just had a bit of fluff on your sweater," Kate confirmed.

"Poor me." He was about to turn and walk off in a pretend tantrum, but Kate caught his arm and made him look at her.

"But now I come to think of it . . ." She blinked and then lowered her eyelashes, wondering what it would be like to kiss him, "I wish you would . . ."

"Would what?" They stood on Waterloo Bridge with the traffic trailing by and the odd tourist or commuter pushing past them. She thought about what she wanted him to do but felt too confused to ask.

"I wish you'd take me home." She bit her lip and felt the goose pimples rise on her arms as the breeze got up. "I'm freezing."

Chapter Seventeen

Kate was awakened the next morning not by Mirri hammering or by a naked man kissing her but by the sound of rain on the shed roof. It was drumming incessantly on the shingle and then sloshing into the gutter. She cast her mind over the previous evening to see what she'd said that she shouldn't, drunk that she wished she hadn't, or not done that she ought to have. Claridge's. Waterloo Bridge. Louis being in love with her. That was enough to make her open her eyes. Oh hell. Louis loved her. The thought made her want to run. And not because it suddenly made the whole thing incredibly awkward between them—she saw now that it had always been awkward for that very reason. Mirri had been right that day that she'd said sexual tension was the problem. Kate couldn't comprehend how someone as out of her league as Louis might feel that way about her. She thought about the hothouse girls and the sweetpea girl and how he'd strode through the Tate with her tripping along at his heel. Louis had it. Kate could hold her own as his pal but never in anything more than a tomboyish way. He made her feel nineteen—as if she'd still die of embarrassment if he so much as *asked* her for a slow dance.

She got up out of bed and put on the kettle, feeling overwhelmingly tired from all the champagne and cocktails, and then trailed back to her duvet without making a cup of tea. The air in the shed was damp and smelled of mildew. Today she was going to go to the estate agents and look for somewhere to live, there was nothing else for it.

"Got to get real," she said, and dashed over to the boiling kettle.

"Two sugars for me." She turned around to see Louis peering through a crack in the door.

"Am I disturbing you?" he asked. His hair was still wet and hung about his eyes in shiny, licorice-colored strands; his white T-shirt matched his grin. It wasn't often that Kate saw Louis's teeth, but they were unexpectedly perfect for such a laid-back man with a fondness for looking shabby. Kate was flustered. She hadn't even gotten around to recalling what had happened when he'd brought her home last night. Though she knew that they hadn't had sex, because that memory would have hit her like a sledgehammer to the head the instant she woke up if they had. In fact, all she could recollect was that they'd finished the champagne in the cab home and he'd seen her to her door. And that was it. No lingering looks, no kiss, no nothing.

"Did you sleep outside my door?" she asked, mentally computing what she was wearing. First for decency and then . . . and this was new for her . . . for attractiveness.

"I'm not *that* crazy about you," he said.

"Right. So we're obviously not going to pretend that the whole thing never happened then?" Kate glanced at him and was impressed by how relaxed he appeared.

"You're kidding. I've been wanting to say that for ten years. You've no idea how great I feel this morning." He took the cups out of her hand and put them on the counter.

"Are you going to kiss me?" Kate took a step back so that she could better assess the situation.

"No, I'm going to make myself a cup of tea. Since you're about as much use as a wet weekend at the seaside."

"I feel like I was taken out by a sniper's bullet and then had my brain sucked out through the hole." Kate shuffled back over to her bed.

"Caipirinhas. I ought to have warned you." He sniffed the carton of milk before sloshing it into the cups.

"What are you doing here anyway?" She flicked the heater on with her foot, pulled on a cardigan, and sat on the end of her bed as she watched him make tea. "Apart from the fact that you look good in my kitchen."

"I'm not staying." He handed her the tea. "I just came around to see if you wanted a lift into work?"

"Oh hell. I forgot." Kate moaned and flopped backward on the bed. "You're my boss." He sat down in the armchair and reached out to touch the zebra with his free hand.

"I also wanted to say that you don't have to worry about what we talked about last night. I didn't mean for anything to happen and it's not going to change anything."

Kate looked at him and suddenly felt shy in her old nightdress. "It's not?"

"I promise. Though occasionally you have to know that I'll be checking out your legs or thinking that your eyes are a pretty color."

"Really?" Kate sat up and pondered Louis—who for all his confessions and flattery didn't actually seem to her as if he gave a damn about her. In fact, he looked positively indifferent to her as she lay there in her practically invisible old cotton nightdress, which you could definitely see her nipples through. He nodded and took a sip of his tea.

"Are you sure?" She knelt up on the bed and noticed how long his legs seemed in her shed. They stretched practically all the way over to the bed.

"Only occasionally," he reassured her.

"Louis?" she asked, trying to get him to notice the see-throughness of her nightie. "What is it that you like about me?"

"Oh, I don't know. Everything. You're cute." He shrugged.

"Cute?" She scowled at him. "Like a puppy?"

"You're funny."

"Big deal."

"I like your nose."

"Louis." Kate sprang off the bed indignantly and stood up with her hands on her hips looking down at him.

"What?" He was clearly surprised at how feisty she'd suddenly become and looked faintly bewildered.

"I don't think you fancy me at all."

"Don't I?" He couldn't help but smile at her now.

"No. You think I'm cute. Like little-sister cute. You probably had a crush on me the first time we met because I looked after you when I maimed you but really I don't think you're in love with me at all." She was completely put out by the idea. As if Louis had somehow cheated her.

"Don't you?" He was enjoying himself now. And he could see her nipples through her nightdress.

"No. I don't." Kate's hands dropped from her hips to her side in defeat.

"Oh, well."

"What do you mean 'Oh, well'? Louis, are you or are you not in love with me?" she demanded.

"I'm in love with you." He could barely keep a straight face anymore. She was like an outraged child.

"I don't believe you."

"Well, I am."

"Prove it." She put her hands back on her hips and waited.

"Are you expecting me to die for you or something?" He sat forward in his chair as if thinking of his next chess move.

"I don't know. I'm not the one who's supposed to be in love." She frowned.

"Okay then." With which Louis stood up. He placed his hands on either side of her face, looked at her for a moment, and then leaned toward her and kissed her on the lips. It wasn't a long kiss but it lasted just long enough for Kate to know that she didn't want it to end. "Now do you believe me?"

"Perhaps," Kate said quietly, and this time *she* kissed him. Of all the things that had surprised her about Louis lately this kiss surprised her the least. Because for some reason she realized that she had always known exactly how it would feel to kiss him. She knew how he would taste, how he would smell, and how soft his neck would feel beneath his hair. She also knew that it had been worth waiting for.

Nick waited for the dogs to follow him through the kitchen door before closing it behind him.

"Shut up, you heathens," he yelled, and pushed one of his hefty black Labradors out of the way with his leg. It was eleven o'clock and he'd just made it back through the woods before the downpour had begun. Which meant that he and the dogs had to run across only one field in the rain. His housekeeper had lit a fire and he stood by the inglenook and dried his trousers out. The dogs barked furiously until he gave in and fed them.

"Okay, okay," he mumbled impatiently as he poured biscuits on top of their meat. Then he began to think about his own breakfast. He was supposed to be cutting back on the bacon sandwiches, but when it came down to it, he just never felt like eating the rabbit food that the girls tried to force on him.

"It's for your own good, Daddy. We just don't want you to die," Jasmine said whenever he looked like he might be weakening.

"Well, since you put it that way, sweetheart," he'd respond, and cram in another mouthful. At least there was someone to care about him, he supposed, but the lot of a single father was not an easy one. Neither was it a guilt-free one. Every time he had a cigar, one of the girls would mention throat cancer. Every time he had a second glass of wine, they practically checked him into The Priory.

"Somebody's got to look after you," Ella would say as if she were a hospital matron from the 1940s.

"And what about your mother. Are you as bossy with her as you are with me?"

"No, Daddy, she's got Simon to look after her." Jasmine wasn't as diplomatic as her sister, who always ended up elbowing her sharply in the ribs when she said things like that. Not that Nick minded. He was relieved that his ex-wife was happy. Everything she'd said was true after all—he was emotionally shut down, didn't know how to show affection, and would be happier on his own. She was much better off with Simon. The girls were the only thing in the world he really cared about anyway. As long as he had them he was happy.

He waited for the kettle to boil and looked at the front of the *Evening Standard* that someone had left on the table. And there she was. It was strange, he'd looked for her picture every day since he'd known she was back in the country, but it had begun to seem as if she'd vanished. Or at least as if he'd dreamed it last time. He'd glance at all the papers in the newsagents when he went in, he'd scan the red tops in the petrol station—but nothing. Until now. He dripped HP Sauce onto a picture of Tony Blair and stared at the photo of Mirabelle Moncur—walking arm in arm with a man young enough to be her son. But definitely handsome enough to be her lover—lest he try to deceive himself. It was the story he'd been waiting for:

Mirabelle Moncur Steps Out with Toyboy

God, they were so unoriginal, he thought as he wiped the goblet of sauce from the page and let the dog lick his finger. He didn't read any further. But what he did do was finish his sandwich and then go straight to his office, where he pulled a half-written letter from his top drawer. He glanced at it once, before screwing it up and throwing it into the bin.

"So what happened with Jonah the other night?" Kate asked as she added the finishing touches to Bébé's ears. The portrait was coming along much better than she'd expected. She'd been worried that he might end up looking kind of cheesy—but he didn't. He looked ruffled and beautiful. At least so far. There was still a long way to go before she was home and dry. She always tried to resist the temptation to do a few strokes of paint too many, as there was a fine line between finishing a painting and messing one up. Still, right now it was good.

"I love him," Mirri said as she came around the back of Kate's easel and stood beside her.

"So are you going to let him leave his wife?"

"I mean your painting of Bébé. I love him." She touched a corner of the canvas where the background paint was dry.

"And Jonah?"

"He'll be fine," she said lightly. "I told him that there was no point in leaving his wife. We can continue to have an affair. Although now she has found out so I'm not sure whether he'll be allowed out for a while. Still, I can amuse myself."

"Did she see it in the newspaper?" Kate asked. She had picked up an *Evening Standard* yesterday when she and Louis had been driving home from their slightly surreal day in the studio. A day when Louis was so cool and professional that she had begun to wonder if "the kiss" had been a figment of her imagination—until six o'clock, when Louis had dropped Kate home at her gate and asked her for dinner on Friday at his place. If it hadn't been for that, she would have been convinced she'd dreamed the whole thing. Though as dreams went it was a pretty good one—and when he brought her a latte and stood over her drawings and helped her to assemble the vast canvas, she was looking at his arms in a very unprofessional way and thinking of them doing far more exceptional things than hammering in nails. "It was on the front page," Kate reminded her. She'd thought that Mirri looked fabulous next to Jonah, holding his hand lightly with her head slightly lowered, her hair buffeted by the evening breeze, with her devastatingly photogenic young lover by her side. They looked iconic and enviable.

"I don't see how she *couldn't* have seen it." Mirri sighed. "Though to be honest she can probably make herself feel better that it's me and not some perfect twenty-two-year-old. And he won't be leaving her. So as far as these things go she's not going to suffer too badly. I've experienced far worse ways of finding out that a man was cheating."

"Still, not much fun." Kate winced. "So have worse things really happened to you?" Kate wondered whether she might be referring to the mystery Nicholas. Though that was a long shot.

"Of course," Mirri said. "Now, how are your sketches of me coming along?"

"Fine." Kate mixed her paints and squinted at Bébé's markings as he lay on the bed, deep in sleep. She was deliberating whether she ought to come clean about the portrait she'd been working on. She decided to take a leaf out of Mirri's book and embrace honesty. "Actually, there's something I wanted to ask you."

"Hmmm," Mirri said as she lay back on the bed next to Bébé and picked up a book. This was the new pattern for the sessions now— Kate brought her paints and easel up to the house, spread newspapers over Mirri's carpet, and worked on Bébé. On these days she would sketch Mirri as she read and then they'd break for chats and tea and sometimes they'd get a rush of excitement about something— laughing either about old boyfriends, the oft-mooted idea of Kate coming out to Africa to visit Mirri at Christmas, or simply a cute way that Bébé was sitting—then Mirri would race down to the kitchen and bring up a couple of glasses of champagne. They'd clink to something meaningless and then feel the crisp, appley bubbles at the back of their tongues as they sat back in the sunshine flooding through the vast open windows. It was the most enjoyable work Kate had ever done, relaxed and stimulating, and every day she learned something about life or history or people from Mirri.

Though Kate had to admit that yesterday had come pretty close in the enjoyment stakes, too. Despite Louis's business-like demeanor, there was still a feeling of mutual support between them. Perhaps it had always been there, but she was only just becoming aware of it, that feeling of warmth that could exist between two people. And even though the idea of *Kate and Louis* hadn't yet registered on her

consciousness, she didn't feel pressured into having to make a decision about Louis and whether she wanted to "be" with him, just
stunned by the passion of their kiss and thrilled at the feeling of two
people wanting the best for one another. Rather than being engaged in a constantly vacillating power struggle as she had with
Jake, who incidentally, only this morning, had sent Kate another
CD in a brown envelope. This time it was Ronnie Lane's "How
Come." Kate had hesitated to play it, feeling somehow guilty that
she might be encouraging Jake by listening. But again it was a song
she loved, and she did take the note that came with it and put it in
the wastepaper basket. It had read,

How come I ain't a superstitious fella but I love you so?

Kate had ignored the lyrics in a determined way and played the
song as she got dressed. Poor Jake. If anyone was a day late and a
dollar short it was him, she'd thought.

"So you wanted to ask me what?" Mirri said again as Kate tried
to get "How Come" out of her head, from where it was melodi-
ously refusing to shift.

"Well." Kate stopped painting and put down her brush on the
ledge of the easel. "I wondered whether you would mind if I did a
portrait of you rather than just a sketch. It's okay if you say no. I
won't take it personally, because I know that if you'd wanted one
you'd have someone else do it—but this would just be one for me,
to remember you and the summer by and to see if I could actually
draw people and not just animals and—"

"Yes," Mirri said plainly.

"Yes you'd mind?" Kate asked cautiously. "Or yes I can?"

"Yes, you can paint me."

"Oh my God, Mirri, thank you thank you. That's so cool. I was
so nervous about asking, I was sure you'd say no and I promise I'll
make it my best work." Kate wanted to hug Mirri but instead she
stood by the easel and shuffled about excitedly. She didn't want to
seem ridiculous.

"There's one condition, though." Mirri sat up on the bed and put her book to one side. *Oh, here it comes;* Kate half closed her eyes in dread. The rules: *No wrinkles, only smooth-like-an-egg skin; the neck has to look as if it belongs to a twenty-year-old; the pensive, far-away look will have to be a sultry pout instead.* Well, if that was the case, then Kate supposed she had to comply with Mirri's wishes.

"I want to commission you," Mirri said. Kate held her breath. "And then if I like it I will give it to the National Portrait Gallery, who have been asking for one for years. They only have photographs of me. So I will pay you. How is that?"

"Really?" Kate was stunned and thrilled. But terrified and fearful at the same time that she'd definitely have to airbrush out the crevices in Mirri's face now and also that she wouldn't be able to deliver anything to the standard of the National Portrait Gallery. *That* went without saying. "But what if . . . ?" she began.

"No what-ifs." Mirri raised the palm of her hand for Kate to stop. "I will not have a peep from you about not being able to do it or not being good enough. You will paint me as you see me and I will pay you twenty thousand pounds."

"What?" Kate almost fell through the floor.

"Is this a deal?" Mirri asked, without the hint of a smile that might suggest that this was anything other than a matter of business. Certainly she didn't imply that she was doing Kate a favor of any sort. Which perhaps meant that she really trusted Kate's work, though this was not a notion that sat easily with Kate.

"Absolutely," Kate replied, as she knew she must at some point in her life—with seriousness and self-belief. And in her head she planned the paint colors for her new house.

———

"I'm looking for something small. And cheap. But nice," Kate said to the woman with the slick blond hair and the remnants of a skiing tan. She had strolled into the estate agents on Regents Park Road on her way to buy a pint of milk. The office smelled of expensive perfume and the walls were hidden behind glistening photographs of stratospherically expensive houses with swimming pools and peach-colored soft furnishings that Leonard would have been deeply offended by.

"How much did you want to pay?" the woman inquired disdainfully, in possibly the poshest accent Kate had heard anywhere but a 1950s BBC radio broadcast. Kate hadn't thought that people spoke that way anymore, but it was good to know, from a historical point of view, that there were pockets of it still in existence.

"Well, I was thinking maybe . . ." And Kate mumbled a figure so far at the top end of her price bracket, it was almost obscured by the mists of fantasy.

"Around here?" the woman asked as she checked her cell phone for text messages from her Swiss boyfriend who drove a vintage Porsche. Doubtless.

"Well, I don't mind going a bit farther out of Primrose Hill. Obviously," Kate said meekly.

"Obviously," Blondie replied as she giggled at her message and keyed in a reply. Probably something about dirty sex and dinner at Sketch, Kate thought. This was supposed to be an exercise in liberation and empowerment, buying her first flat, with her own money, a place to call her own. Instead she thought that she might just have to move in with Robbie and Tanya after all.

"Never mind, then. If you haven't got anything then I'll just hang on, maybe until the market falls a bit and then . . ." She trailed off dispiritedly and was about to leave when Blondie clearly had a moment of clarity.

"There is one place in Primrose Hill. I mean, *just* in Primrose Hill. It's small. But it is incredibly, almost unbelievably cheap. Do you want to see it?" She pulled out a piece of paper from a filing cabinet, without moving one inch from her chair, and handed it to Kate.

Actually "unbelievably cheap" still managed to make it a solid fifty thousand pounds over Kate's budget, but it did look sweet. It had high ceilings, what was described as an "interesting" layout, and a roof made of something other than corrugated fiberglass.

Which, as things stood right now in Kate's life, was a marked improvement.

"I'll see it," Kate said. "Please."

"Sure," the girl said, and pulled out a Smythson diary. "I can fit you in on Saturday morning before I take a client to Chalcot Square." She said this so that Kate would know how low The Blondie was stooping to show Kate her hellhole of choice. Kate wondered what she'd think if she knew she lived in a shed. Unfortunately when it came to filling in her details Kate had to give Leonard's address, which was grand enough to make Blondie blink twice at Kate before reassuring herself that she must be the au pair at the grand house so it was okay to be snotty to her again.

"It really is supersmall. But I'm sure you'll be able to do something with it," she sneered.

"I could fill it with brooms. Like the cupboard it is," Kate said brightly. Blondie was unamused.

Chapter Eighteen

By the time Friday night came around Kate was yearning for her evening with Louis. It was strange that she was suddenly so excited about seeing a man with whom on practically every day of her life for the past ten years she could have hung out, but hadn't been interested in. But still, this was the way it was now. They'd seen one another at the studio almost every day as she'd progressed with the polar bear, but they hadn't so much as had lunch together. So by the time Friday arrived she'd been storing up every observation, every joke she heard, every thought she'd had to share with him. She wanted to hear everything he had to say, too, to lounge around with him in his flat and swap news and stories. She wondered if this was how all couples always were. Not that she was thinking in terms of couples right now, she was just dying to be in his presence for more than the two minutes he flew in and out of the studio.

"Are you playing hard to get?" she'd joked nervously yesterday as he dropped off a sandwich for her and checked out her work.

"Oh, I'm always like this when I'm in the middle of a piece. You know that, Kate," he said to her as comfortably as if he'd been married to her for years. Actually she didn't know that. She barely knew him at all, she was beginning to realize, as she marveled at the way he was revered and admired by the people who worked with him. All week people had dropped in and she'd overheard him chatting to builders, gallery owners, and the PR girl for the exhibition in a way that made him seem so far beyond her reach that she could barely focus on him, let alone recognize him as the Louis she'd known only a week ago. He was self-assured and jocular and they all loved him.

Kate hated the PR girl and hoped Louis could see for himself that her dress sense was cheesy and her cleavage the result of a clever bra—though she feared that he probably couldn't. But the glimpses she caught of him were perfect for building up the suspense of dinner. She wondered whether he'd cook or whether they'd order in and of course whether she'd stay the night. She also had hours and hours in the studio of climbing up ladders and outlining the polar bear, during which she thought of little else than what it would be like to have sex with Louis. She'd imagined them in every room in his house, every windowsill, every way, and a few more things besides. In fact, at one point she was so busy having sex on his workbench, with her left breast tumbling out of her dress, that she failed to notice that he was at the bottom of the ladder asking her whether she'd prefer mozzarella or ham sandwich for lunch.

"Any tips for my date?" Kate asked as she passed Mirri, who was lying in the hammock reading Flaubert while Bébé dug up Leonard's lilies in the flower bed.

"I think you will be just fine," Mirri said.

"I was hoping for a little more practical direction than that," Kate complained.

"Then just remember that it's the things that are most *you* that are most appealing," Mirri said as she shooed Bébé away from the precious plants.

"No, it's the things that are most me that are most *appalling*. That's why I need your tips."

"Okay, then remember that his balls are very sensitive and you should hold them and pay them lots of attention." She shrugged.

Kate cringed. "I was thinking somewhere in between French airy-fairyness and too much detail. But thanks."

"If the man is right you won't have to think about anything. His balls or your appeal. He'll love you for your experience, or he'll find your inexperience adorable. He'll love you for your dirty hair or your soapy clean smell. If you burp he'll laugh and if you don't he'll think you're a lady. You can't lose if it's love."

"That's much more like it." Kate smiled. "Now, what shall I wear?"

When Kate went back to her shed to get dressed, after a very lengthy and slightly heated discussion with Mirri about wardrobe, she found another of Jake's packages pushed under her door. It was the fifth day in a row she'd received one. Annoyingly each song was more beautiful than the last, and she had to play them even if she did make a point of ignoring the notes. Today's note seemed longer than the others; clearly Jake was reaching out, she thought cynically. Though when she slipped on Tammy Wynette and George Jones with their sweet country duet "Take Me" she felt the same tightness in her throat as she had every other day. She pulled the sticky note off the front of the CD and tried not to notice Jake's scrawl:

The very first moment I heard your voice, I'd be in darkness no more.

She turned up the volume and opened the shed door. If Jake had one thing going for him, she had to concede, it was great taste in music. But then that was supposed to be his job. Though it didn't stop her from sitting on the edge of the bed for a moment as she put on her shoes and thinking, for just the briefest of moments, of Jake in his flat flipping through his records, pulling one out, holding it carefully between his index fingers as he blew the dust from it and then dropped the needle onto it. She could hear the crackle of dust at the beginning of the recording and it made something inside her lurch.

"Probably just my lunch." She shrugged as she pulled on the other shoe and picked a thread from the rug off the bottom of her long, cream lace skirt. Kate had wanted to go short but as ever Mirri had been correct in her instinct.

"You must wear the long skirt if you're going to his house. If you wear a short one he'll feel as though he has hired you for the night. If you wear a long one it will seem as if you belong there," she'd said simply.

"Pretty song." Mirri tapped on the shed door before putting her head inside.

"Yeah," Kate said, hoping that Mirri hadn't seen Jake come around earlier with a package. She was slightly curious herself as to how and when he was delivering them, and didn't want to alert Mirri to the fact that The Slug was behaving in a faintly stalkerish way.

"Pretty skirt as well."

"Thanks." Kate did a floaty twirl and then picked up her handbag. "I suppose I'd better be off."

"Of course. I just called in to tell you to have fun." Mirri watched wistfully as Kate fussed over her keys and lipstick and purse.

"I will." Kate kissed her on both cheeks and was about to race out the door when Mirri sighed.

"Oh, to be young again."

"Mirri, you don't want to be young. You'd hate it." She laughed. "It's hell."

"No. I wouldn't." Kate looked at her friend to see whether she was being serious or just maudlin in the French way. She seemed to be intensely serious.

"Mirri," Kate said imploringly, not because she didn't have time to get into this now, but because she couldn't bear to see Mirri looking so defeated. "You're you. It doesn't matter what age you are. You know that."

"Sometimes I think that's true. But right now I wish I could have it all back."

"What, the panic and not knowing who you are and the worrying about men and other pointless things?" Kate tried to be logical but Mirri was talking about something much deeper.

"No, the time." She looked frail as she sat on the arm of the chair. "You go. He'll be waiting for you. Hurry." Mirri tried to chase Kate out but she remained fast in the doorway.

"You always said you wouldn't do a thing differently. You've done more living than any other human being I've ever met. Or read about," Kate added.

"I lied. I would do things very differently."

"Like what?" Kate took as step back into the room and rested against the sink.

"I just want it back. I turned my back for a moment and all my life had slipped away."

"But what? What would you do if you could?" Kate asked quietly and waited for the answer she knew was coming.

"I was in love with a man and we've spent our lives apart."

"Nicholas?" Kate knew that she shouldn't have said his name but it seemed pointless to pretend.

"Yes, you saw the film of the wedding?" Mirri seemed unsurprised.

Kate nodded. "What happened to him?"

"You mean where is he now? I have no idea."

"What happened between you?" Kate rephrased her question.

"Darling, you have a night out with a handsome man." Mirri roused herself from her torpor.

"I was going to cycle but I'll get a taxi instead," Kate said practically. Mirri looked at Kate for permission to begin. Kate moved toward the bed and sat down near Mirri. "So tell me."

"Really?"

"Yes," Kate said, and Mirri leaned back against the chair. Without moving her gaze from her knee she began to speak.

"It was 1974 and I was in London for Tony's wedding," she said. Then she thought about something for a second and looked up at

Kate. "It's not as though you go through all your days thinking about the love of your life who you lost, you know? You hardly notice it. You have lovers and you may even have a husband or two." She smiled wryly. "And you have fun. It's just that there are rare moments when your life is flooded with a kind of light and you see everything so clearly. Then you know that there is nothing else that matters. That as a person you're not made up of what's on the outside, that you're not the way you look or the things you own, you're not even your memories—you're just what's inside, perhaps that's what they call the soul, I don't know. But all that really exists of you is that. And that's the part of you where the love of your life lies. And waits for those moments when you realize that it's all that counts. All that's ever going to count."

"Mirri." Kate let out a deep sigh. But Mirri didn't want sympathy.

"And that's where Nick Sheridan is. He's in my heart or my soul or whatever you like to call it. And most of the time I don't think about him. Well, I didn't used to. I spent years not knowing that I had missed him for the last thirty years. I mean, of course I knew that I had wanted him, and I knew that I'd loved him. But not that I still did. Then late last year I began to think of him on evening drives in Africa. I'd get in the Land Rover and drive across my land and I began to remember him. Some evenings I would imagine that the reason he was in my mind was because he had just died and he was haunting me."

"I don't think he's dead." Kate recalled what Leonard had told her about Nick still working as an architect, though he had said he wasn't sure. But Mirri was hardly listening.

"Then I decided that it was just my life reaching the point where I'd done so much living that it was time to start looking back. The reflections of old age—though of course I deny them and dye my hair and make love to young men—I suppose they will always catch up with you. And it was then that I realized that Nick Sheridan was the love of my life. The man who shone out at me as the only one who really mattered." Mirri walked over to the sink and poured herself a glass of water from the tap. "And the more I thought about him, the more I knew that I had to come to England." She caught Kate's eye.

"Ha, so it wasn't my legendary skills as an animal portrait painter that drew you here after all." Kate smiled kindly.

"Of course it was, darling. You're wonderful." Then she stood beside the window and looked out onto the grass. "But I think that I must find him. I think I have to know. Do you think that means I've finally grown up?"

"I hope not."

"So do I." Mirri looked over her shoulder at Kate and smiled. Then she turned back to the window and watched the leaves on the cherry trees stirring in the breeze. "We were at Tony's wedding and he had no idea who I was, which was very rare then because everybody in the world knew who I was. Anyway, Nick had never seen my films or my posters or magazine covers. Today you'd say he was a nerd. He loved architecture and buildings and we were at an old church in Chelsea and he was examining the pillars and stone and I laughed at him. He was quite serious to begin with. Anyway, we talked and I liked him. He was sweet but he didn't have a clue about anything apart from architecture, I swear." Kate lay on her front on the bed and glanced at her watch discreetly as Mirri continued. She had to be at Louis's soon, but supposed she'd have to be a bit late. "Anyway, to get to the point," she said, as if she'd sensed Kate's close eye on the time, "we had a love affair. For one weekend. We talked and laughed and we burned with interest in one another and our lives. He was engaged to another woman who was at the wedding briefly but who left early because she wasn't feeling well. You probably saw her in Leonard's film. I can't remember what she looked like. Anyway, it didn't matter because he was going to break it off. We were so swept away by one another." Mirri's look when she turned to Kate was as naïve as a schoolgirl's. All her cynicism was gone and instead she just looked vulnerable. Like every other woman on the face of the planet who has ever believed a man when he lied to her. "And you may think it was stupid of me to believe that, but it was true. He would have done it. Except the next day, when he went to tell her about us, then she told him that she was having his child."

"Oh my God. Was it true?" Kate asked as she swiped away a tear with the back of her hand.

"I don't know. But he made the decision. And it was the hardest night of my life. And I didn't want to pick myself up off the floor of my hotel room ever again. But I knew that if I didn't move then and tell him that it was okay to leave me then I would never get up again. So he went. And that was Nick Sheridan."

"And you want to find him?"

"No, I don't *want* to find him. But unfortunately I have to." Mirri walked back to the middle of the shed, and the color returned to her skin. "The thing is, I used to think that it didn't matter. That unrequited love was somehow noble and romantic and better than a love that runs its course and fails as it invariably does. It was an ideal that I could never mess up and never tarnish. That's why it shone so brightly, I suppose. But now . . ." Mirri looked with indifference at her face in the mirror over Kate's sink. "Now I don't want to be like Jay Gatsby, standing beside the lake looking out at the light on Daisy Buchanan's pier for years and years, just being happy that she exists in the world. That's not enough now. I used to be comforted by the mere *thought* that Nick Sheridan existed. Now I know that it was just fear that kept me away. And I hate to be a coward," she snapped angrily at herself in the mirror.

"Do you want me to help you?" Kate asked, making a note to herself to read *The Great Gatsby* one of these days. She was longing to tear down the garden path right this minute and force Leonard to spill all the beans he had on the subject of Nick Sheridan.

"I want you to go on your date. We'll talk about it later," Mirri said tersely. "Now go. Leave. And don't forget his balls."

"Yuck." Kate scowled and then tapped Mirri on the arm. "We'll find him. I promise," she said as she and her handbag fled the shed.

When Kate walked into Louis's sitting room the first thing she noticed was that the sweetpeas had gone. There were no flowers on the table, just a bottle of red wine and a couple of glasses.

"Red?" he asked as he gave her a barely there kiss on her lips.

"Lovely." Kate took the huge balloon glass. She had half dreaded turning up to find the table laid in a candles and napkins cliché of a romantic dinner. But then she ought to have realized that Louis was much cooler than that.

"I bought some steaks from the Edwardian butcher. I thought I'd just put them on when we get hungry," he told her as he went over to the bookcase. "This is for you, by the way. If you're going to paint Mirri's portrait you might want to take a look."

" 'Lucian Freud's portraits,' " Kate read as he handed her a large coffee table book.

"Some of them are all right. You can keep it."

"Thanks. I finally have her permission to do it properly by the way. Which is great. No more sneaking around."

"Great. Only Picasso to compare yourself to, then." He laughed.

"Thanks for reminding me. She hates his one, though. Says it's in her kitchen in Africa." Kate sat on the sofa balancing her glass of wine and flicked through the pages of the book. "Mirri and I had a bit of heavy-duty talk before I left actually," she said. "That's why I'm late."

"You're late because you're Kate. Late Kate. You always are."

"I'm late because I was involved in a metaphysical discussion on the nature of love," she said, taking exception to the accusation. Then laughed.

"Really?" Louis looked interested and sat on the sofa opposite her. "So tell me about love, Miss Disney."

"Well, sometimes you can be in love for just a day or two but it can be the only one true love of your life," she said as though she were reciting algebra in school.

"No kidding." Louis winked. Kate blushed furiously.

"I keep forgetting."

"I don't."

"Louis . . ."

"It doesn't matter. Let's not think about anything. Let's just have our evening and see what happens, shall we?" he said, anticipating Kate's reservations about where they went from here.

"Is that okay?" she asked, feeling slightly guilty. Because even though his kiss had blown her out of the water and she'd thought of little else all week, she still hadn't had time to so much as ponder the idea that they might become a couple. And though it was as clichéd as the dinner table with two candles to say so, she just wasn't ready yet.

"That's fine," he said. "I've had ten years to get used to the idea. You have what's commonly referred to as a grace period."

"Thanks," Kate said, meaning it.

"So medium rare with chips okay?" He tilted his wineglass back and drained it. "I hope so because the menu here's not very extensive."

"Lucky for you it is very okay," Kate said, and followed him into the kitchen.

As Louis expertly threw together a dressing and salad, Kate sat on the counter nursing her glass and chatting inanely to him. At one point he needed to get a plate from the cupboard behind her head so she ducked out of the way—only to collide with his shoulder. The soft wool of his sweater grazed against her cheek and she felt the urge to nuzzle deeper. But resisted. She was shy of Louis no matter how clear he'd made his intentions.

"I don't think I'd be here if I hadn't met Mirri, you know," Kate said as she watched Louis slice avocado with a contented smile.

"What, here in my kitchen?"

"Well I might be in your kitchen but I wouldn't be . . . well, on a date or whatever it is that I'm doing here."

"Seriously?" Louis looked around for a second.

"I used to want to get married and have children and lead the same life that all my friends were. I don't think I even stopped to care whether I'd be happy when I got it. I just didn't want to be left behind."

"Oh, come on, Kate. You were never going to be left behind." Louis watched her as she swung her legs against his cupboard doors and gnawed away at a sugar cube she'd found by the kettle. "And stop eating that thing. You'll ruin your appetite."

"But that's not even the point. Sure, I'd like to have children by the time I'm forty, but why should that mean I have to rush into a relationship with some man who most likely isn't right for me just because everyone else is?" Kate wasn't sure if she should be so candid with Louis—she wasn't used to being honest with a man she was kissing—but she wanted to talk and he hadn't shown any signs of looking like she might be transgressing some sacred law, so she carried on. "There are so many different ways of doing things, that's what I've learned from Mirri. She had love affairs, she married, she divorced, she did all the conventional things but never out of a sense of fear. Only because she passionately wanted to do them. And that's the way we all should be, right? Especially now that we, women I mean, aren't socially obliged to behave in such a staid way. I just wonder why we all continue to do it."

"Well, some people *want* to get married and be settled," Louis said reasonably as he sought out some salad servers from the dishwasher.

"Yeah, but not all the people who do it want to. By any means. They're just scared." As Kate said this she thought how entirely opposite to this Mirri's situation was. She wasn't scared to *not* be in love, she was scared to *be* in love. Which was proof that everyone had their foibles—maybe the way things were turning out Kate could teach Mirri something in return for all that she'd learned. "Anyway, the point is I'm not afraid to be a bit different anymore," Kate said. "I mean, it's not as though I'm going to go and live in a castle and have fourteen babies by different men or anything, but I think that if that really grabbed me, I might be brave enough to do that now."

"Well, if you do go and live in your castle I'll happily sort you out with one of the babies." Louis grinned. "Now, shall we eat steak? You're going to need all the energy you can get."

After supper, over which Kate and Louis continued to discuss life and love and choices—but not themselves—they took their glasses and wandered through the flat and out onto the balcony.

"Louis," she said as they sat on chairs next to one another and looked out over the canal, which in the dark, when you couldn't see the foaming filth stagnating on the surface, almost shimmered under in the light of the moon. "What about other women. I know you said you've been in love with me all this time but there must have been other girls you've been in love with."

"There were one or two." He didn't seem to be at all uncomfortable with this conversation. "And it's not like I wouldn't have gotten by without you. It's just that I always saw so many possibilities for us."

"Like what?"

"Well, strangely it wasn't all about wanting to have passionate sex with you." He smiled cheekily.

"It wasn't?" Kate pretended to sound outraged.

"No. I wanted to hang out with you. I wanted to show you my work. I wanted to talk about yours. I wanted to go to galleries on Sunday afternoons with you," he told her as he looked out over the water. "I also wanted to take you to Florence and drink wine with you in little bars; to read to you as you sat in the bath. To do what we're doing now, just sitting around and talking. It's not very exciting, is it?" He turned to her at this point to gauge her response.

"It sounds lovely," Kate said. She'd been watching him as he spoke and she was overwhelmed by the sense of who she was that he seemed to have. He knew what it was about her that he liked. She was only just beginning to see things in him that made her feel the same way.

"I like the idea of the bath." She had been looking at his mouth and the way his long legs were sprawled out in front of him, crossed at the ankles, and she wanted to be entangled with him.

"Do you?" He raised an eyebrow naughtily and Kate was surprised by the ripple of excitement that she felt.

"I think so."

"Come here." Louis beckoned her over with a curled index finger, as if he were going to tell her a secret. Kate shuffled apprehensively in her seat for a moment and then got up and walked toward him. She glanced at his face only once, though; the rest of the time she looked at her feet. "Sit down." He took her hands and guided her onto his knee, where she sat with her feet dangling over one side of his legs. She put an arm around his shoulder and finally managed to look at him properly.

"Louis, I'm not very used to all this," she said, for want of anything else to deflect her trepidation.

"Got to admit it's a bit surreal." He laughed. "I can see the chip on your front tooth for one thing. I've never noticed that before."

"Oh, God, has it put you off me?" Kate said, and covered her mouth.

"Yeah, in fact I don't think I'll ever be able to kiss you again. It's pretty off-putting. Do you mind?"

Kate scowled and then hit him on the arm. "You're so rude. Jesus, Louis, you go on and on like a broken record about how awful Jake is to me but I think you're just jealous because he got to abuse me and you didn't."

"You got it." He threw his head back and laughed and Kate whacked his arm again. Only this time he moved his hand up to stop her. The next second she'd lost her balance and toppled off his knee, where she'd been perched pretty precariously because, well, she hadn't wanted to get too close to his crotch—contrary to Mirri's advice.

"Shit," she screamed as she hit the ground, using her arm to break her fall. Louis was up already by the time she opened her eyes and saw the blood that streaked her knee and elbows. "Are you okay?"

"I don't know," she said in a slight state of shock as she considered each limb in turn and whether it was still there, or hurt, or looked as if someone had poured ketchup down it. "I think it's just cuts."

"Kitten, I'm so sorry," Louis said as he knelt beside her and eased her leg from under her.

"That'll teach me to hit people bigger than myself." She winced.

"Here." He helped her to her feet and sat her in the chair. "You're quite bloody."

"Nothing's broken, though. I just scuffed myself on your horrible chairs. Do you think I'll get blood poisoning?"

"I doubt it." He grinned. "I'll clean you up. Wait here." Louis ran indoors and came back out with a dampened face cloth. "I'm not sure this is going to get the rust out, though. Ouch. Does that hurt?" He dabbed at the cuts and scratches, which ran down her knee.

"Stings a bit. Acutally I quite like the look of my grazes, makes me seem like I've been skateboarding or something cool." She watched the top of Louis's head as he bent in concentration. His hair was so dark and thick that she felt the urge to tug it to see what would happen. She put her hands underneath her and sat on them to stop herself. Then she remembered that this was Louis, so if she wanted to touch his hair she could. She reached out her hand when he wasn't looking then got cold feet and whisked it back again. She wasn't used to making first moves.

"Yeah, it's quite sexy," Louis said, and fleetingly raised his head, casting her a glance through his bangs.

"Do you think maybe I need that bath?" she asked suddenly. "You know, to make sure that we get all the rust out."

"Maybe." He didn't seem sure whether this was an advance or not. Kate held his gaze to let him know that it was. Then she took a deep breath and reached out her hand to touch the side of his hair. The next instant his face was level with hers and he was leaning down to kiss her. Kate lowered her hand from his hair to around the back of his neck and tugged lightly at his hair. It was so soft and dense, she got to her feet and the pair stood kissing for who knows how long. The next thing Kate knew they had moved indoors, toward the bathroom, where Louis had both the taps on full force and rushing water was flooding into the tub.

"Bubbles or oil?" he asked in between long kisses to her neck.

"Either. Both. Don't mind," she said as she slid her hand down his back and dipped it under the waistband of his jeans, where she let it rest for a moment or two, lightly stroking his skin.

"Bubbles," he said. "Spare your blushes."

"I don't blush." Kate wanted him to go on kissing her neck all night. Until he slipped the strap of her bra off her shoulder, anyway.

"You might," he said as he unbuttoned her shirt with both hands, all the while kissing her on the lips again.

"This is purely on medical grounds, this bath, right?" she asked. "So I don't get an infection and die."

"Yeah, it's a vital procedure," he said as he continued to undress her. And yes, she was beginning to blush, especially as her skirt fell to the floor and he unhooked her bra very deftly.

"For which I need to be naked." She smiled.

"It's better that way. Clothes tend not to work underwater."

"Right," she said, and realized that she was standing there in nothing but her knickers. "Now turn around."

"Do I have to?" Louis's grin collapsed.

"Go and find a book to read to me," she instructed. After which he gave her one last kiss on the lips, shot a very meaningful look at her bare boobs, and did as he was told.

The second he left the room Kate whipped off her knickers and leapt into the bath. The water was much too hot for her but she'd be buggered if she was going to wait around for the cold water to run. She took deep, scalded breaths, especially as she immersed her bleeding knees into the water, but the alternative—hanging around butt-naked and undignified in front of Louis, who was still comfortably clad in jeans and a sweater—was not an option.

"Byron or the *News of the World*?" he called out from the sitting room where he was madly scrabbling for something interesting. He may have been fantasizing about this moment for years but his imagination hadn't made it as far as what reading matter he might amaze her with. In fact, he'd never gotten much beyond the running water and her nipples in the steamy bath, he thought with satisfaction as he rummaged through his newspaper rack.

"Byron, of course," Kate called out. Though she hoped she wasn't missing an especially salacious revelation about David Beckham in the paper.

"Okay." He pulled down his school copy of *Byron's Collected Poems.* "Can I come back in now?"

"As long as you don't read 'She Walks in Beauty,' " Kate instructed him as he went back through the flat, which was never going to win awards for most private space in England.

"*Don Juan?*" he asked dubiously.

"Sure." Kate was now carefully covered with strategic banks of bubbles. "The only thing missing . . ."

"Is me?" Louis asked hopefully as he walked back in the door and settled down on the loo seat with his poetry.

"Is a drink. I think I'm in shock."

"So am I." Louis looked at the woman in his bathtub, with her shoulders peeping above the water, her ponytail dark and wet at the end and her knees poking out of the bubbles.

"I'll get us both a brandy."

"Good idea." Kate nodded and closed her eyes as her scratches and grazes were soothed by the water. "But could you make mine a whiskey?"

"Done."

"You can stay if you like," Louis said as he passed Kate a towel and watched her ascend from her bath as if she were Venus. He'd read a couple of stanzas of Byron and then the two of them had gotten sidetracked with the idea of Italy. Then a Greek island. By the time Kate's skin had turned pink and wrinkled, they'd escaped to live on four continents and more cities than they could remember. They'd gotten lost in so many dreams of where they'd like to travel together and treasures they'd like to see and sipping hurricanes in New Orleans and marveling over Canova's tomb in Venice. There seemed so much that they wanted to do, so many dreams to be lived, that Kate's mind was as light and heady as the bubbles in her bath.

"I'm going to go," she said as she kissed him. "There's a lot to take in."

"Too much?" he asked with a concerned look.

"No, just so much to do and so many plans to make." She laughed. "You know that's a lifetime worth of stuff we've just committed to, don't you?"

"Sure do." He gave her a hug and breathed in the smell of her wet hair.

"I'm glad," Kate said as she circled her arms around his waist. "I can't think of much else I'd rather do than hang out with you. For a while."

"I'll call you a taxi before you go too far and say something you regret." He laughed. "You don't give much away, Kate Disney, did you know that?"

"I'll try to be more open," Kate said, knowing he was completely right. That was partly Jake's fault and partly just the way she was made. "But I'll get better. I promise. If you help me out a bit."

"Deal." He took her hand and shook it. "I'll hold you to that."

Chapter Nineteen

Kate arrived home and found not another brown envelope on her doormat—but Jake. He was sitting on his jacket and smoking a cigarette.

"I only want to take you to dinner, angel," he said dejectedly when she emerged from the shadows of the garden and into the light spilling through the window from her bedside lamp.

"Jake. What are you playing at? It's three in the morning. I've had my dinner."

"Tomorrow then." He sat up straighter but made no attempt to stand.

"No."

"You look beautiful. Where've you been?" He looked at her with awe, as though she were some goddess of the moon.

"Out." She walked past him and opened the shed door. He tumbled slightly but quickly righted himself. Then he stood up and began to follow her in the door.

"Jake, you don't get it, do you? You can't come around here anymore."

"Did you get my songs?" He clearly thought she was Little Bo Peep and he was one of her sheep.

"I liked your songs. I always liked your songs, Jake. But they weren't the problem. Now please please leave me alone. There was this whole three-year window in my life when I would have been thrilled for you to follow me around. But now it's closed and I'm not thrilled."

"I want to give you something." He gazed imploringly at Kate as she shrugged off her shawl and dropped her bag onto the bed.

"Jake, do you want me to scream for Leonard?" she threatened. He smiled and leaned in close to her; for once he didn't smell of whiskey. He just smelled of Jake.

"Angel, Leonard sleeps like the dead and Mirabelle Moncur's gone out with her boyfriend on his motorbike. I saw them leave." Amazingly he didn't even try to lunge and kiss her. He stood up straight and looked remarkably earnest for Jake.

"You're creepy. Stop hanging around."

"I'd like to give it to you tomorrow night. Please have dinner with me? I promise not to do anything you don't want to," he said so seriously that Kate started to laugh.

"Jake, you're mad. Now go." She put her hands on his chest and pushed him like a bulldozer toward the door.

"You don't have to throw me out. I'll go. But for old times' sake you have to say yes."

"No."

"Kate?" he pleaded.

"The old times only count if they were good."

"Okay. The time I took you to Morocco," he said in a flash and watched her face. She remembered them lying on the bed for hours in the afternoon and talking and then sex.

"I came downstairs in the hotel after my siesta and caught you trying to persuade the chambermaid to give you her phone number."

"Glastonbury."

"Mud and tears."

"Venice?"

"Gondolas and tears."

"Kate, give me a break."

"I did. We broke up." She pushed him another two feet toward the door. "I want to go to bed."

"Just say you'll have a drink with me then. Tomorrow." He looked fresher than any daisy Kate had ever stepped on. He wasn't going anywhere in a hurry and she was exhausted. Plus, she wanted to lie on her bed, stare at the cobwebs on the ceiling, and think about Louis and the way he'd touched her. She closed her eyes and inhaled deeply.

"Okay. A drink. Tomorrow. But only one."

"I love you, Kate," he said as he lifted her hand and kissed it.

"I hate you, Jake."

"I'll pick you up at seven." He smiled like a child with a new bicycle and let himself out.

Kate flicked her shoes across the room. One hit the wall and the other landed in the sink. Two men had told her they loved her in the space of a week. She looked out the window and saw that Mirri had left her light on. She thought of her tearing around London on the back of Jonah's bike and smiled. She also wondered whether anyone at all would have told her they loved her if Mirri hadn't arrived in her life. There was definitely something of the lucky charm about her. Kate leaned back on her pillow and felt something hard under her head. Before she'd even looked at it she knew it was another of Jake's songs.

"Bloody hell, Jake. What are you trying to do to me?" she complained as she went to take it out of its envelope. Then she thought of Louis. She remembered how incredible it had been with her face buried deep in his navy-blue sweater and instead of looking in the envelope she Frisbeed it across the room. This time her aim was better than her shoe flinging—it landed squarely in the bin with a gratifying tinny thud.

"Where you belong," she said firmly then pulled off her dress and crept under her duvet.

———

"I've never been so busy in my life," Kate told Tanya the next day as they sat on a bench by the river and sipped cans of ginger beer on Kate's lunch break. She had run into Louis briefly this morning as she padlocked her bike up outside the studio. He'd been with some huge-deal guy from the gallery so he'd only been able to wink at her discreetly as he walked by, engrossed in a heated debate about the Chapman Brothers' latest piece.

"Well, I knew if I didn't hike down here to see you I might forget what you looked like." Tanya scowled jokingly. "So what have you been up to?" she asked. Kate's eyes widened.

"Oh, just work." She grinned then added devilishly, "And Louis." Tanya looked confused.

"Working for Louis?"

"No. Working *and* Louis."

"No." Tanya sat back.

"I don't know what it's all about yet. Just that I went to dinner at his place last night and we kissed. I feel so safe with him, Tan. But not boringly safe. Terrifyingly, excitingly, breathtakingly safe. If that makes any sense."

"Yeah, I think so." Tanya nodded. She looked as radiantly pretty as ever in a simple butter-yellow shift dress with a diamond necklace at her neck. Her hair fell in blond waves about her creamy cheeks, but her eyes were sunk into deep rings of translucent blue—suggesting that she and Robbie still hadn't had any luck in conceiving and the strain was taking its toll. Kate hadn't asked if there was any news, simply whether she and Robbie were okay. Tanya had stoically replied that they were fine, though he was going to his mother's alone this weekend, clearly because the incessant baby hounding was too much for Tanya to cope with, though a weekend in London with its ubiquitous, hip mothers with push chairs who littered the pavements and cafés and organic food stores of the city was enough to make anyone depressed. Whether they wanted desperately to have a baby or not. "So what on earth happened?"

Kate filled Tanya in on every detail of her slow-burning affair with Louis, though it was obviously as hard for Tanya to see him in the role of romantic lead as it had been for Kate.

"But it's Louis. I mean, I suppose he is fantastically sexy, in that baggy-jeans-around-the-bum, artistic way," she said thoughtfully. "And he does go out with the prettiest girls you've ever seen."

"Like who?" Kate was instantly insecure, though she was fully aware that it was true.

"Well, once we saw him at this drinks party at Saatchi's." She dipped into her horrible-looking sprouting salad with a plastic fork. "He was with this girl who I honestly thought must be some airhead actress because she was fluffing around practically wearing underwear and then when he introduced her she turned out to be the Middle East correspondent for Radio Four."

"Thanks."

"Sorry. But that's not the point anyway. Do you want to go out with him?"

"I don't know. I want to be with him. Every minute I want to be with him. And I want him to kiss me and look at me and chat to me and take me out."

"So you want to go out with him then?" Tanya spelled it out for Kate, who chewed on her lip and thought about it.

"I do, don't I?"

"Yeah, you do," nodded Tanya.

"Right. So what do I do about it?"

"I suppose you tell him. Isn't that what he's waiting for?"

"Well, sweetly he doesn't seem to be waiting for anything but if I think about it, yes, that's what he's waiting for. An answer of some sort anyway."

"Perfect. Then tell him tonight. Ask him if you can see him and then tell him. God, he's been waiting ten years for you. It's so incredible." Tanya completely forgot her own problems for the moment and rested her head back on the bench to feel the sun on her face.

"I know. I'll do it," Kate said excitedly. Then gritted her teeth as she confessed, "I just can't do it tonight."

"Why not?" Tanya opened her eyes and looked lazily at Kate.

"I'm doing something else." Kate screwed her face up tight.

Tanya thrust her head up and looked Kate in the eye. "You are not?" she said menacingly.

"I am," Kate replied sheepishly. "He wouldn't get out of my shed. It was three in the morning and he's been sending me songs all week."

"It shouldn't matter whether he's been sending you fleets of Rolls-Royces, beluga caviar, and Scottish castles, you should have told him to piss off."

"I did."

"What, 'Piss off, Jake, and by the way can we have dinner tomorrow?' " Tanya's eyes were filled with venom. Kate always underestimated the strength of her friends' disapproval of Jake until she was confronted with it.

"Look. I'll have a drink with him and then come home, okay? You might think that I've still got a soft spot for Jake but I haven't. It's over."

"Do you want me to come with you?" Tanya was playing devil's advocate.

"You don't need to, I promise. I'm not remotely tempted by Jake. There's so much water under the bridge since then," Kate said. Tanya looked forbiddingly at her, praying that she was telling the truth.

"So how's the house hunting going?" Tanya put her protests to one side for the moment.

"I'm going to see the place in Primrose Hill tomorrow morning. Do you want to come, since Robbie's in the country?"

"Yeah, I'd love to. Maybe we can have lunch afterward?"

"It's a deal," Kate said, and tossed her empty sandwich packet into the bin beside her. "How's everything going by the way?" she asked. Just because she couldn't *not* ask. The subject of baby making always sat between them like an albatross until one of them brought it up. And it was always better once it had been said. It was, after all, such a major, overwhelming part of Tanya's life that it was too odd not to bring it up.

"Things are fine. I'm doing a round of IVF so I'm being completely weird with the hormones. Mostly with poor Robbie. Though I did go out and buy an amazingly short miniskirt last week because I've reverted to being a hormonally rampant fourteen-year-old. So at least there's something in it for him." The girls laughed. Then Tanya looked anxiously at Kate. "If I get my period next week then it hasn't worked. And I'm trying not to think about it 'cause I know the stress won't do me any good but I can't help it."

"Fingers crossed" was all Kate could say. Tanya smiled. "So how short's the skirt exactly?"

"Short enough for me to only have worn it in the bedroom on my own so far," she said. "And before you ask, I won't lend it to you for your date with Jake."

After Tanya's practically allergic reaction to Kate's going out for a drink with Jake, she decided not to bother telling Mirri of her plan. She couldn't face the same onslaught and besides, it was irrelevant, because the last thing she really wanted to do tonight was see him. She did, though, have to go home and talk to Mirri about last night's conversation about Nick Sheridan. Mirri had helped Kate so much and now there was a chance that she might be able to give something back. Even if it was only the encouragement Mirri needed to find Nick. But when Kate got to the house Jonah was there, sitting on the bottom stair, chatting to Leonard.

"Hi, gorgeous," Jonah said, and grabbed Kate for a kiss on the lips, which was Jonah's flirtatious way.

"Jonah, it's good to see you," Kate said. She hadn't seen him for weeks. Obviously, though, Mirri wasn't letting the pain of lost love get in the way of sex with a handsome man. And Jonah was so handsome. As usual he hadn't shaved and his eyes glinted out from his tanned face. "Have you been on holiday? Your arms are the color of mahogany."

"A week in Thailand with the family." He raised his eyebrows naughtily. "Doing my penance for being a bad boy."

"Yeah, well, watch out being that color. Leonard might mistake you for a Regency table and put you up for auction," Kate said. "Is Mirri around? I wanted a quick word with her."

"Upstairs in the bath." He rolled his eyes. "I'm taking her to some smart dinner and she's taking forever."

"Woman's prerogative." Kate patted him on the shoulder as she walked by him and headed up the stairs.

"Thought that was to change their minds?" he called out.

"You won't have to wait long," Kate said then instantly regretted it. It was pretty much the truth, wasn't it? Quite soon Jonah would have to move on to the next pretty thing and Mirri, all being well, would be reigniting her love with Nick Sheridan. Though of course Mirri wasn't in quite such an optimistic frame of mind.

Kate could hear the idiosyncratically French sound of Johnny Hallyday drifting from Mirri's bathroom when she knocked.

"Come in," Mirri called out. Not having a clue whether it was the TV repairman or Nick Sheridan himself.

"Ah, it's you," she said dismissively when Kate walked in. Maybe she had been hoping for the TV repairman after all.

"Do you want me to wait till you've finished?" Kate asked, and took a step backward. Mirri was, after all, up to her ears in her evening bubble bath, her hair was wet and hung around her shoulders like a mermaid's.

"No, but I don't want you to nag me," she said, and turned off the dripping tap with her big toe.

"I just thought maybe you'd want to talk about what we do next," Kate said. There was no point beating about the bush with Mirri. She'd pretend not to know what on earth Kate was talking about.

"I'm not sure that I want to do anything. He's probably dead," she said glibly.

"He's an architect and he did something famous in Madrid. It's not going to be hard to find out."

"No, but it's going to be hard if he's married to a woman he loves." Mirri looked sidelong at Kate, who had tucked herself up on the floor by the bathroom radiator.

"I can find out for you and if he's married then I'll let you know. There are ways and means."

"I prefer to be direct," Mirri said.

"So direct that you've pretended he didn't exist for thirty years."

"What do you want me to do about it?" Mirri shrugged.

"Well, if you hadn't made it sound like the most romantic thing I've ever heard then I wouldn't expect you to do anything."

"I was being foolish." Mirri tugged her towel from the rail and pulled the plug out of the bath.

"You were being more honest than you've ever been before. Certainly with me anyway."

"So?" She stood up and wrapped the towel around her as Kate pulled peeling polish off her toenails.

"So"—Kate glanced up at Mirri's face—"I think when you're at dinner I should look him up online and then we'll discuss what to do next." Mirri stood still and looked as vulnerable wrapped in her towel as a child who'd just been rescued from a swimming pool.

"Really?" she asked. Though Kate knew that this was her way of giving her consent.

"Don't even think about it. We'll talk later," Kate reassured her in what she hoped was a light way. "You go and have your dinner with Jonah and I'll have my drink with . . ."

"Ah, Lovely Louis." Mirri tugged a comb through her hair.

"Not really," Kate said, loudly enough to be telling the truth but too quietly to be heard. Well, by anyone other than Mirri, whose hearing was accustomed to hearing hippos on the loose in her vegetable garden at four in the morning.

"Who then?" she asked as she looked in the mirror at Kate, who was now sitting on an old damask-covered armchair in the corner of the bathroom.

"Jake," Kate said flatly, hoping that Mirri wouldn't remember Jake and The Slug were one and the same person.

"The Slug?" Mirri spun around.

"It's just a drink."

"Why?" Mirri looked closely at Kate.

"Don't tell me you've always done the right thing," Kate began, then realized that excuses might serve her better than defensiveness so changed tack. "It was three in the morning and I couldn't get him out of my shed and he's been sending songs to me all week and I feel a bit sorry for him. Anyway, what difference does it make? I'm just having a drink with him. It's the intention that counts and I've moved on so far in my life that there's no way this means anything," Kate ran on breathlessly.

"Okay," Mirri said, "I understand." She wandered into the bedroom, where she began to rummage through her wardrobe, which was filled with enough vintage Ozzie Clark dresses and fabulous capes and shimmering gold-threaded African caftans to begin a museum of costumes right under Leonard's roof.

"Do you really?" Kate was taken aback. She'd at least expected a small war over the matter. Then she realized that Mirri had just shown trust in her, which was much worse because now she had to prove worthy of that trust.

"Do you think this one?" Mirri held up a chalky-green cocktail dress to her body.

"Yeah, that's lovely," Kate said. "Now I'm going to go and do my research and we'll talk later."

"À bientôt, cherie," Mirri said as she put the dress back in favor of a man's shirt and an old pair of Yves Saint Laurent smoking pants. She didn't want Jonah to be too hopeful of his luck tonight. She was tired.

"Leonard, are you using your computer?" Kate asked as she skipped down the stairs.

"Gracious me, no," he said. "Not if I can help it." Leonard was actually much more competent on his computer than he let on, but he considered it vulgar to be seen to know too much about technology.

"I'm just going to go online for half an hour or so," Kate said as she shuffled by Jonah and into Leonard's office.

"Help yourself," Leonard said distractedly as he showed Jonah a catalog of eighteenth-century fine art on auction next week.

"And if you're looking up nude photos of me," Jonah called out to her wickedly, "it's not the real thing. Just my head on some unlucky bastard's body."

"Yeah, don't worry, Jonah. I won't be looking." Kate settled down into Leonard's office chair and waited for the computer to make its welcome noise.

First of all she typed in Nicholas Sheridan's name. She looked down the thousands of results and swiftly eliminated the Nicholas Sheridan who in 1796 had been an Irish Flax Grower. She also mentally crossed off the Nicholas Sheridan in Year 12 who was a Math Olympiad somewhere in Glasgow. Then she came to a crop of results that sounded much more promising: Great Buildings Online. From Here to Modernity. Clearly these were of a more architectural nature. She found Nicholas Sheridan Partnerships and decided to click on that one. It had a royal blue and listed NEWS, PROFILE, AWARDS, and CONTACT. Well, hopefully if this *was* right she'd get to CONTACT later. She navigated her way to NEWS and found a list of buildings three pages long, beginning in 1975. God, that was practically historical—maybe he was dead after all. But she skipped to page three and saw that his firm's latest project, which seemed to be an airport in Switzerland, wasn't due for completion until 2007, which gave her some hope that he might still be breathing somewhere. Clearly, whatever else Nick Sheridan had done in his life he had stayed at the office late many nights because he'd designed more buildings than she'd managed to ruin paintbrushes.

"What are you looking up then?" Jonah walked into the office doorway, startling her. She doubted whether Jonah had any clue that Nick Sheridan even existed, much less that he was Mirri's lost love. But still she flipped the page back to a horoscope to be on the safe side.

"My stars."

"Load of nonsense." He grinned. "If it's love, you haven't got time to read your horoscope."

"If it's love, you wouldn't tease young girls. You'd be nice." Mirri appeared beside Jonah with a look like thunder on her face.

"Of course it's love." Jonah grinned at Mirri who clearly felt a bit guilty about having Kate look up Nicholas Sheridan. She changed her tune and smiled at Jonah as sweetly as she ever did at anyone, then threw Kate an anxious look.

"It says to expect interesting news of an old flame," Kate said meaningfully.

"What a load of crap." Jonah laughed and then pulled Mirri close to him for a kiss.

"We'll see," Kate muttered under her breath and flicked back to her Nick's pages a few minutes later when Mirri and Jonah were finally dispatched to their taxi and on their way to dinner.

So it seemed to Kate that Nick Sheridan certainly couldn't have had much time to pursue love affairs and marriages and a social life, because he must have been so damned busy for the past thirty years. He'd designed squares and parks and civic buildings and train stations and then a project in Madrid—that must have been the one that Leonard had mentioned. There was absolutely no doubt in Kate's mind that this was *the* Nick Sheridan they were looking for. Next she went to the AWARDS page—which was endless and ran the gamut from small and pointless-seeming awards for which it hardly sounded worth the bother turning up at the ceremony—like the Concrete Society Award—to much more impressive things that had very grand initials beginning always with *R,* which was obviously the Royal-something-something award. Nicholas Sheridan was clearly big time in the architectural world, Kate concluded as she moved on to the CONTACT page—the one that counted. But if she expected to find a house address, telephone number, and cozy-sounding e-mail address, Kate was clearly underestimating the might of the man Mirri had fallen in love with all those years ago. All that was on this page were his offices in Tokyo and London and some very intimidating and impersonal e-mail addresses. There was no way she could e-mail his international partnership and mention an affair that the company president had enjoyed three decades ago. So what next?

Kate went back to her search and looked for articles that might tell her more about the man than the buildings. She looked at Leonard's clock. Jake would be here in ten minutes and she still had on her jeans. Still, what did it matter? She clicked on several articles but only gleaned a bit about his views on development of green-belt land. Eventually she saw one that she knew would be more helpful—*House and Garden* magazine. There it was, the Oxfordshire home of Nicholas Sheridan, architect—a seventeenth-century manor house with a river running through the woodland and an art deco swimming pool and pool house. And while it didn't tell her any more than the other website about what he might look like or be like or whether he lived alone or with a devoted wife, she did know that his master bedroom was painted sage green (how likely was it that a wife would endure this, Kate wondered) with a bed-spread from Kurdistan. Now all she needed to do was call directory inquiries tomorrow and find a Sheridan in the "picturesque Oxfordshire village of Letcombe Bassett." After that it was up to Mirri, but as Kate closed down the computer she considered her research well done.

"Did you find what you needed?" Leonard asked on his way out to dinner.

"Sure did." Kate nodded in a satisfied way and felt relieved that everyone was going to be out when Jake arrived.

Chapter Twenty

Back in her shed Kate had fewer clothes to contemplate than Mirri. She couldn't be bothered to change from her jeans so she just took off her grotty T-shirt and pulled on a cardigan of Tanya's that she'd borrowed last winter. She'd worked really hard not to return it as it was one of the few cashmere items in her possession. While she waited for Jake to arrive, she flicked on the J. J. Cale in her CD player and texted Louis.

I'm out with old friend for drinks. Hope you're having fun. Thanks for last night. Kxx

It wasn't that she felt the need to inform him of her every move. Just that she would feel better if she was somehow busted on a night out with Jake and she'd at least told a semblance of the truth to Louis. But before she could agonize over the whole thing too deeply there was a loud, confident knock on the door.

"Good evening, Miss Disney." Jake was standing before her looking smarter than she'd ever seen him. He was wearing a shirt and jacket and possibly even had styling product in his hair. Kate took a step backward.

"Did somebody die?" she asked with a nervous laugh.

"What do you mean?" Jake appeared puzzled.

"Well, you look so smart. I've only ever seen you dress up like that for funerals or job interviews."

"No, I just wanted tonight to be special," he said, and kissed her on the cheek, despite the fact that she'd practically pinned herself to the far wall of her shed in order not to kiss Jake. Because even though he used to intimidate her terribly by being cold to her, now she was much more nervous about him being so overfriendly. It was too odd for words.

"It's only a drink, Jake," she reminded him.

"So did you like the song I sent you last night?" he asked anxiously as he watched her face closely.

"The song?" She thought back to last night but all she could remember was how tired she'd been. Then it dawned on her: He meant the envelope she'd thrown in the bin. "Oh, yeah. Well I didn't actually get around to listening to it. But I will."

"Did you open it?" He scrutinized her expression and Kate couldn't lie.

"Actually, Jake, I threw it in the bin."

"You did what?"

"I was tired. I couldn't hear another song that reminded me of you," she said honestly.

"Then you still care?" Jake's face lit up.

"No, Jake, I haven't been able to afford to care for a long time. But I do still have memories and they sort of tear me apart so you can't really blame me for not wanting to listen to your very pretty, sad songs."

"I suppose so." Jake began to look around the room for the rubbish bin. "But it might have been a bit harsh of you to throw it away."

"I'm sorry," Kate said as Jake located the wastepaper bin and sure enough, there, amid the rubbish that was thankfully only a few tissues and some screwed-up sketches, he found the envelope.

"I'll keep it, then," he said as he retrieved it and put it in an inside pocket of his jacket. "Waste not, want not."

"Good," Kate said. Thinking with only the faintest of pangs that he'd just give it to some other girl tomorrow night anyway. It wasn't that she wanted Jake to be all over her, but she had been secretly pleased this week that he'd put so much time into trying to win her back. It wasn't that she wanted him, or even that she wanted the pleasure of turning him down. It was just that in a strange way it made up for all the time he hadn't been sweet to her when they'd been together.

"Oh, and Kate?" Jake was eyeing up her jeans. "Are you wearing those?" Kate looked down at her jeans and felt the flood of old insecurities swamp her. Did they make her look too fat? Too frumpy? Too unfeminine? Or was it just that Jake claimed never to have seen a woman look her best in jeans? Kate cast her mind back and tried to remember. Then she stopped dead in her tracks.

"Yeah, I'm wearing these, Jake. I like them." It no longer mattered what Jake thought of her jeans or legs or femininity.

"So do I. I think you look great in them," he said hurriedly. "It's just that I'm not sure that you'll be allowed in . . ." Then he stopped. "You know what. Fuck it. If they won't let you in then we'll go somewhere else. You'll look hotter than any other girl there." He took Kate by the hand and led her out of the shed.

"Right. Well good," Kate said, with the wind well and truly taken from her sails. "So where are we going that's so fancy I can't wear jeans?"

"Just wait and see," he said, and led her down the garden path. Not for the first time, she noted drily.

"Your chariot, m'lady." He smiled as they walked out of the side gate and onto the street. Jake had rushed over to a 1970s cream Mercedes with the top down and opened the passenger door.

Kate stopped in her tracks. "Jake, what are you playing at?" She wasn't cross, just really surprised. He'd never pulled a stunt like this. Ever.

"I'm taking my girl for a night out," he said with a flourish.

Kate didn't move. "Jake, I'm not your girl anymore. You know that." She was concerned and a little bored at having to cover this old ground yet again.

"I know," Jake said, "but will you get in anyway? We're late."

"Jake, we're going for a quick drink. That was the deal," Kate reminded him as she got into the car and he walked around to the driver's seat. "Whose car is this, by the way?"

"Enough questions, angel. Let's just have some fun, shall we?" He turned the keys in the ignition and pulled out into the traffic.

"So I'm going to look at a flat in Primrose Hill tomorrow," Kate said to fill the dreamy silence that Jake seemed to have fallen into. "All part of moving on, you know. Growing up and getting out of the shed."

"Sounds good," he said, but his mind was elsewhere.

"So how's the music going? Any joy with those distributors who were interested?" She was trying to be as all-business as possible.

"Yeah, it's fine. Music's fine," he said as they drove along with the warm evening breeze whipping through their hair. He was playing with the stereo and at that moment a Nick Drake song, as haunting as the others he'd sent, filled the car. Kate wondered whether this had been the song in the envelope last night. She guessed she'd never find out now.

"Where exactly are we going?" she asked as they drove south toward Chelsea.

"You'll find out."

"Jake . . . I can't be out too late. I've got an early start tomorrow," Kate complained.

"I won't keep you out." He put his hand somewhere near his heart and promised.

Ten minutes later, after Kate had tried and failed to converse with Jake and had eventually given up and succumbed to Nick Drake's absurdly, and for Kate irritatingly, romantic "Northern Skies," Jake stopped the car and parked by the pavement next to the river.

"Here we are." He got out and came to open her door but Kate had managed to get out herself already and was looking around to see if there was a nearby pub that they might be going to. For a moment she was relieved. At least there were no swanky restaurants or fabulous bars around here, so clearly Jake wasn't planning to wow her too well. Jake pulled the roof up on the car and locked it.

"Where are we going, then?" Kate asked. "And why wasn't I allowed to wear jeans?"

"I was going to stop off at the Blue Bar for cocktails first but you seemed a bit impatient"—he winked at her—"and inappropriately dressed. So I thought we'd come straight here."

"Here being which pub, then?" Kate asked, almost wishing they had gone to the Blue Bar—the cocktails there were spectacularly good and always put her in the best mood.

"Angel, have you got so little faith in me?" Jake laughed and then ushered her toward the wall overlooking the river.

"Oh, Jake." She couldn't help herself from blurting out when she realized what he'd planned. "Don't tell me . . ."

"This way," he said as he led her onto a small jetty and down to a houseboat. "It looks a bit rotten but I'm told it's completely safe." He jumped onto the deck of a racing green houseboat with flaking paint and held out his hand to help Kate down. The sun was bouncing off the ripples on the water; the only sound was the soft, rhythmic lapping of small waves against the side of the boat and the neighboring vessels, which all seemed to be deserted.

"Jake . . . ," she began to protest. But then she noticed that there was a picnic blanket at the prow and on it was an ice bucket with a bottle inside it and two glasses next to it.

"I thought we could watch the sun set on the river."

"I thought we were going out for a quick drink," she said sternly, wondering whether she ought to just turn back now and tell him to take her home. But his eyes were so soulful and excited to see her reaction that she just couldn't.

"We are. I just wanted it to be nice," he said. "Now, come and look at the view from the top deck."

Kate followed Jake around the boat and he held her hand the entire time to make sure that she didn't fall through holes or overboard. He led her down the steps into the cabin, showed her the kitchen which was doll-like in size, and then he showed her the berth and bed, without once making her feel uncomfortable or as if he was about to pounce. Which was a good thing because if he had she would just have hit him over the head with a saucepan and headed straight for the Embankment to hail the nearest taxi.

"Drink then?" he asked as they emerged into the golden light of the sunset from the dark, mildew smell of belowdecks.

"I suppose so." Despite being a decaying heap the boat was pretty enchanting and definitely the kind of place Jake loved. And though she didn't want to admit it to herself it was the kind of place she loved, too. In her early twenties she'd longed to live on a houseboat, and had even gone so far as to look into renting one, but her bourgeois nature got the better of her when she learned that you couldn't get insurance for them so if they sunk you were scuppered. Still, it was so beautiful here now and she wondered whether she ought to want to be here with Louis. But it was such a Jake thing that she couldn't imagine it.

"Cheers," he said as he handed her a glass of champagne.

"Cheers." Kate sat down on the blanket, because it looked dry, and couldn't quite believe that for a second time this week she was drinking champagne with a man overlooking the river. Perhaps Mirri was her fairy godmother who'd arrived twenty-nine years too late, she thought as she grinned at the latest twists in her boring, shed dweller's life.

"So I know you think we've said it all, but I have a few things I want to tell you," Jake said without even taking a sip of his drink. Which made Kate nervous enough to practically bolt hers down in one hit.

"Oh, come on, Jake. Let's just have fun like you said. It's not as though both of us haven't moved on. We don't need to go over all the things that went wrong. Let's just look to the future."

"I have. That's why I brought you here." Jake looked unusually serious. Kate winced and took another large mouthful of her drink. Just enough to take the edge off her fear, anyway.

"Kate, I've missed you," he began.

"Please, Jake, don't," she interrupted. "Let's just look at the sunset."

But he was like a ship in full sail and wouldn't be silenced. "I didn't realize at first that I was missing you but when I did I had to do a lot of thinking. About how I'd treated you over the years. About how much you meant to me. About the fact that I've never gotten on with any other woman as well as you. You were my best friend, Kate," Jake said. Then he smiled at her, with the look of dread etched on her face as she helped herself to another glass of champagne. "And I also loved you." Kate looked for the first time that night at his face and was surprised to see that nothing had changed. She claimed to hate him now but it was still the same face that until very recently she had been mad about. The face of the man who had broken her heart but kept her hanging on long after she ought to have left. Maybe she'd expected him to have changed by now—to have become less attractive to her because she'd finally decided that she didn't want him and his behavior was too despicable to bear—but he hadn't changed. His eyes were still the same and his lips were still the lips she had loved to kiss. He was still Jake and she suddenly wasn't sure whether she'd ever stopped loving him at all. Or whether she'd just been momentarily distracted by the sheer fun and novelty of Felix and Louis having crushes on her.

"Jake, don't," she pleaded as she realized that she just might be in real trouble here.

"Kate, I know what I was like and I couldn't help it. But I am sorry and things will be different from now on." He tried to take her hand but she kept it determinedly in her lap.

"No, things won't be different. It's over," she said as gently but firmly as possible.

"I love you. More than I've ever loved anyone. And if you just give me a chance I'll try so hard to be what you want me to be."

She'd never seen him so sincere and so vulnerable and she found it painful and disconcerting.

"I wanted you to be you. But nice to me. That was all I ever wanted, Jake. But I don't think you're capable of ever changing. And even if you were, I'm not the girl for you. If I had been you'd have known from the start that I was and you'd have known that you loved me. You're just panicking now because you're about to lose me."

"I can't lose you, Kate." He looked as if he might cry. Kate took a deep breath and let him hold her hand. They looked as far into one another's eyes as it was possible to see for a long moment and then he reached into his inside pocket. He lifted out the envelope and glanced at it closely before handing it to Kate. "This is for you."

"Can I open it later?" Kate asked as she felt his fingers squeeze hers hard enough to bruise them.

"Kate, you're the sweetest, mellowest girl I've ever met. You've been an angel to me and I know I'm not easy." Jake paused and gave a hint of a smile. "In fact, I know I'm the meanest, most difficult guy you've ever come across. But I do love you. And I want to be with you. Forever."

"Jake . . ." Tears sprang to her eyes. She brushed them aside with her knuckles and tried not to be in love with him. She tried to concentrate on how happy and at ease she felt with Louis, how sexy she'd felt with Felix, and how she'd never felt either of these things with Jake. But then she finally had to admit to herself that there had been good times—the best times even—it's just that she'd had to block them out in the name of self-preservation. And the instant she realized what she'd done the deluge of amazing memories and good times and love for Jake washed over her with the force of a tidal wave. She was sucked in and swirled under and pummelled by the remembrance of every kiss and every time he'd cracked her up laughing and the times he'd held her so tightly in bed in the morning that she got dead arms and could hardly breathe. He really did love her and he really did want her. But he'd fucked up so many times that she hadn't allowed herself to see this anymore.

Jake must have known precisely what was going through Kate's mind because just as she was being lashed by waves of memory he took her drink from her hand, put it on the blanket beside her, and kissed her as if both their lives and the future of the planet depended on it. She didn't know whether he was sucking life from her or breathing it into her but she felt faint with the intensity of it.

"Open the envelope, angel," he said to her when they'd both drawn away in light-headed amazement.

"Okay." Kate picked it up and ran her finger along the seal, all the while not taking her eyes off him. She finally got it open with her trembling fingers and reached inside with her hand. She felt for the CD to slide out but there wasn't one. She searched the small, bubble-lined envelope harder but nothing. Until she came across a small, hard nugget in the bottom corner.

"Jake, there's no CD, it's . . ." she began as she numbly lifted the thing from the wrapping.

It was a ring—a white gold ring with a round emerald and three diamonds on either side. Kate dropped it on the ground.

"No," she said, more in shock than refusal.

"Here." Jake put his hand out and picked up the ring. He held it out in front of Kate, who just stared at it. "It's for you," Jake said calmly, not taking his eyes off her. "I want you to marry me. Please." They were words that Kate had waited so, so long to hear. She'd imagined this moment on just about every hill they'd climbed together; she'd pictured it happening as they sat on a log in the woods one Sunday afternoon; she'd thought that it could have taken place in Paris or on the motorway on the way home from a long and blissful day out in summer. Then she'd given up hope altogether. And now here they were on a lilting green houseboat on the Thames and it had just happened and she suddenly hadn't the faintest idea whether she wanted to marry Jake or not.

"It's a very pretty ring," she said in a practical, Daisy-Pulls-It-Off way.

"It's a 1930s sugarloaf, cabochon emerald," Jake told her, as if he'd been rehearsing for days. "Kate, will you marry me?" He had the ring in between his fingers now, ready to slide it onto her ring finger if she said yes. But she was mute. She couldn't think of a thing to say.

"I love you."

"I . . . I just have no idea." Kate was flummoxed. It was as if someone had asked her to answer an incredibly complex mathematical equation and she knew that she could work it out given time. Just not right this second.

"Say yes and I promise I'll make everything okay. Whatever we have to go through again in our lives we'll never be alone. We'll always be together. From the moment I put this ring on your finger." Jake was biting his lip and looking imploringly at her. She closed her eyes in her desperate search for a clue as to what to do.

"Really?" she asked. She'd meant to ask a more profound and taxing question. Like *What makes you think this will make any difference to our dysfunctional relationship?* or *Will this stop you from wanting what you haven't got in the future?* But she wasn't capable of forming the words. Instead she was tugged under by the riptide again and all she could feel were old feelings—of love, of longing and remembering how she would have given anything to be the girl she was now: the girl sitting on the deck of a boat in her jeans and old cashmere, being offered a stunning emerald ring by Jake, who wanted to spend the rest of his life with her.

"We need to be together, Kate, you're the only thing that gives meaning to my life." Well, that was Jake's needs taken care of. But what, Kate struggled to ask herself, was in it for her? Well, Jake of course. The one and only thing she'd ever truly wanted. Until a month ago anyway.

Then, just as she was about to do the sensible thing and tell him that she needed some time to mull over her decision, a terrible thought struck Kate. What if she was as bad as Jake? What if she had wanted Jake only because she never really had him? What if now he was here, asking her to love him, she had decided to flake on the whole thing? Certainly it wasn't as though anything had happened to really change her mind about Jake—apart from the fact that recently the balance of desire had shifted in her favor. There was Louis, of course, and as recently as two hours ago she'd thought she might want to be with him. But then again she might not like Louis next week—she might go through her entire life never meeting anyone again whom she loved as much as Jake. Her feelings for Louis hadn't stood the test of a week, let alone three years. If she were going to be sensible she wouldn't even factor him in the equation. All she had to think about was how she would feel about spending the rest of her life with Jake. Day in, day out. Waking up with him each morning. Having him be the father to her children. Watching him sprout hairs from his nose and gradually grow deaf. She'd told herself a long time ago that she could and would love Jake into old age. Until the day she died. So what had changed, she wondered. She thought hard and looked at the ring. Nothing. Absolutely nothing had changed. Had it? She loved Jake as much as she always had. Of course she did. Nothing else made sense.

"Yes, I will," she said before she could think again. It was like jumping off the high board into a swimming pool. Once you'd stepped off the edge you were free-falling into a future you had no control over.

"You won't?" Jake looked at her with disbelief. Obviously she'd done a very good job of looking dubious and reluctant.

"I will." She said it with more conviction this time.

"You'll marry me?" Jake had hold of her arms now, as if he was about to shake her. He was staring at her.

"Yes, I'll marry you." She laughed, almost hysterical with the realization of what she was saying. She was also completely carried away in the moment—in the idea that after twenty-nine years of living on this earth, she, Kate Disney, was going to get married. Quite apart from anything else it was a complete trip.

"Bloody hell." Jake said as he took the ring in his hand and slipped it onto Kate's shaking finger. "We're getting married." And then they hugged one another so tightly that there was barely room for air between them, and they cried. Until eventually Kate pulled her soaked face away from the damp wool lapel of his jacket.

"Your jacket smells like sheep." She sniffed back her tears.

"Does it?" Jake lifted his collar to his nose. "Yeah, you're right. It does."

"That's what happens when wool gets wet," Kate informed him. Then they both looked at one another in utter shock. They weren't sure whether to be embarrassed or happy or terrified by what had just happened to them.

"You've got snot on your nose," Jake said, and pulled a tissue out of his jeans pocket.

"How attractive." Kate took the tissue and wiped her nose. "Anyway it's not snot, it's emotion." She giggled.

"Yeah, right," Jake teased and then kissed her on the end of her nose. "It's beautiful. You're beautiful. I love you," he said hurriedly.

"I love you, too," Kate said. Then realized that it was the first time she'd ever told Jake that she loved him.

Chapter Twenty-one

How was she going to tell everyone? This was the second thought Kate had in the morning when she woke up in the stiff cotton sheets of the boat's berth. It was just getting light outside, which for English summertime probably meant that it wasn't much later than five A.M. Kate burrowed deeper into Jake, who was folded around her body. The first thought she'd had was that there was something uncomfortable digging into her cheek. She pulled her hand where it had been sandwiched between her face and the pillow and saw that her engagement ring was the culprit.

Her engagement ring. For a second her heart stopped. Then she held her hand out in front of her, careful not to disturb Jake, who was wrapped around her like a python, and examined it. It was, above and beyond its prodigious emotional significance, which she couldn't comprehend right now, a very lovely thing. It was smooth and the color of a forest in sunlight. Kate tapped her tooth against it to see how it felt. Then she ran her tongue along it. She looked at it one more time and then finally buried it back beneath her cheek. Jake had proposed to her last night and she'd said yes. Then they'd sat on the blanket on the deck and looked for stars but it was cloudy and the lights from the city meant that they couldn't see a thing. Still, the moon was bright and the evening was balmy and they'd sat up for hours in a state of shock and discussed everything from what they were going to call their children to where they'd go on holiday when they were sixty years old. It was the first time Kate had ever been free to indulge her dreams of a future with Jake, even though she knew all the answers already because she'd thought about these things a million times before. So they'd talked until the air became damp and cool and they'd retreated to the berth. They hadn't even had sex afterward, they'd simply fallen asleep midsentence as they talked about the idea of an engagement party.

If Kate remembered correctly they'd decided that they were going to have an intimate celebration in Leonard's garden this Sunday. They'd invite all the people they had time to invite and not make a big fuss over it. They'd save the fuss for the wedding. Which was going to have a musical theme and to which Kate would wear Janis Joplin's boots beneath her dress. She hadn't been entirely convinced of this last detail but couldn't remember whether she'd won the argument or not because she'd been so wiped out at that point that her brain was no longer functioning.

"Good morning, angel." Jake kissed the back of her neck and Kate felt a wave of happiness settle over her.

"Hi, handsome." She half turned her head so that she could kiss his hair, at least.

"You haven't changed your mind have you?" he whispered.

"Surprisingly not."

"Good. Because I meant every word I said last night. I love you and want to spend the rest of my life with you."

"Jake?" Kate asked as she shuffled over until she was facing him.

"Yes?"

"What made you decide you wanted to marry me?"

"Apart from the fact that you're beautiful and charming and you love me like nobody else could?" He stroked her hair back from her face.

"Apart from those things."

"Fate," he said simply. Because saying that he'd gambled and she'd won didn't seem like the right answer just now.

"Were you drunk?"

"No."

"Then why?"

"Because I love him."

"No you don't."

"I never stopped loving him. I realize that now."

"You can't go through with it."

"I can. I will. I want to."

"Then you're mad."

Kate had gone straight to Mirri's room after Jake had dropped her off.

"Don't you want me to come in with you so we can tell everyone our news?" he'd asked her before she'd hopped out of the car.

"*Break* the news to them, more like," Kate said ruefully. "You've hardly been the most popular person around here lately."

"Yeah, but when they see how much I love you, when I tell them, they'll be thrilled for us," he said optimistically.

"Let's save the thrills for tomorrow night," Kate said as she leaned over and kissed her fiancé.

"Whatever you say, angel." He took her left hand between his hands and gazed at the ring. "I've got the rest of my life with you. I can wait until tomorrow to show you off."

"I'll call you later. After I've seen the flat," Kate told Jake as she opened the car door. Much as she didn't want to leave his side right now, her stomach was churning like a washing machine with nerves. First she'd tell Mirri. Then Leonard. Then she'd call her mother. She wasn't doing it in order of importance—simply getting the worst bits out of the way first. Her mother was likely to be most tolerant and happy, as she knew Jake the least. Oh, hell, and what about Robbie and Tanya? Kate looked at Jake and was about to suggest they elope when she noticed the curtain twitch in Mirri's bedroom. Too late.

"See you soon." Jake kissed her passionately on the lips.

"What about Louis?" Mirri was in her dressing gown on the landing and Jonah was asleep in her bed. She had closed the door when Kate knocked so as not to wake him.

"I'll talk to Louis. He'll understand. I mean, it's not as though we were really together or anything," Kate said with more confidence than she felt. The thought of telling Louis had been haunting her since she first woke up. She had even contemplated not telling him until their project was over, because the idea of seeing him every day and knowing how he'd be filled her with dread. She'd prefer it if he were angry because then she'd feel less guilty. If he were noble and understanding she'd want to die. She had tried to cast the whole thing from her mind but it kept creeping back in, like knowing you have a trip to the dentist to have a tooth out that niggles away in your head.

"I wouldn't understand if I were him."

"Well, thankfully you're not," Kate said irritably. Then she looked at Mirri's disappointed face and nearly burst into tears. "Please, can't you be happy for me? Your approval means so much. Maybe you could spend some time with Jake getting to know him and like him. He's pretty winning. And now he's changed his ways, well, of course we'll be happy."

"You look so pathetic that I might just try to be happy for you." Mirri shook her head and gave Kate a reassuring hug. "Now let me see the ring. See how much he really thinks of you."

"It's pretty." Kate held out her hand to Mirri.

"Oh, yes. I rather like it. Sugarloaf, cabochon emerald. Antique?"

"I think 1930s," Kate said. Proud that Jake had done something right in her friend's eyes.

"Well then. I think we have to have champagne," she said.

"We're celebrating?" Kate asked as the weight of the world lifted momentarily from her shoulders. With Mirri's approval and advice she felt she could tackle all the other detractors easily. But she badly needed her support.

"Champagne is for funerals, too, you know," Mirri said gravely. Then, when she saw Kate turn an unearthly shade of gray, she laughed and took her hand. "But today we'll celebrate, okay?"

"Thanks," Kate said. It wasn't exactly putting out the flags but it'd do for now.

Leonard, because he was too well mannered not to be, was delighted for Kate. He even shed a tear, as a surrogate father ought to.

"I think he should have asked Leonard's permission," Mirri said as she handed out glasses of champagne.

"Actually I'd prefer tea if that's okay," Kate said. "I've overdosed on champagne lately."

"Lucky you, darling," Leonard said. "But it'd be bad luck to toast with tea."

"Start as you mean to go on." Mirri grinned wickedly. Leonard threw her a filthy look.

"To Kate," he said as he stood up and raised his glass. *"Le coeur a ses raisons, que la raison ne connait point."*

"C'est vrai," Mirri said and took Kate's hand.

"Shouldn't I be able to understand what the toast means since it's about me?" Kate asked with a puzzled frown. "Unless it's 'a plague on both your houses.' "

"It means 'the heart has its reasons whereof reason knows nothing,' " Leonard explained.

"So what you're saying is that even though it doesn't make any sense that I'm in love with Jake, it's okay because that's the way love is," Kate said.

"Precisely." Leonard raised his glass. "I wish you all the happiness in the world, my darling."

"So do I," Mirri said, and took a huge swig of her drink.

"Now I really have to go. I'm seeing a house in half an hour and I'm still wearing last night's clothes," Kate said as she edged her way toward the door.

"A house?" Leonard was taken aback. "A marital home, already?"

"No, just somewhere that I can live that I don't have to share with earwigs." Kate smiled.

"Ah, yes. But you're marrying a slug so you can't object too much to the creepy crawlies." Mirri shrugged nonchalantly.

"Mirri, please be nice," Kate said. "You'll like Jake when you get to know him."

"He does have a certain charm," Leonard agreed.

"I think so." Kate let herself out of the door. "See you both later. And so it's okay about the party, Leonard?"

"You know how I love a party. Leave it to me and invite as many people as you like."

Kate blew him a kiss and then hared down the garden path toward the shed. Tanya would most likely be waiting outside the estate agent's already.

If Kate thought that accepting Jake's proposal was hard, she was discovering that her friend's accepting Jake's proposal was even harder. She hadn't even dared to tell Tanya until they had seen the bathroom, kitchen, sitting room, and limited storage space of the Primrose Hill flat. They were standing in the middle of the very pretty bedroom that overlooked the postage stamp of a garden, admiring the white-painted floorboards, when it became impossible to hold back any longer.

"It's perfect for one person," Blondie, the estate agent, who looked as if she'd been out servicing an entire rugby team the night before, said as she chewed lethargically on her pen.

"Yeah, your own little kitchen, your own bathroom, and there's even space for you to have a small studio built outside." Tanya almost sounded envious.

"Well, it won't exactly be for one." Kate scrunched up her face at Tanya.

"What do you mean?" Tanya asked as she opened the built-in wardrobe to see how big it was then quickly shut it when she saw it wouldn't even have housed her collection of knickers.

"Last night . . ." Kate pulled the ring out of her handbag where she'd been hiding it. She held it out to show Tanya. "Jake gave me this."

"Why?" Tanya took it from Kate and squinted hard at the stone.

"Well, because he wanted me to marry him," Kate explained.

"But why have you still got it?" Tanya was genuinely bemused. She handed the ring back to Kate, who decided to brazen it out and slip it onto its rightful finger. "Oh please, Kate, tell me that you didn't." Tanya looked askance at her friend.

"Yup. I did."

"You're getting married?" Tanya squealed. But not in the way she was supposed to squeal. "To Jake?" She might as well have said *Satan* because even Blondie, who wasn't blessed in the brain department, now fully understood what it meant to be marrying Jake.

"Does he beat you?" Blondie asked, suddenly animated by the drama.

"No, he doesn't beat me," Kate snapped.

"He is pretty mean, though," Tanya confided.

"Tanya, just leave it." Kate darted from the room and into the bathroom. She sat down on the edge of the bath and looked up at the ceiling so that the tears couldn't escape and would have to roll back to where they came from.

"I'm sorry." Tanya was instantly at her side with her arm around her shoulders. "I didn't mean to be like that. Of course whatever you do is fine by me and I'm your friend and—"

"It's okay. I know the speech," Kate said. "I've heard it a thousand times. Do you still mean it?"

"Yes, I mean it. I don't dislike Jake. I just love you more."

"I know. But I think I've learned a lot since I split up with him," Kate said as she gathered up a handful of loo roll and pressed it against her eyes. "And I think it's going to be different this time. I'm not the same person."

"I know. So let's see the ring again. Was it sugarloaf emerald?" Tanya asked as she picked up Kate's left hand to examine it.

"How does everyone know about jewels except me?"

"Because you're not a superficial gold digger and the rest of us are," Tanya said as she nodded in an impressed way at Kate's ring. "So how did Louis take the news?"

"He hasn't yet. Do you think I have to tell him?" Kate didn't even want to think about Louis right now.

"No, I think you should just carry on seeing him and kissing him and doing whatever it is you do with him and have him be in love with you until he notices that you always have to be home by eleven o'clock and the name on your checkbook changes from Disney to Mrs. Jake Moore. Don't you?" Tanya suggested. Kate saw her point, and groaned.

"Louis, it's Kate."

"Hi, sweetheart. I was just thinking about you. I was wondering if maybe you wanted to come to see a film with me tonight?"

"I'd love to but . . ."

"You're busy? I know, I ought to stay in myself and do some work for the show. It's just that I'm going stir crazy and I thought that some human contact and, well . . ."

"Louis, I'd sort of like to talk, if that's okay."

"Yeah, go on," Louis replied with only the faintest hint of suspicion in his voice.

Certainly he wasn't expecting to hear what Kate was about to tell him. She put her engagement ring out in front of her to remind her that this was good news. For her at least. And she hadn't led Louis on in the slightest, they'd just been having a fling. And now they weren't. It was really simple.

"Can I come over?" she asked, and twisted the ring between her teeth.

"No," he said firmly.

"I can't?" Maybe he'd gone off her, she hoped, that'd be perfect.

"No. I need to get out of the flat. Let's meet somewhere." Kate was supposed to be meeting Jake for dinner with her mother at eight. She wondered whether she'd have time to meet Louis without Jake finding out. Then her mother's words sang out in her head: *Oh what a tangled web we weave when first we practice to deceive.*

She ought to have told Jake about Louis. It wasn't as if she'd been doing anything she shouldn't. Certainly the odds were on him having seen a few girls in their sabbatical, as Jake liked to call it. But she hadn't really had a chance . . . and now she was engaged.

"Okay, let's meet at the zoo in twenty minutes," she suggested. "Giraffes." She hoped nothing could get too serious with giraffes around.

"Great," agreed Louis. "See you there."

Kate was already waiting when Louis loped over to join her by the giraffes. He looked slightly frazzled, doubtless from all the work he'd been doing, and was carrying two lattes. He handed one to Kate. Thankfully she'd secreted her engagement ring away in her handbag this time.

"Just what I needed. Thanks," she said, and wondered whether the lattes would come to an end now. In fact she wondered whether the whole polar bear project would come to an end. She really hoped that it would; the idea of being around Louis after this was not going to be the most fun she'd ever had.

"I had a great time the other night." He kissed her on the lips. Then put his free hand on the small of her back and moved closer to her. Kate kissed him back for a brief moment and then shook her hair back in a bid to pull away without seeming like a scalded cat.

"So how's the exhibition coming along?" she asked, and rested her back against the fence of the giraffe enclosure. Louis leaned one arm against it and smiled goofily at her as she took a sip of her coffee.

"I'm so behind, I ought to throw myself out of the window but I suppose if I'm a piece short it's not going to matter, I can just rearrange the space and—"

"Louis, I want to tell you something." Kate decided to abandon the gentle lead-up and get straight to the point.

"Okay." He nodded patiently.

"Well. Something really unexpected happened to me last night," she began.

"Yes?"

The bitter irony was that Louis looked so frayed around the edges today that she fancied him more than she ever had. She wanted more than anything to be tucked up under the sheets in his flat, hiding from the world. Then she stopped herself. These weren't the thoughts of a woman about to be married. She focused on the ground. "Jake proposed to me." She waited a moment before looking to see his expression. Louis's eyes were barely visible—they were squinting tightly in the sunlight. She waited.

"Go, Jake," he said, and then burst into amused laughter. "Well, I'll say this for him. He doesn't give up, does he?"

"Louis . . ." Kate sounded the warning bell and his laugh quickly died away.

"Kate?" He was glaring at her now. Pretty much the way that Mirri and Tanya had also glared at her. Only behind his glare was something else, a look of stunned pain.

"I'm so sorry, Louis, I really am" was all she could manage to get out. There didn't seem much point in justification. She just wanted to leave.

"Come on, you're not serious. You said yes?" His voice was filled with disbelief.

Kate nodded. "I loved what we had, Louis. But I couldn't be sure about us. There was no time to find out. With Jake I know that I still love him after three years and all that we've been through. You and I might only last a week."

"You're not fucking serious?" Louis could no longer look at her face-on. He had half turned his head away from her when he spoke.

"Who knows whether we'd have been anything more than a really great fling?" she said, getting the hang of her defense now.

"Oh I see, is this you having the courage to live your life as you want to?" he snarled.

"What do you mean?" Kate took a small step backward. She couldn't remember having seen Louis angry, ever.

"The other night. All that bullshit about how you've learned that you don't need to conform, you don't need to marry the wrong man just to fall into line with everyone else, how you want to make brave choices. And what do you do? Marry the first person who asks just because it's more time-efficient than finding out whether you and I might be in love and have a chance for the future." He shook his head contemptuously.

"I love Jake," she argued. "And before you say that he treats me badly, he's changed. He understands what he did wrong and it's going to be different in the future."

"Oh, for God's sake, Kate. That's one of the most pathetic, hackneyed things I've ever heard." He began to laugh bitterly.

"I am being brave," she said defensively, "I'm going to marry a man I'm taking a chance on. There's no guarantees with Jake, either. That's courageous."

"No, Kate, that's stupid."

"I'm sorry." Kate closed her eyes.

"Yeah, me too. But I think maybe you'll be sorrier than me in the end."

"We'll see." There was an interminable silence as they both clutched their drinks and Louis scuffed his sneakers in the dirt. "Do you still want to work with me? I completely understand if you don't," she said quietly after a while.

Louis lifted his head. "Sure. It's not really going to change much. Like you said, we had a fling. It's over. Let's not get too overemotional about the whole thing." His voice had a steely edge to it. "Clearly you haven't."

"Okay," Kate said. "I'll see you Monday. Unless . . ." She hesitated. "Unless you want to come to the engagement party tomorrow." There was another long silence as Kate bit her lip.

Eventually Louis sniffed, "Yeah, I think I'll give that one a miss if you don't mind." Then he tossed his coffee cup in a nearby bin. "I'll see you Monday, then." He shrugged and walked away down the path. Kate leaned back against the fence with a sigh of relief. That was that, then.

Chapter Twenty-two

On Sunday afternoon the English summer came to an almost apocalyptic end. It was only July but it felt like November. The temperature had dropped, the skies hung low, and gray and rain threatened. Kate had unearthed a thick sweater and some green socks from a box under her bed and put on the heater in the shed.

"Well, I'm definitely going to buy the flat now," she told Leonard and Mirri as they sat around the kitchen table folding tissue paper into garlands for tonight's party. "Every fox, badger, and hedgehog in London's going to want to make the shed home if this weather carries on."

"Where do I tie the cotton again?" Mirri was glowering at a spindly paper flower in her hand.

Kate laughed and rescued the disaster from her grasp. "I'll do it. You can just cut out these. See where I've made the circles." She handed Mirri a pair of scissors.

"I don't know why you can't buy these from Harrods," she snarled.

"Because I like making them," Kate said good-naturedly. Since she'd gotten all the dirty work out of the way and told her friends and Louis of her unpopular decision, she felt a lot better. The truth was out, it was downhill with her feet off the pedals all the way now.

"Are you going to make your own wedding dress, too?" Mirri was unashamedly bad-tempered this morning. She'd had a row with Jonah last night and had been chain-smoking all day. It was now three in the afternoon and she still hadn't gotten dressed.

"Oh, dear, Mirabelle is depressed," Leonard had said as she walked into the kitchen first thing. It wasn't exactly hard to spot.

"What did you argue about?" Kate asked in a hushed voice when Leonard went down to the cellar to fetch up some wine for the party while they carried on making flowers.

"I have no idea. I made something up," Mirri replied in a surly voice.

"To argue about?"

"Why not. He was being banal. It annoyed me."

"What are you going to do about Nick?" Kate asked. She'd filled Mirri in on his architectural achievements and the fact that he lived in a village in Oxfordshire and that there was no discernible wife in the wings, but Mirri had virtually ignored the information.

"The idea of it makes me feel sick," she said as she stubbed out a cigarette in the bottom of her coffee cup.

"That's no reason not to do it."

"I'm not sure that I would like him anyway."

"You used to like him. People don't change that much." Once again Kate was Mirri's alter ego.

"I don't think I'm capable of loving anyone. And the idea of being with someone in a relationship is intolerable. Look at Jonah—he's sweet and yet a lot of the time I want to bite him."

"It's not as if you have to spend the rest of your life with Nick," Kate said, getting a butterfly as she realized that she'd just agreed to precisely this with Jake. "You only have to meet for a coffee for old times' sake. You don't have to declare love straight away." Kate was feeling remarkably sage and pleased with herself until Mirri let out a hiss.

"If you say one more sensible thing I'll bite you as well."

"Oh." Kate deflated slightly. "Fine. But you can't deny love. It'll catch up with you in the end."

"Jesus, what are you? Kahlil Gibran?" Mirri snorted. Kate shrugged and continued to tie the paper roses to her chain. Not much could dent her mood today.

"So what are you going to do?" she persisted.

"Okay. I'll write to him tomorrow. If I'm in the mood," she snapped and then shut up and cut out the next sixty paper circles without speaking.

An hour before the party the heavens opened. Kate's roof sprang a leak and the dress she was going to wear, a white satin number that she'd spotted in the window of an antiques shop in Primrose Hill yesterday, got covered in a particularly nasty strain of leaf mold as it lay on the bed under the drip. Kate drafted in an old sundress of Mirri's instead and refused to see the whole thing as a portent, despite Mirri's dark mutterings.

"It's not a good sign that your dress is ruined. It's an omen from God that you're not doing the right thing," she mused as she attached one of the paper roses to the clip in Kate's hair. Mirri had done a flowing-tendril number on Kate that was worthy of a bride. "I'd have the wedding hair now in case you never make it to the altar," she said as she pinned away.

"Mirri, will you stop it?" Kate said. "You sound like my evil godmother."

"Don't worry. I will try very hard to like The Slug," she said as if she were offering Kate the world. With a cherry on top.

"I don't want you to try. I'm sure you will. Now, you're not going to row with Jonah in front of everyone, are you?" Kate asked. "It's only that Tanya's trying really had to get pregnant and she's just read a book on how negative energy can adversely affect your chances of conception. She can't be around it 'cause it's bad for her eggs."

"*Boffé,*" Mirri said. "Anyway, Jonah's gone to his youngest child's christening so he won't be coming. And so I told him, neither will I," she said haughtily.

"Poor Jonah, do you have sex with him at all anymore or are you just punishing him the whole time?" Kate asked.

"Oh, I punish him all the time. But when we do have sex it's even better," Mirri said tartly as she held up a pair of diamonds to Kate's ears.

"Don't you ever get tired of all the game playing?" Kate asked. Not, for once, being supercilious. She was exhausted by the very thought of Mirri's life, and she didn't have to live it.

"Of course I do," Mirri said in a suddenly melancholic way. "That's why I can't ignore Nick Sheridan anymore. My past's caught up with me and now my life only seems very frivolous, ridiculous, and sad. I'm too old to chase men."

"You don't chase them. They chase you," Kate reminded her.

"But now it looks as if I have to do the chasing."

"It's not chasing. You're looking him up after thirty years. It's not as if you've been stalking him since the day he left."

"No. I don't think I can do it." Mirri shook her head furiously. She was sitting on the floor cross-legged with Bébé on her lap.

"What do you mean? You can't back out," Kate protested as she looked out the window to see Leonard instructing two men as to where to place the tarpaulin of a tent he'd drafted in at the last minute. "Bugger this rain," Kate said, and turned back to Mirri.

"He doesn't want me. If he did he'd have found me," she said and buried her face in the lion cub's fur. "It's not as though I'm hard to find. He must know I'm in the country. It's been in the papers. No, Kate. That's it. I'm not doing it."

"You haven't got anything to lose." Kate sat on the edge of the bed and pleaded with her.

"This love affair you had. It's thrown a shadow over your whole life. Don't you think you should find out whether it's as significant as you think?"

"What about Louis? He could be the love of your life. You didn't give it a chance," Mirri said petulantly.

"Don't turn the tables on me. I'm getting married. Now, promise me you'll call him. I know you want to. You're just chickenshit."

"Chickenshit?" Mirri didn't understand what Kate meant.

"You're afraid."

"If he's bald I'm going to walk away without saying hello," she threatened.

"Wow, thank God you're not superficial. And I agree, it's completely reasonable to discard your soul mate, the one man you've ever loved in your life, because of his bald spot," Kate said sarcastically as the rain continued to flood the garden.

"I'll do it. Okay? Now leave me alone. I need to look young for this evening. I don't want everyone thinking I'm your mother."

From the magical moment when the tent in the garden was hauled into the sky, Kate was in a dreamworld. Jake had arrived earlier and they'd had an hour of mellow chatter as they made last-minute phone calls to invite friends, dashed to the shops to buy extra tonic water and lemons for the drinks, and finally took a shower together in Kate's bamboo cubicle.

"Why do we need a house anyway?" he'd asked as one of the green bamboo shoots tickled Kate on the shoulder and Jake kissed the other one. "I like your shed. I could begin married life in your shed."

"Too late. I'm going to make an offer for the house on Monday," Kate said. "I've got rising damp in my bones from staying here. Don't forget that I've lived here for months. It's not a novelty anymore."

"I know, but it's so romantic." He hugged her tight and nuzzled her neck playfully.

"We'd better get out there. Everyone's going to be arriving in ten minutes," Kate said as she readjusted her shower cap, which was protecting Mirri's handiwork.

"Let's get married straightaway. Next week." He gave Kate one final squeeze before she ducked out of the shower.

"You're so impractical sometimes." Kate laughed as she grabbed a towel. "Are you afraid I'll change my mind?"

"No." Jake was adamant. "I just don't think we should lose the moment." He called out, "Is there any soap out there, angel?"

Kate and Jake ran down the garden path with an old golf umbrella shielding them from the downpour. They ducked into the tent to discover that they were almost the last at the party.

"I told you we didn't have time for a quickie," Kate whispered in his ear with a giggle as everyone turned to welcome them. Despite the fact that it had been a last-minute party, there were a surprising number of people there. Kate's mum came forward and kissed them both and from then on a steady stream of people bombarded them with questions and sighs and requests to see the ring.

"Yeah, it was on a pal's houseboat on the Thames," Jake said for the umpteenth time that day. Kate felt another of the alien flutters in her stomach when she wondered how many times she'd hear this story throughout the rest of her life. She smiled at Jake's cousins Lizzy and Jemima, whom she'd barely met before, even though they were supposedly close, and politely made her excuses to duck from under Jake's arm and find Mirri, whom she'd spotted grilling Jake earlier. She was longing for a report.

"Are you having a good time?" She spied Mirri chatting to Robbie in a corner.

"Darling, I'm having a marvelous time." Mirri had her hand on Robbie's knee.

"Where's Tanya?" Kate asked. Hoping that Mirri wasn't going to cause any fireworks between her best friend and her husband.

"She's talking to your mother," Mirri replied. "I'm just giving Robbie some advice."

"Very useful advice actually." Robbie elbowed Kate in a conspiratorial way. "But you're not to tell my wife about it."

"About how to have babies." Mirri winked and the two laughed. Kate held out her glass as it was refilled by one of the very smart waiters whom Leonard seemed to have conjured from thin air. They were wearing Nehru jackets the same color as the cornflowers that were wound around the tent poles. The whole party really couldn't have looked more stunning if they'd spent a year organizing it and hired the bossiest party planner money could buy.

"Well, I think that Robbie understands the general principle of making babies," Kate said, "unless you were planning on giving him a practical lesson." She gave Mirri a warning look.

"Darling, I may have adored his father but I like his pretty wife enough not to mess around with the son." She laughed her throaty laugh and Robbie looked as starstruck and transfixed as he had been when he first met her. And Kate had to admit that Mirri was breathtakingly seductive this evening—sitting here in her corner of the party like a queen bee with all the honeybees swarming to her for approval. She had her hair down around her shoulders, a cigarette wafted smoke in the eyes of anyone who looked too closely, and her scent seemed to make the men fall under a spell. Or perhaps that was her cleavage, which flashed into view from behind her fitted, barely buttoned shirt every time she leaned forward to whisper in their ears.

"Mirri's given me a pretty great tip about getting Tanya pregnant," Robbie revealed under his breath.

"That's interesting," Kate said, wondering when her goddess had become a fertility guru as well. "So, Mirri, I want to know what you thought of Jake?"

"I like him. But I don't trust him," she said nonchalantly, and lifted her cigarette to her lips. "Which I suppose is all right. Sometimes when men aren't trustworthy and you feel that you must marry them—well, it's a good thing not to trust them. That way you can't be disappointed."

"You're such a cynic. He's been so sweet to me," Kate said, hardly even bothered by Mirri's dismal warning.

"I think he's great," Robbie said. "We had a bit of a chat about the football. He's nicer than I remembered."

"I told you," Kate said victoriously. "He just needs to be given a chance."

"A chance is exactly what he doesn't need. A tight rein is. Don't get too comfortable with him and it may be fine," Mirri said with foreboding in her voice.

"Why are you so suspicious of him?" Robbie asked with the sort of ingenuousness that makes women look like jaded old tarts.

Not that Mirri seemed to mind. "I have met his type. I know," she said, with the ring of omnipotence.

"God, it's like sitting with the Delphic oracle." Kate laughed. "I'm going to talk to Tanya and my mum. At least they'll want to know what color my dress is going to be."

Which of course they did. In fact, by the end of the evening Mirri's was pretty much the only dissenting voice at the whole gathering. The rain stopped and the bonfire—which Leonard's gardener had been hastily preparing, and then carefully covered up before the first spots of rain—was lit. As everyone gathered around the leaping flames, the women with shawls and men's jackets thrown over their shoulders, the men forming a breakaway group with folded arms, everyone seemed genuinely convinced that the marriage of Kate who had never stopped standing by her at-times-naughty man, and Jake, the naughty man with rather too much charm for his own good, was a brilliant idea. They thought they'd be the perfect match. No one doubted that Jake might be a handful and that Kate would have her work cut out for her, but then when had that ever stood in the way of a marriage?

"Darling, I think he's terribly handsome. And he has wonderful taste in wine," Leonard pronounced as he flitted excitedly over to Kate, having been on the receiving end of some of Jake's ministrations for the past twenty minutes. "And I never knew he was so bright. No, I must say I'm very impressed and looking forward to having him be one of the family."

"Leonard, are you drunk?" Kate asked her slightly more-sparkling-eyed-than-usual champion.

"Of course. I'm roaringly drunk. But that doesn't mean I'm not right in the head."

"I'm so pleased you love him," Kate said, and tucked herself close to Leonard's orange tweed waistcoat for a hug. "Everyone does. Except for Mirri of course." She caught sight of Mirri chatting animatedly to her mother. Despite the fact that the two of them were like chalk and cheese—Kate's mother was passionate about her garden, her dogs, and, rather bizarrely, birds of prey. Her idea of shopping for clothes was a new pair of pruning gloves, and glamour meant brushing the dog hairs off her skirt. But still the two seemed to be getting on famously. As long as she and Mirri kept their talk of slugs to the kind that play havoc with your geraniums and not the kind that play havoc with your daughter's heart, Kate didn't mind.

"I hope the wedding's going to be as much fun." Kate said to Jake at the end of the evening as they put the last guest into a taxi and bolted the garden gate. Though most of the paparazzi loitered only during the daytime now, there was still the odd one who came in the dead of night in the desperate hope of finding a drainpipe to shimmy up to catch Mirri at it with Jonah. Or whoever. The Jonah story seemed to be old news to them now. Kate hoped that soon they'd vanish completely. Unless Mirri started dating someone else— that is, Nick. In which case it'd be flashes galore all over again.

" 'Course it will." Jake put his arm around her and they walked back down the garden to the shed. On the way he picked one of the cornflowers from the tables and tucked it behind Kate's ear. "We're going to be happy. We really are," he promised. And Kate knew that he meant it and that his intentions were the best. But she still wished on the full moon, just to be on the safe side.

Chapter Twenty-three

"So how's the work going?" Tanya asked as she and Kate sat in the ruins of the kitchen in Kate's new flat. It had been a month since her and Jake's engagement party, and she'd finally had the builders in to rip out all the old bathroom kitchen fittings. The girls had a bottle of wine and sat on two rotting chairs they'd found in the garden.

"It's fine. I've finished Bébé and Mirri's thrilled with him, but she's going to stick around a bit longer until I've finished my portrait of her. I've had to put it on the back burner to get the polar bears done for Louis. I daren't piss him off," Kate said as she wondered whether the chalky-blue kitchen she had in mind would work in a small space. She'd have to ask Jake; he was pretty good at that stuff at least, even though he wasn't exactly forthcoming with the dirty work like getting in the plumbers and electricians. He claimed not to have a clue about anything like that. As if Kate might be fully cognizant with it all. Still, he'd been tirelessly looking for the right country-and-western band to play at the wedding, which she wouldn't have been able to do in a million years.

"Is he still being cold with you?" Tanya asked.

"He's so professional, it kills me." Kate sighed. "You know I really do love Louis. Of course it's irrelevant whether I fancied him or not now but we were great friends. I feel like once this project's over we'll probably never see each other again. But I can't stand to think too much about that. "

"It's sad," Tanya said as she sloshed Evian water into her wine.

"It makes working with him hell. He hardly ever comes to check up on the work but when he does he doesn't look me in the eye, he doesn't talk about anything except the piece. I thought he'd have gotten over it by now. Well, not exactly over it but, well more accepting maybe."

"Yeah, he will," Tanya said, then couldn't help but break into a smile. Kate looked at her across the wallpaper paste table that they'd set up for their little take-out supper party to christen the house. "Kate?"

"Yes?" Kate leaned back in the chair and looked expectantly at her friend.

"I'm going to tell you something. Which means absolutely nothing, by the way. It's just something. But it could be something important. Or not . . ." She looked sheepishly at Kate, who was holding her breath, hoping that Tanya was about to say what she thought she might say.

"You know that Robbie and I took a break from IVF this month. You know, so I could let my hormones settle down and he could not be yelled at by me for breathing in the wrong way when he watched TV?" she asked.

"Were you that awful to him?" Kate grinned at the thought of Robbie not being able to put a foot right.

"Really awful," Tanya admitted guiltily. "Anyway, we're taking a break from it all but . . ." She looked unsure of what she was about to say. "I'm late."

"How late?" Kate asked, not wanting to get overexcited just yet.

"Only about six days, but I feel a bit different," Tanya whispered, as if there might be someone in the next room or next house who might hear.

"That's properly late," Kate said cautiously. "Do you think that you might be . . . really?"

"My boobs are sore. And huge," she said as she looked down at her neat chest. "Well, huge for me, anyway."

"Have you done a pregnancy test?" Kate poured herself another glass of wine but didn't fill up Tanya's glass. If there was any doubt she didn't want to poison the baby.

"Not yet. I haven't even told Robbie." Tanya was blushing as she said this. "I just don't want him to get his hopes up. But I really think I feel something. Unless I'm having a phantom pregnancy or something." Her face deflated again.

Kate shook her head. "No, you might be right. I mean, you know your body. Why don't we go and buy a kit from the chemist now?" Kate looked at her watch to see whether the emergency chemist down the road would still be open.

"It won't show up yet. Besides, I ought to wait until I'm a bit more sure and then do it with Rob. 'Cause he did have to shove the injections in my bum. He ought to have a bit of the fun, too."

"I'd have thought he might have enjoyed that part." Kate laughed.

"The thing is. And this sounds really silly." Tanya leaned forward onto the table and lowered her voice even farther. "I think I know when it happened."

"What, getting pregnant?" Kate was surprised. Tanya never discussed her sex life, and she was so awkward that Kate didn't know which of them would be more embarrassed if she began to talk about it now.

"It was the night of your engagement party," she said as she finished her watery glass of wine in two gulps. "We came home and I was just putting the key in the front door. I was about to rush in and turn off the alarm when Robbie sort of grabbed me from behind," she said shyly.

"Grabbed you?"

"Well, he sort of got hold of my waist from behind. I still had the keys in my hand and I could hear the alarm beeping in the house but he didn't seem to notice. Then he started to kiss the back of my head, kissing my hair really furiously." She was looking at her fingers, which were spread out flat on the table in front of her at this point. There was no way she would be able to tell this story if she was looking at Kate. "Then, well, then he sort of spun me around and pushed me up against the wall." Tanya looked up at this point and caught sight of Kate's surprised face. "Oh, he wasn't hurting me. It was just sort of . . . passionate."

"Sounds great." Kate smiled.

"Yeah, it was." Tanya was lost in the memory. "Anyway, then he started kissing me frantically on the lips and all I think at first is that I had to tap the code into the alarm or it'd go off. But then I forgot about it. And about the fact that we were outside." As Tanya told her this, Kate was picturing Robbie and Tanya's house, which was right on the street in Belsize Park. No front yard; barely a front doorstep. You just stepped right out of the door and into the London square. And all she could picture was Tanya, in the pale blue, chiffon print dress she'd worn to the engagement party, and Robbie getting it on on their front doorstep with taxis bringing home stuffy neighbors and passersby copping an eyeful. "So, well, then he lifted up my skirt and practically ripped off my knickers and then we were . . . well, you know . . . having sex outside our front door and I could feel the knocker against my back."

"I'll bet you could," Kate couldn't help butting in. But there was no distracting Tanya.

"And then the alarm started to go off. And we just kept on going. I had my high heels on and we were doing it on the doorstep and we didn't stop until one of the neighbors put his head out the front door and saw us. But by that time we'd already finished and were just sort of collapsed against one another." Tanya drew a deep breath. "And I think that's when I got pregnant. If I am pregnant, that is. But I just feel so sure, Kate."

"Well it sounds like you had a damned good time. Whether you're pregnant or not," Kate said.

"And you know it's all because of what Mirri said," Tanya told her.

"Mirri?" Kate wondered how she might fit into this particular story.

"That night. At your party. She told Robbie that if we wanted to get pregnant then we needed to have fabulous, exciting sex. Apparently you're much more likely to conceive if you have a mind-blowing orgasm. One-night stands are supposed to be the best time to get pregnant—for that reason."

"Well, I never." Kate's eyes widened. "And Mirri told Robbie this?"

"Apparently she told him to"—Tanya leaned across the table in a conspiratorial way—"fuck me senseless."

"Sounds like Mirri's kind of advice." Kate nodded. "So when are you going to take a test?"

"I'm going to give it another week. Just so I don't get too carried away. Then I'll tell Robbie."

"Well, fingers crossed." Kate held her hands in the air. "Though I don't know who I'll eat sushi with if you get pregnant. It'll be a real drag." Kate winked and Tanya smiled, hardly daring to hope that she might soon have to forgo yellowfin sashimi.

"Mirri, it's me." Kate made her way up the stairs of Leonard's house later that evening. She'd put Tanya in a taxi, locked up her brand-new, desperately scruffy house, and come back to Leonard's. She was dying to stay at the flat but it wasn't anywhere near ready yet. And though Kate didn't want to admit it she was slightly disappointed with Jake, who even though he'd played three gigs last week said he hadn't enough money to pay the plasterer who needed to come and fix up the holes in the walls before they could so much as spend the night there.

"Come in," Mirri called out as Kate gave the bedroom door a perfunctory tap.

"I just came to see if there was any post," she asked. Mirri was working at her desk, doubtless looking at endless columns of figures for the trust. She put her pen down and stretched her hands above her head when Kate walked in and sat on the bed.

"Oh, I've been here too long." She stood up and took a few paces around the room, then went to draw the curtains. "No post," she said. "Just bills and an invitation to a Moroccan theme party in Somerset. Which I shall live without."

"Maybe he's away," Kate said with very little conviction.

Two weeks ago Kate had sat down with Mirri and they'd written a note to Nick Sheridan. It was very simple and didn't hint at anything other than friendship. It had read:

Dear Nick,

You may remember that some years ago we met at the wedding of my friend Tony. In fact I saw some footage of the wedding recently and was reminded of you. I'm currently in England for the summer and in between business am finding some time for pleasure. It would be lovely to catch up with you, perhaps for tea one day.

With warmest wishes,
Mirabelle Moncur

It may have been a brief note but my God it had taken an age to write. Kate and Mirri had sat through packets of biscuits, cups of tea, countless drafts, and what felt like the rise and fall of whole empires before they got it right. There had been poetic and quite morbid French-notes; there had been very dry, unfriendly English-notes; there had been love-declaring versions; even one that was an almost fully realized autobiography of France's greatest sex goddess. But in the end they'd prosaically opted for short and sweet. Despite the hours they'd put in, however, they still hadn't heard back from Nick Sheridan.

"They have offices in Tokyo. I saw it on the website," Kate told Mirri for the sixth time in as many days.

"It obviously wasn't fate after all," Mirri said as she dropped down into her armchair and drew her legs into her chest. "Though it's a little irritating that I got rid of Jonah. I'm missing his cock. Still, at least Isabella has the benefit of it now." She shrugged.

"I still can't believe you did that," Kate said. Two weeks ago, the day before she posted the note to Nick, Mirri had experienced a huge pang of conscience and thrown a dinner party for her prettiest goddaughter to meet Jonah. That way if anything happened with Nick, her faithful young Jonah would be wonderfully taken care of. And as Mirri knew only too well, there was no way he wouldn't fall for her. Isabella was twenty-eight years old, her mother was a dead poetess, and her father was a South American arms dealer who was a great friend of Mirri's in the 1970s. He still contributed a very generous donation to the trust every year.

"He's a pussycat," Mirri was fond of saying, though if his firecracker daughter was anything to go by, Kate doubted it. Isabella was studying for her Ph.D. in philosophy at Cambridge and was about as spiritual as General Pinochet. She blew into dinner in a black mood because of the London traffic, even though she had a driver, and practically declared war on Jonah when he helped himself to the last piece of lobster. Needless to say he hardly noticed because Isabella had black eyes, caramel-colored hair, and the tiniest, prettiest hands Kate had ever seen. In fact, she would have asked Isabella if she could paint them but she was terrified of her, and by the end of dinner one of them was also firmly attached to Jonah's inner thigh. She spoke with a barely perceptible lisp, and the day after the dinner party she and Jonah had flown to her grandmother's avocado plantation in Venezuela to get to know one another better, and possibly to throw things at one another. The avocados must have provided ample and ready ammunition, Kate imagined.

"I don't mind. I never gave Isabella very much so as my goddaughter it's the least I can do. Make sure her education is finished off in the best way possible," Mirri told Kate.

"Are they back?" Kate asked.

"Tomorrow. I hear that Jonah's wife has finally found herself a lover so everybody is happy, no?"

"Perhaps." Kate was skeptical of French marriages, though if she were married to Jonah she suspected she'd have done just that a long time ago.

"So what shall we do about Nick?" Kate asked.

"I think we need to take a day trip," Mirri replied. "Now that I have no lover I'm bored. We'll go and see his house. See if he's there. If not, then good. If so, then I'll kill myself," she said matter-of-factly.

"My God, you're going to stalk him?" Kate was surprised. Up until now Mirri had barely had the will to stick the stamp on the envelope to write to the man. Now she was planning to take a flask of coffee and a baseball cap and camp in a car outside his house until he showed. Practically.

"I have a friend in the same village. A girl I knew from school who married an English banker and they retired there," Mirri declared.

"Do you?" Kate wondered why she hadn't mentioned this before; it was the perfect foil for them.

"Of course not. But you believed it. So a man definitely will." She waved her hand in the air dismissively. "What are you doing tomorrow?"

"Tomorrow?"

"Yes? I think make hay while the sun shines, *non*?" Mirri went into the bathroom to brush her teeth.

"Okay. I'll come. I'm supposed to be going in to finish off with Louis but he's never there anyway. I'll go in for an hour or so first thing and shuffle my paints around then we'll set off." Kate sighed. "Do you think Leonard will let us borrow his car?" Kate had never driven the Aston Martin in the garage—in fact, she'd seen it only a few times—but she suspected that he might be reluctant to let a Parisian woman and a girl who mostly traveled by bicycle and bus take his precious car out for the day.

"He will if we don't tell him." Mirri grinned wickedly. "I'll pick you up from the gallery. And we'll take Bébé."

The next morning Kate caught the tube into work at dawn. She arrived before the night security guard had finished his shift and had to turn the lights on in her studio. She'd been working hard on the polar bears and had even spent a couple of weekends in the studio recently, she suspected as a way of assuaging her guilt over what had happened with Louis. Also, because she had never quite gotten over the idea that he had just hired her so that he might be better placed to pursue her, she wanted to make it brilliant. So that he wouldn't regret his decision no matter what the motivation had been. And the piece was done. It was staggeringly, mind-blowingly enormous, and when you entered the vast white space it had real impact. Clearly Louis had known what he wanted and his vision had been spot-on. There was no question that he deserved every accolade he received for his talent. Jake, on the other hand, wasn't exactly thrilled that Kate had been putting in extra hours but was consoled by how much she was being paid to do it.

Kate made her way through the silent corridors toward the back of the building where her studio was. She pushed open the door.

"Louis?" As she flipped the switch she spotted Louis sitting on a windowsill near the painting.

"I didn't know you came in this early." He stood up and ran a hand through his hair. It wasn't clear to Kate whether he'd been there a minute or all night.

"I don't usually." She didn't want to let on how strange she found it that he was there. "I just wanted to get some things finished while it's quiet."

"Then I'll go." Louis bent down for his bag, which was on the floor beside his feet. "I just wanted to check out the piece. Try to hold the whole exhibition in my head one last time before I start to prepare the space."

"Stay if you need to," Kate said, hoping that he wouldn't. "I don't mind you being there while I work."

Louis sat back down on the windowsill and looked at the polar bear again. "It works, doesn't it?"

"Yeah. I think it does. You're great at that. I couldn't begin to

imagine it when you first talked about it. But now I completely get
it. I was just painting by numbers," Kate said, with sincerity.

"So how's things?" Louis asked. "Wedding plans going well?"
Kate looked carefully at his face for signs of sarcasm but found
none.

"Fine," she said quietly. Louis wanted to hear more. And looking
in his eyes she felt oddly compelled to tell him. "It's okay. I mean,
Jake . . . well, he's Jake. You know. Sometimes he's good and sweet."
She paused before continuing. "And then sometimes I don't think
it matters that it's me he's with, just as long as someone will laugh
at his jokes and tell him his songs are great. And if that happens to
be me then it's fine by him." Kate didn't expect to say this and she
couldn't be sure that she wasn't just trying to get Louis to feel better, by letting him think that maybe she'd made a mistake. But she
did mean what she said.

"That's tough," he said without much emotion.

"Yeah. It's like I know exactly what I love about Jake. But I don't
think that he has a clue what makes him love me. Apart from the
fact that I love him." Kate laughed as lightly as she could. She'd
never said that before. But she realized now that it was true.

"But you do love him? You're going to marry him?"

"I know you think that I'm taking the easy way out, Louis. But
it was the only decision I could make."

"I understand," Louis said flatly. Then he stopped looking at her,
he stopped watching her rub the hardened tips of her brushes
against the palms of her hands, unwrapping the colors she'd made
yesterday, and he stood up again. "I've got to go. We should talk
about moving the piece over to the Tate in the next few days. If I
don't catch you here I'll give you a call," he said without looking her
in the eye.

"Great," Kate said. Then she felt a sudden fear of him leaving.
She didn't want him to go from the room. "Louis?"

"Yeah?" He turned and caught her eye. She was almost knocked
sideways with the memory of the kiss they'd had that last night after
dinner at his flat. After she'd lain in his bath and wanted to drift

away on bubbles and his voice reading to her. Right now she wanted to walk over to him slowly and bury her face in his sweater, breathing in Louis and all the love he had for her. She needed to be fortified by him. But she couldn't. She'd cut him out of her life and her future. He was waiting for her to ask him a question but she couldn't. She gave her head a hurried shake.

"It's okay. I'll figure it out." She dismissed him. He shrugged and walked out of the room.

———

"Mirri, do you think it matters that I don't know what Jake sees in me?" Kate asked as they finally made it onto the motorway in Leonard's car. As they'd driven through the traffic in London it had attracted more attention from men than Mirabelle Moncur's bare breasts ever had. Kate had declared the fact depressing. Mirri simply revved up the engine and left the admirers with exhaust fumes in their nostrils.

"Of course you know what he sees in you—he thinks you're beautiful, sexy, and interesting. That's what you tell me every time I ask you this question anyway," Mirri said as she moved up into fifth gear.

"But those aren't things you see in someone. They're things that exist. I just worry that he doesn't get me." Kate sucked in her lips and dug her teeth into them. "Sometimes it feels like I'm just there. That he can't see all the things about me that make me me."

"Maybe he can't. It doesn't mean he doesn't love you." Mirri was uncharacteristically rational and apparently defending Jake. "It's not very often in this world that we find men who really see something in us that we didn't know was there. Something better than just prettiness or sexiness. They're rare." She pulled out in front of a truck whose driver almost blasted her off the road. Kate wondered if she ought to have driven them. "That's why we're doing this today—trying to find Nick Sheridan. I met one man in my life who saw that in me and I have to see if it was real or not."

"I think Louis sees it in me," Kate said starkly as she looked out

the window at the white clouds scudding across the sky ahead of
them.

"Really?" Mirri turned to look at Kate, who couldn't meet her
gaze.

"I saw him in the gallery this morning and I remembered why
for those few days I'd been so captivated by him. He looks at me as
if he can see into my soul," Kate said then stuck her tongue out.
"God, that sounds ridiculous. I'm picking up all this intense bullshit from you." She laughed but Mirri didn't.

"I know what you mean."

"He sees all the things that I don't really want anyone to see but
he accepts them. And he loves me for them. Well at least he did. Before I shattered his faith in me and trampled on him." Kate winced.
She didn't like to sound pretentious and she liked even less the idea
that what she was saying might be undermining the seam of her
life—her relationship with Jake—but she carried on. "And the part
of me that doesn't have any faith in myself hates him for loving me
for my faults. But the grown-up part of me"—Kate sighed—"the
grown-up part of me knows that I shouldn't even consider being
with a man who doesn't see me in that way."

"Like Jake?" Mirri spent as much time looking at Kate as she did
at the road, which was pretty hairy. Kate gripped the corners of her
seat discreetly.

"I wanted Louis to run away with me this morning," Kate confessed. "But only for the briefest second. It's not real."

"Why don't you break it off with Jake? Ask for some more time?"

"I can't. I love him."

"Is it how you expected it to be? Being engaged?" Mirri probed.

"No. But then that's because I'm beginning to think that I'm
fickle. That I can't be completely happy with what I've got," Kate
said dismissively. "Sort of like men are supposed to be."

"That's not men, it's human nature. But how about maybe what
you've got isn't right? It could be that simple."

"I blame you." Kate turned to Mirri and slapped her lightly on
the arm.

"Me?"

"Before you came along I didn't know what else there was. I would have stayed with Jake and I'd have been happy to marry him," Kate said.

"Darling. Jake would never have asked you to marry him if I hadn't come along," Mirri said, while managing not to sound wildly egotistical. "You're a different woman now. And that's why I worry that you can't just slide back into your old habits with him. It's like your life with him is a jigsaw and you don't fit into the hole anymore."

"But he's what I always wanted, Mirri," Kate said plaintively, wishing they'd never gone down this road. She was surprising herself by saying these things. Until she spoke them they weren't even half-formed thoughts in her mind. And now, jolted by her run-in with Louis, she seemed to be confiding far too much in Mirri—a woman who didn't even like Jake, and who certainly wasn't going to stand up for him. But then perhaps that was subconsciously her intention in telling Mirri, Kate thought. Then she bashed her head on the inside of the car door. She had to stop. Now.

"Don't worry too much. Things will work themselves out," Mirri said as she wound down her window. "I promise."

The two women spent half an hour driving around the idyllic village of Letcombe Bassett before they eventually saw a house that resembled the one that Kate had seen online.

"It has pineapples on the gateposts. I promise," she said firmly as Mirri dismissed the house as too bourgeois to belong to the man she'd known all those years ago.

"Well, he's a successful architect now," Kate argued. "The chances are he is bourgeois."

"Then we have to turn back. This house is large and gray and it gives me the creeps," she said as she drove on and refused to pull over.

"You're being hysterical." Kate threw her hands in the air. "It's a house. And I think it's a bloody beautiful house. I'd kill to live somewhere like that. Now turn back."

"I don't like who he's become," Mirri said, and nearly knocked a dog walker and his Labrador off the road and into the hedgerow.

"You're being a coward again. You're so predictable," Kate said scathingly as they drove at breakneck speed past the local post office. The second Kate uttered this Mirri slammed on the brakes.

"I am not," she snarled.

"Then let's go back. You can park up and I'll take a stroll past the front gate. See if I can see him."

"Not without me," she said ferociously. Kate shook her head. Honestly, it was so easy to manipulate Mirri. You just had to employ the same tactics you might with a five-year-old.

Unfortunately, despite having baseball caps and large Jackie O sunglasses, Mirri and Kate managed to look more conspicuous than any visitor to the remote village for the past two hundred years. By the time they'd parked the dove-gray, vintage Aston Martin on the village green (with an appalling amount of screeching, cursing in French, and narrow misses with pedestrians), they had garnered a crowd of teenage boys large enough to hold a rock concert. They were all photographing the car with the cameras on their cell phones, leaning in the windows to ogle the dashboard, and stroking the paintwork as delicately as if it were the head of a newborn baby. Mirri and Kate looked at them in alarm.

"Who are they? Have they nothing better to do?" Mirri spat.

"I had no idea the effect cars had on men," Kate whispered as one boy leaned through the window and aimed his camera at the gearshift.

"Cor, me brother's gonna love this. He's gonna be so jealous he missed it. How old is it?" the car paparazzo asked.

"Oh, really old," Kate improvised. "Older than you."

"No way." He was awestruck.

"How fast does it go, miss?" another boy politely inquired. Kate was convinced that it was Leonard's car that made them respectful; they looked like they'd be your common or garden-variety surly teenagers otherwise.

"I can make it go at a hundred eighty miles an hour," Mirri said as she opened the door, gently nudging the boy out of the way. "Now, if you excuse me, we have to go. Come on, Bébé." As she said that the lion cub, who'd been lying on the backseat for an hour and a half, bounded out the door and onto the cricket green for an almighty pee.

"That's better, isn't it darling?" Mirri said as she snapped a leash on his collar, barely noticing that their audience had suddenly multiplied from being every male in the village under the age of forty to, quite simply, every person and dog in this village and the one down the road. They were all standing around and staring at the bizarre new arrivals with more wonder than if they'd been zipped into silver space suits.

"Do you have the map?" Mirri asked Kate as she locked up the car and set off on their stroll. "I don't want to take a wrong turn and get lost in the woods."

"Got it," Kate said as she pulled the peak of her baseball cap down over her sunglasses and hurried to catch up with Mirri and Bébé.

Kate and Mirri wandered the mile or so from the car to the house they suspected of being Nick's in silence. Mirri was clearly nervous, and both of them seemed acutely aware that every step they took could be one closer to finding Nick Sheridan again. Mirri was weak at the thought of the implications for her life if he turned out not to be the love she had imagined him as. It was all very well harboring notions of lost love for thirty years, as long as he turned out to be the person you hoped he was. Or more poignantly—as long as he was dead. To find him and realize that you had been wrong—well, it would shake the foundations of your world. There was no doubt about it.

"It said in *House and Garden* that he had an eight-foot-high stone wall. Does that look eight feet high to you?" Kate asked as they approached the leaning, moss-coated wall of the house through the long grass and wildflowers of the shoulder.

"Perhaps," Mirri said as she tugged at Bébé's leash for him to get a move on. She couldn't bear to be hindered now. She needed to get there almost as much as she dreaded getting there.

"Yeah, I think this is the one," Kate said as they finally reached the gateposts with the stone pineapples and the vast, wrought-iron gates. "Look, there are lions on the gates. It said that in the magazine."

"Look, Bébé, my darling," Mirri whispered to her cub as if it were a mystical sign from heaven. "There are lions on the gates."

"Shall we walk up the drive?" Kate turned to Mirri, who seemed to be transfixed on the house beyond the gates.

"Do I look old?" she asked suddenly.

"Mirri, I'm sure he's not going to be there. And even if he is he doesn't need to see us," Kate reassured her. "But no, you don't look old. You look beautiful."

If Nick Sheridan had been in his house at that moment it was very likely that he would have looked out the window to see if he could spy the two strange women with a lion cub who were heading in his direction from the village green where they had left a dove-gray vintage Aston Martin and a pack of transfixed locals. Mrs. Ogden from the post office had already dialed his number to telegram the news. As had his cleaning lady, who considered it her duty to warn him of the imminent arrival of the circus troupe. Fortunately for Mirri and Kate, Nick Sheridan's phone rang off the hook in an empty house.

"There are two cars in the drive," Kate felt compelled to whisper, even though they were still a good three-minute walk from the house. The gravel drive wound around a corner and up a small hill. The front lawn was as green as Kate's engagement ring and tufted with small clusters of oak trees. The house itself was a neat, three-story Georgian house whose rows of windows looked like kindly eyes peering out over the valley.

"Do you feel like Elizabeth Bennett seeing Pemberley for the first time?" Kate asked dreamily as she stopped to admire the house and its gardens.

"No, I feel like I might be sick," she said.

"If both the cars are here it might mean he's in," Kate warned.

"Or he's on holiday. There are no dogs barking. In England these houses always have dogs who come tearing at you with their bad breath, muddying your clothes."

"Good point, Miss Marple." Kate nudged Mirri, who was in no mood to be nudged or called after an old lady.

"That could be him." Mirri suddenly stopped dead in her tracks. "He's going to turn around and see us any second." She was pointing to a man who was leaning over by the front door. Kate couldn't make out any more than that he had graying hair, was wearing a green jacket, and appeared to be taking off his boots in the porch. "Go and talk to him." With which Mirri disappeared behind a tree with Bébé. It was like being fourteen again and going to look at the house of the boy you fancied. Only Kate was almost thirty and Mirri was sixty.

Kate stood on the driveway, not sure what on earth she should say to him. After all, she was trespassing. She'd be lucky not to be arrested or turfed out of the gates by a poker-faced butler. She tried to remain silent, in the hope that he wouldn't see her and would just disappear inside. But the man's sixth sense obviously told him that he was being watched because he looked up and scowled in Kate's direction. Then he called out, "Can I help you?"

"Hi there," Kate said, trying desperately to invent a good excuse for prowling around a stranger's garden. Kate walked slowly over to him. As she got closer she decided that if this was Nick Sheridan, then the years had not been kind to him. But then if he'd been as lovelorn as Mirri, maybe it was inevitable he'd look like this, from sheer suffering and heartache. Kate decided not to take any chances.

"I was hoping to speak to Nicholas Sheridan," she said in her best American accent. Which was the worst. "The famous architect."

"He's not here," the man said. Kate wondered whether he was Nick and he was just lying so he didn't have to become embroiled in a discussion. This sort of thing might well happen to him all the time as the architect of controversial buildings around the globe.

"I'm a student from Arizona," Kate said unconvincingly. "I just wanted to shake his hand and tell him how much I admire his work." At this point the man softened visibly. He was standing in purple socks on the gravel, doubtless ready to put on the black brogues that were under the wooden seat in the covered gray porch.

"I'm the gardener," he said. "But I'll tell him you called. He's in Tokyo, I believe."

"Well, thanks very much, anyway." Kate smiled broadly. As an American might. She hoped he wouldn't notice the chips on her teeth as Louis had or they'd give the game away.

"Good day to you, miss," he said as Kate turned on her heels and retraced her steps toward the gate. She wondered how Mirri was going to sneak out from behind the tree now and escape without being seen. But then she decided that she didn't really care if Mirri got caught. She'd thrust Kate forward and she'd made a complete fool of herself. Mirri deserved all she got. Kate smiled and strolled in a jaunty manner toward the gate, drowning out Mirri's stranded hissing noises with the crunch of gravel underfoot.

Chapter Twenty-four

Kate stood in front of the mirror and checked out the white cowboy hat from every possible angle.

"I'm not sure, do you think it's too big for my face?" she asked Alice, an old friend from art school who was now dressmaker to the stars with a very bijoux grotto-type shop in Notting Hill. Alice was as tiny as a fairy with long blond curls that belied her formidable honesty.

"I think it makes you look stupid, actually."

"I sort of do, too." Kate turned her back to the mirror and then whipped her face around to catch herself by surprise. "It might look better in motion."

"It's your wedding day, not a rodeo," Alice pointed out. "You're not going to be in motion all that much."

"I like the idea," Kate said as she reluctantly took off the hat. She did like the idea of a cowgirl bride—a country-and-western twist to go with her boots and her groom, who had planned it all. It had always been his dream, apparently, though Kate had no clue of this because until the night he'd proposed he'd never so much as spoken the word *wedding* in front of her. If he had she might have dreamed up her own theme, or ways to dilute his a bit. But now she was stuck with a hat that no matter which way you looked at it, and she'd looked at it all ways, wasn't working.

"Yeah, on someone else maybe," Alice said. "How about I show you some of the headdresses I made last season. They're not expensive but they're a bit more you. And they'll go with that dress you liked out the back." She went to rummage in her office.

Kate put the hat back on her head one more time. She didn't know how she was going to tell Jake that she looked like JR from *Dallas* rather than Emmylou Harris. She would much prefer a medieval look, or a Cecil Beaton debutante look—anything, in fact, but this bloody hat.

"We could do a really cute white sparkly suit with a miniskirt and jacket." Alice came out from the back of the shop and hung a couple of new outfits on the rail. "But it's more Elvis than cowgirl."

"That might work," Kate said hopefully. "Jake loves Elvis. Let's try it." She stepped into the white suit, and it did look fabulous.

"It's like Jackie Kennedy might look in heaven," approved Alice.

"And on my head?" Kate asked tentatively.

"No way the cowboy hat. Though you might, just might, get away with the boots."

"Great." Kate hugged her friend excitedly. "I think Jake's going to love it."

As she was changing back into her jeans Kate's phone rang. It was Tanya's cell.

"Hi, Tan," Kate answered as she hopped up and down with her foot in one leg of her jeans while also trying to hold on to the dressing room curtain for support.

"Okay, can you talk?"

"Yeah, I'm in the changing room at Alice's shop," Kate said. There was rarely a place she couldn't talk, in fact; when it came to chatting on the phone she was as adept as an ambidextrous octopus.

"Great. Now, I'm not supposed to tell you yet because our parents are meant to be the first to know and we're on our way to Robbie's mum's now . . . but I'm . . . well we're . . . having a baby." Tanya practically screamed the last part of the sentence down the phone at Kate.

"No way!" Kate shouted. "Oh my God, congratulations." She stopped putting on her jeans and sat down on the floor to absorb the amazing news.

"I'm pregnant. Can you believe it?" Tanya was obviously trying not to let Robbie hear but Kate suspected that the entire street knew by now. "We did the test last night. We sat in the bathroom while we watched it and suddenly there it was. I'm a month gone, Kate."

"Darling, that is such amazing news."

"I know. And I'm not going to get too carried away, because it's such early days and you never know but . . . ," Tanya spilled out hurriedly, already very carried away.

"I'm sure you'll be fine," Kate said, then sounded a note of caution. "And the most important thing is that no matter what happens, you've gotten pregnant once. So even if anything goes wrong—which it won't—you'll do it again. And again."

"I know . . . I can't tell you how happy I am."

"You don't need to, I can hear it." Kate smiled and tossed the cowboy hat to one side. There were so many more important things in life than what you looked like on your wedding day.

"Robbie thinks it's totally thanks to Mirri and that amazing"— she sounded as though she was cupping her hands over the phone so Robbie couldn't hear—"orgasm I had that night after your party."

"Do you want me to tell her the news?" Kate asked. "She's been kind of down since she wrote to that guy Nick. She hasn't heard back yet."

"Okay, and tell her thank you so much. She's magical. But she mustn't tell anyone yet," Tanya said sternly.

"Well, let's hope that her definition of not telling anyone's a bit more stringent than yours," Kate said, and the two girls laughed. "Darling, I have to go, and so do you. But let's meet up to celebrate tomorrow when you're back. I'll bring Jake along."

"Brilliant," Tanya said. "Thanks Kate, you've been amazing through all this. I love you."

"I love you, too," Kate said, and hung up the phone with a warm smile to herself.

———————————

Mirri was dropping off to sleep in a garden chair in the baking afternoon sun and Bébé was lying next to her on the grass. She was alone for the first time in weeks. Kate was out shopping for wedding dresses and Leonard had gone to Scotland for the Glorious Twelfth—the beginning of the grouse-shooting season. The peace was just what she needed. She'd been to dinner with three different men this week—including last night's visit to the palace, which had been entertaining, but she'd drunk far too much delicious wine and was feeling the effects. Still, that was the price she paid for not letting the grass grow under her feet. Not only had she not heard back from Nick Sheridan yet—and she was sure that he must be back in the country now; nobody went to Toyko for more than a fortnight, surely—but she was also missing Jonah. Purely as a lover, but nonetheless it wasn't a happy feeling, having a void. And she didn't really have the energy or inclination to fill it right now. She was still waiting to see what, if anything, happened with Nick. She pulled her sun hat down over her face to stop the wretched wrinkles etching their way like a road map across her skin, when she heard the garden gate slam.

"Who's that?" She tipped the sun hat up over her head and lifted her chin to see. Striding down the garden path was not a photographer with his wide-angled lens pointing at her cleavage, but Jake. He was heading for Kate's shed and didn't appear to have seen, or heard, her. Though Mirri didn't assume anything, she found him insufferably rude and wouldn't put it past him just to ignore her.

"Kill, Bébé." She patted her lion cub on the head and pointed in Jake's direction. He'd disappeared into the shed now. But Bébé simply turned over and showed his face to the sun. Mirri tried to go back to sleep but didn't like the idea of The Slug sniffing around in Kate's shed while she was out. Eventually she took off her hat and sat up. She fastened her sarong around her bare breasts and stood up. Padding down the path silently, without shoes on, she wondered whether she'd catch Jake in some compromising act. Maybe trying on Kate's underwear.

"Are you looking for something?" Mirri walked in to find Jake flipping through Kate's paintings.

"Hi there." He hardly looked up as Mirri walked in the door of the overheated shed. "Just looking through Kate's pictures to see if there's anything we can give to my aunt Catherine for a birthday present. I completely forgot to get her something." He lifted a small watercolor of a mill house next to a pond out and appraised it.

"You're doing what?" Mirri asked.

"Oh, Kate won't mind. I'll check with her first, you know to make sure it's not priceless or anything." He laughed. But Mirri didn't respond. She stood with her hand on the open door, as if blocking his exit.

"That's her parents' first house, where they lived before she was born. She went down last summer and painted it on the anniversary of her father's death," she said fiercely, then added, "but you probably didn't know that, did you?" Unfortunately for Jake he was too involved in trying to find the right painting for Aunt Catherine, before her birthday supper this evening, to notice the menace in her voice.

"No, I didn't know that. Right, well I won't take that one then. Thanks for the tip." He moved on and was checking some still lifes, including one of a stuffed zebra head next to some paintbrushes, when Mirri moved inside a few more steps and closed the door gently behind her. She went over to the bed and sat down on the edge of it.

"Have you booked the honeymoon yet?" she asked as she crossed her legs beneath her sarong.

"The honeymoon?" He looked blankly at Mirri, vaguely wondering why she'd come in rather than leaving him alone with the paintings. He was in a hurry. "No, I was thinking maybe we'd go to Umbria in October. My mother's got a house there."

"Ah, so Kate wants to go to Italy?" Mirri asked.

"Well, I don't know. I haven't asked her." He looked up impatiently at Mirri. "It's supposed to be a surprise, you see."

"But it'd be so much more romantic to take her somewhere that she'd always wanted to go."

"Probably. I think she'll like Italy," he said, and pulled out a painting of some tulips. They were ordinary but Aunt Catherine would probably like them.

"Jake, how do you feel about Kate?" Mirri was looking down at her toes, which were painted glossy fuchsia. She didn't want him to see that she was trying to catch him out.

"Kate? Well, I'm marrying her, aren't I?" he said casually as he set the tulip painting on one side. Mirri nodded, unconvinced. "Which means I love her. Kate's the kind of woman you should marry. She's great. She cares for me. I don't know what I'd do without her."

"Does she bring magic into your life?" Mirri looked him in the eye now.

He blinked and then frowned for a moment. "Magic?"

Mirri nodded again.

"Yeah, I mean. Probably." Then he was hit with a thought. "Especially in bed. She's great in bed. I mean she looks really sweet but she's a rocket." He nodded in a satisfied way. "Especially lately."

"And she's the only woman you're interested in?" Mirri asked as she uncrossed her legs and leaned back onto her arms.

"Yeah, pretty much. I mean I wouldn't be human if I didn't think there were some cute chicks out there, but . . . well, I'm marrying her. She's getting what she wanted."

"Isn't it what you want, too?"

"God, what are you, a shrink?" Jake pretended to be lighthearted but Mirri was getting under his skin now. He hadn't a clue what her game was but he knew, in the way women were so bloody good at, that she was playing with him. "I love Kate. When we weren't together I missed her and I asked her to marry me, which means that I want to be with her. What's your problem?"

"You know that if you marry her she'll expect you to be faithful for the rest of your life, don't you?" Mirri raised an eyebrow at Jake.

"Maybe."

"No, she will. She believes you've changed. That all those nights she knew you were out with other women are behind you."

"Well, they are," Jake said defiantly. "At least for now."

"But not forever?" Mirri gave him a coquettish look. She didn't want to do this, but she knew that he needed to be needled a bit more. She had to know whether Jake had really changed, and there was nothing else for it.

"Well, I mean . . . maybe not forever . . ." Now he was looking at Mirri in a different way. The knot of her sarong, which was only an inch or two above her cleavage, had loosened. Her hair was spilling out of the clip it was in and tendrils hung about her face.

"I could never manage to be faithful," Mirri said with her most kittenish pout. "That's why I stopped getting married."

"Why do you think I haven't taken the plunge before now?" Jake said, his smiled glued to Mirri's diaphanous sarong, which was slit open to the thigh. "But Kate's great. She'll forgive me if I mess up. That's why I love her."

"Sex is like eating sweets," Mirri said, echoing a line she'd once had to say in a movie. "I can never have enough and yet I get bored of the same one for too long—I prefer to have the whole shop to choose from." At which point Mirri stood up and walked over to where Jake stood, rooted to the spot.

"I know what you mean," he said as she fixed her hooded, goddess eyes on him. Eyes that despite the years were still as suggestive of unspeakable things as they ever had been.

"I thought so," Mirri said as she waited for him to come to her.

Kate was planning to go straight home and get ready for Jake's aunt Catherine's birthday, where she was supposed to be meeting all the family members she'd never encountered—soon to be her own family. But as she cycled along Regents Park Road she couldn't resist stopping in a shop selling the smallest, cutest baby cardigans she'd ever seen. She rode up to the window and stared in for a few minutes at hats, booties, and dresses. Then she thought better of buying any of them. Perhaps it was bad luck to buy clothes at this early stage of someone's pregnancy. Maybe she'd wait. She spotted a blue gingham dress with lace culottes and nearly died at how sweet it was. She couldn't help wishing that Tanya would have a girl, immoral though it might be to want anything other than a healthy baby. As she got on her bike again and cycled up the hill to Leonard's she also wondered whether she and Jake might have children before too long. She and Tanya could have babies together and do all the things that she got so irritated at other mothers for doing—like talk about baby yoga all day and take screaming children to cafés—it was a whole new world. For the first time in days Kate felt excited again about getting married. She'd found an outfit that looked great, she and Jake were going to have a rosy future in the new flat and maybe even have babies—despite what Mirri preached, and what Kate on some level believed—it didn't seem to be the soft, smug option in life at all, just a really natural, normal idea.

Kate leaned over her handlebars to open the catch on the garden gate. She cycled through and closed it behind her. The sun was bright over the garden and Bébé was lying asleep on the lounge chair beneath the cherry tree.

"Hey, Bébé, where's your mummy?" Kate swung her leg over her bike, hopped off, and propped it against a tree. Mirri couldn't be far away if Bébé was on his own. She wandered over and kneeled on the grass next to him as she gave him a stroke behind the ears. She looked up to see if Mirri was fixing herself a G&T in the kitchen, but it didn't look like it. "Wait here, I'll go and make sure she hasn't forgotten you." Kate kissed him on the head before heading

for the house. It wasn't a very sensible thing to do, leaving an endangered and potentially dangerous species wandering the garden
alone. "Mirri, it's me. Are you there?" she called as she went into the
kitchen. But the house seemed to be empty. A bottle of suntan lotion lay on the kitchen table with its top off, and the familiar sound
of Mirri shouting down the phone in French from the top floor
couldn't be heard.

———

"How do you want me?" Mirri said as she lay back on Kate's bed
and watched Jake strip off his shirt.

"Christ, you're sexy," Jake breathed and watched as Mirri devoured him with her eyes. With one hand she unknotted the
sarong, which fell open to reveal her voluptuous, freckled breasts.

"Come over here." She beckoned to him with her finger. Jake
stepped out of his jeans and across the floor. Mirri wanted to get
this out of the way before Kate came home. She didn't really want
Kate to find them—just to be able to tell her about it later. She'd be
hurt enough when she heard, but Mirri felt it was a necessary step.
Though when Jake sat down on the edge of the bed and leaned
down to kiss her lips she wondered at the wisdom of it. She'd kissed
more men in her life than she'd had cigarettes almost, it was practically her profession as an actress and her hobby as a woman, but
kissing Jake wasn't easy. Not because he wasn't cute—Mirri found
him surprisingly sexy as he lightly brushed his lips against hers and
stroked her stomach with the back of his hand, it was no wonder
Kate was so hooked on him, she thought as her nipples hardened to
his touch—but she found it difficult to do this because for the first
time ever Mirri understood how awful it felt to betray someone.
Kate had become a friend, one of the few people whose spirit Mirri
admired, and now she was doing something designed to hurt her.
She wondered whether she should put a stop to it.

"You know, I'm not sure . . . ," she murmured in Jake's ear as he
moved his hand over the front of her bikini bottoms.

"It's okay. Kate won't be back for ages," he said. "She's shopping for a wedding dress."

When he said that, Mirri suddenly opened her eyes and saw him leaning toward her, his eyes closed in pleasure, his naked body so close to hers.

"We can't," she said. She had a flashback to the day that she'd first come into this shed. She'd stood at the bottom of the bed and watched as Kate and Jake had sex. She hadn't liked him the first time she met him and she liked him even less now. He might have been a romantic but it didn't stop him from being far too careless of Kate's feelings. Sure, Mirri knew that in a way he really loved her. He believed that she was the only girl for him. It was simply that Kate deserved so much better. Mirri put her hand up to his chest to stop him from going any further. "Let's not, Jake," she said. He opened his eyes and at first appeared bewildered, but then he saw on her face exactly what it was they were doing.

"Maybe you're right," he said, and paused for a second with his hand on Mirri's cheek.

"I am." Mirri was about to take hold of the corner of her sarong and cover herself when the door swung open. Kate walked into the dimly lit shed from the bright sunlight.

"God, Mirri, I'm sorry," Kate said, assuming that Mirri and Jonah had for some unknown reason appropriated her shed.

Then Jake called out, "Kate!" He spun around before she had a chance to duck out again and leave them to it.

"Jake?" As her eyes adjusted, Kate stared uncomprehendingly at him. He shuffled off Mirri, leaving her naked on Kate's bed, and stood in suspended animation for a moment as he couldn't seem to decide whether to grab Kate or his boxer shorts.

"Kate, this isn't . . ." He watched as the look of bewilderment on her face failed to shift.

Kate looked from Mirri to Jake and then Jake to Mirri but nothing seemed to add up. "What were you doing?" she asked, as if they might have been watching the news.

"Kate. I know what you think." Jake grabbed his boxer shorts and thrust his legs into them. Then he pulled on his jeans. "But it wasn't anything it was just . . ." Mirri sat up on the bed and grabbed her sarong. She wrapped it tautly around her body and though she knew she probably ought to leave Kate and Jake to sort this out between them she was too furious with him.

"Of course it was something," Mirri said as she stood up. "If you weren't such a pathetic man you'd tell her the truth. You'd tell your fiancée that we were about to fuck."

"You what?" Kate said. It was as if she hadn't seen them lying naked on top of one another a moment ago.

"It wasn't like that . . ." Jake went toward Kate with his hand out.

She ignored it and took a step backward. "You and Jake were having sex?" She was looking directly at Mirri now; Jake didn't even seem to concern her.

"I'll talk to you about it later," Mirri said as she walked contemptuously by Jake and then shrugged at Kate. She wasn't hypocritical enough to pretend to be sorry; she'd achieved what she'd wanted in a way. She just hadn't expected to feel as horrified at having hurt another person as she felt for having hurt Kate.

"Where are you going?" Kate said as Mirri walked past her.

"To the house."

"Oh, no, you're not," Kate suddenly exploded in Mirri's face. "You're not going anywhere until you explain to me why when I walked in you were about to have sex with my fiancé."

"Why don't you ask him?" Mirri pointed at Jake, who was shaking his head from side to side with a pained expression on his face.

"You're my friend," Kate said.

"I know, and I'm sorry that you saw us. I meant to stop but . . ."

"You're sorry that I saw you? But not that you were having sex with my boyfriend?" Kate's face was contorted with pain. "How could you?" She turned to Jake. "How could both of you do this to me?"

Jake and Mirri steadfastly refused to look at one another. Jake was looking at the ground and Mirri was attempting to look Kate in the eye, though that wasn't as easy as she'd imagined, either.

"You didn't really want to marry him," Mirri said in her most measured voice. "And I knew that he wasn't ever going to be right for you. He loves you but not in the way you should be loved."

"So you decided to sleep with him?" Kate said. And in that second, the realization of what had actually just happened on her bed seemed to dawn on her. She looked to her rumpled duvet, she looked at Jake's discarded shirt on the floor and the two people in the world who were closest to her, and she walked out, still clutching her bag as she had been when she'd walked in.

Chapter Twenty-five

Kate sat on a bench at the top of Primrose Hill and stared numbly at the view. She looked at the London Eye in the distance but no emotion registered with her. She thought about the night that she and Louis had stood on the bridge and drunk champagne but she felt nothing. She thought about her father—about what he'd say to her now if he were here, about how much he'd loved her and wanted to protect her, about the fact that she'd never see him again—but still she didn't feel. She didn't feel sadness or pain. Then she thought about Mirri and Jake again, how they'd stood defiantly in front of her and not even apologized. She understood very clearly that she was no longer getting married, that the ring on her finger didn't mean what it had done half an hour ago, and that she and Jake would never live together in the flat now, but for some baffling reason she didn't seem to be hurt by these thoughts. Nothing Kate could think right now seemed to touch her. It was like watching one of those hospital dramas where someone's been paralyzed and they're sticking pins into his body and he doesn't flinch. Kate couldn't feel a thing.

"Tanya, the weirdest thing's just happened," she said into her phone after she'd dialed her friend's number and gotten voice mail.

She remembered that Tanya was in the country so probably had no reception on her phone. "I just went home and found Jake and Mirri in bed together. Anyway, the thing is, I'm all right but I'm sitting on Primrose Hill and I don't really want to go back there right now so I just wondered whether you kept house keys with any of your neighbors so that I can go around to yours for a bit. To have some space. Give me a call if you get this message." Kate hung up.

She thought about calling Leonard in Scotland but he'd be out on some grouse moor up to his ears in heather. Besides, there was nothing Leonard could do right now. Kate just wanted somewhere to go. She knew that she was going to have to cry eventually and that her detachment was just an extreme form of shock, and she knew that when she started to cry she didn't want to be out in the open frightening dog walkers and mothers with push chairs who might think that she was a mad person instead of someone whose world had just been tipped on its axis. She looked out at the skyline for the next half hour while several things occurred to her. They were:

1. Whether Jake thought Mirri was better in bed than her. She found herself genuinely curious.

2. That she wouldn't be paid to finish Mirri's portrait now. And even if she was paid, there was no way she'd be able to look at her for a second, let alone stare at her to paint her.

3. She might never get married and have children.

4. She would have to change the sheets on her bed, which was her least favorite domestic chore in the world.

After she'd thought these things she felt her chest begin to tighten in panic and her head begin to throb at the temples. She knew it wouldn't be long now before her eyes started to prick and tears would push hard from behind her eyeballs. She wanted to go to her flat and sit in her ramshackle shell of a kitchen and cry for as long as it took, but her keys were on the bookshelf in the shed and she couldn't go back there. Her mum had gone back to the country last night. She had nowhere to go.

When Kate arrived at Louis's front door she paused a moment before knocking. She was here because he was her oldest friend and the only person she could turn to right now. She wasn't thinking about how she'd dropped him as soon as Jake came back, she wasn't thinking about how little sympathy he'd seemed to have for her in the gallery the other day when she'd told him her doubts about marrying Jake. She wasn't even thinking how all the while she'd been trying on wedding dresses to marry Jake and thinking about the future, she actually began wondering what it would be like to be marrying Louis. Louis was the dream, Jake was the prosaic reality. Louis would be the man who would treat her well, who'd help with the children, whom she'd talk to every night into old age; who shared a passion for work and art with her. In comparison, she'd come to realize, Jake was the kind of boyfriend you're supposed to have as a teenager—badly behaved, rough around the edges, uninterested in you, lazy, and yet for some reason you want to kiss him in the phone box late at night and steal out to see him when your parents are asleep. In short, Jake was the guy who Kate should have grown out of. Louis was the one she should have grown into. But the whole marriage thing had been a red herring and taken her down the wrong street.

Of course, as she stood outside Louis's front door and anticipated his sympathy, tears began to stream down her face. There was nothing like someone feeling sorry for you to make you dissolve into your own sadness, no matter how stoic you thought you were. And as Kate stood on Ladbroke Grove, with the cars tearing by, she wasn't conscious that she'd elevated Louis to perfect-man status before Jake had messed things up and proposed to her—she was aware only that Jake and Mirri had just brought her world crashing down around her and the only person she really wanted to see and be with was Louis. He'd make her feel better, no matter what had happened in the past few weeks. She was sure of this.

"Louis, it's me." Kate said as the entry phone buzzed. There was a click as the front door opened. Kate pushed the handle and went up the stairs, past the bikes and scrap metal, toward the familiar, fluorescent light of his studio. The door at the top was open and Kate walked in, expecting to find Louis in his jeans, leaning over a bench with a pencil in his hand and a frown on his face as he finalized the details for the exhibition, which was only ten days away.

"Louis?" she called out when she saw that he wasn't there. The door to the flat was wide open so she walked toward it.

"Louis, it's me." She tapped her knuckle on the door to the flat in a perfunctory way and walked on in. But as she was about to put her head around the kitchen door she saw not Louis, but a woman emerging from the office.

"Oh, I thought you were Louis. He's gone out to buy some milk." She had a low, soothing American accent and was clearly surprised to see a strange woman in the hallway.

"I'm Kate, a friend of Louis," Kate said, then added, "We're working together on the Tate project."

"Right." The woman nodded. "He's told me about that." Kate looked at the stranger and took it all in. Not only was she wearing Louis's shirt over her jeans, with the buttons undone to the point of indecency, she was also extremely beautiful and slightly older than Kate. And Louis, for that matter. She wasn't cute or sweet or pretty and she wasn't fragile, either. She was quite simply beautiful, with the face of a woman—a wide straight mouth, intense brown eyes that seemed to understand everything, a delicate, serious nose, and slightly ruffled brown hair with heavy, Julie Christie bangs.

"But if he's not here I'll come back later." Kate began to back out the door. Standing beside this woman made her feel utterly wretched. Kate had a tear-streaked face and had come running to Louis out of a pathetic sense that he might actually want her and make her feel better. But looking at the woman in front of her,

Kate completely understood everything that she herself wasn't—she wasn't smart, she wasn't interesting, and she had just taken for granted this man who could clearly do so much better than Kate. Kate was the lame girl who thought that the world revolved around her and really nobody was that interested—not her friend Mirri, not her fiancé, and now not even Louis it seemed.

"You can wait." There was no way this woman would ever flake on Louis. Neither did she feel insecure about Kate. She was so at ease with herself that Kate just wanted to run away. And grow up. She'd lost Louis to this self-assured, beautiful creature and she suddenly determined that this was the last thing she'd ever lose. She'd lost everything and now she was done with losing and losers. For good.

Kate hurried down the stairs and out onto the street, banging the door shut behind her. But as she was about to catch a bus to who knows where she saw Louis walking up the sidewalk with a plastic carrier bag in his hand. She was going to do an about-face and scurry off in the other direction but she remembered her resolution. No more losers—and that included herself.

"Louis," she said as she got closer to him. She held her hand up in a small wave. "I just called by at yours."

"You did?" he asked, computing the facts. "I wasn't there."

"No, I met . . ." Kate hadn't even asked the woman's name.

"Grace."

"Exactly," Kate said. "Anyway it's fine. I just came around to say that . . . well . . . it doesn't matter anymore."

"What doesn't matter anymore?" he asked, switching his shopping to the other hand.

"It doesn't matter that I came," Kate said. But clearly he wasn't going to let this go too easily. He looked quizzically at her.

"I came to tell you that Jake and I are finally over. For good. Not that it makes any difference to your life at all," she said, thinking he was probably longing to get back and drink coffee with Grace. Or maybe even have sex with Grace and then drink coffee.

"Of course it makes a difference to my life," he said with genuine softness.

"Really?" Kate averted her gaze from her feet to his face.

"I care about you too much to see you with a prick like Jake. I want you to be happy." He rubbed his hand up and down her upper arm.

"Great. Well, there you go, then," she said, suddenly feeling sick at his avuncular patting of her. There was no doubt about it—Louis was lost, too.

"Was that it?" he asked.

"What?"

"You came all this way to tell me that you'd split up with Jake. Did you want anything else?"

"No, that was it," Kate said, and faked a big smile. "See you at the opening."

"Sure thing," Louis said, and walked on, back to Grace.

It wasn't that there weren't a million things that Kate had wanted to ask Louis about Grace, it was just that there was no point. It suddenly seemed to her that she had no right whatsoever to know whether he'd been seeing her for six hours or six months and if he was in love with her and whether he'd simply made the moves on Kate for old times' sake. None of it was going to make any difference to the fact that Kate had well and truly fucked up. Somehow she didn't even feel as if she needed to ask Jake and Mirri for explanations anymore, either. From the moment she took Jake back it seemed inevitable that things were going to end up like this. She'd had her doubts and she'd ignored them. Mirri had tried to persuade her that she deserved better than Jake but to Kate's mind she deserved every bit of misfortune that she'd gotten. She'd lacked the courage to do what she knew in her heart was the right thing, and now she had to live with the consequences.

Kate walked toward the bus stop and decided that she was going to face the music. She caught the bus back to Primrose Hill and Leonard's house. She walked down the path as she'd so innocently done a few hours ago and took a deep breath as she approached the shed.

"Kate, can we talk?" She heard Mirri's voice from somewhere down the garden. She reluctantly looked up and saw her sitting in the hammock. She'd changed and was wearing jeans and a baggy T-shirt. It was the least sexy Kate had ever seen her look.

"There's nothing to say," Kate said, and made a beeline for the shed door.

"Please. I want to explain," Mirri called out. Kate stopped and waited to hear more. "Come here. Please."

"You're wasting your time. I know what happened and nothing's going to change what I think of you or that shit-for-brains ex-fiancé of mine. Has he gone, by the way?" Kate looked apprehensively down the garden and toward the house. If both of them were lying in wait for her she'd lock herself in the shed and never come out again.

"I knew exactly what I was doing," Mirri said.

Kate looked at her with some interest. "Which makes it even worse." She decided that she wanted to hear Mirri's excuse. She didn't want to look the bitch in the eye but she was suddenly curious. She walked over toward the hammock and stood up against a tree. She had to be standing—she had the moral high ground and she wanted the literal high ground, too.

"You didn't love Jake. You told me so—," Mirri began.

"For God's sake, I was going to marry him. We had a house. I wear his ring." Kate noticed that the ring was still there when she looked at her hand.

"Of course you didn't tell me you didn't love him in a straightforward, honest way. That wouldn't be English of you. But I knew you didn't. And you knew you didn't." Mirri fired Kate a challenging look. "Tell me that you were in love with him then."

"I was going to marry him" was all that Kate could manage to say.

"Exactly. You needed to be set free. And I watched you and I hoped that you'd be able to do it but you couldn't. You're too nice.

Too sweet. And luckily for you I'm not. So I did it for you. He was in your shed taking the pictures you've painted, looking at them with no sense of appreciation—which is the way I've seen him look at you—and I went to confront him."

"Why was he taking my pictures?" Kate was puzzled.

"Because he was too cheap to buy his aunt a birthday gift and he is used to taking things from you. Has he paid anything for the deposit on your house?" Mirri asked. Kate shook her head. "Has he paid for the builder? The electrician? The plumber? No, because he thinks you'll take care of him. Which is fine. It may even be the modern way, what do I know? But what is most wrong is that there's one thing you have asked of him. You have asked him to be faithful. To not break your heart. Am I right?"

"It's not as if he was serially unfaithful. He just liked a pretty girl," Kate said defensively.

"Maybe," Mirri said sagely. "But I wasn't sure that he wasn't going to cause you pain again. So I had to see for myself."

"Oh right," Kate said sarcastically. "So you decided to seduce him yourself."

"Yes."

"No," Kate screamed at Mirri now. She felt anger pouring from her but Mirri remained calm. "I'll tell you how it was. You are a bitter, envious woman whose one hope of love has turned to dust and you couldn't bear to see me happy. I was engaged to a man, I had a future, and you were jealous."

"Oh, come on, Kate." Mirri was genuinely shocked. It hadn't occurred to her that Kate could even begin to construe things this way. "You know that's not true. You're like a daughter to me," she said, for the first time voicing a feeling about Kate that she'd had since she'd arrived. She'd felt protective of her and frustrated by her bad decisions, but she had firmly believed that she wanted only the best for this girl who was so unlike herself, yet perhaps had all the qualities of selflessness and naïveté that Mirri lacked. In a way they were like the perfect pair. But it dawned on Mirri now that maybe Kate had never seen things this way. Sure, she'd seen Mirri as a helpful friend at times, but Kate didn't need a mother. She had one. It was Mirri who wanted a daughter.

"You are nothing like a mother to me," Kate said in a hard, even tone. "A mother would never behave like you've done. You're so self-obsessed that you wouldn't know how to think about another human being. That's why the only creatures you can actually persuade to love you are animals."

"Kate, you can't say that." Mirri looked as if she'd been slapped around the face.

"The truth hurts, doesn't it?" Kate said. "And I know that Jake was a cheating bastard, I wasn't as stupid as you thought I was. But I also wanted to believe in something and I wanted to be part of something and he was a chance for me to have that. Which may not have been the most noble, pure reason for getting married but it's as good as most people's reasons."

"I'm sorry," Mirri said.

"Yeah, well, it's fine. If you're really sorry you can do something for me," Kate said, pushing herself away from the tree trunk with her hands.

"I'll do whatever you want me to," Mirri promised.

"Great. Then wait here."

Five minutes later Kate walked out onto the lawn carrying a bundle of bed linen in her arms.

"What's this?" Mirri had been expecting a more profound gesture.

"It's my laundry. If you're sorry then the least you can do is clean up your mess." Kate dropped the pile to the floor beside Mirri. "I don't iron the sheets, by the way. Just the pillowcases and the duvet cover."

"But Kate . . . ," Mirri called out as Kate strolled back to her shed with a satisfied spring in her step.

"Tomorrow's fine to bring them back. I've got a spare set," Kate called out without turning around. Then closed the shed door behind her for the night.

Chapter Twenty-six

For a whole week Kate had managed to resist Mirri's charms, flowers, apologies, excuses, and even a box of chocolates from Fortnum and Mason. She had flatly refused to carry on with the portrait of Mirri, suggesting that Lucian Freud might be delighted to take up where Kate had left off. Even Leonard had been down to the shed, sheepishly looking for the magic formula that would persuade Kate to pick up her brushes again. But she wouldn't budge. She'd accepted the loss of her relationship with Jake, and in a way she had even accepted that in the long run, and totally inadvertently, it really did seem as if Mirri might have done Kate a favor. But what she couldn't accept was the betrayal of her friendship with Mirri. She had grown to love Mirri in a way far beyond the way she loved the men who'd come and gone over the summer. Kate had learned to be adventurous and exacting of herself and she'd learned to let go and have fun. And even though she'd fallen at the last hurdle—by accepting Jake when really she didn't even want him—she'd still come a long way thanks to Mirri. And now her idol had been shattered and her feet of clay well and truly exposed. It wasn't so much that she felt betrayed as she was just disappointed.

"You don't have to speak to her. Just come and finish the painting. It's very important to her." Leonard had cornered Kate in the kitchen. She'd tried to wait for Mirri to leave the house each day, or for the curtains to be drawn on the top floor, which meant that Mirri was taking her siesta, and then she'd bomb up to the house and collect her post, show her face to Leonard, or raid the fridge. So far she'd avoided Mirri. But now it seemed she had enlisted him as messenger.

"I don't want to be in the same room as her," Kate said.

"Don't you think you're being a bit sanctimonious?" Leonard asked in a concerned way. "You've admitted to me that seeing the back of Jake was secretly what you wanted. And misguided though Mirabelle might have been—her intentions weren't bad."

"I can't do it."

"Ah, well, I tried." Leonard shook his head ruefully. "I'll be sad to see the back of her, though. I know she can be a royal pain in the backside but she's brought a bit of life back to this place. The pair of you have."

"What do you mean see the back of her?" Kate asked as she plucked a grape from the fruit bowl.

"She's off back to Africa at the weekend." Leonard pointed to a British Airways ticket on the table with the rest of the post.

"She's not?" Kate immediately felt her legs weaken. She knew that whatever she felt about Mirabelle Moncur, she didn't want her to leave. Not yet anyway. Still, she tried to hide how unsettled the thought had made her. "But why?"

"Well, she came for the portrait of Bébé and you've delivered that. And she wanted one of herself, which you quite understandably don't feel able to complete. So what else is there?"

There's Nick Sheridan, Kate thought. *That's why she came.* But now that dream was shattered for her. Kate felt a deep pang of sadness for Mirri. Strangely she felt much more sorry for her than she did for her own situation. Kate was young and she'd move on, but Mirri—without Nick she'd probably turn her back on the idea of love forever.

"I'll do it," Kate said in a split second. "But tell her that it doesn't mean anything apart from the fact that I'm a professional, I never renege on my promises, and I need the money to pay the mortgage on my new house since my boyfriend and I split up."

"I shall tell her," Leonard said with a twinkle in his eye. "And I must say that I couldn't be happier."

"It's a work thing. Not a friendship thing," Kate reminded him firmly.

"I know, I know, and I can't wait to see your splendid portrait," he said as Kate took a handful of biscuits and some strawberries back to her shed.

Chapter Twenty-seven

"You've given me a mustache." Mirri walked over to the easel and scowled as she looked closely at her upper lip in the painting.

"It's shadow. I'm going to lighten it later," Kate told her.

"Do I have a mustache?" Mirri walked over to the mirror and tilted her lips toward the light. "I don't want to be like one of those old women who look like a nanny goat with a beard."

"Would you mind just sitting down, please?" Kate said in a humorless voice.

"Of course." Mirri was chastened and sat down in her chair again. "Maybe one day you'd like to see the Picasso?"

"I'll go to a gallery if I want to see a Picasso. I think Africa's a bit far to travel. Especially to see a bad one."

"But it might not be as bad as I think. I mean what do I know? You'd be able to tell me whether it's really any good or not."

"I doubt it," Kate said, and determinedly mixed her paint. It had been like this for three days now. Mirri trying to make amends and Kate being truculent.

"Do I have to tell you once again that I am sorry for what I did?" Mirri asked with a frustrated sigh.

"No, it's okay. I heard you the first time," Kate said. Although she really hadn't wanted Mirri to leave London she was also stubbornly refusing to acknowledge to herself that she would have been desolate without her around.

"Do you miss Jake?" Mirri asked.

"I wouldn't have thought you'd have cared whether I did or I didn't."

"I care about you. I care that I made you unhappy." She tried to keep her head in the right position for the portrait.

"Maybe it's just guilt that you feel," Kate said dispassionately.

Mirri stared at Kate for a minute before she opened her mouth. "No it's not, it's love that I feel." She stood up and looked as if she might tear her hair out. And if not hers then Kate's. Kate froze with her paintbrush in hand as her sitter suddenly began to rail at her. "I thought that we were friends. I thought that for once in my life there was a woman I liked who I learned something from. And I thought that I was helping you, which it's obvious now I wasn't. But if you continue to be such a stick-in-the-ass, uptight *rosbif* then I would prefer it if you didn't finish my picture because right now you're just trying to punish me and I'm sure you're planning to paint horns on it." Mirri was standing right up close to Kate and glowering at her. They glared at one another for a long moment, Kate in a state of shock, but knowing that she deserved to be yelled at, and Mirri with a face like an elastic band that had just snapped.

But as they stood face-to-face, staring one another out, Kate was struck by a massive and irrepressible attack of the giggles. It started as a quiver in her upper lip but became a twitch around her mouth, then it spread to her nose and developed into full-blown hysteria.

Mirri was more furious than ever. "What is so funny?" she demanded.

"Actually it had crossed my mind," Kate spluttered between laughs.

"What had?" How dare Kate not take her seriously? She'd been taking Kate's fury seriously since the day she'd seduced Jake. And now the girl was laughing in her face.

"I was going to paint horns on you." Kate bit her lip to control her laughter.

"You were not," Mirri protested crossly.

Kate nodded. "I was."

The two women looked at one another again before both gave way to demented, snorting howls of mirth that drifted through the house and out into the garden.

"Are we friends again then?" Mirri asked, wiping the tears from her face.

"I think we probably are," Kate said as she finally got her breath back. Mirri took Kate's hands and then caught her in her arms. They hugged one another tight.

"I'd much rather have you in my life than Jake," Kate said in Mirri's ear.

"Am I supposed to be flattered?" Mirri pulled back a little and smiled.

"Well, yes, actually, because as you probably know, he's a great kisser." Kate threw herself onto the bed and lay on her side, her hand propping up her head.

"Ah, this is true." Mirri grimaced at the recollection of what she'd done. "But I have had much, much better."

"Me, too," Kate announced.

"You? Really? Who?" Mirri was surprised.

"Louis."

"Lovely Louis?"

"*Mais oui.*" Kate smirked. Then a look of sadness washed over her face. "Well, it was fun while it lasted anyway."

"You should go after him," Mirri said seriously.

"Somebody else already has. She's called Grace. She's got hair like Julie Christie."

"Ugh, Julie Christie. Who cares about her hair?" Mirri waved her hand dismissively.

"No, it's too late. But that's okay. I'm taking a breather from men."

"Can I show you something?" Mirri asked.

"Yes." Kate rolled over onto her stomach and watched as Mirri walked over to her dressing table. She pulled something out of her top drawer. "This arrived yesterday." She handed Kate a cream envelope.

"From Nick?" Kate sat up on the bed and crossed her legs. "Is it?"

Mirri stood still and nodded.

"Can I read it?" Kate carefully opened the envelope and took out the creamy card notelet with a red border.

"Of course you can read it." Mirri waited expectantly.

"He wants to meet up," Kate told her.

"I know."

"Next time he's in London."

"I know."

"He wants to take you for tea," Kate continued. "He can't tell you how delighted he was to hear from you."

"Isn't it exciting?" Mirri clapped her hands together.

"Why didn't you tell me?"

"Because you weren't speaking to me," Mirri pointed out.

"I'm sorry."

"No, *I'm* sorry," Mirri reiterated. "Now what on earth am I going to say to him on the telephone? What am I going to say to him when I see him? Shall I tell him I'm in love with him? Pretend that I just want to have tea? And what—" Mirri looked truly anxious. "—what shall I wear?"

At which point Kate burst into fresh peals of laughter. "Oh my God, don't tell me that I have to spend the rest of my life worrying about things like that," she groaned. "Am I really going to get to sixty and be as superficial as I am now?"

"Probably not, darling." Mirri looked at her disdainfully. "I'm sure when you get to sixty your hair will be gray, your stomach will be held at bay by your enormous beige knickers, and your nanny-goat beard will have little bits of your lunch stuck in it."

"That's disgusting," Kate yelled. "Anyway I think you're wrong. I think I'm going to be every bit as tarty and muttonish as you."

"Muttonish?" Mirri asked quizzically.

"Mutton dressed as lamb." Kate smiled cheekily. "Just like you."

―――――

When the day of Mirri's date with Nick arrived she didn't look remotely muttonish. She had tied her hair back in a ponytail with just a few wisps falling out, a rose-colored scarf knotted around her neck, and a raincoat.

"Is it okay?" Mirri asked.

"You look perfect," Kate said, "like you should be meeting your lover at a railway station."

"Well, I am meeting him in St. James's Park for elevenses, it's almost as romantic." Mirri looked at herself one more time in the mirror. "He's going to think I look so old," she lamented.

"You'll probably think the same about him."

"Do you think we'll have anything to talk about?" She turned to Kate and squeezed her hand nervously.

"You've never had a problem talking before." Kate was trying to get Mirri out the door and into the waiting taxi. She looked at her watch. "You're going to be late. At this rate he'll have left."

"I wouldn't mind. I don't think I want to go. What do I want a man for anyway?" Mirri fussed with her scarf.

"You don't. You've had plenty of men. You just want this one in particular." Kate opened the front door to usher her out.

"Or not."

"Only one way to find out." Kate was about to give Mirri a good-luck kiss on the cheek when she clutched Kate's hand again.

"Please come," Mirri pleaded.

"I can't. It's a date."

"No, just take me to the door. Then you can see what he looks like and whether he seems to be happy to see me and—"

"Okay, I'll come to the door. But I'm not going to spy on you. If you can't tell whether he likes you or not with all your experience, then you should just give up and go back to the cats forever." Kate grinned and pulled a jacket off the coat stand by the door.

"Thank you, thank you." Mirri tugged Kate by the hand and out the door.

The taxi pulled up on the mall and its engine hummed while Kate tried to eject Mirri from the back. "You have to get out," she hissed, "he might be walking down to the restaurant, too, and watching, and you don't want to look like a fourteen-year-old."

"I'd kill to look like a fourteen-year-old." Mirri remained glued to her seat. "Can you see him?"

"I don't know and I'm not about to look because it's silly. You'll see him for yourself when you get out and meet him like you're supposed to." Then Kate turned to the taxi driver, who had already done his "Eh, ain't you that Catherine Deneuf?"—which hadn't made him popular with one of the passengers in the back.

"How much do we owe you?" Kate asked.

"Fifteen quid." He pointed to the meter, which had just ticked over another forty pence as Mirri dragged her heels. Kate had decided to get out in the park and go for a walk while Mirri had her date. And afterward they'd meet up for a debrief. Unless of course Mirri was having her debrief elsewhere, in which case Kate would just get the tube home. Finally Mirri budged from her seat and Kate practically dragged her along the path toward the Inn the Park restaurant, with its turf roof and shadowy verandas.

"Have fun," she said, and then vanished into the verdant, jungle-like lushness of the rainy park.

"Mirabelle?" A man in the corner of the room, in a navy-blue sweater, with dark hair graying slightly around the ears and temples, stood up as Mirri walked hesitantly through the doors of the restaurant. He had a newspaper open on the table in front of him and beckoned her with a generous smile. Mirri raised her hand in a gesture of recognition, although she didn't recognize him even slightly, and meandered through the small tables toward him. As she stood before him her hands shook. She didn't feel as though she were "coming home" or any of the things she had imagined might happen in his presence again. She simply felt a rush of nausea.

"Nick." She was going to clasp him by the hand when he took her shoulders and looked into her eyes and then at her face as though he wanted to memorize everything. In fact, he was really just remembering. Then, without warning, he hugged her into such a bear-like grip that her scarf slid around her neck and her arms were clamped to her sides. Which was just as well, because she didn't know whether she would have returned the gesture even if she had been capable.

"Oh my God." He pulled away and looked at her. "I can't believe it's you." Then he checked himself. "Sit down, sit down, now, what can I get you?"

"Oh, well, tea will be fine," Mirri said politely. She stole a surreptitious glance at him as she repositioned her scarf and slipped off her raincoat. He was taller and broader than she'd remembered— she'd shrunk him over the years to the point of being able to fit him into her pocket—but then maybe he'd also grown in stature, which always made men seem larger. His eyes were the softest, warmest brown and his face was tanned in a countryside way that was much more fly-fishing than yachting on the Costa Smeralda. And the feathery breaks of gray in his black hair just made him look more appealing and watchable than he ever had been at thirty. Mirri cursed men for the glamour they always seemed to acquire with age. Then she noticed he was stirring his tea and unabashedly staring at her, so she had to hope that she still had a few of her charms left.

"Don't tell me you've gone English on us?" His laugh was as soft as his eyes.

"Never." She relaxed a little as he put his hand on her forearm. "But do you think they serve café au lait?"

"I expect so," he said, then confided, "We've become quite smart around here. Quite cosmopolitan."

"No?" Mirri pretended to be horrified and the two of them

melted into the secret laughter of lovers as effortlessly as if they'd been breakfasting together since the day they met.

———————

"So tell me." Mirri braced herself for the worst as she dropped a sugar lump into her coffee. "Are you married to the same woman as all those years ago?" Nick pensively narrowed his eyes. Mirri watched the swirls of coffee spiral into nothingness in the middle of her cup. She waited for what felt like another thirty years.

"No." He looked out through the windows and onto the park beyond as if the past were located somewhere beyond the trees. "We were engaged when you and I said our goodbyes, weren't we? Cecilia and I?"

"I believe so," Mirri said. Why was it that men seemed to have such appalling memories for the things that mattered most to women? "And then she became pregnant."

"So she did." He drew in his breath and remained focused on the view. "Well, she didn't, as a matter of fact. Although she told me that she had. I think she wanted to secure me at all costs. By which time we had been through a lot of hoo-ha and you had left and"— he turned to Mirri, who realized with relief that he hadn't forgotten a thing—"it was too late. We didn't get married, but by the time we'd broken it off"—Nick turned to Mirri as if assessing how honest he ought to be—"well, by that time you'd met someone else," he said very matter-of-factly.

"I had?" Mirri was surprised, and also desperate to know what happened next in his life.

"I read it in the newspaper. *The Times* no less." He pretended to be impressed. "They said that you were engaged to be married to a Pulitzer Prize–winning novelist and had moved to Mississippi to live in his colonial home."

Now it was Mirri who seemed not to remember something important. She cast her mind back. "Oh my God, him," she said with disbelief. "You know I can hardly remember his name. I stayed for two weeks and got so tired of his sitting all day in his study and then playing poker all night that I left. In fact, I walked with my suitcase through the fields and past the swamps all the way to the nearest town to catch a train home and never saw him again." She marveled at the memory. "You know, he probably thinks I am still waiting for him on the porch."

"That was it? That was the news that haunted me for years afterward?"

He was being surprisingly candid, she thought. "You were haunted?"

"I was. For a long time. And then I threw myself into work and then, well, then I got married . . ." He played with the handle of his spoon. Mirri had just begun to think that she was home and dry. That he had never been able to fill her place, that he'd been as faithful to her memory as Jay Gatsby was to Daisy, and that he'd felt the same as her for all these years. And now, this blow.

"Of course you did," she said as lightly as she could manage.

"I did. And I have two beautiful little girls . . . well, they're horrors actually . . . but I like them." Mirri saw her past and her future collapse in on her like a house of cards. "Anyway, of course it seems that I'm not cut out as the uxorious type at all because Jessica, probably quite rightly, left me. Apparently I'm difficult." He smiled. Mirri smiled, too. When she'd first walked in she wasn't sure how much she still liked him; her expectations were too unearthly to know how she'd felt. But in the last few minutes, since they'd been chatting, she knew that he was the same. That he was the man who would be able to make her feel secure and happy. More so now than he had when they'd first met, in fact, and it now looked as if maybe there was a chance. Could he really be as single as she was? And as difficult to live with? She stopped herself from getting carried away but all her Continental ardor made her want to fling herself at him. Though equally she was as shy as a girl anticipating her first kiss.

"I'm impossible," she boasted.

"A sweet-looking creature like you? I don't believe it," he teased. She laughed and lowered her head. "You are pure trouble, Miss Moncur. I can tell."

"Moi?" She treated him to her dirtiest laugh.

"Oh, yes. Absolutely." He shook his head and gave her a despairing smile. Then seemed to become serious. "But then your young boyfriend might know more about that than me."

"Boyfriend?" Mirri was beginning to feel like a slut—forgetting lovers like this. "Who?"

"I've admired you from afar for a long time," he told her, "and I've found the newspapers to be most informative. I believe he's a young actor."

"Jonah. Ah, Jonah." Mirri was delighted to dispel another misconception, albeit erroneously. "He goes out with my goddaughter, actually."

"The press, eh? Never let the truth get in the way of a good story, do they?" He seemed thrilled by this revelation.

Never let the truth get in the way of a good romance, Mirri thought. If this romance was going to go anywhere, she'd tell him about Jonah eventually, but right now she was keen to seem as good as gold.

Later on, however, as she sat in Nick's car, hitching a lift back to Primrose Hill, Mirri suddenly got the urge to be anything but good. They'd stayed in the restaurant for a long, boozy lunch and talked nonstop until the last of the customers had gone and they'd drunk so much peppermint tea that they felt they might drown if they consumed another drop. Then they'd ventured out into the park, gasped in the fresh air after hours in the stuffy restaurant, and wandered around. They'd pointed at the ducks, laughed at strange people, and had eventually collapsed onto a bench to draw breath. It was then that their date seemed, inevitably, to be over: They'd toyed with the idea of going to a gallery or to Harrods to look at strange, expensive things, but they'd decided against it as they were both shattered with the excitement of the day, like two-year-olds after a playdate. While Mirri was in no doubt that this was just the beginning of everything, they still decided that Nick would drive her home before heading back to Oxford where his gardener's wife was babysitting for his girls.

"Maybe I won't go to Primrose Hill," Mirri said suddenly as they waited in comfortable silence at a red light.

"Are you thinking a hotel?" Nick asked cheekily. Mirri loved the way he wasn't afraid to say what was on his mind; he was open about his feelings for her, even though as yet they hadn't done more than hold hands as they walked around the duck pond.

"No," she replied prudishly, "I'm just thinking that I don't want the day to end. So maybe I'll come back with you to Oxford-shire."

"Really?" He was thrilled.

"Would that be okay?"

"Okay?" he repeated, putting his foot on the brake and acceler-ating madly along Holland Park Road so that Mirri was flung back into her seat. "That's the best idea anyone's ever had."

Kate had never received a phone call from Mirri suggesting they meet up so that she could hear all about it. In fact, she'd never re-ceived any phone call at all and it was now two in the morning. She'd waited up in Leonard's sitting room, watching TV, and she was beginning to worry. Leonard had gone to bed hours ago, with a smirk on his face at the idea of Mirri on a date with Nick Sheri-dan. At first Mirri had wanted the whole thing kept quiet because really she hadn't enjoyed any of the buildup to meeting up with him again. But Kate assumed, by eight o'clock, that their relation-ship was official because technically they were on their third date already—elevenses, lunch, and now, presumably, dinner. Crafty old Mirri—how to have sex on the first date without it being a travesty of The Rules. Still, it didn't stop her from being slightly worried as to whether Mirri was okay or not. There was after all nothing on Nick Sheridan's slick website to suggest that he might not be an ax murderer. Kate dispelled her paranoia and turned off the TV. She took a shortbread from the tin on the way out and headed back to her shed.

As she sat on her bed, listening to the BBC World Service and munching her biscuit, she had a searing sense of loneliness. Mirri was out on a date and if all went well, and Kate prayed that it would, she'd soon be in love and out of commission as a friend. There were no longer any suitable distractions in terms of men in her life. She'd well and truly dispensed with Jake, that was for sure—apparently he'd gone to Thailand with his two young cousins for a month—so where did she go from here? She rummaged in her drawer for an old photograph that she knew was there. Kate and Louis about five years ago. She had no idea where they were or what they'd been doing or even who'd taken the picture, but they were both pouting in an outrageous and silly way, with their heads together. Kate looked dumb as they come, but Louis looked exquisitely beautiful. He was all cheekbones and sexy eyes and she wanted to be with him so badly right now that she felt as if she'd been punched in the stomach.

How could she have been so stupid? First of all not to have noticed him when he was right on her doorstep for all those years, but then to finally see him and be crazy about him and yet walk away. She flipped the picture onto her bedside table and turned off her lamp. Where might he be now? she wondered. Probably in bed, fast asleep, or not, with Grace. Kate wondered whether there'd ever be another chance with him. Not now but maybe in twenty or thirty years' time. Certainly she could never make a move. Maybe they'd have friendship, though. That would be something. A poor second compared to the dreams of him sharing the next part of her life with her—the really big part—the traveling and the family and building lives together. Still, as she drifted off to sleep the thing that seemed to matter most was something that Mirri had said about Nick—that it didn't matter whether you were with a person sometimes, if it was a true love then you felt better for simply knowing that person existed in the world, with or without you.

———

"Darling, wake up. It's me," Mirri whispered. Kate opened her eyes and flinched as the bright dawn light flooded in.

"What's going on?" Kate lay the back of her hand over her face. "What time is it?"

"I have no idea." Mirri was sitting on the edge of Kate's bed, still wearing her raincoat, exactly as she had been when Kate left her yesterday outside the restaurant. Only as Kate opened her eyes she noticed that her hair was considerably more lived in than it had been then.

Kate shuffled up in bed so that she was half sitting and propped against a pillow. "Where have you been? Do you have any idea how worried I was about you?" she said in her semicoherent morning voice. "I thought something terrible might have happened."

"Darling. It's so sweet that you care." Mirri swooned back onto the bed as if she were Doris Day in pink pajamas, not the most bewitching sex kitten of the last hundred years.

"It was completely inconsiderate of you," Kate grumbled. Then she rubbed her eyes and straightened the pillow behind her, getting into position for the good stuff. "So come on, tell me, how was it?" she demanded bossily, as if she were Mirri's mother.

"It was the most incredible night of my life." Mirri was gazing at the ceiling.

"Really?" Kate sounded suspicious.

"We've been in love with each other since the day we met," Mirri said, as if she couldn't believe it herself. "He's thought about me. He kept cuttings from newspapers. He thought about coming to Africa to visit me but always assumed that I wouldn't remember him and he couldn't bear that. We felt the same, Kate, we've gone through the last thirty years knowing that we were the loves of one another's lives. But not daring to think that the other was going to feel the same. It's the fairy tale I've waited for all my life. And we're old. We've wasted so many years that we could have spent together, but that's okay. I think."

"It really was *it*?" Though Kate had hoped for the very best for Mirri, somewhere she, too, didn't believe that it would ever happen like this. But here was Mirri, the tireless cynic, telling her the most implausible story of love that she'd ever heard.

"It was it." Mirri sat up and put her hand on Kate's. "It is it." She shrugged as if she could hardly believe it herself.

"So what happened?" Kate asked as she settled in for the long haul.

It was lunchtime when Mirri had finally filled Kate in on every word of the previous day and every brush of hands and shared thought. Mirri and Nick had gone from London down to Oxfordshire, where they had sneaked in on the sleeping household. Nick had taken Mirri upstairs to see his daughters asleep in their beds, at which point she'd almost cried because of how proud he was of them. Then she'd met the dogs, who were pretty much as she'd expected—noisy and smelly and overfriendly. But she'd pretended to find them entertaining for Nick's sake. Then she'd been introduced to the babysitter, who was the wife of the gardener. She was asleep on the sofa with dribble navigating its way along her jowls. She'd been delighted to meet Mirri and said she'd been a big fan of her films when she was young. Which made Mirri want to slap her across the face because the woman looked about 103 years old, but once again she forced a syrupy smile and pretended to be flattered.

Nick might even have taken her to meet the entire village if it hadn't been far too late. He was boundless in his energy and desire to show off the woman he'd waited a lifetime to see and be seen with. Even though in his mind he'd taken her to a thousand summer fêtes, carol concerts, and lunches in the pub. In fact, now he could face the truth he realized that almost every breath he'd ever taken since the day he'd met her had been with her in mind. He'd decorated his house, designed buildings, collected awards, and cooked elaborate dishes with a small part of his mind always wishing that she might be there with him.

When they'd finally met everyone there was to meet and Mirri had seen the lake and the pool and woods, Nick began to relax a little. Then they'd walked back to the house through the inky black night and he'd taken her to his library for a nightcap. They'd shared a whiskey as she didn't really want one, but longed to taste his, and then he'd kissed her. That was all. But it was a kiss that they'd both waited a very long time for.

"So how did you get back?" Kate asked as they sat at the kitchen table at midday. Kate was still in her pajamas and Mirri's mascara had now streaked down around her eyes.

"I borrowed a car. He wanted me to stay but I said I needed to collect some things."

"Are you going back?" Kate was surprised. She'd expected Mirri to have more dates and then who knew what. But not really for her to go back so soon.

"We've got catching up to do and a lot of time to make up for." Mirri winked.

"But his children?"

"Their mother was collecting them this morning anyway. I'll meet them next weekend."

"Are you sure?" Kate hated to sound a note of caution, but it seemed pretty fast. "I mean, it's not going to be like the days when you took men home and then spat them out after you'd finished?"

"I don't know," Mirri said, for the first time not sounding like a smitten teenager. "I suppose I'll find out. If it is then that's fine. But it doesn't feel like that."

"Good," Kate said. "So how does it feel?"

"It feels as if there aren't going to be enough moments left to spend with him as it is. I can't waste even one of those moments," she said, not quite believing it herself. "Though of course we haven't made love yet so it could all still go terribly wrong. He'll be the oldest man I've ever made love to, you know."

Chapter Twenty-eight

Without Mirri around, Kate had all the time in the world to finish her portrait. With nothing better to do when her back began to ache and her head began to ache from hours in front of the canvas, she paid a visit to Green and Stone art suppliers on the King's Road. Here she spent far more than she ought to have on things that she didn't need—a new Russian sable paintbrush, some cloths, fresh tubes of acrylic, and some handmade inks. She loved the woody smell of the shop and the old crumbling Chelsea painters who dawdled for hours near the turpentine and oak easels. It was as therapeutic for Kate as going to a spa and being drenched in sweet-smelling oils was for other people. She also had some canvases stretched for her next work and looked for an age at possible frames for Mirri's portrait when it was finished. She decided on a simple limed oak one, but knew that when she came in with the painting in a few days she'd change her mind a hundred times and leave the ever-patient staff wrung out.

"Leonard, what are you up to tonight?" Kate asked when she walked back into the house with next month's mortgage worth of painting paraphernalia under her arm in a brown paper bag.

"Some art opening at the Tate," he said as he hung up the phone on a very stressed-sounding customer.

"Louis's?" Kate asked. "And mine I suppose."

"Let me see." He looked in his desk diary and nodded. "You're right, he sent me the invitation a while ago. Will you still be going?"

"Yeah, I'm going to go, but I wanted moral support. I was going to ask you to be my guest 'cause I've got spare tickets but I forgot you're the most invited man in London. Maybe I'll get Robbie and Tanya to come, too."

"We could all have supper afterward." Leonard loved a gathering. "Shall I call Louis and ask him along?"

"I think he'll have other plans," Kate said. "I'm sure that Amazing Grace will have booked something very intimate and special."

"Just the four of us, then." Leonard shrugged. "And you never know, we might pick up a few strays on the way."

"I'll give Tanya a call," Kate said, and was about to disappear when she turned back. "Leonard, do you think that Mirri's done the right thing?"

"In which respect?"

"In swallowing her pride and going after Nick." Kate knew what the answer was going to be but she had to check. There didn't seem to be any drawbacks from where Kate was standing but in the eyes of the world maybe there was a downside to running headlong into a relationship with a man you'd loved for most of your adult life.

"Well, it certainly looks as if she's done the right thing," he said as he searched under piles of paper for something he'd lost earlier. "I've spent the past few days desperately trying to remember if I have a lost love, as a matter of fact, just so that I can look him up and relive my youth. Can't say I've had much luck." He shrugged. "I did remember a chap from Sotheby's the other day whom I'd taken rather a shine to but I gather he's an MP now so it's probably starcrossed."

"Yes, maybe best to leave that one alone." Kate smiled as she headed back to the shed. She was going to miss Leonard when she moved out and had already made him swear to twice-weekly suppers around the corner at Lemonia. Though he'd been afraid it might interfere with his bridge playing, so they'd settled for two coffee mornings instead.

Kate felt completely schizophrenic about tonight's party. While she embraced any possible opportunity to see Louis, she dreaded him being there with someone else on his arm—and also the indifference with which he now seemed to view her. He'd called her briefly yesterday to say that he was putting the final touches to the exhibition and that everyone who'd seen it so far seemed to be very impressed, especially with the polar bear, and he wanted to make sure that she was going to come. That was it. Business-like and as if she were just the guy who'd wired up the installations or the girl who'd mailed out the flyers for the show. She was no more than a part of his team, and she no longer seemed to matter a bit to him. Which was no more than she deserved, she understood, but it was a bitter pill. She needed to know what Mirri would do in her shoes but didn't want to disturb her. Eventually, though, she couldn't bear it anymore. Mirri had been in Oxfordshire for a week and Kate needed advice.

"Mirri, it's Kate Disney," she said, as if she might have been forgotten already.

"Ah, *cherie*." Mirri was slightly breathless, and Kate worried that she'd caught her and Nick in bed. It sounded as if Mirri might just have been reveling in the fact that despite being her oldest lover ever, Nick still seemed to be in complete working order.

"Am I disturbing you?" Kate asked tentatively.

"No, hang on a minute," Mirri panted.

"Okay, I'm sorry, I'll call back later." Kate was about to hang up when the heavy breathing subsided.

"There we are. I can speak now. I was in the river and I had something hooked." Mirri was now sitting on the riverbank in her green waders, watching Nick farther down stream as he reeled in a fish.

"You were fishing?" Kate sounded alarmed.

"No, I was fly-fishing, it's much more exhilarating. And very wet."

"That's pretty bourgeois for you, isn't it?"

"I went duck shooting yesterday." Mirri laughed and put down her rod.

"And heartless, too." Kate was looking at her portrait of Mirri in the corner of her shed. Mirri was sitting on a chair in her bedroom at Leonard's with an intelligent, contemplative frown on her face. She looked like a woman who hadn't quite found peace but who was on a path, at least. She was serious and focused on doing her best for animals.

"It's amazingly good fun." Mirri laughed down the line. "I'm a great shot."

"Your picture's finished." Kate yelled to be heard over the rushing water of the rapids in the background at Mirri's end.

"I can't wait to see it," she shouted back. "We're going to be in town this weekend. Will you be around?"

"Sure," Kate said. She was permanently around at the moment. "Mirri, can I ask you something?"

"Always."

"It's about Louis. It's just that I miss him and I don't know what to do and tonight it's his exhibition and there's nobody else I can trust to tell me and . . ." Kate stopped speaking. There was nobody at the end of the phone. Perhaps Mirri had been tugged into the water by a giant salmon or something. Maybe it was just a bad line. Now she couldn't ask her. She had no clue what to do.

Mirri had sounded so full of life on the phone. If Kate had to paint her at this moment she suspected she'd have to start all over again. She pictured Mirri laughing on the riverbank in the damp grass. She was doing things that two weeks ago she would have been full of scorn for. And she was loving them. That's where Kate had gone wrong and Mirri had gotten it right, it seemed. Kate had done what she thought she should do in agreeing to marry Jake, and she'd lost out on something better. Mirri did things that nobody expected of her and that she didn't expect of herself, even, and she lost nothing. Kate unpacked her paintbrushes and wondered how she'd play it tonight now that she hadn't Mirri to guide her.

For the first time all summer she'd have to work something out for herself.

———

Kate arrived at the doors of Tate Modern with Tanya and Robbie. Leonard, true to his word, had met somebody on the street outside and promised to come in and join them in a moment.

"I can't wait to see it," Tanya said as they walked inside and merged with the crowd. Everyone looked amazing. Even the strangest-looking people in the art world managed to look fabulous; here rubbery lips and cross eyes and hook noses were simply assets to make you look more interesting. And the clothes were striking beyond the imaginations of the fashionable, who were always too sheep-like and nervous to stand out. Kate felt an old rush of belonging to something whenever she stepped into an art opening. Much as she felt like the poor relation to all the famous faces and personalities and numinous talents here, she also knew a lot of the people in the room—she'd gone to college with some of them; had met them through Louis over the years; and though she didn't know much about the work they were doing, and they certainly didn't lose too much sleep over Kate Disney as a competitor, there was some mutual respect. Which gave Kate a slight buzz when she smelled the freshly painted room and saw glasses of champagne swinging between people's fingers as they mulled over a piece or caught up with old friends. She looked around for Louis but knew he'd be the nucleus of an admiring posse somewhere.

"So which one's yours?" Tanya asked as she glanced around the room.

"I can't see it yet." Kate hadn't even thought to look. She'd been too riveted by the old faces and wondering whether they'd be graced with Grace's presence. Kate wondered how differently she'd feel tonight if she were the girl with Louis.

"Let's go and find it," Robbie said, and took his wife by the hand. Kate followed closely behind and felt a rush of happiness for them. Though it was still too early for Tanya to be able to tell the world about the baby, it was so obvious from her face that she was going to be a mother that Kate thought she might as well get T-shirts printed. She looked so preternaturally relaxed that even in a room of solipsistic freaks, Tanya was the most stared-at person. Kate was terrified to think how lovable they'd be as a family unit, and had joked that she would only buy the child baby clothes made out of horsehair and sackcloth so that it would develop a character beyond being the cutest thing on earth.

"There it is," Kate said as they approached the farthest corner of the room. Towering above the other works was the polar bear painting, but in a context so alien that Kate couldn't recognize it as her work. It had been transformed into a metaphor for destruction and isolation and the loss of innocence in the world. Well, at least that's what the respected art critic next to her was telling to the camera of the BBC news team. To Kate it looked lonely and sad. But maybe she was projecting. She thought back to the day at the zoo when she'd been making sketches and she'd run into Louis. Maybe it had started as a metaphor for his isolation from her. And now, ironically, it ended up being Kate's narrative. She wondered if she ought to thank the art critic for helping her out with her interpretation of the piece, but the next minute he was beckoning over "The artist himself, Louis Alcott." He tugged at the corner of Louis's sleeve as he wrested him from conversation with some fascinated Germans.

Kate couldn't exactly run away when Louis was placed in front of the camera, just a couple of feet in front of her. Instead she smiled in case he looked up. She'd imagined for some reason that tonight Louis would be wearing something smart. That he'd look important and serious and commanding, being the man of the hour. But he wasn't. He looked exactly the same as he always did. He was wearing his worn-out jeans, with frayed edges hanging over the back of his sneakers and a T-shirt that had been rescued from the laundry basket. His hair fell over his forehead in the same schoolboy way it always did. The only concession he seemed to have made to it being a special occasion was that he was wearing a snakeskin belt. It was one that Kate had helped him to choose in Barcelona years ago on a college trip. Kate remembered standing in the shop while they looked at about twenty different belts. She'd thought they all looked the same and was impatient for him just to pick one out. But Louis had taken his time and knew exactly which one worked for him. And that seemed to be the way he was with everything. Louis knew who he was and what he wanted. Unfortunately it no longer happened to be her.

Kate listened to the first part of the interview. Louis told the cameras how he believed in a democracy of ideas and how high and low culture could coexist and that was what his work was about. Then Kate felt an elbow nudge her.

"Come and see this piece," Tanya whispered to Kate. "Robbie thinks it's meaningless but I like it. Anyway what does he know. He spends all day writing about manure." It was good to have her old friend back, Kate thought as she allowed Tanya to lead her away from the crowds, who were gravitating toward Louis and the cameras. Tanya seemed to have lost a bit of the preciousness that had crept over her of late and become her fearless, feisty former self.

"Have you spoken to Louis?" she asked, much too loudly for Kate's liking, as they walked past a group of exotically shod girls with thrilling faces to match—all of whom would undoubtedly leap at the chance to take home the star of the show tonight, Kate noted as the last vestiges of hope deserted her. He hadn't even caught her eye earlier as she watched him in front of the cameras. That was how important she was to him.

"Not a chance," Kate said as they entered a dark screening room and let the curtain drop shut behind them.

"I didn't know Louis did video installations." Kate said in her friend's ear as they sat down on the back bench. The film began and the audience of about fifteen people fell silent.

Kate watched with only half her mind on the piece at first. The piece seemed to be a moving film of airport X-ray machines. Each one was a different suitcase as it appeared on the monitor above the security machines. Kate had watched a hundred times as her cell phone and the blobby outlines of her belonging showed up on screen. Once or twice she'd noted with horror as a pair of scissors were revealed and it meant she'd have to hand them over to security as she'd forgotten to put them in her suitcase.

"It's clever," Kate said to Tanya. "I love watching other people's stuff."

"It's sweet," Tanya said, so Kate looked closer. Sweet had actually passed her by. Then she noticed that amid all the blobs, the white shapes, and the odd metal object like a gun or a knife, or even the famous scissors, was something unexpected. In the image on the screen now was a flower. Barely visible, but it was there. Next there was a bracelet wedged against a laptop computer. Kate looked more closely and then recognized the bracelet as the same kind of charm bracelet her dad had given her for her twenty-first birthday. She waited for the next image. She sort of knew that it would mean something to her but at the same time didn't expect it to be. This time there was no doubt.

"Isn't that your zebra head?" Tanya asked in too loud a voice. "I didn't see this bit before."

"Yeah, I think it is." Kate leaned forward. In the next few images were a toy car, a chunky watch, and a brilliant white credit card. Kate began to wonder if she'd been hallucinating the bracelet and the zebra head. Then there came a suitcase with a blurred photograph in it. Kate instantly recognized it as the one she had in her bedroom drawer. She waited until the film stopped but nothing else came. Only more obvious, hand luggage objects.

"I liked that," Tanya said as everyone filed out of the room and back into the dazzling white of the gallery. "You didn't tell me he'd borrowed your zebra head."

"He didn't. It just looked like my zebra head. Mine's only got one ear." Kate was trying furiously to figure out what all that had been about. Was it a coincidence that things of Kate's were in there? She paused by the wall on the way out and noticed the white piece of card with the name of the piece on. She waited for some people to move so that she could check it out. She hoped that it would say something like, THINGS BELONGING TO THE WOMAN I LOVE. But as she nudged closer it only read TRANSPARENCY. Kate rolled her eyes. She bloody well hated conceptual artists. She agreed with Robbie, it was meaningless.

"Did you like it, then?" Louis was standing in front of her when she turned around.

"The piece?" she asked.

He nodded.

"I thought it was . . . sweet," she said. She couldn't read his face.

"It was about you," he told her.

"Was?" she asked. "In the past?"

"I did it a few years ago and never showed you. It's pretty dated now and obvious but hey, it's supposed to be a retrospective. I can put it in if I like, can't I?" He looked tall tonight and Kate could see people hovering and wanting to speak to him.

"If only I'd known," she said.

"I don't think it would have made much difference." He shuffled in the way he used to in front of her. "In the long run anyway."

"Is Grace here?" Kate asked, not able to help herself.

"Somewhere." Louis looked around and about five of the hovering people looked ready to pounce.

"Before you go," Kate said, suddenly fearing that this would be the last contact they had, "I just want to say thanks for giving me the chance to work with you. It's been a great experience and I love the piece and . . ." Louis was looking at her but it was as if what she was saying meant nothing. Which actually, if she was honest with herself, it didn't. She thought of Mirri on the riverbank in a ridiculous coat, getting water down her waders and making a fool of herself in front of Nick. Nick wouldn't mind, Kate thought. And if he did, well, as Kate had discovered, it would just mean he wasn't the right person for Mirri. It was impossible to lose something that wasn't there in the first place. Kate had lost Jake because he was never truly hers. She had lost Louis because she'd never accepted the side of herself that he loved. And he'd lost her because she'd been too fearful of taking chances to take anything but the safest of steps. Even though that so-called safe step of getting engaged to Jake had been the wrong one.

"Louis, I messed up," Kate said. "I'm really sorry for who I was. I'm sorry that I didn't listen when you told me about Jake. And I'm sorry that I didn't see a good thing when it was right in front of me. And if it's any consolation I know that I'm never going to be as happy with someone as I would have been with you. And I know it's my loss and I don't expect you to do anything about it, but I just wanted to tell you," she concluded as one of the exotic-shoe girls tapped him on the shoulder.

"Louis Alcott?" she said. He nodded. "I'm Tatiana, I work at a gallery in New York, and I love your work. I was just wondering . . ." She was dazzlingly pretty with her raspberry python-skin shoes and leopard-print coat.

"Tatiana, would you mind just giving me a moment with my friend Kate. It won't take long." He smiled winningly and Tatiana retreated with a satisfied swoon.

"Kate. Thanks. I appreciate it," Louis said, and touched her arm. Was that it? She looked at him, waiting for him to tell her that he was in love with Grace now or that he was glad that she still cared because he couldn't stop thinking about her. But he didn't.

"I'll see you around, I'm sure," he said as he tugged at the hem of his T-shirt.

"I hope so," Kate said as emphatically as she could manage, but it didn't seem to matter. Louis gave her one last smile and then turned to Tatiana.

Kate stood like a lemon behind Louis for a second or two. She looked at the people filing in to the video piece. What bloody good was transparency, she thought, if it got you nowhere? She'd done what Mirri would have done, she'd been honest to herself and to Louis, and where had it gotten her?

"Transparency's bullshit," she said as Robbie arrived at her side clutching an exhibition program.

"Couldn't agree more," he said, sneering at the piece of card outside the entrance to the room. "I could do better myself."

Chapter Twenty-nine

It was the first week in September and Kate had been living in her flat for just a few days. She really just spent most of her time wandering from room to room and marveling that it actually belonged to her. Not that it was wildly exciting just yet—some of the floorboards had been sprung up by the plumbers and were lying in wait to trip up unsuspecting visitors, most of the walls were still pink with plaster, and though there was a kitchen and a shower now, that was pretty much as sophisticated as it got. In fact, in its current state it wasn't much better equipped than the shed had been. But it was home and Kate had been waiting an age to find where she belonged. She was at the top of a ladder when there was a knock at the door.

"Just a minute," she called out as she put her paintbrush down on the top of the tin. She'd spent all day painting her walls a chalky-gray color, but whenever she came back into the room they looked more and more like a prison cell.

"Parcel." The postman was standing at her door with a huge, flat package resting against his legs.

"Great." Kate signed for it and got gray paint all over his pen. He handed over her parcel. She was surprised at how heavy it was.

"Mind you don't put your back out with that," he said when it

was too late. Kate staggered into the hallway and was about to tear
it open when there was another knock.

"It's open," she called out and turned around. It was supposed to
be Leonard because he'd promised to come around and give her an
honest opinion on the Cell Gray color. But she could tell by the
shoes that it wasn't.

"What's *that* doing here?" Today was Nick Sheridan's first full day
in Mozambique. He'd just gotten back from visiting the site where
the Mirabelle Moncur Wildlife Trust had asked him to design their
headquarters. He was tired and dusty but walking up behind Mirri,
with her bottom hanging just a bit below her indecently cut denim
shorts, he knew that he'd done the right thing in agreeing to spend
six months here. His daughters would come and visit for Christmas, he'd take them on safari, and they'd all go down to Victoria
Falls. They'd definitely test Mirri's patience, but not as much as it
was going to test her patience to try to share her life with anyone
other than Bébé. And possibly not as much as his patience was
going to be tested if she kept on behaving like a willful child.

"I like it." Mirri moved back a few steps and stood beside him.
She squinted slightly at Kate's portrait of her, which she'd hung over
the fireplace. "I like the way I look in it."

"But it's not yours." He shook his head disapprovingly. "You
gave it to the National Portrait Gallery."

"Well, I didn't give it to them, actually. As you can see." She
pointed to the painting. "I kept it."

"You can't keep it. It's not yours. You gave it to the nation."

"They won't notice." Mirri bit her lip guiltily.

"They'll have made a space for it." He slapped her bottom playfully. "And a little white label to hang beside it. You have to send it
back tomorrow."

"But it makes me think of Kate." Mirri played the sympathy
card. "I miss her. She's like a daughter to me."

"You speak to her every night." Nick folded his arms and looked more closely at the picture.

"It reminds me of you," she said with a flourish of inspiration. He didn't believe her. "It was a time when I used to sit and look out the window and think of you. I didn't know if you were dead or alive or married or even remembered me," she said tragically.

"I can't believe you were an actress." Nick walked over to the drinks cabinet and poured himself a gin and tonic. "You're so terrible at it."

"It's true. Look, can't you see the loss in my eyes." She pointed at the portrait, which he had to admit did reveal all the depths and complexities of Mirri that most people never saw. It was a stunning portrait of a beautiful woman, but it wasn't the most flattering picture he'd ever seen of her. When he thought about it he was pleased that she liked it. It meant that she was at ease with herself.

"Please, darling," Mirri said as he handed her his drink for her to take her customary long sip before giving it back to him. She followed him toward the endless glass doors that looked out onto the plain. There wasn't much of a garden, just a baobab tree, better known as the upside-down tree because it looked as if it has its roots in the air, and some very scratchy grass where Bébé was rolling with one of his brothers. The sun was setting in the distance and Nick gazed with wonder at the horizon, which was the widest and farthest he'd ever seen.

"Only if you marry me." He turned to her as if he had her in checkmate. He'd asked her every day since they'd met up again but she'd resisted. This painting could be a bargaining chip.

"If I like your building then I'll marry you," she told him.

"It's a deal," he said. "I'm going to build you the most spectacular structure you've ever seen. It'll be like a cathedral to our love."

"Oh, good." Mirri laughed and took another sip of his drink. "That seems very fitting, because you know you're the answer to my prayers, don't you? I used to go up to the hills over there in the evenings and think about you."

"Mirabelle Moncur, are you getting sentimental in your old age?" Nick turned his head to hers.

"No." She smiled naughtily, "It's just that I like that painting a lot, it reminds me of a wonderful summer in England. Besides, I can't send it back. I like to get my own way."

"That's more like it." Nick laughed. "If you weren't a tricky, devious, spoiled pain in the backside I'm not sure I'd like you."

"That's why I love you," she said as she hung her hands around his neck and kissed him.

"I have to remind you, though," he told her, "I like to get my own way, too, now and again."

———————

Kate recognized the scuffed sneakers standing on her mat. She looked up to see Louis in the doorway.

"You did it." He knocked on the door. "You've got your own front door."

"I have a kitchen sink, too," she said proudly as she stopped cutting the string on the parcel and stood up.

"But no running water?" He pointed at Kate's face, which was streaked with the dubious gray paint.

"Ah, yes." Kate rubbed her cheek, but it didn't come off. She was wearing an old pair of dungarees and an orange-and-pink scarf in her hair. "But the loo flushes."

"Thank the Lord for small mercies." Louis smiled. "Do you mind if I come in?"

"God, no, I'm sorry. I'm not used to owning a house to invite people in to." To be truthful Kate was just so shaken to see Louis again that she couldn't think straight. She couldn't imagine what he wanted, but experience had taught her not to expect anything too promising. Besides, she was just beginning to feel as if she could stand on her own two feet. For the first time she wasn't borrowing Leonard's garden shed, she wasn't asking Mirri's advice, she wasn't craving Jake's love. She was finally sleeping under her own roof, albeit in a sleeping bag on a yoga mat, and doing things for herself.

Since she'd finished her portrait of Mirri, Kate had been encouraged enough by the response of Leonard and Nick and Mirri to advertise in Green and Stone for anyone who might want a portrait. Of themselves or their children or lovers, and not just their cats and iguanas. So as she felt the familiar feelings of yearning as she looked at Louis, she reminded herself that she'd be fine, no matter what he'd come to say. As long as it wasn't to invite her to his wedding. She wasn't improved enough as a person not to throw a paint tin at his head if that was the reason he was here.

"I wanted to ask you something," Louis said as he closed the door quietly behind him and stepped onto one of the dangerous floorboards.

"Mind that one," she said as he nearly disappeared through to the cellar.

"Ah, yes." He walked with extreme caution into the sitting room and found himself a safe-looking piece of windowsill to perch on. Kate followed him and sat on the stepladders.

"I've been really pissed off with you," he said, and looked down at his feet.

Kate was taken aback. The last thing she wanted was a telling-off. "Really?" she asked, thinking maybe she'd just ask him to leave now.

"I thought that what you did to me after you got engaged to Jake was unforgivable." He sounded cold and she didn't like the way he wouldn't catch her eye. "I pretended to be civil, you know, for the sake of us working together and for the project, but it was really hard."

"Louis." Kate stopped him. "If you've come here to give me a bollocking, then I'd rather you went away and wrote it down in a letter or something. Only I'm not sure that I want to hear it."

"I thought we were being honest." He pushed the fallen piece of black hair back from his face.

"Oh. Okay, go on." She didn't like this honesty game and she cursed Mirri for having started it. What was wrong with subterfuge and white lies and hiding from your true feelings? Hadn't she been happier in those days? She thought back and realized that she hadn't. "But can you make it not too brutal? Only I've just moved in and I don't want loads of negative energy flying around."

"Fine." Louis chewed his bottom lip thoughtfully for a second. "The thing is that I fell in love with Grace. She was lovely and bright and great company," he said calmly. Oh God, here came the invitation to the wedding. Kate looked for a nearby paint tin to hurl.

"But every night when I was at dinner with her I thought about you. When I went into the gallery in the mornings I'd go and look at your work, hang around your paints and things to feel close to you. The piece I said I made years ago? Well, I made it after you'd split up with Jake." Louis began to chew his fingernail. Kate pushed the scarf back off her face. "I told myself I didn't give a damn about you, but I did. And when you told me that night at the opening that you were in love with me . . . well, walking away was the hardest thing I've ever done."

"Right," Kate said without much emotion. As she sat here, in her new house, surrounded by her new beginnings, she suddenly wasn't sure whether she was brave enough to hear him out. For the first time in ages she felt as if nobody could hurt her. She didn't know if she wanted to be shaken up again so soon. She took a deep breath. "I'm going to get us some tea." She walked out into the hall without letting him finish.

"Kate," he called after her. "Just hear me out. Please."

"I can't, Louis. I just want to be by myself for a while." She stood in the hallway and looked down at the parcel, which was leaning against the bottom stair. The brown paper was peeling back at the top. She wondered what it could be. It was very badly wrapped.

"Don't walk away from me." Louis came after her, then stopped as he watched her take the first layer of paper off the parcel. "What's that?"

"I don't know. It came in the post just before you arrived." She knelt down and peeled off the paper. "I think it might be a picture."

"It is." Louis stood over her.

"Oh my God." Kate moved away from it when she felt her finger brush a corner of canvas and oil paint.

"What?"

"This better not be what I think it is," she said as she very carefully stripped away at the package. "She can't have sent this without so much as HANDLE WITH CARE written on it. Can she?"

"It's incredible." Louis looked over Kate's shoulder as she gazed at the painting in front of her. A card was stuffed into the bottom corner of the frame. It read,

A HOUSEWARMING GIFT FOR MY FAVORITE ARTIST AND GREATEST FRIEND. LOVE MIRRI XX P.S. PUT NOVEMBER 21 IN THE DIARY. WE'RE DOING THE UNTHINKABLE. WILL YOU BE A BRIDESMAID?

"No way!" Kate screamed as she read the card. "No way."

"What?" Louis touched Kate's shoulder and tried to get some sense out of her. "What's going on?"

"She's getting married." Kate laughed in disbelief. "They're getting married."

"Mirri?" Louis guessed.

"I can't believe it." Kate looked at the picture on the bottom stair. It had to be what Kate thought it was. Kate stared at it. If it was Mirri then she was virtually unrecognizable—her nose was where her ear was supposed to be and her head seemed to turn a corner—but the colors were spectacular. Then Kate tilted her head and looked at it again. Suddenly it seemed to make sense: the feline eyes, the tempestuous pout, and the yellow hair. It was definitely Mirri.

"It's mine," Kate said. She stood up and looked at Louis.

"It's a Picasso." Louis could hardly believe it, he didn't know whether to look at Kate or the treasure on the stairs.

"So what was it that you wanted to ask me?" Kate was suddenly curious. As they both gazed at the Goddess in the picture Kate knew that she wasn't ever going to get away from the lessons she'd learned. She could close her front door and not invite them in and she could walk out of the room when she was confronted with them, but she couldn't ignore them anymore. Because what she'd learned from Mirri was no longer just the things she knew. It was who she was. She had no choice.

"It doesn't matter," Louis said as he turned away from the picture and toward Kate. "You said you wanted to be by yourself for a while."

"I lied," Kate admitted.

"Okay then." He smiled. "Do you want to come out to dinner with me?"

"I'd love to," Kate said. It was much easier than she'd thought it would be.

"Great." He reached out to touch her cheek. Kate lowered her eyes, waiting for him to kiss her. She felt the familiar thrill being near him. "Are we still being honest?" He looked at her face and screwed up his nose.

Kate frowned. This wasn't what was supposed to happen. Where was her kiss? "Yes," she said suspiciously.

"Great. Because I have to tell you that you have the worst taste in paint and if you paint your bedroom that color then you're going to be spending most of your nights at my place." He laughed.

"How dare you?" Kate kicked him in the shin and glared at him. Then she looked down at Mirri's portrait and remembered something the Goddess had once taught her.

"Well, you won't be saying that when I've finished with you," she told Louis. "In fact, you'll be begging to sleep at the foot of my bed."

"Really?" he asked as he grabbed her by the hand. "Is that a promise?"

"Trust me." Kate smiled as she stepped over the Picasso and led Louis up the stairs. "I learned from the best."